# RESTORATION AND RETRIBUTION

## THE LIFE AND TIMES OF GEORGE CARTERET

### Royal Chess Series Part Three: 1660-1680

JOHN DANN
First published 2024

Other publications:

Walking the Acamus

Konyatice 1250-2000

Pole Dancing as a Pastime

**King's Gambit** – (Royal Chess Series, Part1)

**Fool's Mate** – (Royal Chess Series, Part2)

ISBN: 9798321811771
Imprint: Independently published

## DEDICATIONS

This book is dedicated with gratitude to the friends who made the concept possible, offering advice and assistance with proof reading, especially, Valerie, Bruce and Simeon and also Kathy Norris who saw the Royal Chess Series through to publication. I owe particular gratitude to Vanessa for the tolerance and understanding she has shown in the years since I began this project.

I owe gratitude also to the archivists of Essex Record Office, the Special Collections Office of the University of Aberdeen, and the Royal College of Physicians, for adding valuable original material. My thanks are also extended to Valerie Noel, Librarian of the Societe Jersiaise, Gemma Hynard of the Hampshire Record Office, and Naomi Seckett of the Wiltshire and Swindon Archive.

Grateful thanks also to the many local historians, professional and amateur, who have shown me Parish Registers, memorial stones and buildings, providing valuable insights concerning the individuals described in the book. I hope that in constructing a narrative around the events of their lives and the events they may have witnessed, I have not done them an injustice.

# THE ROYAL CHESS SERIES.

The **'King's Gambit'** is the first of three books examining the lives of three closely related families and their associates during the years 1610-1680. The Carteret, Dowse and Paulet families were representative of a large number of middle class families who lived through a time of cataclysmic change and events which affected them deeply. Their social standing, and total dependence on the arbitrary decisions of central government, which affected their everyday lives, made them easy victims of policy changes. They had so much to lose in terms of money, property, and power, and no means of defending these assets if the Monarchy withdrew its support.

It was a time when statesmen and even a King, were executed; when the great Plague raged killing thousands; when London was destroyed by fire, and the war between Britain and Holland led to unnumbered deaths. In addition, the British nations waged internecine war over matters of religion and morality.

George Carteret was born in Jersey of a ruling family, who came to England as an adventurous teenager to join the Navy. **'King's Gambit'** traces his travels to Newfoundland, the Mediterranean and in British waters, defending the coast from invaders and slaves traders. His career saw him promoted him from Lieutenant to Captain. In 1639 Charles I appointed him Commander of the Royal Navy. George and Elizabeth celebrated their marriage and prepared to settle in London. Theirs was a long and happy marriage and, the happiness of their children and their hospitality was admired by many.

The second book, **'Fool's Mate'** follows them to London and the dreadful contest between King and Parliament which lead to Parliament's dismissal of Carteret from his command. Refusing to accept Parliamentary orders George took a third of the Naval ships to Jersey, since the King had not dismissed him from office. In Jersey he was promoted to High Sheriff, and Jersey gained wealth as a trading nation. When Charles I was executed in 1649, Carteret proclaimed his sixteen year-old son, Charles, King of Great Britain. Charles was his family guest in St Helier. After the capture of the island, George and his family were exiled to France by Cromwell's government, and his money and property confiscated. He continued to work as a trader from St Malo, and to give his financial support to the Stuart cause throughout the Civil War. The book concludes with the plans leading to the restoration of the Monarchy. George is confident that Charles II will reward him for his years of constant support.

The third book 'Restoration and Retribution' will reveal whether Carteret's hopes are realised.


## RULES of the GAME of ROYAL CHESS (Adapted)


A KNIGHT has a dual role: to attack, and to defend the ROYAL pieces. He operates within the parameters of six squares and in action must leap over other friendly or opposing pieces. This privilege is not granted to any other piece on the board. He must attack at an angle and thus ambush and capture unwary pieces, removing them from the field of battle. He is dedicated, at whatever risk to himself, to support the Queen in defence of the King.

# A select bibliography

Calendar of State Papers, Domestic series 1600 -1690

Aubrey, J. (1692) Brief lives

Balleine, G R . (1976) A biographical dictionary of Jersey. London

Balleine, G R . (1950) A history of the island of Jersey

Balleine, G R . (1951) A Balliwick of Jersey

Davies, J.D. (2023) Kings of the Sea

Dunton, (1637) The journal of the Sallee Fleet

Carteret, G. (1633) The chase of a pirate

Carteret, G. (1639) Return to Africa

Falle, P. (1694) An account of the island of Jersey

Hakluyt, R. (1600) Navigations, voyages, traffiques and discoveries

Poingdextre, J. (1889) Caesarea, or a discourse on the Island of Jersey

Padfield, P. (1999) Maritime Supremacy. London

Partlett, D. (1979) Card games. London

Syvrey, M and Stevens, J. (1981) Bailleine's History of Jersey.
Jersey: Phillimore & Co

The diary of Samuel Pepys (full edition)

Wells, H. G. (1911) Floor games. London

# The Carterets

Rachel née Paulet:                   Mother of Elias and Philippe

Elie (Elias) de Carteret, b. 1585   Attorney General for Jersey
Elizabeth, née Demaresque       Wife of Elie b. 1590
George de Carteret               Their eldest son, b. 1609
Philippe de Carteret             Their second son, b. 1612
Reginald de Carteret             Their third son, b. 1615
Anne de Carteret                 Their eldest daughter, b 1617

Philippe de Carteret, b. 1583     Seigneur de St. Ouen
                               Governor of Jersey
Amyas de Carteret              Brother of Philippe, b. 1587

Gideon de Carteret             Brother of Philippe, b. 1591
Anne, née Dowse               His wife, b. 1585
Philippe de Carteret             Their eldest son, b. 1620
Elizabeth de Carteret          Their daughter, b. 1625
Amyas de Carteret              Their son, b. 1627
François (Francis) de Carteret Their son, b. 1630

Amice de Carteret, b. 1559       Seigneur de Trinité
                               Governor of Guernsey
Catherine, née Lemprière       His wife, b. 1559
Dr. Philippe de Carteret, an MD Their eldest son b. 1608
Joshua de Carteret, a lawyer    Their son, b. 1611

# RESTORATION
# AND
# RETRIBUTION

# INTRODUCTION TO BOOK THREE: RESTORATION AND RETRIBUTION

CHARLES II was called to the British throne eleven years after the execution of his father, Charles I for waging war against his people like a tyrant and crushing their traditional freedoms.

In 1649 Parliament set up a Republic intended to choose ministers to ensure the "rule of the People by the People". Unfortunately, few were willing to take on the onerous duties of Government. As a result Cromwell, who had defeated the King, was forced to choose generals to take public duties which led to a military dictatorship. When Cromwell died in 1658, no effective successor until could be found, until Hyde, Montague and Carteret, offered a solution in the form of a monarchy with powers limited by parliament. This gained the full support to the Uncrowned Charles II, who accepted the offer of the Crown.

George Carteret returned with the new King from eleven years of exile, and almost £3,000,000 wealthier than before his exile. This volume is an attempt to give a clear account of the many and various areas of business he took on at the age of fifty. The ever-increasing sources of information are available from the National Archive records.

I have made an attempt to construct a coherent account of the range of tasks Carteret undertook to secure the reign of Charles II, a King for whom he worked tirelessly. Book Three begins with the restoration of Charles on board a ship commissioned by Carteret.

# ~ ONE ~

## CHAPTER ONE

Blood! Hot and glutinous, it showered over his head and clothes, so that he could even taste it, and smell the metallic aroma. of newly shed blood. He was calling aloud for help when, amid a frenzy of confused sounds, a piercing cry of outrage rang out," You villain!" The voice rang in his head and, with heart pounding, he woke from this nightmare, vividly real, to find Bess restless beside him, a lock of hair quivering as she breathed.

It appalled him every time the horror of this recurrent nightmare came upon him. Indeed, it was nowadays more infrequent, though no less terrifying when it occurred. He was no longer woken by his own shouts, to the alarm of his family. Buckingham had been dead for more than thirty years, but strangely retained the power to disturb his sleep. Calm returned, leaving him with the usual uneasy feeling of guilt, as a helpless observer, which lingered for some minutes. He knew he could not have prevented the murder… and yet!

Sleep abandoned, and his time-piece showing six o'clock, with a sunny May morning in progress, he rose and considered the day's plan. He heard William bringing hot water, and smelled fresh rolls and coffee. While dressing, he noticed fishermen unloading their catch on the quay below. He had an appointment at 9.00; not the early start he made when at sea.

Later, spruce, and wearing a fashionable tailcoat, he murmured thanks to Pernel, the maid, who poured him a final coffee.

'Bernice told me, Sir, that her Ladyship is awake now, and hopes that you will go up to pour chocolate for her before you hurry off to work.'

'Thank you, Pernel. I will do that. Please remind Will Jarvis I shall leave in fifteen minutes. And I need to speak to him before I leave.'

'My darling, I hope you have not put on your beautiful coat to impress me. I had hoped you would still be in your nightshirt, George!'

'I apologise, dear heart, but I have much to do today.' The temptation was too strong, however, and he moved the breakfast tray and embraced Bessie. 'Oh Bess! I notice you are wearing a chocolate moustache this morning:

come, let me kiss it away! There! It has gone, and now I will drink chocolate with you, before I go to speak to the Mayor.'

'Has a message come this morning, George? I hope you will not have to leave Jersey until next week. You must not miss the party on Saturday. Philippe will be very upset if you are not there to congratulate him on his eighteenth birthday. All our friends, and his, will be coming and a ball has been arranged for the evening. Have you decided whether to make him a full partner in the business? He surely deserves to be.'

'I promise I will be there, and claim the first dance with you, before the younger people make the musicians play those new dances. How much responsibility I give him, will depend on the demands the King has for me. I might have to wait to be told in London, although I hope for some news from Edward Hyde.'

'No message has arrived today, then?'

'It's a little early in the morning, my darling, for a pigeon, flying from London, to reach St Malo. I'm expecting its arrival soon, since yesterday's fore runner. I was told to expect a personal message, and it may have been sent to the Hotel de Ville!'

'George! Not the old forerunner joke again! It's a quotation from Macbeth. I thought plays bored you.'

'Not since I realised Will understood the problems faced by Kings. If I hadn't read his plays in the Bastille, I would never have known.'

'Well, George, if you are so well informed, perhaps he will make you Master of the Revels!'

'Far too onerous a post for a simple fellow like me, my sweet!'


'Will, while you are delivering the letters in town, ask old Hubert whether a pigeon has brought me a message. It is highly confidential, and he must not read it and memorise it: it is absolutely confidential.'

George climbed the slope to the Hotel de Ville, and entered the Mayor's office. No preparations had begun for the family celebration they would be holding in the reception rooms in a day or two. It must be finalised that day. He hoped, if the news from London permitted, that his son Philippe would become a full partner in the firm and receive the congratulations of their business partners. He certainly deserved it. He wanted to inform his fellow Burgesses of his intentions before he spoke to Philippe. Politeness required George to inform them of his decision to relinquish his position, to his son.

Philip had shown his ability during his father's frequent absences overseas and deserved promotion. George was reasonably confident that the King would require him to attend to issues of importance when the message arrived, and he would probably have to go to London. If the King's business required that they must live in London, Philippe might be needed there. Fortunately there were other Carterets who would be ready for promotion. He had not been visited London since the Parliamentarians exiled them.

He had learned that Monck and Hyde had travelled to the Low Countries, to discover the new King's wishes, and the conditions to be met before he would come to claim his throne. He would learn later the King's negotiations with Hyde had been successful and were disarmingly simple. He offered co-operation with a new parliament and no desire to exact retribution. The provisional Council of State was relieved and willing to smooth his path. The date for the discussion of a possible Coronation, could be discussed later, although as Charles had been King of Great Britain for eleven years without being crowned, it might not be necessary. A delay of few more months would reveal the need. He was confident His Majesty would have some role to offer him. He must be ready to accept it, bearing in mind the unavoidable delay which would occur if he was delayed in the Channel crossing to England . He hoped fervently, that the pigeon would hurry, and would even now be winging its way to St Helier.

Will Jarvis played a significant part in George's life. Among other errands, Will was to find out which ship could be ready to engage take him to Portsmouth urgently. Since his meeting with the Queen and her treasurer, Jermyn, George was confident that his full value had been realised and he wished to develop his improved reputation. In the past year, both Thurloe and Clarendon had kept him abreast of developments. His actual identity was concealed under the pseudonym, 'Milton,' and the Court and Queen would not have realised how much he had done to assist the Royal family and the new esteem they had gained. Charles had assured him that he would repay all he was owed in cash and in gratitude, but George knew that he must continue to work assiduously to retain the favour he had acquired. He could not depend on the past success: he would need to be constantly applying himself to acts of service to the Monarch. Favour could easily be withdrawn.

Carteret was confident Charles would find him challenging tasks, created by adapting parliamentary regulations to the needs of Monarchy. He was surprised to find that himself eager to read the expected message, carried by pigeon. post He would be expected in London without delay. Fortunately, the king was well aware that there would be delays in crossing the Channel, caused by wind and weather.

He knew the King trusted in him, and he held a document signed by Charles, guaranteeing the repayment of all his past expenses. This included the years 1640 to 1660, when he had served the King's needs at his own expense. So anticipating future expenditure, he would keep careful accounts. While governing Jersey he had hunted down many pirates in the Channel, as Chief Jurat and later, as Sheriff of Jersey. He also took on the cost of defending the island against Parliamentary forces, as a way of safeguarding the interests of the king.

He had suffered exile for the King and confiscation of his property. He and his family had left Jersey with nothing and it was fortunate that he had sound commercial relationships with the traders of St Malo, who had found him a house, and financed him to expand his business from their town. This had been an advantageous move, supported by the Dowse family, his distant relatives in Carteret-Barneville, who provided a safe retreat at Peyrol farm. His skills had come to the notice of Louis XVI, who knew that Charles I had appointed Carteret, Controller of the Royal Navy, a post he had held briefly, until Parliament dismissed him and sent him in to exile. A third of the fleet had remained loyal and he had based them in St Helier, building up a fleet of frigates and yachts to fight for the King.

Louis had become aware that he had an exiled Englishman, exiled in his country, seeking employment and offered him protection if he would make a survey of his Channel ports, to ensure they could withstand attack by the much larger British ships of war. George had set improvements under way. He had then been approached by the French Lord High Admiral, Cesar, Duc de Vendôme, a son of King Louis by Madame de Maintenant, who had no experience of ships, but had been placed in charge of the French navy. The Admiral, with Carteret's help, trapped and destroyed the Spanish Channel fleet in port. He was certain that this had been noted with approval by Charles II and the French King, his cousin. He had every reason to be confident, since he could think of no rival who had such a broad range of naval, financial, and administrative skills. On a personal basis he had amazingly good health, for a man of fifty years, unlike a growing number of his contemporaries.

A first step on the path to the delayed restoration occurred when the Rump Parliament dismissed their army Commander, Lambert, in favour of Monck, who in turn handed command to the King. Monck and Fairfax summoned a Convention which announced the restoration of the Monarchy. This process begun, Monck sent a delegation to negotiate with Charles, who was constantly changing his French refuge to evade possible assassins.

Two days later, Philippe's birthday celebrations took place, in St Malo, in an atmosphere of celebration, and George finally received the delayed message advising him to cross to Portsmouth. George, while making his son a full partner, indicated he would soon to be in charge, when he was summoned to the mainland. He suggested to his fellow Burgesses, that Philippe should be elected to the City Council with a Dumaresq cousin, as deputy, who would take his place if and when it was necessary for Philippe to transfer to London. Everyone in St Malo was fully informed about the changes happening in England, a close trading partner, and wished the Carterets good fortune and increased trade with Britain for themselves.

Bess, who disliked uncertainty, needed reassurance on a number of issues. Was George confident that the King had not forgotten them? After all, they were owed a large sum to repay the constantly increasing loan they had made to the King. She was also anxious about her husband's health, fearing the stress caused by fresh responsibilities.

'You must refuse to take on any dangerous missions, George? I hate it when I hear nothing from you for weeks. I fear you are risking your life or are already dead.'

'I think Charles may notice that my hair is grey, Dear, and will bear it in mind when he distributes appointments. I hope to have largely sedentary occupations, and the opportunity for sailing, It's time he found a younger executive officer and left me to do the administration.

'If only you could take Will Jarvis with you to make sure you eat. Remember you are fifty, and many of our old friends are dead or dying. I want to enjoy a few years of retirement with you in the country, when you decide to resign.'

'Honestly, Dearest, I think the King will remember I am a seaman. I really don't know much about anything else, although I seem to have some talent at making money. I suspect he is lining something up for me as we speak, and we will hear soon,'

George retained a measure of unease with regard to Hyde's attitude to him. He had been wary of placing reliance on him, remembering his talent for causing alarm and despondency. It seemed to him that Hyde enjoyed complicating simple operations so he could enjoy the praise he received when he solved them. Never depend on a lawyer to find a simple solution, he decided.

In the meantime, there were other family matters requiring attention. They could not ignore the possible effects the changes would have on the younger ones. James, four years junior than Philip, attended college in Rennes until the end of the academic year. The three little girls were happily settled at the local convent in the care of an order of intelligent nuns. It seemed best for George to become established in the rôle he was assigned, and for the family to remain in St Malo until he could find a suitable home for the family and servants. This would probably take several months and the details could be left until stability was established. He would take Will Jarvis with him to re-establish his former contacts with London tradesmen.

## CHAPTER TWO

1660 was a year of tremendous change affecting Royalty, the Nobility, the Middle Sort and even manual labourers. The civil unrest between 1642 and 1660, saw the rise to power, largely unacknowledged, of the merchant, trading, and banking classes, and to gain control over the nobility and rural landowners. Those who had formerly controlled society, who had spent their lives, defending the power of the king, were left poorer and no longer held sway in the provinces. The restored King was given total charge of defence, though a Parliament, controlled by the Middle sort, would decide expenditure. Charles inherited the unique role of Defender of the Faith, bestowed and blessed with sanctified oil, empowering the King with total authority over the spiritual lives of his subjects. These conditions created opportunities for ambitious men and women to create and hold public and private offices, unavailable to earlier generations. George and his family were in a position to take prominent roles in the nation's government and they seized it with vigour. The less welcome aspects of the event would be come all too apparent during the coming months.

Carterets, Dowses and Paulets were among the many families of humble origins which rose to eminence with Charles's restoration. Thynnes, Fiennes and Montagues and many others followed this trend. They were ably assisted by refugees from France, the Empire, Holland, Belgium, Scotland and Ireland: all with scientific, economic and mathematical skills undervalued in their own lands and many of whom held religious beliefs condemned in their own lands.

The Government Convention had asked General Monck to negotiate directly with the King, and the resulting terms of agreement were few and simply stated. Neither he nor the King wanted to delay securing the immediate return of the King to his kingdom. The tedious details could be defined later. Charles believed he would be welcomed and was willing to work closely with parliament. He would take the traditional oaths at his coronation, and defend the established civil law, the English church and the Religious Covenant in Scotland. He demanded the punishment of those who had signed the death sentence on his father, but would not threaten the lives or possessions of those who had worked under the Commonwealth Government. On this basis, the Declaration of Breda was agreed and put before parliament for approval, first being put into legal language by Clarendon and senior lawyers, Charles was proclaimed King on 8 May 1660. The King had made it clear to Monck and Hyde, that any agreement they reached, must be with the understanding that all laws passed by the Commonwealth Government, must be rescinded. The powers and privileges held by his father must legally pass to him. On this understanding, the Declaration of Breda might be proclaimed publicly.

In the fullness of time, it became clear that a less eager wish to restore the new monarch, might have created a more structured chain of command in government. It would have taken more care to eliminate those areas of dispute, which Parliamentary Government had solved, and which were now restored to the statute book, to give rise later to the very same difficulties. The very looseness of this agreement was, however, of extreme advantage to the advanced intellectuals and scientists who found merchants and traders, eager to employ them to develop new skills for craftsmen, new trading ventures, and industries. Charles's first command was to invest heavily into one of his own personal obsessions. Two fourth-class battleships were renamed 'Royal Charles' and 'James Royal' to carry their separate households and this was followed by the order of more new ships of war, frigates and sloops, than had ever before been constructed. It was Charles II who called the Navy by its new title, the Royal Navy.

Many privately-owned trading vessels joined the huge escort flotilla composed of ships of all sizes and varied ownership. This was an indication of the way matters were developing a popular momentum. George was not among those who met the Royal brothers on board, but he was closely involved with organising public events surrounding the King's welcome to London. When he reached Portsmouth, he learned that Edward Hyde had been created Lord Chancellor and Charles had already appointed him Assistant Lord Chamberlain. The task had been intended for the 2nd Earl of Warwick, Cromwell's "Great Earl". He had died, exhausted, in 1658. His son, Charles, the 4th Earl, had no discernible ability, and all the Chamberlain's functions devolved upon George. His actual instructor was the Duke of Norfolk who made all the large-scale appointments and commanded agents to carry out his instructions. Three weeks was the time available before the day planned for the Royal procession and welcome to London. George was told of this when he met the King at Dover, who also gave him authority to apply any necessary pressure to persuade the Burgesses of London, and General Monck, to give their full support. Fortunately, Charles made a very slow progress from Portsmouth, hampered as he was by the requirements of his household, his mistress, his children, his horses, his attendant spaniels, and the happy crowds among whom he walked and talked. When he reached London for the ceremony, it was 23 May, and by coincidence, his thirtieth birthday. What could have been more suitable! It may even have been planned.

George, appointed as the King's Household Chamberlain, knew he would be expected to produce a very public outdoor event, the success or failure of which could make or break his reputation. The State procession, timed to follow Charles's three week progress, must be performed without error and with such display that it remained permanently in the memory of citizens. The progress from Dover fortunately, had been rapturously received by every class of citizen along the route. Charles had dismounted to walk among his people, exchanging greetings and "Touching" the afflicted who knelt for his blessing to remedy their ills. George was aware that he had not visited London for eight years and that much would have changed: many former friends might have retired or died. He held on to the hope that his previous reputation for reliability remained strong. The arrangements would be largely at the expense of the City Fathers, but he would have to take charge of a team of eager City merchants, and others whom he had never met. All would be as eager as he was, to have their loyalty noted.

It was essential to familiarise himself at once with the City which seemed to be a busier place than he remembered, and London had grown to be the largest capital city in Europe. The population had increased to 75, 000, and people were gravitating there from all over Britain and Europe, seeking employment in the many new trades available. The former monopolies had been abandoned confining transport of goods to English ships, and closing trade with some European trading cities. Gresham's Stock Exchange was flourishing and growing inadequate for the demands of traders. In the narrow streets and alleys, shopkeepers and hawkers noisily touted oysters, oranges, enamelled patch-boxes, ivory teeth, and miracle cures. The smell of three large Markets: Billingsgate for fish, Covent Garden for fruit, and Smithfield for meat; intensified the general stench of street life and overloaded sewers to new levels of offence. To the north and east of London, commerce and housing was already expanding beyond the encircling city boundaries, while there, and within the walls, farms and smallholdings scratched a meagre existence.

In the event it was fortunate that they were anticipating a new growth of foreign trade. As he went about his work of cajoling and offering favours and rewards to encourage generosity, he met with considerable willingness from the most unlikely officials. The Mayor and Aldermen, determined to retain the privileges extracted so unwillingly from the King's father, were determined to display their firm hold on the right of the City to govern itself. George was a little surprised how, after a slow beginning, the Livery Companies were increasingly eager to open their doors and banquets to him. Initially he attributed it to his fine new uniform and attendant officers bearing his wands of Office. Later he was to find their friendship was offered at informal meetings, and he regained the warm feeling that he met with general approval. George realised that the favourable esteem which he generally received, seemed to survive in this new context. It certainly made his task easier. It certainly helped with the vexing matter of the missing Crown Jewels when it became a pressing issue.

There lingered in the memory of Montague and other nobles, a traditional order of events and the placing of these in order of precedence. Any vacant spaces would be filled by representatives of the City companies and Guilds, or by the surviving regiments, though it would now include Cromwell's own regiment, the Coldstream Guards, who were to be retained. The formal procession, beginning at Aldgate and passing though the City, was greeted by the Lord Mayor and Corporation at the Guildhall, it then wound along through the streets by way of St Paul's Cathedral, where former religious figures, from earlier years, including some Presbyterians, clustered around Juxon, formerly Bishop of London. A sign of things to come! Along the road, triumphal arches, heavily decorated at the expense of London nursery men, had to be negotiated, admired and praised. Everywhere cheering crowds of Londoners, drank wine from the local fountains, and contributed raucous and tipsy greetings to their new ruler. The older citizens would have recalled recent occasions where violence, riot and derision had ruled the day. To general relief events of that kind did not occur.

It was acclaimed a considerable triumph, much to the relief of organisers, and especially gratifying to George. With spectators lining the streets and leaning from the windows, the procession at last crossed the Tyburn River and entered Westminster, where the Abbey bells rang out to welcome Charles to his residence at Whitehall Palace. Somehow, he had assembled regiments of armed guards, and bandsmen to create the right atmosphere. One group of soldiers wore unusual uniforms rousing curiosity as they marched past. They had been given to George years before as a leaving gift, by the Sultan of Morocco, and were worn, to the astonishment of their wearers, by one of the newly formed brigades. George left no diary or notes on the process of his arrangements, but published descriptions are available in the memoranda of other observers, and there is a fine engraving, showing the length of the procession, and the personnel taking part. His uniforms added a bewildering touch of oriental colour and magic and were the cause of curiosity. They can be seen in Hollar's engraving. The King, and Prince James, both wearing tall black hats, and George, leading the Moroccans, can by seen clearly. Bess and the family bought Hollar's engraving when it was published later, to keep a family memory alive.

# CHAPTER THREE

In addition to Carteret's procession, there was other business to attend to in the next three weeks preceding the King's arrival in London. The Rump Parliament gained the honour of passing into law the hurriedly prepared contract settled in Breda. All laws passed by the Commonwealth were subsequently to be cancelled without discussion, in the wave of relief sweeping the country. The King would take Command of the truncated army, and Monck would direct its conduct, confining its duties to royal protection and ceremonial events. James, Duke of York assumed command of the Navy, and Sir George would be Navy Treasurer and general advisor. Bess, on a short trip to London, was delighted to be the wife of a Knight Baronet. The change of business management was underway and the ship 'Ruby' made permanently available as a family vessel. As navy controller Carteret would have the use of the large Admiralty barge and, as Chamberlain, the provision of Barges and Yachts for the use of the royal family passing between the Tower, Somerset House, Whitehall, Hampton Court and Windsor. Oatlands Palace was set aside as a home for future royal offspring, where they would be nursed and educated for their rôle in life.

George was chosen as one of two MPs for Portsmouth, to sit in the new Commons after the Rump parliament had completed its transitional duties. The penalties imposed on the Carterets, Paulets and Dowses, in the form of fines and sequestrations were lifted, and this applied to all families who had been penalised. Their land and property were restored. Daughters and sons of the two power groups, had begun to intermarry to ensure the smooth passage of land and possessions from one generation to the next. Similarly, some non-conformist "readers" were adopted as Anglican rectors where those owning the living felt it to be appropriate. Edward Carteret, from his youth cupbearer to Prince James, was placed in charge of one of the new regiments of guards

George, whose financial brain rarely slept, had kept accounts of the money provided to traders who provided the silks, velvets, horses, stabling, feed for horses and grooms, and money donated to assist dignitaries on the

Royal route, to present gilded goblets and plates as welcoming gifts. Each had provided an estimate of expenditure, and had been reminded that if they overspent, future tenders might be refused. Returning home, engrossed in calculations, he was waylaid by a polite gentleman, who commanded him to attend on the king. He found Charles cheerfully dismissing the last of those lingering to offer congratulations, and indicated that George should remain, escorting the remainder to the door. George was asked to join him at his work table. Throwing himself into an armchair, the King invited him to draw up a seat to a table spread with papers and scribbled notes.

'The Lord Chamberlain and I need food, Peter. Please ask the kitchen to send up some cold cuts, pastries and salads, and a flask of Burgundy, as soon as possible!'

'Sir George, I am grateful for the fine display for my homecoming. I hope it may be a sign that future events will be equally successful. In three weeks you have created a show as good as anything I saw in Paris. You look very well, George, and I hope Lady Elizabeth and the family are all in good health, and of course Sir Philippe. I regret deeply the unfortunate deaths of so many of your family in the recent upheavals. I intend that nothing so dreadful will ever happen again while I am King.' At this point Charles paused and had wine poured and served, remarking that Cromwell had failed to exploit one cellar, which had allowed the bottles time to mature. A toast was drunk and The King expressed his good wishes to Lady Carteret.

'I have always known, Sir George, I could rely on you in difficult situations, and you would give good advice when I needed it. I am inundated now with obligations and regulations and the whole business of discovering how I can rule the country, with the support of Parliament. I have started on a list of some of the urgent matters, and I hope you will offer some help.

'For example, I would like your thoughts on matters to have priority. Perhaps we could run through the most pressing of them. I will of course consult Edward Hyde, whom I have just created Lord Clarendon, who will be Lord Chancellor. I know he will refer me to my father's practices, of course, but, though my father and I owe him a great deal, the past is the past, and I want to avoid past errors. My father was a fine man, always loving to us children, perceptive in his understanding of his subjects and their needs, and scrupulously honest, but it seems that these qualities were not sufficient, or perhaps he was not perceptive of the need to make his decisions palatable to the people.'

'George, I am not my father! I hope that the generous support I have been offered by the people and Monck's Rump Parliament, may continue to support me in my attempt to lay the past errors to reSt I want to regain the support of a freshly elected Parliament as soon as possible. I have no wish to antagonise them before I am crowned.'

George realised, that Charles seemed to draw a distinction between himself and his father, which might suggest an acceptance that he might be willing to accept compromise in preference to confrontation. If this was so it was reassuring, although he was reminded of Amyas saying that depending entirely on the word of an absolute ruler might lead to disappointment. At this early date, Charles, aware that he had no money to repay the large sums spent on his behalf, was inevitably eager to know when he would be told his royal finances.

'I gather the Members will be offering me financial grants to welcome me home. My father was never offered anything at his Coronation, because MPs did not trust Buckingham to spend it on matters of national benefit. I suppose I may regain some of the land confiscated from me and given to dissenters. Is this Palace mine, or any of the other Royal possessions? I would like to know. I have no income, and no idea what income they have in mind. Neither do I know how much to ask for, if I am asked to request an amount. I am not prepared to "live off my own" since at present I own nothing. I hope I shall be offered some of my previous estates, but I need an agreed annual income also, and a guarantee that Parliament themselves will pay for the defence of the realm. I am not prepared to follow my father's example. He went to great lengths to live off his own savings, but in the long run he was forced to go to parliament with a begging bowl, to afford ships and pay their crew.' By this time, much had been taken and more wine was poured, before they continued the discussion.

'I see neither of us has answers to these questions. Have you considered what salary you would expect as Lord Chamberlain? I intend to repay you and your officials, from the Navy Account, when the Commons decide how much the army and navy require. Could you perhaps discover whether there is a traditional allowance for a Palace Chamberlain?'

'May I ask former office holders for advice Sir. I believe those who collect taxes have always kept any surplus remaining after the tax expected has been given to the treasury. It might not be appropriate in this instance.

I will consult experts and bring you information.'

'Hyde tells me the new Parliament is willing to make me a generous award. Failing that, I shall have no freedom of action. My growing number of staff, and you, will require to be paid. This will be my responsibility. I cannot rule in a condition of poverty. A King must be able to live in some style and be able to set a standard in palaces, navies and regiments. I wish to support the arts and sciences by sponsoring those who can add to the accomplishments of the nation. A King must make an impression among other rulers of power to be able to show the nation to the best advantage. The procession you created was a good beginning: my coronation must be even more of a spectacle for the eyes of the world will be inspecting us.'

During the summer of 1660, George made enquiries about Parliament's intentions as to the King's future income. There was discussion, but it was slow to make a decision, and the King required a decision. Finding Hyde in a rare moment of relaxation, Carteret broached the King's anxiety concerning payments to ensure he could afford to rule effectively. Hyde was somewhat dismissive, and told him not to fear, that he would be repaid what he spent for the King's benefit. He was advised to continue to keep a careful account, in case questions arose, and employ an accountant to support his claim. Hyde implied that George was greedily asking purely on his own behalf, and went away feeling that Hyde had once more cast doubts on his probity: he was sorry that Hyde appeared to hold him in contempt; or that he was not significant enough to deserve an answer.

At least Hyde wasted no time or words in Council meetings. There were hundreds of small claims and apparent injustices to be adjusted, many, but not all, pending from the restoration and the changes it caused. Largely to satisfy his son's curiosity about the momentous decisions his father was presumably making, George jotted down a few notes during a typically dull meeting on 20 May 1660. Of course these matters were important to those who made requests, but they were the sort of minor decisions always at the heart of government. The King was now the final decision maker and even such trivial matters as these held potential importance. On the rare occasions when the King was absent from Privy Council, Prince James or Hyde chaired the meeting.

1. Robert Slingsley mentioned the case of Mr Kirke late of the Bedchamber. He had been sent to Calais, by the King's order and had been flung into a "loathsome dungeon" by some misunderstanding, where he remained after three years. (Order sent for his release.)
2. To demand the return of fines imposed on English cargoes by Louis X1V. (demand made for £1000 for every year imposed.)
3. Sir George Carteret to be Treasurer and future Commander of the Navy. John, lord Berkley and Sir William Baber to be surveyors and Samuel Pepys, Clerk.
4. Capt. Burrow's frigate to be refitted for the Queen Mother: "to set men to work!" Royal Party to meet Her Majesty.
5. Repairs to 'Henrietta' and 'Blackdown'.
6. Captain Edward Curtis requests his discounted payments to be paid. He had been slandered.

When his son remarked that he had expected more important matters, George pointed out that, as in book-keeping, it was the small sums which kept the country solvent. A government must deal justly at all levels.

Carteret's duties seemed to bring him ever closer to the King. Dr. Philippe, Adjutant General to Cromwell's army, was among those whom Charles retained for his accomplishments. He had sworn loyalty to the new regime and he and George joined the rota of gentlemen attending on the King throughout the day. George seemed to be a sounding board for the King to tell his personal concerns. The King raised the subject of money with increasing frequency. It was clearly a matter of personal concern.

'I told Hyde that if MPs imagined that I had ambitions to spend a fortune to be a warrior King, they should dismiss the suspicion. I have seen too much evidence of the damage done by armies and navies. I hope never again will war or civil strife afflict my people. My regiments and my county militias will be employed solely for the defence of our peace. If we take part in wars, it will be in other lands, not here. I will never forget the battle at Worcester: So many fine people died for no benefit, and decent men like Goring and Lucas had their lives ruined.'

'Your Majesty, I hear that Hyde will explain Your Majesty's Breda Agreement and believes that the Commons will welcome your intentions. He will suggest they should offer you not less than one million pounds at the very least and it seems their mood was generous.'

'George, you have brought crumbs of comfort. I hope that is not all I shall be offered. I believe we may already be overspent and I have a former Army and Navy unpaid for two years! Then there is the expense of a Coronation and the re-creation of the Order of the Garter. Without Garter Knights and Bishops, there can be no Coronation. I wonder if they realise this'

'I believe Hyde will speak to them about those matters', George remarked. 'As for the estimated cost of your Coronation, Sir. I believe that these may not be fully appreciated by some of the new men who begged your Majesty to return. Hyde will have to put the facts to them calmly, and tell them you are making reasonable demands. It must be pointed as the inevitable result of their own action: it was entirely their decision to request your return. The older members of the House will be able to make this clear to them.'

'I hope you are right, George. I will tell you that these are my basic requirements, and they must be respected. There must be no doubt. In the last analysis, if I am not allowed to be crowned with proper dignity, and receive an adequate income, I am prepared to leave my kingdom permanently. I will not accept an inadequate settlement. I have no wish to leave, of course. Please keep me informed, George. I shall need to address the Lords early next week and I am eager to praise their generosity. I do not want to have matters sprung on me for which I am not prepared. I shall make that clear to Hyde again, so that he has no doubt on this matter.'

'I shall talk to Hyde as soon as I can, Your Majesty. He has a clear understanding of the Constitution as set out by James 1, your grandfather, and I am confident he will wish to uphold it.'

'I shall inform Parliament when we meet next of my new appointments and hope that they will find them pleasing and well deserved. I shall also mention that I shall be seeking for a number of younger men to bring the House of Lords to its traditional size. I have noticed empty stalls in St George's chapel where former Knights of the Bath sat. I must appoint suitable replacements, and as a European monarch, some of the new Knights will represent friendly foreign rulers.

I intend to take a lead in matters of a cultural nature, to take the lead in promoting sciences, learning and Industry, and I shall be seeking those who can provide those skills for the benefit of the country. I hope that my Parliament will support me in these aims so that we may all benefit from the wealth to be gained as the result of our expenditure.'

George was greatly encouraged to hear these propositions and hoped that the promise of future commercial gain would encourage the most tight-fisted MPs to invest in future prospects. At the same time he wondered whether the Parliament would support these aims. There had been some attempt to encourage the concept of buying and storing goods to guard against future shortages, and laying in stocks bought while prices were low. George had some experience of it and had seen that it had brought wealth to the Dutch, but the English tended to trust only in enterprises bringing short term gains. Changes of this kind would demand new procedures which could be deferred for the presenting the need for increased trade at present. Portsmouth and the Navy were being starved of the supplies they needed because no one was prepared to purchase supplies in advance and goods were often unobtainable when they were urgently needed. Perhaps as Naval Treasurer, he could bring about changes. The tediousness of his other daily tasks, was increasingly wearing, but was inevitable considering the large number of worthy individuals who were, on the whole, only seeking for the justice they deserved, if they were to be persuaded to follow the demands of the new government.

The King was an early riser and had inexhaustible energy, however time-consuming his work. Every morning he was attended by his barber, who shaved him, and his valet who bathed him and assisted with dressing. Courtiers, always present, were reminded of his appointments for that day, which always began with coffee and rolls. Exercise normally came next and the dogs were included among the gregarious party of attendants, secretaries, and guards who accompanied him during his morning exercise. Charles walked rapidly, with long, loping strides, greeting passers-by and engaging in animated conversation. As a variation, he frequently gathered attendants and towelling, and took a brisk swim in the Thames, or took a rowing skiff, perhaps setting up a race with his brother, James, or other gentlemen. George found it was sound practice to be present to hear Charles's thought on general matters. Meetings of the Privy Council came thick and fast early in the reign and frequently followed shortly after the morning exercise.

George was often present, but there were large numbers of new members, and the Chair was often held by Hyde or Prince James. Sometimes Prince Rupert presided. Close contacts with wealthy traders and bankers stood him in good stead. Fortunately, discussions between ministers took place openly about the Court, and Hyde took a pride in his openness and frank statements of policies. George was able to present Charles with unmoderated news as it was heard in the exchange, on a daily basis.

George was astonished at the changes made in the life of the City of London. In many ways, its freedom from Royal interference, at a sudden whim, including financial demands, such as taxation levied, had increased the country's standing as a trading nation. Without unpredictable interruptions to trade, there was a natural move towards a commonwealth of shared interest in trading. Meeting William Petty one morning, George enquired whether Cromwell had encouraged these practices now employed in the City and on the Stock exchange.

'I must urge you to exercise caution, George, in speaking of these matters. Confidentially I will say that His Majesty has forbidden me to promulgate ideas without his permission. My land and property in Ireland will be lost if I fail to follow new regulations.'

'I am shocked to hear this, Will. I remember those meeting at the The Bear, where we used to discuss potential government changes to make government policies more transparent to MPs and the people they represent. What does James Harrington say about this stifling of discussion? Does he still conduct meetings of the Rota?'

'Nothing at all, George. All talk of democratic change is banned. The King believes that his father paid to much respect to those who envied his power and discussion of that King is reported by his agents for possible prosecution.'

'What does Harrington think about this? I read his book, 'Oceana,' during my exile, and thought it was an excellent programme. I know it was modelled on the Rules observed by Dutch traders. Amyas told me that before the King's trial, your group, the Sola, had considerable backing from the City.'

'The King also read it with interest in 1654, but regards it as a possible danger to his authority. The book has been banned and copies are being confiscated. James was imprisoned when the King reached Whitehall. Secretly I am informed he is being held in Portsea Castle until the King decides his fate.'

'But surely Harrington had frequent discussions with the late King and thought he had come close to persuading the King to made real concessions and I believe he and Henry Mildmay, another loyal negotiator, had persuaded him to accept Pym as his first Minister.'

'True I believe, but an unexpected difficulty appeared, George. Charles tried to arrest the Commons rebels, and failed: then he made a degrading offer of money and a Peerage to Pym informed the Queen of his intention and she persuaded her husband that Pym was merely a man greedy for power, who would seize all his powers to govern.. She proposed that Charles should offer Pym a peerage and a huge salary to change sides and enforce the king's wishes. Pym was furious and refused to negotiate any longer with the King.

'The news resulted in the street riots and the Queen terrified for her children, They all took refuge at Hampton Court. This led to Civil War and the deaths of thousands. The King should have returned to London and accepted parliament's offer. It might have repaired the damage. Instead the Queen made her husband leave for Oxford and safety. He should never have abandoned London. He was not facing attack. They had never been threatened by Parliament, and no-one seriously opposed the principle of Monarchy.'

'I had no idea of this.'

'You had your own problems to solve in Jersey, of course.'

'Why is Harrington in prison. He was a loyal subject and attended on the King with Mildmay at the execution.

'They were asked by parliament to assist the King. King Charles now believes that they should have refused the offer since by doing so, they agreed with the execution. Mildmay is being held in the Tower. The twenty-nine MPs who signed the death sentence are held in Lambeth Palace as regicides. The King will shortly bring them to trial, and parliament is likely to demand the death penalty.

'I thought the King had promised Albemarle and Hyde, to create an Act of Indemnity exonerating those not involved in the death sentence? I fear that Harrington and Mildmay may not be granted indemnity.'

'How do you see your future, William?'

'I have decided to retire from public life, and cultivate my Irish plantations. Cromwell's government and the City Fathers are adopting some of my recommendations, and the City merchants also, and there will be no stopping them, I believe. If the King seeks culprits to punish, I believe I will be grouped among the harmless ones, like Milton, Montague and

Marvell, who have reputations and wealth. If those are threatened, I would accept most orders rather than lose their friendship. I value your friendship George, and hope to meet your family once more. I suspect we may all be held in suspense by a King who knows how to play a game aimed a gaining his own advantage by allowing us like butterflies, trap ourselves in his net.'

Carteret, always a pragmatist, felt great sympathy with Harrington and sympathised with his certainty that with more effort, a solution would have been found. In his heart he felt sure, even if the King had made concessions, they would never have been sufficient, for the King would never renounce his right to change any agreement undermining his authority. In the meantime he was preoccupied with the business of state, chief among which was the Coronation. He suddenly thought of Amyas Carteret, the uncle who had introduced him to the Courtiers of Charles I, and guided his every action. He had advised strongly that George to seek power and influence but never wholly trust the promises of Kings. He should always have a fall-back position in reserve, and money to protect his family in the event of disgrace and ruin. Perhaps Dr Philippe was held in high regard although a Roundhead leader. As such he was placed close to the King where his actions and words could be observed. George realised that his own closeness to the King might be a variety of house imprisonment.

The King was also in two minds on various subjects apparently. His threat to leave the country if his "reasonable financial needs" were not met, was a threat he held in reserve, only uttered in private and a smile of amusement, but his words passed between his friends and roused consternation. It probably urged Parliament to give him their support. Equally firm was his determination to have a full Coronation ceremony, performed at Westminster, in the sight of his nobility and subjects, by the Archbishop of Canterbury. The London Aldermen must accede to his insistence on a full state procession, beginning at the Tower, and crossing the City, as Charles asserted his right to do so, en route to the Abbey.

He had been King since January 1649, when his father was executed, and it might seem an empty, expensive gesture, and unnecessary. Without a coronation, Charles would be seen as a state appointee and, like the Dutch Stadtholder, could be dismissed if he caused offence. To be valid the Coronation would be attended by European statesmen, some of whose rulers were nervous about their own status. The power of the Dutch Republic, and the republican British Commonwealth, was a very real threat. It was essential to demonstrate that Britain had a strong Monarchy once more. The pressure he could successfully apply on Parliament, was a trial of his strength, and a strong boost to monarchy.

Parliament was so exultant at the Restoration of Monarchy they paid little or no attention to the powers they were signing away, and the strong encouragement they provided to Louis XIV and his plan to establish absolute monarchy. Carteret might well have felt that Charles had the ability of a master strategist in political issues. His clever manipulation of his associates had only just been tested.

## CHAPTER FOUR

Charles would have known that his Royal parents, before the Queen and the children sailed to exile in France, had sold surplus items including some grants of land, to raise money to finance a force of mercenaries in support of a national uprising in favour of the King. Royal Treasures, held in safe concealment, were conveyed secretly to their ships. The most precious Treasures were held in the Tower of London, the most secure place in the Realm. Charles and Henrietta regarded them as objects of personal property, and took the most valuable. In France, these were broken up to pay for arms and soldiers to attack Parliamentary forces. Charles II was probably aware of his father's action, and possibly relished the embarrassment it would cause when their loss was noticed. He may not have been aware of George's part in the sale of the Queen's own jewels, for which he obtained top prices from the gold merchants of the Netherlands.

His new position in the Royal household obliged him to replace the lost items at the expanse of parliament. Tactful approaches must be made first to the previous Warden of the Tower and to inspect the accounts and receipts. The Warden was arrested in the meantime for dereliction of duty and possible treason. How much pressure could he place on Henrietta, the Queen Mother? Some objects might remain in her possession in case of need. The King would have to decide. His frequent disregard for his mother, shown earlier, may have prompted him to award her Wimbledon Palace following her return to Britain, urged by King Louis, who had financed his Aunt's household expenses for several years.

It is probably time to outline some of the more important constitutional changes made by the "Restoration" Parliament. The King had been chosen by a Parliamentary decision to reinstate the monarchic principle. The Declaration of Breda was remarkable for its brevity containing a few intentions guaranteed to be generally popular. Charles expressed willingness to accept the advice of the Royalist Parliament, and they in turn would reward him financially, sufficient to restore the personal privilege of the Sovereign, which the civil war had been fought to restrict.

Charles II was given all the power his father had lost by leaving London, allowing parliament to take on full authority. How different life might have been if Charles I had not abandoned his capital!

Charles II, by cancelling every act passed during the Commonwealth, had rejected all the restrictions placed on his father to curb his ability to disregard Parliament whenever he chose to do so. Carteret was a trusted councillor of long standing, on many issues, and was at once appointed to the Privy Council, remaining a P.C. for life. His appointment was not popular with senior nobles, who regarded him as a tradesman, and few would have known how much they owed to his loyal actions during the past thirty years. He had never previously served in an office of state, and therefore lacked supportive ex-colleagues, or friends in the establishment. Neither was he a member of the English ruling class. Although he was not exactly mocked as a 'Foreigner,' his accent was that of a countryman, assumed to lack culture. This attitude became clear to him when associating with Prince Rupert, who was quite open in his contempt for Carteret, and whose views were adopted eagerly by new and impressionable courtiers. Rupert was third in line for the throne and an influential courtier.

George noted that Charles understood the need for patience, that it would be wise to delay making some decisions until Parliament decided reach his desired conclusion. He had proposed an Act of Indemnity and Oblivion, despite his mother's opinion that those who had served under Cromwell should be executed for Treason, and officially decided to protect those who had acted in good faith, or had been 'misguided'. Some criticised this generosity, for the majority had in fact supported the Commonwealth and, economically, had benefited from improved commerce and trade brought about by restrictions on the strength of Holland. Many nobles and wealthy citizens supported Hyde when he praised Charles for asking capital punishment only for those who had signed his father's death sentence, a few who had benefited by the King's execution.

John Thurloe and his spies, were re-allocated to Hyde, were to arrest the regicides the guilty, and were quite successful in pursuit of those who had signed the death sentence. Thurloe had been Cromwell's chief minister but was excluded on condition that he betrayed former colleagues. Others, including John Locke, Andrew Marvell and John Milton, were spared on condition that they became strong advocates of the King's actions. Of the forty signatories of the Death Sentence, twenty-nine had been rounded up

*Restoration and Retribution*

by September and were held in Lambeth Palace, awaiting parliamentary examination. Six more had emigrated to France, Switzerland or Holland and two to New England. These were dealt with at a later date when captured.

George had been shocked by the arrest Mildmay and Harrington, both of whom were strong royalists. Was it possible that their loyalty was thought to be insufficient? If that was so, would others who had discussed Harrington's moderate proposals, be subject to arrest? He himself had attended and spoken at these meetings. Thankfully his family was in St Malo, but he might need to rejoin them for self-preservation.

He kept his fears to himself but intensified his pursuit of the missing jewels and their replacement. During a September Privy Council there was discussion of the recent Act of Oblivion, passed by both houses of Parliament. Hundreds may have breathed a sigh of relief, confident that the actions required of them under Commonwealth government were to be forgotten. The King proposed, now Parliament had granted them permission, to decide how to proceed. Hyde proposed that they must each have a fair trial and that, currently, twenty-nine persons were detained at Lambeth. They must be brought before a judge, their guilt or innocence demonstrated, and their punishment defined.

One member remarked that it might be a lengthy process and involve numerous attorneys. Hyde was of the opinion that their signatures must be clear evidence of their guilt and if they were to be tried, they should be released from house arrest and sent to the Tower to await trial. Prince James, impatient of delay, proposed the appointment of a small committee of legal officials to question each under oath, and that the Lord Justice should recommend an appropriate sentence, and the appropriate punishment. A group of four were empowered to begin without delay, including the Chief Justice, Sir Richard Palmer, Leader of the Commons and James Prynne. The selection of Prynne, who told George when in Jersey, that his pamphleteering had never been an attack on monarchy, only an attack on the Royal family for taking part in theatrical pretences wearing 'indecent' costumes. Appointing him to judge those who may have supported him seemed to George another example of indirect punishment for past 'offences' as though branding and exile had been insufficient.

The Regicides, whose guilt was already obvious, were brought before the court in groups of six and found guilty. They were condemned to death, and suffered public execution. This mock trial seemed justified by members of the Royalist party. At the end of the month the 29 were drawn to the place of execution near Charing Cross, and each was hanged, revived, tied to a stake and disemboweled while alive, their bodies quartered, and distributed to sites around London and the larger towns, their entrails burned and heads boiled before being displayed on poles on the roofs of most public buildings. The King and ladies of the court observed the proceedings from the Gallery of the Holbein Gate of the Palace. The long ordeal was observed by enthusiastic crowds for several hours but at last the executioners were so exhausted and the surroundings so dangerous underfoot, that they drifted away to their homes. The final executions were postponed to the next day and held at Tyburn. Carteret, who probably kept busy going about his Royal duties, was probably not present. The King had performed his promised Act of Oblivion. Oblivion excluded forgiveness but meant that those executed were never to be mentioned again. The Commonwealth was to be wiped for history as contrary to the British constitution.

Half of the remaining Regicides were dead from sickness and old age. The rest were systematically killed by Hyde's agents in their foreign places of safety. Many MPs felt that the number of traitors was insufficient and penalties were set for those expressing regret or approval of the Commonwealth. All mail passing though the Post Office was opened and senders and recipients of treacherous ideas punished. Non-conformists were forbidden to meet in groups greater than five. The spy system was extremely effective and those guilty were whipped, driven behind a cart, pilloried, or hanged. Many lost their work and their home and were forced to emigrate to New England. Those provinces and their Governors, were subject to inspection by Royal agents and those of extreme views were subject to British punishment. Governors and elected councils were forced to conform under threat of extradition to England for trial. Catholic, the French and Jews were increasingly subject to abuse and assault. Catholics continued to be fined for refusing communion, for taking Mass, harbouring priests, and many were condemned to death.

The standard of repression was as extreme as that used by the Commonwealth but, on the whole the people approved the restrictions imposed on 'cranks and lunatics'. Even after the execution of the last regicides, Parliament took upon itself the task of performing a final punishment of rebels. These were not living people, but the dead. On Jan. 31, 1661, the eleventh anniversary of the execution of Charles I, a party of engineers were sent to Westminster Abbey, entered Henry VII's Chapel, and removed the slabs commemorating the burial of Oliver Cromwell, Stephen Ireton, his son-in-law, and John Bradshaw. They exhumed their corpses, which were dragged through the streets of London to the Boar tavern in Fleet Street, a Puritan stronghold. The public were charged a penny each to abuse the corpses of their oppressors. Londoners were not eager to view these unfortunates it seemed, and the corpses were quartered and nailed to city gateways a few days later. Charles ordered the Bishop of London to permit this sacrilege as yet another example of his justified vengeance. It demonstrated beyond doubt that death should not be imagined to absolve the guilty from punishment. For the first time retribution would be performed on the bodies of the dead. This would serve as a vivid example of the extent of the powers invested in the King, from whom no-one would avoid punishment. The will of the King must be seen as absolute.

## CHAPTER FIVE

'Ah, Carteret a word if I may.' George, who had attempted to avoid the Lord Chancellor, made a cursory bow, and remarked that he was hurrying to the Commons' chamber.

'Then we will walk together, Carteret. I suppose you propose to make your maiden speech, either today, or very soon. I advise you to speak only on naval matters: it's a subject you know something about, I suppose.' George suppressed his annoyance, and remarked that he had received little warning of being made an MP.

'Unavoidable I'm afraid, Carteret. We were trying to fill the Portsmouth vacancies with two desirable candidates, when I thought of you. I knew you frequented the place. Of course, many of your wife's family have been notable Ministers over the years, so I suggest you ask them for advice, if you feel overwhelmed.'

'I feel quite confident in fact, Edward, and I know many members well!'

'I'm relieved to hear it! Don't go into detail answering questions, you will come to grief, I suspect. Here we are! You use the side door, Carteret. Good Morning, Officer!

'If you are asked a question in the Chamber concerning the coronation, simply reply, it is under consideration, and refuse to be drawn. Employ your Chamberlain's prerogative.'

Making his way to the familiar Commons benches, George thought about the many years he had known Hyde: it must be twenty-five at least He was a totally honest man, and knew the law like no one else, but why was he so often disparaging? It was a behavioural issue he supposed, and was not intended to be offensive. It had been very effective in Parliament and had secured the impeachment of Buckingham and an made an end to Charles's arbitrary taxation. He might find it difficult to be reduced to a supportive role, under Charles after years spent exposing the failings and illegalities of so many in government.

Carteret was fully occupied by his duties in Parliament. Prioritisation was among the skills he had acquired, and was more essential than ever. In addition, there remained his obligations to his family. Philippe had made a good start in the business, but George realised that more would be available to him if he separated himself from Jersey. The Act of Oblivion, included the restitution of land and houses confiscated from Royalist owners restored to George his properties and manors in Jersey, confiscated with their exile to St Malo. This, including their Broad Street house and his birthplace at the farm It also made restitution of land and income to other family members and friends.

George was faced with a choice, between life as a landowner in Jersey, or a life committed to offices of State in Great Britain. His choice had been made when he lent all his support to the restoration of monarchy. His exile in St Malo had severed administrative ties with Jersey and he had developed wider commercial interests in Britain. When Bess received the news with enthusiasm, as he had hoped, he sold various properties, and his local fishing and farming interest, mainly to family members. Bringing his wife and family to London would be irrevocable, and he would have to persuade Philip to agree to life in London, and be qualified as a naval officer while he, George, was continuing to co-operate with French traders.

A close result of the Oblivion Act was a death sentence had been passed on the head of the Oxenbridge family, who were close associates. The extreme royalists among MPs', desired to punish Colonel Lambert, who had bravely protected law and order in London, while General Monck negotiated the Breda agreement and brought the Army peacefully back from Scotland to England. Many felt he deserved praise, not blame, but the Commons chose to send him into exile for life. George felt this was severe and offered him house-arrest in Mont Orgueil, where his family settled until he gained his freedom. He also pointed out that the Oxenbridge family "traitor" had died in the meantime, and his heir, William Scott, was a man of known loyalty. He requested that the confiscated property, Hurstbourne House, should be handed to Scott. The Oxenbridge family, like the Paulets and Gage families, had felt compelled to leave their Sussex lands and settle in Hampshire to avoid the brutal treatment dealt to Catholics following the Armada. Hampshire was a less militant region and no-one displayed disloyalty openly. They and the Carterets, trusted that the new monarch would honour his declaration to promote religious tolerance. Several Dowse Members of the Courts of Justice, had resumed their posts in the Law courts, and three, who had served as rectors and suffered sequestration, regained their livings.

All these held posts in the gift of the Crown, so many people were bound by loyalty to one man. George hoped that they had taken note of the fate that had recently ended their lives. They could be grateful they belonged to the Anglican Church and were not non-conformist. Had acquiescence of the Bishop of London to the excavation of graves in the Abbey disturbed them? It belonged to the King so it was fully justified perhaps.

Parliament applauded The King's announcement that: "Sir George Carteret [ is to be] Knight and Baronet, Lord Chamberlain of my Household." His son Philip, thus became the Honourable Philippe Carteret. From that year, however, they discarded the prefix 'de', no longer to be used by male members of the family. At his suggestion, the English spelling of Philip and Francis were also to be used. If George was anxious about bringing the family to England, the King's next decision provided considerable reassurance.

Charles had decided that he needed to fulfil his obligation to defend the realm and protect his subjects. Parliament agreed that in future the Army would be under his personal control: Naval administration would devolve upon Prince James, the heir to the throne. Charles commissioned the Brigades of Guards to be responsible for the protection of Parliament and the Monarchy. Cromwell's own regiment, the Coldstream Guards were reinstated, followed by the Irish and Welsh guards, and other regional formations. All these would have important duties in public ceremonies, under a new command structure. This was entirely acceptable to Commons and Lords.

Traditionally, counties were led by County Sheriffs responsible for taxation and law and order. Charles created "Lords Lieutenant," men with military experience, who were prepared to deal firmly with public disorder and ensure the safety and loyalty of Judges of Assize, on their regular Circuits. Sheriffs would work under their supervision. In future, Sir Francis Dowse, Bess's nephew, could expect an easier task than Sir Francis, (his father), when he became Sheriff of Southampton in 1664. Every Church was to display a large Hatchment above the chancel arch displaying the Royal Arms and inscribed Carolus Rex. They were to be bought by parishioners.

The appointment of Prince James as Commander of the Royal Navy, gave George some anxiety . The Prince congratulated George when he was appointed Treasurer to the Navy. George had known him when he was a mere child, subservient to his brother and fiercely loyal. He had every effort to equal his brother in everything, from asserting his rights, to strong attachment to a few friends, and later to his numerous mistresses and illegitimate offspring. When a child, had been adopted by the Carterets during his long exile in Jersey. He had trained with the militia there, learned to sail, and made a tearful departure when summoned to Paris by his brother. George hoped to be able to work with him, for he was an acknowledged authority on ships, harbours, and all things naval, and had shown leadership qualities under General Turenne with the armies of France. He also knew his weaknesses including mental inflexibility and reckless conduct in battle.

The Puritan Governor of Jersey, John Mason, was replaced by Colonel Carey Raleigh, a descendant of Walter, who had saved Elizabeth Castle from slighting in the reign of Queen Elizabeth. George was awarded payment in compensation for his lost earnings during the exile. As a unique gesture of gratitude, the King presented him with a personal Charter, endorsed with the Royal Seal, expressing his gratitude for George's past actions and undertaking to repay all his expenditure. Before presenting it he added, in his own handwriting and signed by himself, his assurance that he would perform his promise. Even Bess was impressed!

Deptford House, among the orchards on the south bank of the Thames, was to be their official Residence. An official barge went with the tenancy. Bess was more than mollified: this house had been promised to them in 1640 when Charles 1 appointed George Navy Controller. Now, twenty years later, he was to resume his appointment. Contrary to expectation, the fates had relented, and the Carterets were to become Londoners and take their place in the court of the new monarch.

He met the King, soon after his appointment, following an elaborate trooping of the new colours of the regiments in Whitehall. The King, dressed as Army Commander, had just taken the salute, as the foot soldiers and cavalry marched past. It was summer and the parks surrounding the parade ground were looking at their best.

'I think that went well, George. Fortunately we still benefit from Cromwell's meticulous training. I must ensure that standards continue to be upheld.'

'It will simply be thankful that they were not soaked. They look very professional in their new uniforms. The Commons were quite eager to pay for them.'

'The weather was perfect for the occasion.' George remarked.

'Yes. I am pleased we had the bands playing, there's something special about drums and trumpets: it attracted quite a crowd. If only the weather had been as good for the Battle at Worcester. I will never forget the sudden downpour just before the charge. Armour tarnished at once, and swords jammed in their scabbards, I recall. I pray that I may have fair weather for the coronation, when we agree a date. This time next year, would be my preference. Any thoughts on this matter, George?'

'I have, Sir, but I fear there are a number of matters I have to addressed first.'

'I expect you have: I have thought of some myself. Speak, George, but keep it brief, we can compare problems, then deal with the implications. We must get the plans underway while the MPs are still enthusiastic. I'll think about the implications myself.'

'Well, Sir, you are King by right of succession, and with or without a crowning. However, are you also Head of the Church of England? The fact is, however, that hierarchy no longer has legal existence, and Laud, the last Archbishop, was executed for treason in 1654. Parliament negated King Henry's Act creating the English Church some years ago. Without an Anglican Church, clergy, and an Archbishop, who will crown you? In addition, the House of Lords retains members of the nobility, but there are no Lords Spiritual to add their moral strength and Sacred Authority to your rule.'

'There will have to be discussion in parliament on the subject, George. I promised Hyde that I intended to promote a degree of Religious Toleration to eliminate the dissension which led to the Scottish wars and my father's execution. There must be an end to such disagreement and the Bishops and clergy must be drawn from a broader Christian base and truly represent the many mansions and people of goodwill. I believe everyone wants an end to contention. Any new bishops must support this policy. And less than a year to put it all in place, George! Fortunately, the two Houses are solid supporters so far; so, I hope this will not be a stumbling block.'

'Perhaps it would be best to present a small-scale Bill, for immediate attention, a day or so before you prorogue the House for the recess. It might pass 'nem con,' many members having left early.'

'That would be underhanded, George. My father would disapprove strongly. However, I am not as righteous as my father, and I like the idea. Is there anything else worrying you?'

'Concerning the Crown Jewels, Sir. I have searched the Jewel Tower, and there is no St Edward's Crown. It was definitely melted down to pay the Army their wages. There are only a few spare coronets and boxes of semi-precious stones. '

'This is a matter of concern! We cannot have a Coronation without all the regalia. They must be reclaimed, or remade: there must be sales receipts. Contact the buyers and be firm with them. I would rather have no procession that a poor one. Where have they all gone, George?'

'Many of the best pieces were sold to pay your father's supporters. He regarded the Crown Jewels as the personal property of the monarch, since they were personal gifts, or won in battle; some were Ambassadorial gifts. As recently as a year ago, the Queen and Lord Jermyn ordered me to find an honest jewel merchant in Amsterdam to value her jewels. At that time, perhaps you remember, you had to borrow a shirt from Jermyn.'

'Hard times indeed, George. However, search out who now owns them, there will be an account somewhere, and love or money might result in generosity. I could offer them a privileged seat at the Coronation, or a knighthood, I suppose! I must consult with my mother. She may have concealed some for emergencies.'

During the Christmas celebrations of 1660, people may have felt that life had returned to normal, since Christmas could be celebrated once more in the old way, to the joy of children, to whom it would have been a joyful event, giving pleasure to their parents. There was song and dance, Wass-ale gatherings and Holy Communion, celebrated by full churches, minus those whose non-conformity was profound.

Carteret took responsibility for ensuring that the courtiers, eager that the Palace and royal chapels should resound with seasonal anthems, and the hall resound with dancing. Preparations required thorough rehearsal to increase the excitement. The King and Royal family deserved the highest standard of entertainment, and even the Boar's head, when it was carried into the dining hall on its charger, seemed to wear a smile. Everywhere were signs at all levels of society and that a new age was beginning. Six months had passed since the deaths of Prince Henry, the younger brother of Charles and James, and also Princess Mary of Nassau, their elder sister, married to William the Silent, as one of the last acts of Charles I, before her mother's household left for refuge in France. Her one son, Prince Willem, aged seven, was present at his Uncle Charles's wedding. In twenty years' time he would return to Britain with an army to become King. The story which follows will explain how this unlikely event came about.

When January came the new parliament met in the Commons Chamber. They were eager to hear the programme for the coming year and discover what part they were expected to play in the change of Government.

The King himself would command the newly formed Guards regiments, and the previous oppressive army disbanded and permitted to return to their previous employment. Prince James would command the navy and create a force to be reckoned with worthy of its stature as a Royal Navy.

Hyde, now Lord Clarendon, would be Lord Chancellor. George, now addressed as Lord Carteret, became Knight Baronet, Lord Chamberlain of the Palace, MP. for Portsmouth, and Treasurer of the Navy, responsible for its expansion programme. Other appointments would follow in due course. The Coronation would take place on 23 April and all were asked to rejoice with His Majesty.

## CHAPTER SIX

One use made by Carteret of his Staff of Office, was to have the mysteries of the Jewel Tower revealed. The last Keeper of the Jewel House, appointed by Charles I. was Sir Robert Howard. His appointment ended with his death in 1651 during the Civil War. Its contents had been considerably reduced by the Queen before her departure for France, where she sold them to Amsterdam merchants. Those items left in Government hands, such as the gold forms of the crowns, heavy chargers, the sceptre, and orb, and most other Coronation regalia were melted down for coinage, and the precious stones sold to feed the army. It was the second week of June when George was introduced to the New Keeper. In fact, Sir Gilbert Talbot had arrived that very day to take up his post, and he and George made a thorough survey of all that remained. It was a sorry state of affairs. The State crown of St Edward, had been among the first to be melted down. Full details were noted and the King informed, and George was instructed to go to the goldsmiths to create replacements.

In future, the King decided, the Jewels would be kept under permanent guard in the White Tower, to ensure their safety. Office clerks and Assistant Keeper were formed into a permanent guard with a rota to ensure their safe-keeping. While about his business there, George met the new Master of the Rolls, who made the financial decisions for the Court of Chancery. It was none other than his former detainee in Gorey castle, William Prynne, the outspoken Lawyer, now elderly and in favour with the new King. His co-operation was sure, and he was held in favour by City goldsmiths for his uncompromising honesty. Prynne and the newly appointed Speaker of the House of Commons, Sir Harbottle Grimston, assisted Carteret's attempt to discover an appropriate salary for a Treasurer. Grimston, had been a Colchester MP, and like Richard Rich and Thomas Audley, had begun his career there as Town Clerk. He had been instrumental in rescuing Sir Charles Lucas and his family from furious townspeople, determined to burn down his house for entertaining Marie de Medici, in 1639. The county of Essex would feature prominently in Carteret's future business and family affairs.

Operating as an MP Carteret assisted by passing into law the necessary act of restoration. The Rescissory Act rendered all Acts under Cromwell null and void. The Act of Oblivion restored all penalties and confiscations to their previous Royalist owners, except for those where a personal agreement had been made by the opposing parties. Equally popular was an Act of Uniformity, re-establishing the sole authority of the Anglican Church in matters of religion. Charles accepted this with reluctance because unless he asserted his office as head of the Church, no Coronation could be held. This Act revived all the animosity over religion, which had provoked the Civil War. The King was opposed to the act and felt that Clarendon had not opposed it with sufficient energy. It undermined his total trust in Clarendon and the Breda Agreement.

The appointment of the Navy Board under Prince James was accepted, but members were alarmed by the size of the existing naval debt which stood at £678,000. They were disinclined to accept yet another expense and considered it unnecessary. Savings should be made first The King knew this was impossible, and to see the Act through parliament, Carteret used his own security to pay off the debt. It was a private arrangement, made in the spirit of good will, but not one that the Commons, or public accountants would approve. At least it cleared the way for the Coronation to take place, now that the legal barriers had been overcome.

Charles was annoyed and embarrassed by the objections made by loyal MPs by their proposition of an Act of Uniformity, having stressed that toleration was one of his two main promises he had made. It was directly contrary to his wishes made conditional in the Statute of Breda. Hyde's supporters supported it with considerable force, but a majority were unmoved. He expressed the King's concern to Archbishop Juxon, insisting that the Church should comply and appoint nonconformist ministers, known to hold sound Christian principles, by appointing them as rectors in an act of peace and reconciliation. But Juxon refused, insisting that Anglican Communion was the only genuine expression of faith. Everyone must attend their local Church, to register their compliance, and take an individual oath of loyalty to the King as Head of the Church. It was clear that there was to be neither reconciliation nor toleration.

The King may have wondered again whether this was the time to abandon Britain and return to exile. Reason and his advisers would have argued that there would be no second restoration and the fait accompli would have to be accepted. It is likely that Charles thought that the conflict roused might bring about a change of heart. if he exercised patience. On a visit to the waters in the fashionable spa town of Tonbridge, a church, built by popular subscription, was dedicated to 'King Charles the Martyr.' This could be a favourable move, however, in the next ten years, at least six more churches were given the same dedication. Furthermore, the 'secret' organisations, the Sealed Knot' and the 'Fifth Monarchists' were revived and active. Non-conformists and non-communicants were expelled from their employment, and 24 Roman Catholics were tried for treason and publicly executed. Jews, and possibly Islamists, had been permitted to return to Britain by Cromwell. Perhaps it was not passed into law, but adherents of those faiths seem to have escaped persecution.

In the Channel Islands, Jermyn, once treasurer to Henrietta Maria, had become Governor. He had sworn allegiance to the Anglican Church, and began to apply force to Jurats and ministers to adopt Anglican communion and sign the register weekly. He would have asserted that they prided themselves on allegiance to the Duke of Normandy, who was now their King. How could they object? Jersey generally complied with the inevitable, as they had with non-conformity, but Guernsey had had non-conformity imposed by Dr De Carteret's father. Jermyn caused strong and bitter antagonism to his wishes, and when he attempted punitive measures, the fishermen of the island, a determined generation, took their families away by boat, to resettle in Massachusetts. Their settlement adopted the strictest religious principles of presbyterianism, and excluded any who refused to express belief. They named their community 'Salem' and it became notorious some years later.

Much as Charles would have disapproved of these violent responses, he hoped that general tolerance would grow from the pride induced by the splendour of the coronation, and would overcome outdated expressions of sectarianism. When John Evelyn spent a day with the King at the races, politics were not on his agenda. His mood had improved, perhaps due to the birth of a daughter by Lady Castlemaine, formerly Lady Barbara Villiers, and married to Sir Roger Palmer. Charles had brought her from France as his mistress, and Sir Roger, who had expected to be awarded the Navy, was now rejected. To give her respectability at court, his wife was created Lady Castlemaine. Any son of hers by the King, would inherit the title denied to her husband. They remained on good terms, however.

The King was also putting new boats through their paces. Overtaken by a violent storm in the Thames estuary when sailing alone, he was once forced to land at the nearest beach at Leigh on the Essex coast. He spent an uncomfortable night sheltering under the boat, making his way to Rayleigh the following day. Both exploits improved his personal standing, also his early morning walks in St James's Park. These were taken after his levee, and accompanied by a crowd of attendants and numerous spaniels, in increasing numbers, and all claiming his attention. At over six feet in height, he walked at what was described as 'a loping gait' his followers sweating in his wake. He would stop frequently to admire herons, or to exchange greetings with a friend, or perhaps a stranger who wanted to speak to him, or ask for his royal blessing. Frequently the brothers would arrange a swimming or rowing contest Both had tremendous vigour and energy, and engaged in all outdoor activities. Both competed in horse racing, but James was devoted to hunting, and had enjoyed the opportunities given him by Turenne while in France.

Among this complex range of events, Charles accepted George's proposal that his remuneration as Treasurer, should be based on the going percentage rate for a city trader. It was agreed at 3%, which was generally considered adequate. Charles was determinedly harangued by his mother at the same time on the necessity to gain a wife. She was very aware that of her nine children, only three remained living: Charles, James and Marie, Duchess of Orleans.

The King had in fact, set this in motion, seeking a rich heiress with impeccable antecedents, and from a friendly nation with overseas commercial interests. France and Spain were able to oblige but, fearing public opposition, he had sent Fanshawe, his former secretary while in Jersey, now ambassador to Portugal, to discuss with King Pedro IV marriage with his sister, the Infanta. He drew attention to the previous marriage of an earlier Infanta, to Edward III, and their Treaty of Lasting Peace. His proposal was accepted because Fanshawe was persuasive, spoke Portuguese, and had translated the works of Camoens into English. May 1662 was reserved for the wedding, and there would be a proxy marriage in Paris, allowing six months for Catherine to travel, largely by land to her new home, finishing with a Channel crossing. Late in 1661, the King sprang another surprise on George, reminding him that he still had his uses.

Time now to return to the affairs of the Carteret family and their removal to London, which was a considerable undertaking, if their style of living was to be maintained. Fortunately, they had a complete ship placed at their disposal, and a strong organiser in the shape of Lady Elizabeth. She tolerated her husband's commitment to his duties, for the freedom and the challenges it presented. Anne, her mother was always at her side and equally forceful.

At last George received an enthusiastic letter from Bess, sent by the expanding postal service, from Portsmouth on the previous day. Philippe had remained behind to unload their furniture: but she, James, and the girls would be resting at Portsmouth before travelling to London. They intended to visit the homes of Dowse relatives scattered across Hants and Wilts, and visit the Paulets at Hurtwood, whom they had not visited for ten years. She promised to give warning of her arrival in London.

George put Will Jarvis in charge of turning the tall, thin, Whitehall house he and his clerks occupied into a temporary home for a family. The clerks were disgruntled, being crowded into less congenial rooms. Beds and commodes, were borrowed from colleagues, or from vacant houses. George rarely ate at home, but was lucky to find a French chef, looking for new opportunities in England. Maurice soon assembled a small, but adoring staff, and began to produce food so good that Bess would be impressed, although it would not compensate for the shortcomings of his house. George invited Harrington and Thomas Dowse for dinner to try the skill of his chef, and both gave their approval, praising the wines selected.

Philip arrived, bringing the family moveable goods, for which rooms were found. George took him to the Admiralty in Seething Lane, and enrolled him for naval training. Now that he was Treasurer to the Navy, the Admiralty agents were more accommodating than when he had been a humble Lieutenant seeking a ship. Philip gave them a clear account of his sailing experience, and was signed up at once for the Lieutenant's Exam, and became in time, a Captain. In his absence, James was signed up for the exam in 1662/3, and enquiries make for a commander needing an assistant. A Captain Herring thought he might have a vacancy. George's enquiries revealed that the man had a good reputation. However, a decision would be made when he had spoken to James. The naval tradition must be upheld.

Attending the Commons to make his maiden speech, in which he advocated lengthening wharfage for larger ships in Portsmouth, George took the opportunity to introduce Philip to the King. Philip had been seven years old in 1649, when they had met, but Charles remembered him as a mischievous boy with an enquiring mind. His behaviour during sermons in St Helier church, had provided him with welcome entertainment. Discovering that Philip had used telescopes with Huygens and hoped to join the Roto group of scientists, Charles mentioned his intention to create a scientific body, to develop engines to advance progress in the sciences. He hoped Philip and his father might be interested. George noted that the King liked to pick up new ideas and make them his own. The Slave Trade was a typical example, but that came later.

In July, Elizabeth arrived at Whitehall by coach, she and their daughters, Anne and Rachel, in the care of James, now a teenager, aglow with real responsibility! George and he embraced warmly and the girls were excited and open-eyed with wonder on their first sight of London. The younger girls, Elizabeth and Louise remained in St Malo, in the care of their grandmother, Lady Anne. They would remain at school with a teaching order of nuns. No equivalent education for girls was available in England. George and Bess embraced, she and the girls were eager to see their new London house. Bess observed that the girls were gazing enraptured at a tall Guardsman, in full dress uniform, who was about to address them. His face wore a large grin and Bess, momentarily puzzled, suddenly smiled with recognition.

'Edward, it's you, my little nephew! You are so smart! And so tall, but you haven't really changed. Are you still the Duke's Cupbearer?'

'No Bess, one of Fanshawe's boys is the new cupbearer.'

'No Aunt, I'm too old for that. It's wonderful to see you again. I'm an officer in Prince James's bodyguard, and Gentleman of the Bedchamber. Good Day, George, we have walked past each other several times recently: I heard you were expecting the family to arrive. I was the officer on duty at the March Past for the King and you went off talking with him. Dr. Philippe attends on the King from time to time, also, he remembers you from the parties at St Ouen. He sends kind regards.'

They walked together to the house, which Bess declared dark and old-fashioned. Edward and James overcame their initial reticence, and were soon on good terms. Maurice, like a genie from a bottle, brought in a display of delectable French pastries, and endless pots of coffee. George's head began to spin with the exchange of names of family members he had never met. It seemed there were numbers of Dowse folk trading or manufacturing in London in the burgeoning financial climate. Some were hopeful of employments with the Navy. He agreed to a suggestion from Edward that James should meet some of his good friends, and their sons. "Several have attractive daughters,' he remarked.

'Yes, essential! But only after he has signed on with the Admiralty!' George asserted.

He remembered the Fanshawes only had sons, but some of his colleagues certainly had teenage daughters: the Montagues, for example, Pepys often mentioned them. He realised how much he enjoyed his wife's company, her warmth of affection and ability to disarm total strangers. If he could find their girls friendly hosts of their own age, perhaps he and Betsy could escape together for a few days before she became absorbed in home making. He envisaged a lively skiff and a day's sail to Gravesend or Richmond, a lavish picnic on a grassy bank, a friendly country hostelry over-night, perhaps? A visit to Deptford House would be essential, of course. Perhaps a Thursday start and a long weekend, then back to work.

It seemed that the Commons would strengthen the Navy Acts but had agreed to the reinstatement of the best Army regiments. They were probably going to swallow the bitter pill of giving their financial backing for the changes: after all, it was what they had demanded. Perhaps they had not costed the operation carefully. The King was wildly enthusiastic about making new companies, and desperate for freedom to spend money so as to rival the Court of his cousin in France.

'The Royal Adventurers Trading in Africa Company' was encouraged by the King to import ivory and precious woods and was a new registration. George was less keen on his plan for an Act to forbid the export of wool, which George felt made no sense for the French would simply respond by increasing home produced wool and ruin the most productive English export. However, King and Commons were as one on this matter. George's presence at Court was not essential as yet and he and Bess had leisure to discuss the future plans for their children. They were both eager to learn news of their scattered family members. How many had died in the internal conflict? Who were these Dowses in Wiltshire and in London? Bess had heard from the wife of Mr Houblon, their Banker, of his association with William Dowse, Lawyer of Magdalen College who was a friend of Richard Du Cane, a wealthy London trader, and who were Huguenot emigrants. They were shortly joined by Mde Courtauld, who ran a company of silversmiths, and was proposing the production of silks. They were all keen to buy land in Balham, Croydon, and Wandsworth and close to Deptford, in fact, where he had warehouses and workshops. He must try to meet Mr. Crewe, a High Court Judge, who was gaining a good reputation for financial advice. George Jeffreys, another legal expert, was making a mark for awarding firm and severe sentences to discourage those inclined to turn to crime as a profession. These were people he must get to know. Men to watch! Suddenly he remembered Giles Dowse, that ex-army Chaplain, and family member who had been so torn by conflicting Christian doctrines. Had he survived that Commonwealth? He wished him well: would Bess discover any news of him?

Fortunately, Harrington's group had survived social upheaval by closeting themselves in Wadham College, where they continued to explore and develop new sciences, uninterrupted by strife. Harrington was withdrawing himself gradually from these discussions, saddened by the King's execution and feelings of guilt, that he had been unable to persuade the King that he could make concessions to their progressive suggestions without showing weakness. None of those whose views Charles had rejected, wanted to overthrow the Monarchy as such. Charles's obstinacy had the unfortunate effect of allowing the extremists to take control. George, as an old friend, tried to continue to propose moderation, but Harrington viewed his ideas as a lost cause.

Stubbs, Marvell, William and Max Petty, John Aubrey and Thomas Dowse, and sometimes Robert Hooke, continued to meet regularly however, and George was welcomed when he could attend. He had planned to introduce his son, Philip to them. Their discussions had recently come to the notice of the King, someone had referred to them as 'The Illuminati'. Somehow the Italian name seemed derogatory, as though their actions were in some way "not British' the King himself, however, had made a point of engaging some of these individuals in conversation, and expressed an interest in their ideas. They found the King quick of understanding, but easily bored by detail or theoretical debate. He was however eager to take a lead in any trend which might increase his reputation as an intelligent ruler among the Kings of Europe. George's son Philip was fascinated by clocks and the use of springs as a means of driving clocks in place of reliance on weights suspended on chains. He had experimented with Fromantel's controlled-action spring, and the possibilities it offered of making machinery controlled by perpetual motion. This might be the subject for an introduction to the King.

Edward Montague, an effective commander, had scored a celebrated victory for the Commonwealth at sea, but was dismissed for distributing prize money among his officers, cutting out the large percentage gained from selling confiscated articles by the Admiralty. He was to be sent abroad on various embassies as a reprimand. He congratulated George on his appointment, and recommended an able, young Magdalen College, graduate, to organise his Navy office. George met Sam Pepys later at an Iluminati meeting, and presented him to Prince James as a possible employee. James had heard the King mention Pepys, whom he had met on the ship bringing him to England, and to whom he had confided his hopes for the future. Pepys was appointed at once and, with George's assistance, began to lay down the basis for the future British Navy. George was surprised to discover that important appointments were often the result of previous relationships with colleagues, or friendships made at university. Appointments were made always among a privileged group. 'Just like the Navy,' he reflected. Perhaps he should make notes of names and professions for the advantage of his family?

## CHAPTER SEVEN

After initial enthusiasm, business was put to one side, while the King and his brother pursued former racing traditions on the Berkshire Downs. All the Stuart rulers were keen horsemen and Windsor Castle had a race track close by, once favoured by Queen Anne of Denmark, their grandmother. The brothers were excellent horsemen and James was experienced in cavalry actions with the French army. New prizes were created as a reward for winners and Racing Programmes were established at Epsom and at Newmarket and for Flat races and obstacle races. Nationwide country gentlemen established their own racing programmes, steeplechases and fox hunts. Beagling was also popular among the young perhaps without a proficient hunter. Arab stallions were brought to England at great expense to improve blood lines and, since most people could ride, racing became a central interest for the public at large. When the king was forced to be in London, the Royal Parks, especially St James's Park, were used for informal racing and daily exercise. Rowing and falconry were popular established hobbies like archery, and for quieter relaxation, many enjoyed fishing, and trout streams were carefully protected.

Other interests of the royal brothers, and George, were sailing, and Bess and George seized any opportunity to take the Commander's barge out on the river. This splendid vessel was provided with a team of oarsmen and had comfortable sheltered accommodation in the event of inclement squalls. Deptford House, on the South bank, looked as splendid as when they had first been promised it in 1640. Then, recently married, prosperity and happiness seemed to await them. What could go wrong when the past repeated itself in this strange manner? Could their hopes of a secure future be snatched away for a second time? The matter was one of concern.

'Do you think we will ever live there, George?'

'The renovation is making good progress and I am as eager as you to move in. Our house is more like an office than a home and I cannot deal with all my appointments without more office space, and clerks. Pepys, I believe, will get a firm grip on my Admiralty tasks, and ensure I have the right information when Parliament demands answers.'

'I don't like the Whitehall house and the constant coming and going of pompous, arrogant young nobles with giggling girls pursuing them. I know that they are young and happy, but I am concerned for our girls. I know we have sheltered them in St Malo, but sending them to Mrs Makin's college in Tottenham, will stretch their minds. She provides music, embroidery and dancing, but also teaches the languages and the classical languages. The Dowager queen sent her daughters to her and Elizabeth of Bohemia is proof of her method. Unfortunately, most of the mothers, such as Lady Hyde, believe that men want obedient wives to provide meals, not intelligent ones who want to talk.'

'The Puritans, encouraged the education of girls, but few families can afford tutors, even for their sons! If James was two years younger, we could have sent him to one of the schools for young gentlemen. They also set up Artisans' Colleges where they can be taught practical skills like book-keeping, surveying, accountancy and mathematics. James might have had better opportunities there.'

'I hope Mrs Makin will also teach them the uses of calculation. Our eldest seems to have an aptitude for figures and card games. I have been talking to Lord Brounker about the probability of laws of chance. We have been attempting to apply them to trading decisions. I think surveying and architecture might be subjects James would enjoy. He enjoys outdoor work and grasps perspective.'

'Your mother writes that they are happy with the nuns and that she wants to bring them here when we have settled in Deptford House. The sooner the better for all of us, in my opinion, I miss our girls.'

Bess became increasingly concerned to make positive arrangements for the future of their daughters, Anne, and Caroline. Both were well into their teens and plunged headlong into the hectic and challenging street life of the largest capital city in Europe, and a court where young men were eager to dive headlong into the opportunities offered. Their daughters had come from a quiet, sheltered life in rural France and their parents were relative newcomers and had no time to develop a circle of friends with eligible sons who might become suitors in time.

They concluded that while the girls remained biddable they would find them husbands. The eldest was almost nineteen, her sister a few years younger. Several of George's business colleagues were doing well enough for the impulsive purchase of a country estate. They lacked a wide social circle but hoped to marry, make a fortune through trade, and retire to cultivate children and their estate. Introductions were made, engagements arranged, banns called, and at the end of 1661, Anne married Sir Nicholas Stanning of Marystowe House, Devonshire, with John Evelyn as a witness. Two weeks later, Caroline married Sir Thomas Scott, heir to a fortune on his father's sudden death, and a large estate in Kent. King Charles had been her godfather, when she was baptised in St Helier. Although he was at the races on her wedding day, he was rowed to Deptford a few days later to present his wedding gift.

While present, he took the opportunity to broach a commission he had in mind as eminently suitable for a man with Carteret's talents. These were the words he chose. Fortunately, it was largely a matter of facilitating arrangements, placed in the hands of distinguished noble men of high standing, but dubious management skills. He task would be to cover matters they overlooked, bungled, or placating officials they had offended. It was a delicate operation to be negotiated in complete secrecy specifically without the knowledge of parliament. The whole matter must be completed in the greatest possible haste because Louis XIV was eager for an end to negotiations. There was a December deadline, or Charles II would lose a great deal of money. It was exactly the sort of thing George was best at, in the King's opinion.

During the Commonwealth years, the New Model Army had waged war with the Dutch Republic to curb the power of Spain in the low countries. This resulted in total victory for Admiral Blake and his naval defence of Dutch interests. Britain's reward was the coast town of Dunkirk and its surrounding province. There was a good harbour which might assist in the Protestant struggle against the overpowering resurgence of Catholicism. A large regiment of New Model Army was installed and new defences constructed,

At that point the Commonwealth government became unworkable and became a lost cause. The Army, unpaid for two years, was disbanded at the restoration of parliament, and the parliamentary Act of Ownership of Dunkirk was rescinded. The large British regiment and Governing Council was completely abandoned. Charles was astonished to discover that he owned territory in France where law and order had disintegrated and horrified to discover the huge cost of any attempt to restore order. It had become ungovernable and soldiers set up piratical ventures to avert starvation. It would be a heavy burden to subdue, and many men had lost their lives and their families to protect this port.

Charles realised that he must divest himself of Dunkirk, and offered it to his cousin, Louis, for 25,000,000 ls. Louis saw that Dunkirk was not likely to be used to endanger France and therefore offered 8,000,000ls since it was almost derelict. Charles ordered Prince James and the Duchess of Orleans to request Louis, to improve his offer. Louis, appreciating his cousin's desperation, nevertheless declined to increase his offer and made a final offer of 5,000,000ls. He insisted that the sale must be completed before Christmas, 1661, but offered to provide Charles with a safe refuge if his life was threatened by his government, and also offered to made future loans. Urgent action was essential. Quite unaware that his services were to be called upon, George Carteret had begun to look forward to a more restful time with his family, leading up to Christmas.

Charles turned his attention to fresh coinage in addition to his demand for adequate parliamentary allowances. The Commonwealth had made no changes to the British coinage, although a few examples have been found that reveal their intention to make a change. It was probably better left unchanged since it might reassure foreign traders that trade would not be affected. The few Cromwellian coins reveal the underlying problem. Coins usually showed the head of the ruler. Cromwell refused to have his head shown, but what could take its place? No conclusion could be reached.

Charles had no hesitation. His head in profile would be on one side and emblems of the four nations on the other. Six coins were minted: Gold sovereigns and half sovereigns, and four silver coins of lesser value. These became legal currency after the coronation but his father's coins remained in circulation. Details of the pre-Christmas 1661 Dunkirk transaction seem to have evaded the attention of contemporaries but the Louis d'or probably formed the basis of the impressive new currency. The actual details of the exchange are both fascinating and absurd involving so agents, sworn to secrecy. The confusion resulted in so much inconvenience to all concerned, that it provides a striking illustration of the complex pageantry and formalised rituals essential to achieving success. George Carteret's role was, as it was so often, to pick up the forgotten pieces and provide money to cover the unexpected expenditure. George and Elizabeth enjoyed their visit to Hampton Court, and remain totally unaware of the tangled financial affairs about to cast a shadow on their Christmas celebrations. The financial crisis impending in the coming years, caused great untold harm to individuals and companies that it needs explanation in a later section.

George was required to ensure that the royal palaces were ready to receive the royal family if they chose to celebrate Christmas at Hampton Court. Elizabeth was overjoyed when George asked her to accompany him on a tour of inspection. As a woman she would be able to tell him of the deficiencies that a woman would notice that he might not see. Arriving at Hampton Pier, they walked to the Palace, observing that the gardens were immaculate George summoned the housekeeper who would show them round. They had been seen approaching, as George had hoped. He was wearing his Chamberlain's cloak with the gold key emblem, the mark of his authority. They were given a warm, but polite reception, and once George had introduced his wife, any tension quickly dispersed. He was able to assure the housekeeper that the King was planning a visit, but was at present in the process of assembling his household.

The state room shutters were opened and the covers removed from furniture. Bess murmured that the quality of paintings and statuary was even higher than Pyrgo House. (George was unaware that he would learn a great deal more about that estate soon.) As they sat in their barge, after the visit, enjoying luncheon under the canopy, George considered a few of those matters causing him anxiety, which might crop up after Christmas.

Did the new order of government have the stability essential for its survival? The combined energies of the King and his ad hoc Parliament was making rapid progress, but George wondered if Charles realised that a new Parliament, based on an election based on the counties and boroughs, might not favour some aspects of his stated programme.

As he predicted, nothing was going to be easy, everything would receive close examination. Replacing Coronation regalia and creating new Armies and a Navy were relatively simple compared with the tortuous complexity involved in re-establishing the Church of England. Clarendon and the King had reached an agreement that, as part of a reconciliation process, nine of the High Court judges would be reappointed, to begin to reinstate the Upper House of Lords where the new Bishops would also sit.

Juxon, deposed in 1644 as Bishop of London, would be reinstated as the next Archbishop of Canterbury. Juxon hoped to wield the power of Laud, who had total control of Doctrine and appointment of cooperative rectors, but acknowledged that a measure of tolerance might refresh and empower the Established Church. The process of finding compliant Bishops was in progress, but a generation of those appointed by Laud, who remained unemployed and available for reappointment, also shared his intolerance of non-conformists. Charles was clear that the binding promises of tolerance he had made in the Treaty of Breda, were not negotiable.

It was a point of contention. Charles may have restated his reluctance "to go on his travels again," Would this promise become an issue to cause the King to abandon his crown? Much rested on this question, including the effort and money to be expended on the whole process. George, and many others, might find themselves dismissed from office again. Also, what form of Government would emerge from another revolution? George knew that the King was eager to improve on the unyielding firmness of his father by compromising on inessentials, avoiding the raising of issues likely to rouse strong opposition. He was also willing to be patient to gain agreement, although he disliked delay, and would settle for the best offer available. George knew Charles had stated his right to rule but would he be prepared to abdicate over this issue? Every measure must be taken to ensure that Charles kept the promise he had made and Juxon must accept a process of 'gradual' toleration in the spirit of compromise and a change of heart.

Other issues progressed smoothly. Parliament returned private land taken into Government ownership, to its previous owners, or their heirs. Thus, Charles regained his many estates, palaces and castles throughout Britain. Dukes and lesser nobility were restored also, although 'The Vine' near Basingstoke, home of the Sandys family, lacked an heir and the house remained with the occupying Parliamentary General, Chaloner Chute. Its Catholic Chapel was left intact by its new owners. Other owners compounded for their property, paying the Treasury an agreed sum to cover lost revenue. The Paulets regained the remains of Basing House, and its land, and after compounding, the women of the family were granted small pensions. It was thus that the Carterets regained their Manors in Jersey and Guernsey, and George, to his astonishment acquired unexpectedly, a significant source of wealth confirming his established responsibilities overseas. The Pyrgo estate in Essex, had reverted to the Percy family on the death of Lord Hay, and its contents auctioned. Lady Hay, retired to Petworth House, where Thomas Dowse, a convinced Parliamentarian, was a permanent guest, once Northumberland's secretary, and now a distinguished member of the Commons. Pyrgo was eventually demolished, and the land sold to provide country estates for newly wealthy merchants and industrialists. Only the gatehouse was left standing.

The wealth of the Hays had been derived from their monopoly of tariffs from the West Indies. A new Company of the West Indies was to be formed to exploit their resources, and military Governors appointed for the islands already claimed by Britain. This Company would be administered by George Carteret and Edward Hyde. No doubt the King knew that George would ensure the treasury would benefit from his trading skills, and Hyde would create a sound legal constitution. Thomas Dowse had recommended George to the Percy family, of which Lucy Hay was a member, and who would continue to retain some interest. Thomas had worked for the Court of Chancery since qualifying at the Inns of Court, but was also an MP.

Finally, their removal to Deptford House was complete, and by that time Bess, with usual energy, had established her position in court circles. who was delighted to welcome Frances, Lady Clarendon on her return to England, where she shared Lord Clarendon's cramped Whitehall quarters. When his new mansion in Broad Street was completed, she would bring their daughter to England. She and Elizabeth were two among many families shuffling between France and England, awaiting the return of property, before re-settling permanently. Some, particularly Catholics, chose to remain: others were detained by close ties formed following a childhood in France. Frances was amusing and popular, and adopted Bess as a younger sister, ensuring she met the wives of Royalists and MPs. Carriages, barges and horses were always readily available and the Carterets became known for hospitality and good company.

They also became leaders of fashion and James, the Naval cadet, became actively involved in fencing, tennis, riding, dancing and was a worshipper of fashionable women and their maids. Tom Dowse, the younger, had matriculated and would be studying at Oxford where other relatives were already students. Laurence Hyde, aged nineteen, had graduated and was training at the Temple. His intelligence and wit were phenomenal and he studied under Dowses, who were Doctors of Law and Judges. Dryden,

Congreve and Marvell responded to the more liberal spirit of the time, and turned to literature. As Chekov said later with reference to his plays: "I am married to Medicine, but Literature is my Mistress." Milton continued to explore the relationship between man and God in remarkable poetry and was held in great esteem as a man of letters.

It was a life of luxury for the privileged, and the arts, theatre and literature flourished. Uniforms were as colourful as everyday clothing had become. Gold and silver were displayed on regimentals and even George was forced to wear a uniform for official events. It included a broad-brimmed beaver hat with a large semi-precious stone in front and ostrich feather at the side. On the front of his black coat the golden key displayed upon it, authorising him to enter any of the palace buildings. His clothing was brightened by lace, coloured ribbons and silk stockings. When about his work, he carried a long white wand, as a token of authority.

Among Bess's new friends was Barbara Palmer, the wife of Roger Palmer, from whom George had proposed to purchase the Navy office years before. He had been exiled to Paris, where he met and married the beautiful Barbara Villiers, niece of the murdered Duke of Buckingham. Not only was she beautiful, but possessed a flamboyant manner very much in tune with the fun-loving energy of the new French court. At their first meeting Bess noticed Barbara was pregnant and that the father was King Charles. Bess was not surprised by this news, having realised, when Charles was a teenager, that his manner was very attractive to the Ladies of St Helier. There was discussion among her women friends about who the future King would marry. Now that he was soon to be crowned, his supporters would have to learn to accept the existence of his illegitimate children.

In the meantime, the Navy Acts, introduced in 1661, prohibited foreign ships trading through English ports. Goods must always be carried on English ships. The settlements in the New World were required to trade only with Britain. All their raw materials must be sent to Britain for manufacture: the finished articles had to be purchased by the new colonists. Trade with the Dutch was heavily taxed to weaken their financial advantage. These Acts were contrary to the free trade practised by most British traders, and George had always exercised complete freedom of choice. He and many others, tended to ignore these regulations and since Customs and Excise officers only operated out of major ports, smaller ones grew more powerful. Many traders operated from Dunkirk, which had been awarded to Cromwell for his assistance in the war with Spain. The town was maintained by an English Garrison. It operated as though the Navy Acts did not apply and became a base for acts of virtual piracy. George and others faced a difficult choice. Freedom to trade wherever English products were in demand, was surely a right. Our overseas partners would be discouraged from trading if their ships were excluded from our ports. Would the nations of Europe be willing to accept these restrictions?

The newly elected Parliament was, in the coming years, a powerful association of bankers and traders lobbying for their own interests. The newly elected MPs included a wider franchise, including traders and manufacturers as well as country landowners, although landowners continued to be a majority The Upper House had the addition of new Bishops, to provide moral guidance and now attempting to establish a more tolerant Anglicanism, including Christian sects previously considered heretical. Charles confronted his first strong opposition, in these debates. The Bishops refused to countenance any alteration of the practices established by Laud and, moreover, they had the backing of the dozens of re-appointed rectors, dismissed from their benefices by Cromwell. Their refusal to accept even minor changes to Laud's regulations was firm. Charles, John Owen, Milton and other non-conformists worked together with Juxon to attempt to reach an agreement.

The King won a minor victory when the Bishops agreed with Cromwell's decision to allow Jews to re-settle in England and establish synagogues. They were few in number, offering no threat, but were 'non-conformists' like the Roman Catholics, who were regarded as traitors, under the control of unscrupulous foreigners. This threatened to destroy the unity which was Charles's hope, but no compromise by the King to introduce safeguards for Anglicanism was acceptable, and the Church of England was intransigent on this point.

Realising that the project he and Charles had devised was facing rejection, Clarendon swiftly devised an Act re-enacting the previous regulations. Clarendon explained to the Privy Council, that he had acted for the best, but Charles began to distrust him. This suspicion tended to increase from that time forward. At a local level and varying in the severity where large royalist majorities held power, non-Anglicans were dismissed from their employment and many sought a better future in the overseas colonies, which became increasingly sectarian in government.

A later Act, referred to as the Five Mile Act, forbade non-conformists residing within town boundaries, or from setting up businesses there. Fines were re-imposed for failure to attend Communion, and Catholic priests, hiding in England, were arrested and tried for treason. In Guernsey, where Presbyterianism had been enforced, and seventy "Witches" burned to death, the new law resulted in mass emigration to Salem, Massachusetts, where co-religionists had already found a welcome. Later, Salem became notorious for its "witch hunt" trials introduced in imitation of Guernsey. As time passed, with the determination of Anglican authorities to assert that the English Church was Catholic, it was commonly considered to be a virtually Roman Catholic association.

Throughout Europe the extermination of non-conformists, gave rise to the belief that the Anglicans were crypto-Romanists and plotting to massacre Protestants. Louis XIV had chosen this time to impose Catholicism on every region of France, and any who opposed this plan were executed or allowed to escape into exile. Many took refuge in Britain and in Holland. Huguenots were accomplished bankers and industrialists and contributed to the wealth of Britain. Many of the refugees were attacked in the streets, but their arrival added to the public opinion in which Catholics were held. Louis' persecution was pursued relentlessly, and its final success came in 1682, coinciding with the reign of James II. , George and his family were unaffected by this, but he lived long enough to witness its beginnings.

Compulsory Church attendance on Sundays was enforced again, Charles was always a regular communicant. Those in the new Navy office, including Pepys were required to comply and a register of congregants kept at St Olave's, Hart Street, situated close to his home in the former Navy Office building. George's family continued to worship regularly, either in Whitehall or Deptford. He himself often had duties to perform, even on Sundays, if the King sent an order for a barge and rowers to be provided, supplied with a full picnic, for a river party for a score of friends. Pepys enjoyed surveying the attractive ladies among the congregation, and awarding scores for that day's sermon in his notebook.

George's search for the Royal regalia was finally abandoned, and the Treasury gasped at the enormous cost of making replacements. A whole new office of Government was created to protect the regalia from further theft. The Crown of St Edward, the most vital item, the golden Sceptre and the Swords of Justice and Mercy, were replaced, also the Communion plate and chalice. A flask containing consecrated oil was re-discovered, and also the golden Saxon spoon for the anointing. Fortunately, the Black Prince's ruby had survived undamaged. The cost was astronomical for creating robes, crowns and coronets for all those entitled to wear them, made greater by the expense of restoring the golden coach, and other vehicles which were less ornate, plus uniforms for the newly formed regiments. The vast expenditure of a Coronation was a damaging blow to the economy. Some made a contrast with the small amount required to establish a Lord Protector. George found that London goldsmiths and silversmiths were eager to make the new regalia, which would display their skills and ensure future orders. Among suppliants to the Privy Council, George had noted a sad letter from one Edmund Harrington, "Embroiderer to King James, and King Charles" who sought to be appointed to the new King Charles, and mentioning that he would be grateful for the payment of £4,000 owed to him for previous satisfactory work. He added with respect, that he was seventy years old, and had 21 dependant children. He, and many others flourished in the restored Kingdom.

## CHAPTER EIGHT

George kept a watchful eye on matters affecting the King, who had made a careful study of the traditional processes which confer authenticity to the ceremony. No omission was to be permitted to create doubt that he had been properly Crowned. At the Coronation, Charles was to be escorted by the Knights of the Most Noble Order of the Bath. Thirty years had passed since the crowning of his father, and many of the knights had died. Twenty-four new Knights must be appointed, following a week of religious ceremonies to confirm their Loyal Commitment. In addition, a number of 'Stranger Knights' must be chosen, from among the rulers of friendly nations or their Ambassadors. In addition, a Garter King of Arms must be chosen, and other officials, not forgetting the Gentleman Usher of the Black Rod. Without that official, the King was not permitted to enter Parliament to announce a programme of actions for the year. George played a central role in the selection of members, and the Stranger Knights. The King appointed General Sir Edward Carteret, Bess's younger brother, as Black Rod. The whole business kept the members of the court fully engaged for weeks on end.

During these early months of the new reign, the King was granted an annual income of £1.2 million. The ancient financial awards, like ship money, were withdrawn. The Earl of Southampton, Lord Treasurer, offered George either £2,000 per annum, or three pence in the pound, for every Naval transaction. The second was the standard rate for City Traders. The Treasurer regarded the King's grant as parsimonious, and it had been trimmed so that there would be no opportunity for Charles to be as extravagant as his father. Royal expenditure required twice that sum for the management of palaces, to manage land holdings, and for diplomacy. The Royal Princes were given no alternative to becoming traders, as well as rulers, and to accept subsidies from France, although the latter was a closely guarded secret.

George, as Pepys was later to discover, was probably worth £2,000,000 at the restoration, the result of unremitting labour. His various new appointments brought him substantial income and added to his profits from trade. The King continued to make new appointments and each required financing and would not show a profit unless he made personal investments. This obviously raised a moral question. If an office of Government, intended to enrich the country and the King, was financed by George Carteret, how much of the profit gained was he entitled to claim? This question was bound to arise with a Parliament and Ministers advocating a policy of financial stringency. His friends in banking and assurance were there to advise him however, and Petty, Brounker and Samuel Hartlib, were the international financial geniuses forming and guiding the financial systems devised in the City.

There was a growing interest among nobles and the many new and salaried officials of the Government machine. The fact was that he was an astute and skilful financial manager. The financial geniuses just mentioned, George had in his childhood spent leisure time, when confined indoors by the weather, playing card games, involving the throwing of dice, and developed the ability to recall which player held the cards he must capture to win a game. His response to King Charles's offering to pay him an annual salary of £2,000, or to receive 3 pence for every financial transaction, was to choose the latter. He had clearly made an estimate, based on his trading experience, that fresh growth in naval activity, must bring better overall gain. Huygens in 1657, published an account of the Science of Probability, which was probably seized eagerly by William Petty and Samuel Hartlib, who were mathematicians and statisticians. There were accounts kept dating back many years in a number of the Hanseatic ports, from which statistics could be gained. The insight gained assisted merchants making decisions affecting their export trade. London merchants held these practices to be trickery on the part of bean counters, they relied however on their personal insight. This however was the third approach to Probability, known as the Subjective Approach. A balanced choice would come to be seen as a combination of both approaches.

The science of Chance, or probability, and its rules, was in its infancy at this time. In France the mathematicians Pascal, and Fermat. both formerly employed by Mazarin to develop an understanding of the "rules" and how they could be used to financial advantage. George had a natural talent for numbers and patterns, and was able to made complex calculations, rapidly which often caused astonishment.

He enjoyed the challenges made by gambling, and how easy it was to rob the innocent or the unskillful. He would have been fascinated to read Huygens on the puzzle controlling loss at the tables, known as "Gambler's Ruin" He enjoyed the less obvious challenge of estimating the probability of profit from a commercial venture. Therefore, he acquired a reputation as a respectable trader, and not as a reckless gambler. New companies were sponsored by the wealthy, who were willing to invest, but projects often failed though lack of financial skill. Companies were now promoted by Lotteries which tempted small investors to buy shares which were certain to fail, spelling disaster to investors. Lotteries are designed to ensure that the promoter received the best reward, and George thought them basically dishonourable but if well managed by a reliable sponsor, they worked well, and the Dutch commercial empire and the wealth of their people, had resulted from rigidly supervised lotteries. There was a strong case for a less than scrupulous English Government to allow both models to operate.

It must seem that months have passed since the new King rode into London, but in fact, it has been less than a year. We must now move on and explain the nature of Carteret's main occupation. As Treasurer to the Navy Office, he was closely involved with the most significant of senior Government affairs. The organisation was conducted in the same warren of overcrowded rooms which he remembered from his earlier time in London, in the year 1641. James, Duke of York, had recommended strongly, a move to more spacious premises, to match their significance and increasing responsibilities. The Government, advised by Hyde, allocated large financial grants to the army and navy, but had little insight into the requirements of either. Neither of the defence forces had received an allowance to cover pay for two years. Cromwell had refused to award money himself, wanting it to be a matter which Parliament should control, if it was to have real power. His MPs had declined the responsibility, fearing opposition to increased taxation. Consequently, army and navy were in a state of decay. Neither officers or men had been paid and there was uncertainty about the numbers employed. Naval supplies were depleted, and there were ship chandlers owed large sums for unpaid bills. Shipbuilding was largely at a standstill and, worst of all, there was no money for repairs or refitting, which was essential.

The Duke was a keen sailor, like his brother, and had persuaded Charles to appoint Carteret as Treasurer, knowing his excellent reputation for sound financial management. At an initial meeting with the inner team of six, it was clear that minutes must be kept of subjects discussed and decisions made. The King suggested Samuel Pepys, as an efficient secretary, and it proved to be another example of his excellent character judgement. Pepys proved effective, as the executive officer responsible for managing the expansion of the navy, day by day, during the next twenty years.

Meetings of the Navy board took place a least twice every week, and the King and Prince were often both present. Pepys knew little about ships and less about the navy, but he was a quick learner, and Carteret and the princes were prepared to teach him, as though he was a naval cadet, and in addition to meetings, took him on board ships, exploring their construction and introducing him to honest carpenters especially the Pett brothers, both excellent shipwrights. Other brothers of the same family were among a number of famous mathematicians. He also saw timber yards and rope-walks. He made errors of judgement and poor choices at first, but was totally absorbed by the trade. On one occasion he was sold short on the required length of two new masts. As a result, he learned the practical uses of trigonometry. He was a thorough mathematician but slow at accounting. Carteret demonstrated the value of committing the twelve times table to memory. Number bonds became second nature to him.

The Prince made every effort to increase the allowance for naval construction and repairs, but MPs from inland counties, failed to understand, or believe, that ships began to rot from the day they were launched. The ground floor office to which every seaman, from deckhand to Captain, came seeking employment, was a crowded war zone and many sea men were constantly demanding payment for long stretches of duty. There was a lack of staff and space to place a work table. Finally, Pepys, newly married and living in a cramped letting, moved into a newly created apartment carved out of an office building as the board moved to the new Admiralty building. This is where the point at which his Diary begins.

Carteret, Pepys, and Clarendon were among dozens of Londoners building new houses. Many who had returned from exile, had seen and admired the architecture of French, or Italian buildings constructed a century earlier by Palladio, and admired the simplicity and strength of their structure. Many wealthy young men seized the opportunity to see for themselves the splendours of Europe. Portrait painting and representations of the human form as statues had been largely destroyed or burned in the strictest puritan areas like London and East Anglia and those owned by the King sold on the European market. Some, like the Duke of Mantua's tapestries, had fortunately been too large to remove. Charles and his nobles became avid collectors of these missing items. Charles began to form a collection which forms the basis of our national collections.

Elizabeth Carteret and the children soon made adjustments to the demands of London life and variety of entertainments available. Frances Hyde introduced her to ladies of the Court who had never experienced the moral strictures of the British dissenters, having adopted the flexible morality of the French nobility. While repatriated husbands competed for sinecures at court, their wives delighted in the colloquial informal and blunt sentiments of the new dramatic style. With wealth restored and property regained, many acquired horses and carriages and rode out to the Downs where permanent race tracks were being constructed with Royal support. The importation of Arabian blood stock, opened prospects of increased wealth, which would exceed the fever over tulip bulbs. Bulbs, however encouraged market gardeners to supply other new plants imported by the Tradescants, and also to the opening of market gardens to providing fresh vegetables for the growing population.

Gambling was popular with the people, and the new weekly lotteries invited investment in ludicrous scams devised by those whose aim was to encourage the flow of money in their direction. Evidence shows that many ladies invested weekly amounts of cash which would have far exceeded the wages of their domestic staff for a year. Labour was cheap, and workers streamed into London to fill vacancies in an expanding job market. However, the discharging of unpaid soldiers and seamen brought increased unemployment. Many officers sought service overseas in Flanders or France, fighting as mercenaries, including John Churchill, who hoped to gain experience of modern battle tactics and weaponry, unavailable in England.

As wealth increased, fields were turned into estates of new housing and market gardens and livery stables to serve them. These in time spread into ever more remote suburbs where glass works, iron smelting and silk weaving co-existed with piggeries and cess-pits. New Palaces rose on the banks of the Thames, adjoining pleasure gardens, like Vauxhall and Ranelagh. Without building regulations, a factory producing glass, chemicals, or a blast furnace might be built beside them. The population grew to over 800,000. It was a source of wonder to foreign visitors, and expansion continued unchecked. Sir George Downing, a former colleague of George, invested in building projects with Lord Jermyn. Speculative building flourished to the north of Whitehall, and Bond Street, with its arcades selling high-end merchandise, quickly became popular with those seeking luxury goods. The Belgravia streets and squares were popular with the wealthy and successful, and Edward Carteret bought a town house in St James's. Broad Street became publicly known as Piccadilly.

This was an ongoing process, which gained a new impetus from the disastrous Fire of London which occured in 1666. Wholesale regeneration was essential and among the plans for redesigned commercial and dock areas, were those of Wren and Hooke. They proposed to re-position the docks between the Walbrook and the Holborn River, as the dock area from Queenborough to the Tower, and most warehouses had been totally destroyed. However. the Warehouseman asserted their right to rebuild their previous premises in their previous position. Also, on the north bank, the same speculators built cheap housing for aspirant city clerks, carriage builders, and day labourers, and also other larger communal buildings, intended as cheap lodging houses, pot houses, or brothels for travelling seamen and dockers seeking entertainment.

When details of the proposed Coronation route were announced, the demand for balconies commanding a good view increased considerably. The family urged George to reserve one rapidly, though it would not be required until the following year. Clarendon offered his house so that their families could be together. Clarendon House, Piccadilly, was ideal and on the procession route. He had a strong feeling that George and he would be so closely involved in averting disaster, they would see very little themselves. Fortunately, the Hyde family were hospitable and Edward had been made Lord Clarendon, and Lord Chancellor, as reward for making the restoration happen.

An example of their ambiguity in action came to light close to the date of the Coronation, and Elizabeth Carteret was among the first to know. Members of the exiled Court drifted back gradually to England, but many

*Restoration and Retribution*

had established strong relationships abroad. Frances Hyde had returned with her husband, and they had decided to build a new family home when the King returned. Her sons had returned and were creating new careers at the Bar. Anne, her daughter, remained with friends in France but rumours began to spread of reckless behaviour affecting her reputation. She seemed reluctant to leave the exiled court. Her father, anxious for the family reputation, sent her brother, Lawrence to encourage her to leave.

Hyde was dismayed to find, on their return, that his fears were justified. Even George noticed that Edward seemed preoccupied, and somewhat subdued in manner. The reason was soon to be revealed by Elizabeth who had received an unexpected early morning visitor.

They had recently moved to Deptford House, and Elizabeth was considering curtain fabrics when her maid announced, 'Lady Frances is in the drawing room —in tears!' Telling her to prepare coffee, Bess experienced some unease, and wondered what could have urged Frances to come by boat from Whitehall at such an early hour, hurried to be with her and was almost overwhelmed by a red-eyed Frances Hyde, able only to sob and cry, "Edward! Poor Edward!" It took several minutes to calm her and learn of the events which causing such anxiety. Frances seemed to be blaming herself for some awful misfortune.

'My husband has been summoned to attend the King at once: I believe he may be dismissed from Court and lose all his offices. It will destroy him! He has done so much for His Majesty, and regards him as a son.'

'I'm sure it will not be as bad as you fear, Frances. Whatever is the problem, I am confident Edward will provide an answer. Edward is known for his hard work and devotion to the King. What did he tell you, before he left? Why did he think the King was angry? Did he tell you nothing before he left?'

'Oh, Elizabeth! I'm so ashamed! Lawrence brought Anne home yesterday, and she told me that she is pregnant. We had to tell Edward, and he was terribly shocked, and does not know what to say to the King. I should never have agreed to Anne staying in Paris. I could have seen the danger signs, I'm sure.' Further floods of tears followed and when Elizabeth had managed to create some calm, aided by strong coffee and a little cognac, she attempted to present a rational argument.

'Oh, Frances I am so sorry; but it is not a tragedy. It is one of those events which occur despite a mother's best preparation and warnings. Anne is old enough to be married and is an affectionate woman. She will love the child, and think, my dear, what happiness it will bring you! Your first grandchild!' This resulted in fresh floods of tears and incoherent sobbing.

'Come, Frances. Calm yourself and let us eat breakfast together. I expect the King has received bad news from Portugal, concerning his proposal of marriage. I can't think that he is aware of your good news, but I'm sure he would be the first to offer congratulations.'

'That is quite impossible, Bess. You see, the father is Prince James, his brother! And what is worse, they have been married! And by a Catholic priest! I did not imagine my daughter had deserted her religion. We don't know whether James has told his brother, you see!'

Frances Hyde was reconciled to her daughter's situation as it became clear that the King had taken the news in his stride. Hyde had been sent for to allay the King's anxiety concerning his shortage of money. His intended bride would require a generous dowry apart from the cost of bringing her from Lisbon with her royal entourage and the wedding itself. As to the pregnancy, Hyde and George, and others in the close household, learned the news later in the day but had heard nothing more. Clearly the situation was to remain a confidential matter.

He noticed the King and his brother on their way to the river, where they had taken a two-man skiff. An opportunity for private conversation, might perhaps have been seized. Later that day Charles had again broached the subject of his Parliamentary grant. The Lord Treasurer had informed that provisional orders were little short of the necessary allowance. It seemed unlikely that normal taxation and fines would bring in much more. There were the outstanding Navy estimates to pay still requiring settlement. Prince James would inquire into these matters at the first meeting of the Admiralty in a few days' time. "Perhaps George could offer some suggestions." This aside was made by Clarendon, in George's hearing.

"Or perhaps he is suggesting that I should offer another small loan." George thought.

# ~ TWO ~

## CHAPTER NINE

The price of gold had reached a new high since the restoration, and the newly made emblems of royalty were designed by London craftsmen. Fortunately, the recently legalised London Jewish community was eager to thank the King for awarding them domicile and work permits and in response, provided a quantity of gold to be used as the King thought fit. It was employed to purchase timber for two Royal barges for himself and his brother. Clarendon seemed to be invisible at the time, and was extremely busy, engaged in writing acts to be rushed through Parliament. It had been noticed by the Lord Chief Justice that the new Acts of Parliament made to accommodate the restoration, had no legal authority. For example, the re-Establishment of a Church of England was expressly forbidden by Cromwell's Act of Disestablishment, which he had discovered was listed separately in the Statute book. Unless it was rescinded, the newly appointed Bishops had no legal status and a Coronation would be illegal unless the former act was read in parliament and redacted.

Hyde would be eager to conceal this situation from the King, George reflected, since there were several other Acts open to the same legal contradiction. It would reflect badly on Hyde if it delayed the King's Coronation, and it was necessary that the King should remain unaware of it. A few days later a second Restitution Act was presented and a handful of inconvenient legislation was consigned to oblivion by both Houses in one day. They also were eager not to be seen as 'wets'. Fortunately, Clarendon had noticed the mistake before someone who might have exposed their incompetence: George was not surprised that the King remained unaware of the new Acts he was signing into law. Charles had little knowledge of English Law, and no experience of the working of the law. In general he seemed to avoid legal involvement, and indicated policy decisions by hints offered in Council. If he had serious objections to a proposed Act, he preferred to postpone a decision to a later parliamentary session, when it might be less controversial, and could be shuffled out of sight. He always aimed to avoid confrontation.

Since her return to England from France, Frances Hyde had made a close friendship with Elizabeth, as they occupied adjacent apartments. Warm-hearted, sociable and familiar with London and those whose lives were centred about the Court, she took Elizabeth in hand, in the family carriage, to visit the sights of London, introducing her to her own circle of friends. When the Carterets moved into Deptford House, their small skiffs were brought into service for the exchange of visits. George became aware, when he met Frances, that Hyde was fully human, and became more prepared to accept his moments of ungraciousness. Their sons were a few years older than the Carteret boys, and launched into different careers. Henry the elder son, was heir to the family home in Oxfordshire, and had taken on management of the estate. Laurence, highly intelligent, had completed his legal training and was making a name for himself as a skilful advocate. He had political ambitions. He was very proud of both his sons and eager to offer them help to gain success.

Bess was dressed and about to take a carriage to St, Paul's, where fresh silks and damasks had arrived at the stalls, when she was surprised to receive an unannounced visit from Prince James, who was not a man to make informal visits. He seemed uncertain, even embarrassed, and after stilted greetings, asked if she could advise him on an important personal matter. Concealing her belief that it concerned his wife, Anne, Elizabeth politely offered help, and coffee. She was not sure that she was assumed to know about the secret marriage. She and her husband had known James as a diffident teenager, having none of the confidence and charm of his elder brother, and who had difficulty forming relationships. During several months he had spent in Jersey, and largely disregarded by his elder brother, he had often come to the Carteret home, as a welcome visitor to share the company of their family which he came to enjoy. He enjoyed sailing, hawking and riding, but also family meals and card games. Bess had come to regard him as an extra family member and decided that he was perhaps feeling the lack of a stable family life. The Queen learned eventually that he was associating with "country folk" and insisted he came to Paris to acquire the attributes of the nobility. James had been sad to leave and Bess had to remind him of his duty to his mother and brother.

Accepting the offer of refreshments, James took a comfortable chair and gradually relaxed, Bess prepared herself for his frequent inability to make an appropriate decision. She remembered their last meeting clearly. He was often taken for granted by his elder brother and had asked her whether he could disobey his brother's order to follow him to France. 'There was nothing for him in France,' he protested, 'and he enjoyed sailing and riding in Jersey'.

He finally broached the subject of Anne Hyde. 'The fact is,' he said, 'I had no wish to marry Anne Hyde.'

He had known her for nearly four years in Paris, he said, and also several other ladies in their circle. One of them had already given him a son, named Charles, of whom he was very fond. He accepted that he was the father of Anne Hyde's expected baby, but asserted his reluctance to marry her, as a matter of convenience.

'It is unfair! It is my duty to be united with a noble family of international importance and social standing.'

'But are you not married to Anne Hyde? I was told you had married her.'

'Yes, Lady Bess, it is true that we were married in a private ceremony, but only to stop her being unhappy and gossiping. I wanted to prevent her telling her father or my brother, who was making important arrangements to return to England. I knew I had made a serious error.'

'James, you must accept that you are a married man! Have you not spoken to your brother about the situation? You must tell him before he is informed by someone who wishes to shame you. He may already know!'

'Yes, I have of course, and I told him I was sorry for the mistake, and wanted a separation, because it was only a Catholic marriage, which surely counts for nothing in England. I reminded my brother that he has three bastards. This one would be my first. Did you know that when we were in Jersey in 1649, he already had two children and was expecting a third? I see you are surprised.'

'My husband had heard something, I believe. Tell me, James, what has His Majesty decided you must do?'

'He said he was never fool enough to offer marriage to a mistress. He told me to go and think about doing the 'right thing' and wants to know my decision tomorrow.'

'James, I am so sorry to hear this. You have acted on impulse again. You often behaved without thinking of the consequences, when you lived with us. But though you regret it, you have committed yourself. You realise that, surely? Anne is a bright, intelligent girl, and not a silly, empty-headed princess. She is kind-hearted, like her mother, and I am sure she married you for love, not ambition. I know you always try to do what is right. Give it careful thought! I think you could be very happy together.'

There was more discussion along the same lines, and much coffee was drunk before James took a sorrowful leave. As an afterthought, before departing, he asked whether Bess knew why he was so eager to stay in Jersey.

'Because you enjoyed riding and sailing, Perhaps?'

'I knew the reason Charles wanted to go to Paris. It was to show me his son: he did not want my company. I might as well not have been there: he spent all his time with Lucy and the baby. He had named him James and wanted me to be god-father. I started gambling and going after women to pass the time. He sent me to volunteer with the Army when he decided I cost him too much money.'

The next day, the King and his brother arose early and, mounting horses, went racing in St James's Park. Their gentlemen were soon dismissed and the brothers returned separately some hours later. The King called on Juxon in Lambeth to raise issues concerned with the Coronation. The following day, Bess went with Frances Hyde to St Paul's Churchyard, where, while examining lengths of cloth, Frances confided that the wedding would take place in the King's Whitehall Chapel, on 5th. September, with a small family party, and before witnesses. Later she was instructed that any mention of 'the marriage' was forbidden. Anne would spend the remaining months at Oatlands Palace, to await the birth in the place where the children of Charles I had been raised. And so, at a stroke, a situation which might have caused anger, had it been made public, had been made legal and acceptable as the 'secret' gradually became known. A public announcement was neither necessary or desirable.

Once the family removal to Deptford House was completed, Prince James was among their first visitors, and made every effort to support George in his task of setting the Naval Finances to rights. The Commons demanded to see the accounts by 25 March 1661, and Pepys, new to accountancy but a rapid learner, found a current deficit of £685,000. George took on the debt, with the consent of the Prince, to draw a line under past deficits. The Clerks under Commonwealth control, had produced accurate accounts. They had not attempted to provided money for the past two years. In an attempt to allay the justified anger of the Navy, which was becoming a public disgrace, and had led to rowdy protests outside the Admiralty, during which threats had been made to the staff. The Admiralty were sympathetic to the marines and resorted to unconventional means to prevent violence. Those unpaid were offered "tickets," ie. promissory notes, as a temporary makeshift.

In 1660, a Privy Council note records that Pepys requested a second "ticket" for a Mr Grey, who had defaced his ticket. Carteret, who was presiding at the meeting, directed that he must produce the damaged ticket to ensure he did not claim twice. It would seem that this episode roused a hornets' nest, since the other Councillors were unaware that promissory tickets had been issued. Those in the Treasury objected that they should have been asked for permission before the Navy involved them in unknown amounts of expenditure. Later, this decision resulted in a long and bitter Parliamentary enquiry into suspected embezzlement, since the Treasury had not been consulted about this informal decision, others might have been made dishonestly. So many errors went unnoticed at this time, only equalled by the opportunities which went unnoticed, when useful savings or investments might have been made.

Philip and James Carteret adjusted quickly to the opportunities and diversions available in London: the largest European city, with 850.000 inhabitants, which was welcoming such valuable newcomers as bankers, economists, scientists as well as sculptors, artists and musicians. James advanced from captain's assistant, to midshipman with deceptive ease, and was popular among all ranks on board. On shore he was also popular, though tending toward brawling and drinking. Philip's talents were also appreciated, and his knowledge of naval management, and navigational skills impressed the gentlemen of the Admiralty. His Lieutenancy was assured. Harrington heard of his fascination with timepieces and introduced him to Robert Hooke, a difficult man, but an inventive genius. Hooke had begun the development of a balance sprung escapement for timepieces, which might reduce their size and increase their reliability. His other interest was navigational instruments and telescopes of all kinds for the efficiency of navigation and accurate time-keeping. Hooke, although he could not be described as "clubbable" was at the cutting edge of a wide circle of experimental thinkers and mathematicians, with whom he had associated at Westminster School and Wadham, Oxford.

At the same time Philip was becoming indispensable as an aide to his father. He and Jarvis, taken on years ago as a valet, now formed a reliable team as the Carteret businesses grew. Another of his many interests were magnification and Probability theory. He had studied with Huygens, maker of telescopes and microscopes, and had read Pascal's book,'La logique ou l'art de penser,' published in 1657 and discovering that he and his father were able to analyse chance, and make predictions of the fall of dice or cards. He learned the basics of trigonometry from Fermat's papers, and taught it to Pepys, who had been deceived by a dishonest timber merchant over the purchase of a ship's mast. Pepys learned much at Cambridge, but not that new concept. Nor did he learn the traditional 'Twelve times Tables' by rote. He was shown them by George who found Sam one day scribbling mysteriously on scraps of paper while balancing an account.

A generation of University students had their degree studies interrupted by the closure of Oxford University to provide accommodation for Charles I, his court and his family. Those who had wealthy families returned to their homes, but those who had won endowments from Westminster School had no such luxury. A significant group, including some of the brightest men in England, having no College accommodation, took cheap lodgings and commandeered an Oxford coffee shop. Opening in 1653, this was probably the first in England of the establishments which were to become centres of lively debate, in which all were welcome to take part. Their discussions were fruitful and led to an English scientific revolution of great importance. They moved to London after the Restoration, in search of employment, and sponsors to finance their projects. Their social connections in the City, and avid discussion about their difficulty in finding backers, led to entrepreneurs prepared to select the ideas they judged worthy of support. Someone, possibly Pepys, who had established a close relationship with Charles during the long crossing from France to England, introduced Philip Carteret to the King, who was fascinated by scientific experiments, and quickly seized on new ideas. Obsessed by clocks, the king had filled every room with them: in his bed chamber, he had installed seven, which chimed irregularly and drove his attendants to distraction.

Charles was always eager to be at the centre of any exploit which brought clever people together. His father had been rendered helpless by clever lawyers and tradesmen. Having met Newton, Wren and others, who were being talked of as the leaders of English progressive future, he decided their inventiveness needed his official supervision. New technology and industry, which led to increased national wealth was essential and deserved financial backing. He himself had other irons in the fire, and lavish entertainments to attend, but he could give his Royal blessing to a scheme, and encourage an ambitious newcomer to provide the finance. This would add to his reputation as a progressive ruler, the equivalent of Louis XIV for whom he had considerable envy.

Research, he was convinced, must always have clear, practical outcomes: abstractions and speculation wasted time, and could be left to other nations, for example, the French financing of Sèvres Porcelain, seemed to him merely a vanity project, or a pretty irrelevance. Charles had an inquisitive mind and instituted weekly meetings of his Royal Society, expecting to be presented with a new invention at each meeting. This institution was set up in 1662, and George and Philip Carteret were among founder members. Hooke was left the task of finding something to explode or go up in smoke, to catch the King's attention for a few minutes. Newton's cautious theorising was not his style, so he was placed in charge of the Royal Mint to discover how the purity of gold could be raised and to analyse foreign gold for adulteration or impurities. Wren, an engineering genius, was paid to construct Pavilions for the entertainment of customers at Vauxhall Gardens, and to spy on French locomotive engineers and steal the secret of improving suspension for carriages. They continued with their own experiments, like Boyle with his pump, while Hooke remained underestimated by all.

The first appointees to the Royal Society were two of his doctors, his Chaplain, and Sir Robert Moray, who speaking as the King's voice, demanded to know how beer could be improved, why ant eggs were larger than the ants themselves, and why the leaves of sensitive plants contracted to the touch. Undoubtedly the gathered experts would have been amazed by the King's sagacity. Huygens, Boyle, and Wren were among the first members and chose as their policy statement "Nullius in Verba" ('Take no man's word for it!') For the King it seemed, novelty was of first importance but prolonged discussion tested his patience. This was paralleled by the speed with which constitutional issues were dealt with after which decisions often proved to have inherent flaws. Philip's time-piece obsession however gained the King's immediate response, for the King also had a fascination with clocks. It also, fortunately, gave opportunities for regular meetings, often informal, held in one of the coffee houses opening in London. These were probably more rewarding than the more formal sessions.

George was an indulgent father to his daughters and particularly missed the two youngest who remained in France. Philip was constantly in his thoughts, however. During the St Malo years, it was Philip who had supported his mother in matters of family business, and with the care of his siblings. Now that he was in London he dealt with increasing amounts of administration. He was a man of few words, though they were well chosen and to the purpose. He took over the running of their manorial rights and income, settling disputes and collecting taxes, including those paid to the County Sheriff for administration, still referred to as "the Farm."

## CHAPTER TEN

George's many duties required the keeping of a diary of appointments, and he informed Philip of them, and his son prevented double bookings and facilitated prioritisation. The King's demands had priority always. With a full day ahead, the King might demand a barge and musicians to play while sailing, with the result that other necessities were postponed or cancelled. The range of George's duties as Lord Chamberlain were extremely varied and constantly changing. As a monarch, Charles felt it a duty to encourage trade of all kinds, so that the highest quality was worthy of 'Royal Appointment'. Thus, an Arras worker, a bookbinder, a brewer, a coffee maker, a fishmonger, a milliner, a saddler, a woollen draper, a clock maker, and many others needed to be attested and rewarded. More personal appointees included a Surveyor of Stables, Masters of the Mews, Falconers and also, of course, the Provision of Uniforms to distinguish the new regiments. This last was of benefit to the clothiers of London. Two Dowses were cloth merchants, trading with Italy and the Levant.

He ensured that the royal theatres were able to show attractive sets: costumes were mainly garments discarded by members of the Court. The audiences were astonished by the silks and satins on display, and the demand for material was so great that a silk factory was established at Mortlake under Royal sponsorship. The artist, Michael Wright, was appointed to paint the ceiling of the Banqueting Hall at Whitehall, and enormous tapestries were required for the walls of the Queen's Palace at Greenwich. He appointed, and sometimes pensioned off, Gentlemen of the Chapel Royal at Windsor, and engaged Court Composers and instrumentalists, generally providing their uniforms. George never held a sinecure, but knew, from his early experience in Jersey, that ruling a complex organisation was hard work, however rewarding. Any worthwhile achievement was the result of hard work. His was a family who achieved their status by their own efforts.

When it was obvious that they had two marriageable daughters, it might be assumed that, as a man of wealth held in public esteem, he might seek among the ranks of the Nobility for suitable husbands. There were increasing numbers of young and eligible bachelors seeking promotion about the court, but George looked for more successful men as marriage partners. Instead he apprised the sons of his City acquaintances, and found several solid Traders or manufacturers, whose sons, like Philip, showed an interest in following their father's trade. Invitations were issued for family meetings and, since their daughters had not been dazzled by apparently attractive fops, they were able to choose their preferred suitors. Pepys and Carteret had formed a strong relationship almost at once, and he and Elizabeth became welcome visitors. Pepys enjoyed the company of young people, though he and Elizabeth had no family. He was taken by George's children on a tour of the rooftops of Whitehall and enjoyed their company at home. Pepys first mentioned George favourably in a diary entry: "I do find him a very good natured man," and they remained friends long after George relinquished the Treasury post Prince James and his two employees formed a strong and effective partnership and any improvements in the abject condition of the navy, was entirely due to their efforts.

In the following year, Anne and Caroline found their chosen partners and the marriages took place in the August of 1662. Prince James prevailed over his mother, and the weddings were celebrated in the ancient Chapel of the Savoy Palace. Among the many guests, was John Evelyn, an old friend from before the Commonwealth. In August 1649, Evelyn, Lord Cottington, Edward Nicholas and Doctor Earle had paid a courtesy visit to the widowed Queen in Paris and offered her their support. This Chapel had been provided exclusively for the use of Henrietta Maria and appointed for the celebration of mass. James and his wife, a recent convert, were among the guests. James remained a practising Anglican at the time.

Anne married Sir Nicholas Stanning, already a Knight of the Bath, whose father had been a Devonshire Royalist and commander of Sir Philippe's son, who had joined the west of England rebellion twenty years earlier. Caroline married Sir Thomas Scott, whose mother had shared the king's exile in France. Stanning and Scott were both wealthy and industrious: the former held estates in Devon, the latter, near Tenterden in Kent. Lady Anne, and the two younger children, Elizabeth and Rachel, were able to attend these weddings as bridal attendants, but returned to Jersey afterwards to stay with their uncle in St Ouen. While there, young Philippe de Carteret died from smallpox. Anne and the children returned to Peyrol, hoping to avoid the fatal epidemics prevalent that year.

That spring the Navy estimates had been accepted and George set about the resurrection of the navy, with the increasing support of Pepys, who became adept at accountancy after he had been shown the multiplication tables They formed a good partnership. Sharing a basic optimism essential in an age when government spending was discouraged and investment for the future was regarded as reckless. This was a grave handicap for naval progress since it was not understood that ships needed constant repair and refitting. They required a sinking fund to maintain them in working order. Just as an army needed constant feeding and housing, as well as new shells and artillery. Only Richard I and Henry VIII showed some awareness of these facts, though Henry's first concern was always his latest vanity project.

They were fortunately able to make their own choice of experienced experts to make up an extremely efficient committee. Sir Robert Slingsby, a close associate of George before the civil War, now became Naval Comptroller and, like George, had been an effective captain, and also, like George, had trained under Admiral Edgeworth. Sir William Batten of Trinity House, and a former merchant Navy commander, was appointed naval surveyor, and remained in post for the next twenty years. Sir William Menges became Naval Architect, having studied shipbuilding and design for several years. Immediately they laid down the keels of two, two-decked battle ships and set about scuttling ships long past repair, first paying off any remaining crew. Pepys learned the lesson that ships begin to rot on the day they entered service: unfortunately, MPs did not understand this fact, or chose to ignore it, claiming the need to prevent wasteful expenditure.

"Why are there so few ships?" was the first question posed, and the more detailed the explanation given, the more they suspected prevarication. Whenever it was possible, Prince James extracted donations from the Privy Purse. The King was unable to set aside a Naval Fund, Parliament would have been highly critical of such interference. Occasionally, James had some success, but finally a Parliamentary enquiry into the constant demand for money and possible embezzlement, was inevitable.

The truth was that Charles had hardly a penny to his name. The Coronation in 1661, was the last straw. Charles was forced to apply to his nephew, Louis XIV for money to pay the most pressing bills. Louis was happy to help him, but pointed out that Charles was without full Sovereignty in his own country. He recommended his cousin to seize control from bankers, and have them arrested for Treason. Charles rejected this advice, remembering that his father had long ago exposed his own weakness by attempting to arrest elected MPs. In consequence Parliament had effectively rendered him powerless and asserted the power which led to his execution. He considered using the threat of abdication but decided to hold it in reserve. If the financial enquiry into the Navy was successfully concluded, he would have to find other means to finance his plans for creating effective areas of public life over which he could have full control, while increasing the esteem he looked for from the wider population. His decided he must participate in aspects of life which the man in the street would approve.

At the year's close, Barbara Palmer gave birth to Lady Anne Palmer and shortly after, Anne Hyde, now acknowledged Duchess of York, gave birth to a stillborn son, following a timely marriage in the privacy of Windsor. These additional events were yet another burden on the Royal finances. James Fitzroy/Croft, the King's eldest illegitimate son, was made Duke of Monmouth, entitled to his own household and attendants in memory of his Welsh mother, who had recently died He was to be included with others to receive the Order of the Garter, officially recognised as the King's son. Barbara Villiers/Palmer, to enhance her status as the King's mistress, was given the title 'Lady Castlemaine'. Her husband was refused the Lordship, though the son born to Barbara later that year, would inherit her title in the fullness of time. The Garter Ceremony could not be delayed any longer and must precede the Coronation. Charles was probably balancing his options. His recent actions had been taken without parliamentary discussion or approval. He applied again to parliament to keep its promise. He had been guaranteed £1,200,000. He had only received £850,000 as yet and this shortfall was to recur in subsequent years, despite Parliamentary assurances that the deficit would be made up.

Charles's personal Treasurer questioned the sincerity of parliament and asked whether they were having second thoughts about his right as a reigning monarch. While the debate ensued, Charles and his brother looked for other sources of income. The African Adventurers' Company, regenerated and, with a new Charter, was handed over to Prince Rupert to stir it into life. This series of actions formed a clear demonstration of Charles's personal power to effect change. Although moralists questioned these actions as unworthy of the propriety expected of a King, they were approved by the general public Now in his forties, Rupert was hardly recognisable as the energetic, chivalric hero of Naseby and other cavalry actions. He was overweight, disappointed by being denied the throne of Bohemia, irascible in discussion and with a tendency to vent his displeasure employing obscenities in a wide variety of foreign languages. He was becoming the subject of shocked admiration. Charles had given him the detailed report on the Gambia River to exploit as a source of timber, and minerals, especially gold. George had drawn up the report some years earlier for Charles I which had been shelved. The new world was not forgotten, however, and George was appointed, with Lord Clarendon, Lord Proprietor of Georgia, and High Chamberlain and Admiral of Carolina and Caroliola, later known as Grenada. The king obviously knew of George's trans-Atlantic trading links, and expected them to be developed to his financial advantage.

At the same time, King James's claims in the Hudson Bay Area were redefined to include the headwaters of all the rivers feeding Hudson's Bay. This covered the Area now known as Canada and regions feeding Lake Michigan, including Chicago. This created the largest of all the land areas included under English control. Elizabeth I had granted a Charter to the East India Company in 1600 and the Stuart kings had granted a number of Charters including the Levant and Tunis concessions. These established the practice whereby wealthy men, nobles and commoners, came together to commit large sums of money for the development of trading bases, the construction of ships to convey trading goods, and armaments and men to defend their claims against other claimants. Carteret had become the major beneficiary of the Indies company following the death of James Hay, Earl of Carlisle. Charles Dowse had been Hay's business agent at the time of Buckingham's murder, and Carteret's connections with City Aldermen were of long standing. It is often said today that Britain is directed by only two hundred wealthy and influential men. It would certainly have been true in 1660, and the evidence suggests strongly that George Carteret was one of this group whose names crop up consistently during these years.

## CHAPTER ELEVEN

Clarendon, as Lord Chancellor, was responsible for the conduct of these companies whose taxes underscored Parliamentary power. The King also acquired a percentage from these sources, their Charters sanctioned under his authority. These and the Royal Africa Company bore Royal Charters, and were in need of structured Government, operated by local Councils to ensure that British law was followed. Areas not covered by British law, like the possession and sale of slaves, were to be resolved as a local concern, under the general terms for the care of property and livestock. John Locke was tasked with responsibility for devising a model constitution for the Government of any new Crown Colonies. Locke, held the belief that people were entirely responsible for shaping their own lives, in imitation of Christian standards, and humans were born with neither pre-conceptions nor knowledge. Each was a 'tabula rasa' ready to be programmed with a set of principles which would enable him to take an acceptable station in life, including all its pre-ordained social and legal obligations. His was a rigid structure and changeable only by national consent. It was basic to the existing structure of British society, but transformed into a set of rigid laws. All enjoyed rights and obligations and these, if obeyed, would confer the correct amount of personal freedom. An exception was made for the lowest order of society, who were slaves owned outright by the masters who had purchased them. George and Clarendon were not resident Governors, and therefore appointed trusted army officers with the task of setting up legal codes to suit the growth of their colonies. They based their system on the English model, but made alterations over the years. Locke's rigid model found its way to an obscure cupboard and when it came to light, unfortunately, was used when a model for a United States Constitution was sought: rigidly structured, and with no flexibility to adapt to changing circumstances, it is famous for its inability to adjust to changed circumstances. Prince James was appointed Commander of the expansion of British command in America. New Amsterdam was renamed New York, to celebrate his title, and as a calculated insult to the Dutch. Prince Rupert acquired a large new territory as a reward for his loyalty.

James pleaded with his brother for a more active part in the political structure. He was prepared to settle for a posting with the Guards. But Charles was determined to retain control of the army, and in addition, when James asked to be allowed to take up a career in the Army of their French cousin, refused him the major role in the French army, which Louis had offered him. Constantly restless, he was probably over-eager to impress his brother, which may be the reason why he tended to act on impulse, and had little time for prolonged persuasion. As Commander of the Navy, and with its interests at heart, he was disappointed at his lack of success in begging his brother for the necessary money. He therefore decided to exercise his personal authority. He began by demanding that all foreign vessels passing through the "English Channel" must fly a British flag on a conspicuous masthead and sail with all topsails set so that they passed Britain at their greatest speed, demonstrating that they did not intend an invasion.

This was, although petty, an insult to foreign merchants passing peacefully through the "Narrow Seas". This sea passage had not been regarded as English possession in the past, and formed another arrogant challenge. For many years, Cromwell's government had enforced the rule that cargoes imported or exported through British ports, must be carried in British ships. These actions were greeted with general approval as a welcome sign that Englishmen could walk with their heads held high. The Navy office, Pepys and Carteret included, dared to believe that further grants for reducing the Naval Debt might be forthcoming. But Prince James had another card to play, now that his previous acts had been well received. As a man of action he was convinced that only a strong naval action and victory at sea would prove that the navy was a force worth investing in, and that a new powerful force would be created.

A small squadron of warships, would set sail for the Dutch coast to lure the Dutch to leave their safe port, the English fleet would then spring on them with the full force, and take them by surprise. The Admiralty was horrified, although compliance was unavoidable. The Navy office was aware that they were ill-prepared to challenge the Dutch navy, fearing the best ships, repaired at great expense, might be lost or seriously damaged. In precipitate promptness, an English fleet, supplemented by commandeered merchant ships, partially armed or carrying supplies and reinforcements, put to sea, dropping anchor off Lowestoft. The British plan was known throughout England and Europe. The Dutch fishing fleet had observed every stage of the British preparations and prepared their response. On 3 June 1665. the Duke's flagship engaged his Dutch opponent off the coast of Holland. Engaging at once with Van Opden's flagship he destroyed it completely. In the meantime, other Dutch ships surrounded the English ships, sailing in line of battle, and surrounding them picking them off one at a time, inflicting serious damage.

The Dutch fleet then attacked the undefended supply ships. The Duke, well satisfied with his action, and content to have destroyed the Dutch flagship returned to London, making no attempt to pursue the Dutch. Nevertheless, he proclaimed a victory. Victory traditionally goes to the Force which captures the field of battle. Such was not the case on this occasion. The shock felt by the Navy office was palpable. Heavy injuries had been sustained by officers and men, and the British Navy had suffered extreme losses, the most modern ships having been severely damaged. Britain would be unable to undertake any major naval action for years to come. The cream of British officers and seamen died in action, and the finest ships were lost. These results were keenly felt by Carteret, who had achieved so much despite the lack of adequate finance. Whoever held the Treasurership would have a thankless task. It was at this stage that Carteret began to look for a replacement Treasurer. The King realised his brother's action had been unwise, to say the least, and had risked his life unnecessarily. The Duke was relieved of his Naval Command and a committee appointed to make a reorganisation, led by Coventry, the Duke's treasurer and a man of integrity. The King informed his brother that, as heir to the throne, he was forbidden to risk his life again. He was dispatched to Scotland with an army, to strengthen government there.

By the end of the year, Lady Castlemaine had given birth to Charles Fitzroy, named Duke of Southampton. Neither Charles nor James had a legitimate son, although each had increasing numbers of illegitimate ones. Charles had already begun to search for a suitable marriage partner among European Royal families. Three of these could be discounted; Spain as ancient enemy, France, because Louis had recently revived the campaign waged for some years against Protestants, and the Dutch, because a cold war was now in progress.

The Infanta of Portugal was the sister of the new Portuguese king whose authority was open to question, being heir to the province of Braganza. His right was questioned by Spain, and in face of the threat from his larger neighbour, support from Britain would be a safeguard. The wealth of the Portuguese trading posts in Africa and the Far East would be opened up to Britain, and together their traders could threaten the power of the Dutch. The Portuguese had begun to develop a province in south America also. On the whole, the Infanta seemed a wise choice for the King and she and accepted his proposal, for the safety of her brother, with the provision that she would be permitted to remain a practicing Roman Catholic, and that her priests, religion and household would have total protection from persecution. Charles had some reservations concerning his present heirs, of whom the first was James, his impulsive brother. Others were Prince Rupert, who retained some popularity, and was unlikely to regain the Bohemian Crown. There was also his nephew, the nine year old Stadtholder, Willem, and his brother James's two year old daughter, Mary. Catherine of Braganza would bring a large Dowry and a number of trading posts in parts of the world which proved resistant to British traders. The marriage Treaty was signed, and Carteret found that he was to have a role in the ceremony when it occurred.

The King was once more bankrupt. Court ceremonial and household expenses were expanding daily and the Navy had lost its warships. James was despatched by his brother to Scotland, which was mired in internal conflict, and spent the next four years reorganising the administration. The King himself now became Commander of the Navy, and James took the army to Scotland. Coventry, the Duke's secretary was appointed to the Navy Board to see where savings could be made. The King had borrowed so much money from the City that further loans were given only on condition that George underwrote them. No longer threatened by war, savings were able to be made once more.

Charles had one last financial hope. He had a lifelong affection for the sea and was something of an expert with shipbuilding. He appreciated that the navy needed a strong injection of cash. The answer seemed obvious. Dunkirk must be sold to France. However, as an English enclave on the French coast, it was of considerable value to Louis XIV. Long negotiations followed, and the initial purchase price was negotiated downward until a final offer of 5,000.000 écus was reached. Charles accepted the offer and James ordered Carteret to organise transportation for the gold to London. Charles had insisted on payment in gold coin and it must be conveyed to his Treasury in the Tower of London. In the chaos leading to the collapse of the Commonwealth, the acquisition of Dunkirk had not been announced.

Charles had insisted that the money must be paid in gold coin of the realm, and every coin counted individually into strong coffers and conveyed to Dunkirk, where it would be handed over and signed for after being recounted to the satisfaction of both parties. The Lords and their clerks, horses, carriages and servants were in position in Paris. Carteret was asked to stand by in case of problems. He realised that problems were inevitable and that he would have to call upon the help of all his French friends if the plan was to succeed. It was autumn, and a very wet one, the clay soils of northern France would turn to mud. French roads between Paris and Dunkirk were poorly surfaced, because the area was agricultural land left fallow in winter. It was better left unpaved to prevent the passage of invading British armies.

The Lords were delayed by weather. They were to discover how long it took to count out such a quantity of cash. Loading it, and carrying it to a safe place was arduous and more employees were required. Once counted and coffered, it had to be conveyed cross country to Dunkirk, which was British territory. Carteret solved the difficulties by calling on French landowners he knew to provide farm wagons, each drawn by teams of four oxen, to drag the money to its destination. At least fifteen wagons were required. Their owners assumed that they would be recompensed for the use of their men, wagons, and food for both oxen and men. Carteret suggested that some of the gold coins could be used to pay what was owing. The noble Lords thought the suggestion offensive, but did not offer to pay. Carteret filled the financial deficit

At the border, Louis himself insisted on being present to assure himself that the cash was delivered and the keys of the town handed over. The exchange had to be made at Calais on French territory, since Louis life might be in danger if he stepped into "Britain." Once this was done, Carteret's task was over. The British ex-Governor took charge and used his own initiative to hire ships to convey the goods to Dover, transfer it onto English wagons after unloading the ships and conveying it to the Tower, a palace belonging to the King. Remarkably Charles got what he wanted and the few who were aware chose not to speak of it, since it seemed to be discreditable. Possibly, with Christmas approaching, they were eager to forget their task, and too occupied with religious uncertainties.

# CHAPTER TWELVE

The Garter Ceremony and Coronation could now take place. In a remarkably short time the missing regalia had been painstakingly reconstructed by goldsmiths, silversmiths and enamellers, who divided the work among themselves, overjoyed at having the opportunity to deploy their skills. Carteret made a point of searching out Edmund Harrington, embroiderer to two Kings, to whom they had already paid the £4,000 owed to him. He received the honour of constructing the heavy, golden Dalmatic, worn by the King after the crowning. Thus, it became a matter of logistics, because the deaths of close relatives necessitated six months of full mourning, and those grieving wore robes of purple velvet, trimmed with deep lilac. The long delay had been further protracted by the deaths of Mary, the wife of the Stadtholder William, and of Prince Henry, the youngest of the three royal brothers. Both had died from smallpox. Clarendon's papers reveal that he considered Henry a real loss having greater potential as a ruler than either of his brothers. Henry had not suffered the humiliations and poverty they had experienced, and had been brought up as a firm Parliamentarian by the Lord Croft's family of Risley, Suffolk. He was entirely devoted to the Anglican Church. However with two healthy elder brothers it is unlikely that he would have inherited the throne, although he might have been willing to take the throne from his brother James, it is unlikely that he would have committed such an act of betrayal.

A delay for the six months of court mourning had to be observed and, in the circumstances provided time for the missing items essential in the ceremonials of a Coronation and Royal marriage, to be replaced. Parliament, with remarkable generosity, provided a further grant for the Coronation, but the amount was insufficient to cover the total cost. Work on Hampton Court and Windsor Castle was essential in preparation for the Garter ceremony, and to provide accommodation for those to be ennobled. Charles had decided that Windsor would be his most secure residence, since it was a defensive structure, essential in the event of a new revolution, or as a defence against rebellion. As such, its defences were raised to comply with modern weaponry.

*Restoration and Retribution*

The cost of these two ceremonies was borne by the Treasury and amounted to three million pounds. The Garter ceremony, included a night of compulsory prayer and confession of their sins, made them eligible to receive the Honour, which was a symbol of purity! James, Duke of York, Prince Rupert and the Elector of Brandenburg, were principal recipients, also the recently deceased, Dutch Stadtholder. The Duke of Ormonde received his for loyal support of the Royal family in exile. This was essentially a private occasion, and George was in charge of the 'Props' for this extremely theatrical event. Robes, chains and symbols of office must be ready when required, and the guards' regiments were dressed in full regimentals, with gilded braiding and epaulettes, boots and helmets, in constant attendance. Their coats were dyed scarlet, at great expense. The ceremony took place on the 14/15 April 1661, ending with a service of dedication in the Chapel Royal. Charles was a well-informed music lover and appreciated the anthem composed for the occasion. During the imminent coronation, the King was to be escorted by Knights of the Most Noble Order of the Bath.

Thirty years had passed since the crowning of his father, and many of the Knights had died. Twenty-four new Knights were appointed, following a week of religious ceremonies, to demonstrate the assurance of their loyalty. In addition, a number of 'Stranger Knights' from the representatives of friendly nations, were to be present, In addition a 'Garter King of Arms' and a 'Gentleman Usher of the Black Rod' were required. The King appointed General Sir Edward Carteret, Bess's younger brother to that post. George Carteret assisted in the appointment of the foreign replacements, and had to ensure that all wore the robes and accoutrements considered essential. The vast expenditure of these enterprises was astronomical and a damaging blow to the economy. In part it was alleviated by the influx of foreign dignitaries who came to inspect the events to assess whether this new monarch could be taken seriously. Another benefit was the number of skills, old and new, providing employment opportunities. This would increase public affection for the King. These beneficial results Carteret realised, with some amusement, depended to a large extent on this effective management.

When details of the Coronation route were announced, the public could squabble over the best views. The Royal party would spend the previous night at the Tower, their London stronghold, and proceed slowly through the City and numerous triumphal arches, to the Guildhall, where they would be welcomed by the Lord Mayor and Aldermen. Formality concluded they would pass through the expanding areas of new mansions and the Inns of Court, to cross the Tyburn and pass Westminster Hall before reaching the Abbey. For the wealthy, balcony views were in demand so that they could have an uninterrupted view of the passing procession, and so that they could be seen. Bess had arranged with Frances Clarendon that they would stand on the balcony of Clarendon House before making their way to the Abbey. Edward Hyde as Lord Chancellor, would carry the Crown, and play a prominent role as directed by the Duke of Norfolk, who was traditionally organiser of the whole event. The Carterets would be seated to stage left of the throne. Bess was overjoyed to be part of the event, taking an almost maternal interest in the proceedings.

At last her husband had completed his task on time. The staging of the event was his duty. A remarkable circular mosaic had been created on the Abbey floor at the crossing point where the throne stood on a dais, and the surrounding area was approached along a crimson carpet and the central area hung about with purple drapery of pure silk and velvet. The whole building would be aglow with bees-wax candles and with crates full of replacements. Uniformed officials would stand guard among the guests, and escort them to their seats. Most of them would need to be seated and the nave galleries would be crowded to the walls. Within the crossing point, wooden stands were placed for the nobility and foreign visitors.

The Coronation was in complete contrast to the Bath ceremony, being designed as a public show. It was for the enjoyment of the loyal citizenry of London, large crowds from surrounding counties, and the foreign dignitaries and visitors from abroad. England was famed for its ability to put aside political and religious conflicts, and even riots, for the sake of enjoying a spectacular State Processions or Tournament. Even at the height of Parliamentary opposition, Charles I was cheered when he and the Court took part in a public masque performed through the streets of the City. Its success led him to believe that he would be applauded when he attempted to arrest five rebel MPs. He was quite wrong to make such an assumption, which was made painfully clear to him when he witnessed the enthusiasm of the crowd on the day of his execution!

At the Abbey elaborate changes of clothing for the King and other Principal nobles were enacted, and Dymoke, the King's Champion, issued a challenge to fight any man who questioned the King's right to rule. Along pathways covered in fine red carpeting, the King processed to the Abbey, where he was dressed in gold and scarlet, and put on golden chopines with four inch heels. At almost seven feet tall, he towered above all present. These included representatives of every country and City State in Europe. Louis sent his brother, Philippe, Duke of Orleans, and shortly after the Royal wedding, the Duke married the King's youngest sister, Henrietta-Anne.

Bess and the Clarendons had excellent seats in the Abbey and saw Archbishop Juxon crown the King. Following the ceremony, the party adjourned to Westminster Hall for a State Banquet and entertainment. The provision of food, cooks, cutlery and plate was in Carteret's hands and, it was fortunate that he could count on the eagerness of so many skilled practitioners to organise the fine detail. He, Bess and Philip would be guests at the feast.

George had no specific role in the proceedings, now that he had organised the provision of the many articles essential for the ceremony. He was asked, at the last minute, to stand in for the Duke of Exeter, who was unwell, and act as Almoner. He was to extract generous charitable donations from the Guests. The weather on that day had been hot and rainless, and the fountains of London ran with wine, by courtesy of the Vintners. Later that evening, there was a torrential thunderstorm. It was generally agreed that all was as it should be. The omens promised a splendid reign.

As vice-Chamberlain of the Palace, George was entitled to claim the blue carpeting covering the floor of the Hall and the scarlet carpeting of the Abbey floor. In addition, the draperies lining the Abbey, were his to use, and a Tun of fine wine, plus various 'accessories', including 305 ounces of gilded silver dishes. Rest assured, he made careful notes. These were his to sell or give away. The range of responsibilities he was expected to undertake was subject to constant change. George had, for many years, arranged his appointments and recorded his financial dealings. Pepys kept a very strict eye on Naval expenditure, since every pound was vital for naval pay, supplies and repairs. Parliament might grant a subsidy, but the Treasury checked every bill. Therefore, clear distinctions were essential between George's personal gains and his professional earnings. Sometimes this demanded a minute degree of discrimination, as the next unpleasant episode revealed.

The Coronation Feast filled Westminster Hall and was a crowded and noisy celebration, and despite spillages passed off successfully. The building eventually cleared and the guests spilled out into the fresh air many of whom joined in the celebrations in the London streets, where the City Fathers had plumbed the fountains to dispense red wine free of charge. Clarendon invited the Carterets and other friends to his magnificent mansion, its exterior complete, but its several empty rooms soon echoed with sounds of laughter and celebration. The whole series of recent events could so easily become a disaster. Between the Garter ceremony and the Coronation a considerable disaster struck at the heart of a Royal family still shocked by unexpected family bereavement. Once more, the Carterets were fully engaged. It began early one morning.

Charles' clear duty as King was to find a wife and provide an "Heir of the Blood". The proxy marriage to the Infanta of Portugal in 1661, had taken place in Lisbon, assisted by Sir Richard Fanshawe, of Valentines, Essex. He was a former Secretary to Prince Charles when he was living in Jersey. He spoke fluent Portuguese and had translated the Travels of Camôens into English. He and his wife remained close friends of the Carterets.

In April, George undertook an inspection tour of the Royal Dockyards and directed his attention to Plymouth. His tour had been arranged to coincide with the expected arrival in Portsmouth, of the future Queen. Such arrangements were unfortunately subject to alterations since communication with ships at sea was impossible, and no-one could guarantee that wind and weather would be co-operative. Since he was one of two MPs. for Portsmouth, he had been familiar with its needs for many years. In the event, the Queen's ship was delayed but his party had a perfect opportunity to meet the leading citizens. It was believed that the Infanta had set sail. Thomas Dowse was the other MP. The combined Inspectorate/welcoming party also included Sir William Penn, William Hewer, the assistant of Pepys, and a fine accountant, also William Bodlam, a businessman, and Dr. Clarke. George, travelling by coach, met the others at Havant for lunch, before they moved into lodgings with "Wiard the Chyrurgeon." During the next two days they made a thorough inspection of harbours, and ships, and discussed the possibility of constructing a dry dock. They discussed this need with the local experts, Edmund Dummer and Richard Haddock. There was undoubtedly a need to improve facilities on the west of the Island, for without it, the newer ships would be forced to make the longer trip to London docks. The future of Portsmouth depended on it. George reserved rooms in the home of Mrs Steven, and the team joined him there in the evenings, for the next few days, to inspect the accounts. Another day was occupied with the accountants in the Pay Office. The three areas chosen for inspection were commended and the port received the Royal Seal of Approval. The work was not completed for several years but when it was completed it transformed Portsmouth, making it the main port of the Royal Navy.

On the day for the Infanta's expected arrival, reports revealed that she had met with a storm at sea and had been landed at a French port where she was recovering from severe sea-sickness. She had decided to remain there until the weather improved. George and the welcome party had enjoyed several formal dinners with the mayor and corporation, in the interim, but a farewell Feast was arranged, at which the mayor asked them to carry a Wedding gift to London to celebrate the Marriage. A silver and crystal salt-cellar, was duly presented from the people of Portsmouth.

Possibly at this time, and on 30 May, Anne Hyde, Duchess of York, gave birth to a daughter at St James's Palace. This event passed almost unnoticed, apart from those present at her Anglican christening in the Palace Chapel as Princess Mary. It would have been a reckless person to predict she would one day be Queen of Great Britain.

A messenger brought the fresh news that Catherine would take the shortest crossing. Several days later it was reported that her ship had been observed at Mount's Bay. George left Plymouth, knowing it would be a week at least before her arrival, because he had another palace to inspect, namely Hampton Court which was chosen as a remote location for Lady Castlemaine to give birth to Charles's latest child. The new birth might distress the Queen if she became aware abruptly of it too soon.

New messages arrived advising the Queen would soon arrive in Dover, and Charles travelled there to greet her, to find a considerable group of officials assembled. Carteret made a swift survey, and ordered a cleaning up programme around the dock, and the placing of red carpet and bunting. The local Militia would present arms, and the Mayor deliver a welcome. The castle and its approaches needed rapid renovation and the Royal apartments made ready for a private reception. On 13 May, Catherine landed. Her ship was escorted into port by the Royal Charles, commanded by Lord Sandwich, Pepys' cousin. The King greeted her as she stepped ashore and brought her to the castle after the public welcome. Food, wine and coffee were available, but her first request was for a cup of tea. This was an outlandish request for tea was nowhere available in England. Carteret's face was saved by the King's amusement and he persuaded her to try the English national beverage, and she was contented with a mug of English Ale! They lodged in Dover Castle and, two days later, she and the King arrived in London, where Charles declared himself well satisfied with her appearance and character. He then rode off to Hampton to be with Barbara Castlemaine for the birth of her new son, born on 12 May, and named Charles Fitzroy, Duke of Southampton.

Among the changes needed at court, Catherine's precise rôle had to be defined. Was the Infanta to be crowned Queen? This would allow her to deputise for the King in Parliament and elsewhere, as Catherine of Aragon had done, before her divorce. If so, as a British ruler, she must become an Anglican, and any children must be Christened as Anglicans. The marriage contract stated that Catherine could remain true to her catholic faith, and had promised that a team of confessors and mass-priests would be always at her side. A chapel, appointed for Catholic worship would be always available for her daily devotions. She agreed that their children would be Anglican. The Dowager Queen, Henrietta, was angry at this concession, which she had refused, and advised against it, but Charles, as always, ignored his mother's advice.

To confirm these arrangements, there was a brief Catholic blessing on the marriage in Dover Castle, which was performed in private. The Carterets may have questioned the status of the bride, but Charles arranged for an Anglican ceremony to be performed in the Great Chamber of the castle on 21 May.

Fresh arrangements at Whitehall were indicated and apartments for the Queen provided, and for her personal staff, numbering a hundred. It was at best a makeshift arrangement and Charles's rooms were extended, and the Queen given her own Palace in Somerset House. Numbers of household officials were also required to take responsibility for the Queen's horses and carriages. Edward Montague was appointed Master of the Queen's Horse, and a Chamberlain of the Palace to ensure smooth management.

Now that these adjustments were complete, Carteret, officially appointed Gentleman of the Presence, received a fresh appointment as Controller of the Royal Forests. The new Court Chamberlain would have more onerous duties as Master of Ceremonies, as the Court expanded its artistic, theatrical and sporting interests.

# CHAPTER THIRTEEN

Prince James, engaged in re-shaping Scottish Government, retained the keen interest in Naval vessels which he shared with other Stuart kings. He filled notebooks with sketches and information about the constantly changing reefs and sandbanks of the east coast. He had a deep understanding of naval jargon and sailing was his favoured mode of transport, whenever it was possible. His Secretary, Coventry, scrupulously honest, kept a close eye on Naval expenditure, seeking to save money. Although he respected his thoroughness, Pepys disliked his interference and what seemed to him his implication that he, and other administrators were less than honest. Coventry looked with interest for details of George's contractual obligations and salary, and found that there were none. As has been previously described, George had made a special financial arrangement with the King, based on the King's absolute trust in him, with freedom to run the navy as a virtual monopoly, drawing down a 3% allowance whenever a profit began to be made. All other employees, including Pepys, were paid a fixed annual salary. Coventry was concerned that MPs skilled in fiduciary matters, would be dissatisfied with such an arrangement.

Coventry informed James of his concern. James, who knew nothing of his brother's decision, asked him for clarification. Pepys, when Coventry asked, confirmed by reference to the accounts that the arrangement existed, but could offer no explanation. Carteret informed Coventry it was standard City practice and, as a City Trader, and not a government employee, it must be legal, since the King had approved it. Coventry offended both Pepys and George, by suggesting that Carteret's financial gains were unjustifiably large: he added that perhaps he was draining money which could repair ships. George disagreed, and explained his contract, repeating its terms firmly. The whole business caused great ill-feeling between them, and resulted in a series of public enquiries since neither was prepared to make concessions.

The business rankled. During the years to come it would give rise to a lengthy Court of Enquiry into naval affairs which would impugn George's reputation for years, causing the family great distress. Clarendon faced similar accusations three years later, and though one can understand that both men were open to criticism for their manipulation of the collapse of Cromwell's rigid system of rule, for something less structured, since no precedent existed in British Law.

In the long term, the Naval committee had to be replaced by a stronger management structure, when it became obvious that the Navy required larger and more regular funding and no amount of 'savings' would supply its deficit .A strong Commander was required and the King selected Admiral John Lawson, a man of strong character and administrative experience. He had trained under the methods of Carteret and Admiral Edgecombe. On 7 March 1665, the 'London,' flagship of the British Navy, sailed on a sea trial in the Thames Estuary, having on board celebrated guests, and the Admiral's friends and family. That evening there was an enormous explosion, so loud that it was audible in London. The "London" sank in the Thames close to Southend-on-Sea. There were few survivors and the cause could not be established. To many pessimists, its wreck seemed to parallel the state of the nation, and the financial market reacted with shock. The newly appointed Admiral Lawson, was not on board. The trip had been intended to accustom new officers to the ways of the ship. Pepys and the Admiralty were deeply shocked at such a dreadful blow to British esteem and reputation abroad. To Pepys the ship was a visible image of the city and all it stood for. The Dutch were enormously amused and, expecting public unrest, took the opportunity to prepare an invasion of England by way of the Thames.

George relieved of many of his duties found compensation in his appointment as Controller of the Royal Forests. These were extensive areas of open country, mainly to the south of Oxford, but also to the north and east of London in Hertfordshire and Essex. In essence they were areas in which the pleasures of hunting could be enjoyed by the King and his Courtiers. Forest law was administered by Wardens and Verderers, taxed with the prosecution of infringements, including poaching and attempts at enclosure. The enforcement of these laws was George's prerogative, and also the preservation of vegetation, the planting of new trees, coppicing, and the preservation of streams and ponds from draining and pollution. As always Carteret sought the best advice, consulting the keepers of the Oxford Horticultural garden, and specifically John Evelyn, who had seen and analysed the customs of the Horticultural gardens of Italy. The insatiable demand for timber for ship building and housing, was laying waste to the once well-stocked woodlands of England, to such an extent that timber was frequently imported from Europe and Scandinavia. Evelyn's advice for the planting of new forests, was acted on by the King, and laid the basis for renewed forest cover for the benefit of the national wildlife.

George continued to use Deptford House as his London family home, where John Evelyn was his neighbour. They were distantly related by marriage, Rev. Giles Dowse of Broughton, having married a Joan Evelyn of West Dean near Salisbury, where they were adjacent landowners. The Forestry appointment came with an official residence, a Jacobean gentleman's residence named Cranbourne Lodge, set in Windsor Great Park, on rising land, commanding prospects of Windsor Castle and the Thames, two miles distant. It required changes to make it suitable for the family, but it rapidly became the favourite Carteret home.

The forests in his care were confined to the south and east of England. They were extensive and still covered large areas of country-side, in parts forested but also included large areas of open land and moors. Probably a royal hunt, scheduled for several days, might range widely over county boundaries and were devised as a way of culling surplus deer, hares, beavers, partridges and other game, depending on the season. Gamekeepers and huntsmen were employed to protect the game, and care for the hounds and horses. Verderers were employed to police the Forest Law to prevent poaching or illegal tree felling.

Hunting, like horse racing or steeplechases was seasonal. Each eventually had its own race tracks. At this stage these distinctions were not entirely established, and the state of the ground and inclination of the riders over-ruled strict definition. Cromwell, like most countrymen, had enjoyed the thrill of the chase and steeplechases and used his ability to train the Parliamentary cavalry. Prince James was a devotee. His pursuits often occupied whole days and most of the counties of southern England.

The enforcement of forest laws and fines for transgressors was his task but also involved the preservation of vegetation, the planting of new trees, coppicing, and the preservation of ponds and streams. The king was instrumental in the sciences of plant cultivation and land improvement and encouraged plant studies at the Oxford Horticultural Garden. Such work was essential economically for the insatiable demand for timber, for building houses, ships and wagons over the centuries, had decimated the forested areas and timber was now being imported from Scandinavia and Europe to supply the demand. John Evelyn, was the first to publish a study of trees and their cultivation for the Royal society and the King adopted his ideas in all his extensive estates.

As the father of teenage sons, Carteret understood their need for physical challenges to encourage strength and health. Both boys had learned to row and sail since childhood, and had turned from short-staff fighting, to rapier contests and practice, skills that every gentleman had to possess, together with dancing and the ability to join in a part-song. Their father was a skilled swordsman. and, in earlier life, had owed his life to his skill with a rapier. His usual expression of anger or impatience was 'Garda mi spada' or 'Watch for my sword!' Spoken with hand on hilt presumably, these were not empty words: it would be a warning to take care what one said. In London sports were rife. Fishing on the Holborn or River Lea: tennis, cricket, even kite flying joined horse-racing and carriage-racing, as alternatives. Bare-knuckle fighting, bear-baiting and cock-fighting were also popular and Will Jarvis, Philip, and the other clerks went to cheer on the participants and lay bets on winners.

There was a well-patronised fencing club in Fenchurch Street where Philip was a member. He went regularly for training with foils, which demanded close attention and had strict rules of play to prevent serious injury. It was becoming popular with duelists, because victory or defeat came quickly, were open to a referees judgement, and participants generally avoided injury. By 1665, Philip and James were quite proficient among their groups of acquaintances and equally ready to dance for the entertainment of their latest girlfriend. Women who could enjoy increasing leisure, continued to pursue falconry, archery and riding as well as hunting for venison. Skittles and quoits were games enjoyed by all, and darts boards were in use.

George and Bess had their own circle of friends, an inner group with whom they could share concerns, and a wider circle of those who were good company on a country or river picnic. Concerts and plays were often attended by the King, and there were musical Church services in St, Paul's, Westminster and at Windsor. Elizabeth rode whenever possible and was a keen gardener, often busy with cows and chickens on the home farm. The King encouraged composers and instrumentalists, and was building up a band of 24 violists. Some were from Italy and France, and played the latest string music. There was no doubt that entertainment, for those who had leisure and money to spend, was there for the asking, and that included the Carterets and their inner circle.

The latest fashions were as extravagant for men as for women as a contrast with the practical and discreet style associated with the Commonwealth. Visits to the theatre were extremely popular and provided opportunities for displays of fashion, and to associate with the celebrities of the day. Bess and George patronised the King's Theatre in the Haymarket and also the Prince's Theatre, closer to the City. Women of the court also had their plays performed. The Inns of Court had dramas performed in their great Halls, which were famous for spectacular candle-lit performances. The King's Theatre was managed by Davenant, and the latter by Killigrew. Both were forceful impresarios and in strong competition. Davenant may have been among Shakespeare's illegitimate children. Outdoor performances sprang up in Inn courtyards and in country fields, throughout England. The plots were busy and bustling with comic activity, and included lovers meeting and parting, and dramatic deaths.

There was ready acceptance now of women playing female roles, and of opportunities for singing and dancing, particularly when it was performed by the women of the cast. The Royal brothers were as fond of a shapely figure as most men. A well-turned leg had a strong appeal for Pepys who fought often with his addiction for the Theatre. He began to record his many theatre visits, and relished the chance to sit close to Lady Castlemaine, whom he admired intensely, to such an extent that he had her portrait hung on his dining-room wall, to his wife's displeasure. When the play ended, he liked to entertain the women of the cast to dinner, Mrs Knepp was his constant favourite and was a frequent guest when he and his wife entertained a company of singers and actors. Elizabeth Pepys enjoyed the theatre also, and went often with her friends, on one occasion to see "The Knight of the Burning Pestle."

Jonson's masques and the whimsical romantic comedies of James Shirley remained popular, if only for their use of London slang and salacious innuendo. Beaumont and Fletcher plays were more frequently acted than Shakespeare's plays, which did not appeal to Pepys. Prince James was frequently in his brother's company, but led an independent life for much of the time. The brothers were adept at creating a display of public unity, although in private James was often compelled by loyalty to agree to orders he could not refuse. The King knew that James would never challenge him and was inclined to mock his brother in more private situations. He regarded James as slow witted, humourless and stubborn. James, although not a model of morality or integrity himself, was one of many who reproached the king for his public display of immorality.

Returning home by river following an evening spent at the King's Theatre, where the Carterets had spent an enjoyable evening with friends, seeing a performance of The City Ladies'. George noted that Bess seemed to be preoccupied.

"Mrs Behn seems to catch the tone of the 'ton', ie. "the smart set" don't you think?"

And Bess quoted to him almost verbatim, a passage which had surprised her with its running sexual innuendo:-

"Mis. Car. First you shall not desire that I should love you.

| Fair | That's first; proceed. |
| Mis. | Car. No more than "proceed"? Do you know what I say? |
| Fair | Your first exception forbids to ask. That you should love me. |
| Mis. Car | And you are contented? |
| Fair | I must be so. |
| Mis. Car | What, in the name of wonder, will you ask me? (Aside) You shall not desire me to marry you. |
| Fair | That's the second. |
| Mis. Car | You shall neither directly or indirectly, wish me to lie with you. Have I not clipped the wings of your conceit? |
| Fair | That's the third. |
| Mis. Car | That's the third! Is there anything a young man would desire his mistress, when he must neither love, marry, nor lie with her? |
| Fair | My suit is still untouched." |

'Bess, my dearest love, I suspect, from your expression, you have some strong objection to the play we have seen. Yet you seemed to be thoroughly enjoying the rapid exchanges about whether Fairfield will ever have his "wicked way" with Mistress Carol before the fifth act ends.'

'No, I have no such concern: I enjoy rapid repartee in plays and the skill with which they convey the innuendo to us, while the actors pretend to absolutely innocent of naughty thoughts. To judge by the chatter of some of my friends, I think that Aphra has picked up the slang and manners of the court very well. If only the courtiers were as nimble-witted as Mrs Behn', she added.'

'Not worrying about Edward Hyde, surely? He had survived his daughter's fall from grace and remains Lord Chancellor. When the birth occurs, the bride's father will be a Lord, not a mere Knight, and making him socially acceptable to the Royal circle. Our King is a wily customer, as we both know.'

'I'm not unaware of that, George. Certainly not that. Have you noticed that young fellow roaming around with that group of wealthy layabouts. You can hardly avoid seeing them. They make enough noise, roistering about Whitehall, as though it is a playground.'

'Of course I have, and they seem to have gained a new leader for all their pranks. He is James Croft, the son of the family Charles selected to educate his brother James'. They were famous for their riotous lifestyle and encouraged James in his own lascivious proclivities. They seem to have teamed up with John Wilmot, who has just inherited his father's fortune and seems to be determined to waste it as soon as possible. His father was hard working and loyal to the late King. But why does this concern you, Bess?'

'Unfortunately, our daughters have both noticed him: I've overheard them giggling and wondering how they could attract his interest without blushing and stammering. If we had enjoyed normal lives, they would be married, or at least engaged, at their age. Our eldest is almost nineteen, the same age as Anne Hyde, and she is about to be a mother. We must do something about it as a matter of urgency, or I can foresee problems.'

*Restoration and Retribution*

## CHAPTER FOURTEEN

To some extent, this year, 1664, was to mark the zenith of George's public career. By coincidence it was also a year marked by personal tragedy. In that year he was elected Master of Trinity House, responsible for all coastal defences, lighthouses and Harbour defences, and was promoted to Admiral. His portrait was painted by Lely, wearing his robes of office. Portrait painting had become the fashion, as though those with sufficient wealth doubted whether their virtues would be remembered by their descendants. A portrait in oils by a reputable artist might perhaps give them a kind of immortality. It is noticeable that hints to lead to their identity are often provided by the artist. A profile in relief carved as a marble monument in the chancel of a church conferred immortality in a public place.

George's new post led to increased contact with the King, who had an increasing passion for ships. He was impressed by the Dutch "yacht" given to him by De Witt, the Dutch Pensionary, and the foremost English shipbuilders were ordered to build improved versions for the King and his brother. Their cumbersome "barge" was consigned to the past and the order books for naval vessels and 'Yachts' for the nobility and wealthy men, benefited shipyards and brought income to the treasury. 'Yacht' racing became the sport of the wealthy, and the years 1650-1670 were a period in which the royal brothers, plus the enterprise of Pepys and the Navy officials, established the basis for Britain's command of the seas. The London shipyards expanded to match the demand and merchant ships also were in demand. The Pett brothers, John and Christopher, developed new technologies for a new class of ship, and with the increasing numbers of trading companies, Pepys and Carteret were among those whose wealth challenged rival Dutch merchants. It was their State sponsored economic growth, against unpredictable private enterprise at the whim of an individual which evened the score.

Clarendon was delighted that the prevailing climate of optimism gave a considerable boost to free trade. His personal desire to enhance his influence with the panoply of greatness was to build a Baroque styled mansion in Piccadilly. It dominated the older buildings and exceeded the buildings in the Bond Street area, financed by Jermyn, Downing and the King. George and family owned nothing in London, where their three London residences were tied to his three main appointments. He was expecting the arrival of Lady Anne, and his daughters, Elizabeth and Anne, and his youngest, Louise. His mind dwelt on the probable needs of a growing family, two of whom would soon be thinking of marriage and starting their own families. In the interim they would require their own rooms and maids to assist with dressing and bathing: dress-makers, hairdressers and probably horses, waiters… The list was endless.

He would give thought to a suitable London home: a family home (there were Philip and James to accommodate) and it might be a saving to include office accommodation for his expanding business activities. It would be sensible to invest his savings in a secure base for their future needs. He was in his mid-fifties, and ruefully reminded himself that some of his contemporaries were threatened with replacement by younger men with high ambitions. The new Parliament was not as compliant as the Restoration stalwarts of the first parliament. Half the Lords and Commoners had been infected by Commonwealth zeal and enterprise, and despised old conventions, attempting to curb the powers of non-elected Ministers. Basically, this was what Coventry was attempting and he and Clarendon were becoming the 'old guard'; two among many. They began to realise that the freedoms the Commons had gained under Cromwell had been encouraged by the Statute of Breda, which had swept aside earlier conventions. Unless Charles II was very accommodating, the battles of the past twenty years, and the resulting loss of life, would be forgotten and dismissed, in an attack of mindless euphoria and change for its own sake.

From their safe refuge in Brittany, and by way of St Malo and Jersey, Lady Anne and their daughters, Rachel and Elizabeth, finally reached London. Louise, aged ten, would remain in the care of her nursemaid and the sisters of the convent. To leave France was a relief. There were fears of a recurrence of the plague, which was endemic in eastern Europe. Cold, wet winters and hot, damp summers encouraged it, but it spread as the result of population movements. French armies, for example, sailed the Mediterranean, attacked the Flemish Lands, England sold Dunkirk, and its soldiers returned to England, accompanied by French traders, Not only were these changes unwelcome, so also was the apparent policy of the King to restrict the power and influence of dissenters and so-called Huguenots. The King was eager to persuade the Pope that France was a Catholic monarchy, in alliance with Spain and the imperial states in unity against the Dutch.

One day George was compelled to recognise that the King had a long memory for personal insult, and that he had not yet declared Oblivion which he had promised for Regicides. Two more met a sad fate in New England and to his astonishment, Harrington and Mildmay, were brought from prison to face trial. They had spent months in prison awaiting the Ling's pleasure. The earlier panel of judges were recalled and both men were declared guilty of permitting the execution of Charles I. It was decided that by standing by the King during his execution, they were acting as willing agents of Cromwell's government. Their statement that they were strong supporters of the King was seen as hypocrisy and confirmed their guilt. They were condemned to life imprisonment and to be dragged on a hurdle to Tyburn annually and there to be stood in the pillory for a day.

George and the family were shocked at the cruelty of these punishments but once more were forced to the realisation that they had supported the overthrow of Parliamentary rule for restricting their freedom. Charles, like all his forebears, was now the sole embodiment of law, and would tolerate no questioning of his right. Discussions about government policy, had been too protracted for subjects of Cromwell to tolerate. Nor did they wish to join in the discussion of policy, which was a waste of time preventing them from following their own pursuits. They had chosen to recall a King to rule over them and make their decisions for them as before.

Harrington suffered his punishment once and was then released from prison. He was compelled to live in a house in Lincoln's Inn, he was forbidden to publish new books, and "Oceana" was destroyed and its possession forbidden. Only certain visitors were permitted. John Aubrey, an old friend, reported that he became subject to alarming delusions during his remaining years. Mildmay continued to suffer his punishment for several years, probably because he had written in favour of the Commonwealth, although he was a Royalist. He was released from prison and exiled to France, where he spent his last years supported by his family.

The Carterets traded in Europe, and moving from France to Jersey and London, was part of a trend. It was noticed that many French manufacturers were moving their factories and families to England. This did not go unnoticed in London, where all levels of society were fearful of unemployment by a wave of foreign immigrants, or of a vast amount of material goods, selling at lower prices than they chose to charge. If foreign wares were also of a higher standard, this added to the fear of the strangers. British memories were of the Catholic threat from Catholic France in the 1580s and the Medici persecution of the 1620s, but above all lingered memories of the Spanish Armada, when Britain was threatened with invasion by a Catholic army in support of King Philip's attempt to seize the throne as heir to Queen Mary I. All these events, revived in popularity when the next virulent infection of the plague appeared.

Sir Philippe de Carteret, for example, died showing some plague symptoms, although, as a result of mutation, symptoms frequently changed. George's brother, also named Philippe, who had assumed George's Magisterial duties to enable him to join the navy, now became Bailiff of Jersey, and occupant of St Ouen Manor. George and Bess may have visited to the island to commiserate, celebrate the changes, and greet old friends, but they realised that island life was now a thing of the paSt They were now joining the hundreds of 'new Londoners' creating new lives for themselves in a foreign land, transforming the traditions of London with new social customs brought from overseas. These would include persons of colour arriving as employees of business, as wine importers or silk weavers and other business concerns emigrating to Britain, and also musicians and entertainers, and domestic employees, who settle here and established families.

The Plague, or Great Plague, when it arrived, was neither unexpected, nor new. Present investigation asserts that it was probably a version of the Black Death, endemic in Britain since the 14 Century. It was also endemic in the French population, which had encouraged the Carteret's to bring their family to England. They may not have developed immunity from the disease due to their isolation in Peyrol. The King's brother and sister had succumbed to smallpox in London due to lack of natural immunity. The strength, and frightening death rate, of the 1665 Plague seemed to be stronger in England than elsewhere. The plague seemed to increase particularly virulently in the poorest, overcrowded areas of London, in the South, east and north, where large new settlements of the rural poor were packed together with immigrants from Europe and ex-soldiers returning from serving as mercenaries abroad, congregated in poor housing lacking pure water and effective sanitation. The parish plague registers show this

*Restoration and Retribution*

to be the true, although the City and Westminster seemed to remain poor breeding grounds for the spread of the sickness.

Deptford House was in a rural position, and the air salubrious. Bess was delighted to be among farm and fields where there were cows and chickens. Too late, unfortunately, they realised that the new virus seemed particularly lethal to children and the old. Sir George, who was a proud father, insisted on introducing his beautiful daughters to friends and colleagues, including Prince James. Pepys would certainly have wished to meet the girls and gossip about their elder, married sister. Caught one mid-day in a drenching shower, and muddied to the knees, Pepys was invited to shelter in George's carriage, which happened to be passing. George's passenger was his nine-year-old daughter, Elizabeth, whom he addressed by her pet name, 'Per-pot,' as Pepys recorded. He mentioned George's enjoyment of his daughter's company.

Sadly, their aquaintance was to be brief since Elizabeth, and her eleven-year-old sister, Rachel, died soon after showing plague symptoms. News arrived, at almost the same time, of the death of Lady Anne Stanning in Gloucestershire, from the after effects of childbirth. Pepys does not mention her death, but had already mentioned in his diary, exploring the roof tops of Whitehall Palace with her. Fortunately, Caroline, Lady Scott, gave birth to a son, and survived the ordeal, despite her youth.

Deptford House had become a house of sad memories, and perhaps they blamed their decision to bring the children to London. If George and Elizabeth were grief stricken, Lady Anne, intimately involved in their upbringing, would have suffered deeply. As an exemplary teacher of young minds and bodies, she must have felt that all her efforts were wasted. She experienced perhaps, feelings of failure, or even guilt. Both are possibilities. There were no more young people to care for: what purpose was there to life? Increasingly her time was spent at Cranbourne Lodge, in its rural calm. Lady Anne, organiser of Georges' career, and mother of his wife, struggled to overcome her grief at the deaths of her two grandchildren.

Fate was about to intervene once more. On a visit to London, to view the new house in Broad Street, Anne developed a chill, following a wet drive to Windsor. A fever quickly followed until she developed the visible symptoms of plague. Mercifully her suffering was brief. She died within a few hours, and was buried at St Mary-le-Bow Church. Her death came as a severe shock to the whole family. Bess was particularly close to her mother and in strength of personality, shared her strong-minded self-reliance. George was certain how much he owed to her strong support when he was seeking to follow his own choice of career, in opposition to family tradition. Following the death of her husband, Sir Philippe, she had shared all the privations of the Civil War with George and his family and their banishment to France. Her practical common-sense was key to the support of the children during their father's long absences in his determination to ensure that they would survive the hazards they faced. Thus, strong educational foundations were laid on which future success could be built when the restoration came. Above all, perhaps, was the memory, passed to the children of her strong defence of Mont Orgueil, and refusal to make an abject surrender to superior force, and demand that their banishment would be honourable and on her terms.

The effect of these deaths was devastating for them all. Philip, who had seemed at times to be largely unaware of the world about him, such was his fascination with the new technologies and mathematical theories, was shocked by the removal of a person who had provided a secure place of safety for him. It also seemed to be a wake-up call. He, who had been encouraged to pursue his scientific interests, found that he had reserves of strength, to fill the vacuum caused by the loss of family members. It was probably Lady Anne who had succeeded in forging those bonds which existed between the several branches of the family and refreshed the bonds with their Dowse and Paulet relatives. Without his aunt's support in his teenage years, George might have been forced to become a farmer or fisherman which he knew would not provide satisfaction, placing him in competition with his brother, James. George owed his varied experiences of the wider world to her foresight and support. Her support for Philippe's different ambitions allowed him to become an island Jurat and next in line as Bailiff. Without Anne's support, and the influence of her father, Sir Francis Dowse, George could not have attained his social status, or gained the confidence of his King.

For Bess, her mother had been a formative and supportive influence. Realising the strength of her daughter's will, in comparison with her accommodating brothers, she was at first anxious about the bond Bess had formed with her cousin. She saw in her teenage years, that Bess's affection for George grew stronger, even when he was absent at sea. Despite their relationship as cousins, Anne accepted their affection and welcomed their

*Restoration and Retribution*

delaying an engagement until George had taken his first naval command. Bess enthused about his visits to distant countries and was among the first wives of that century to tolerate the lengthy overseas absences made by their husbands in search of new trading opportunities. She always retained her own adventurous spirit, and the ability to adjust to new relationships when necessary. George knew that although for a time his wife seemed cast down by grief, her resilience would at last return.

Prince James was among those who attended Lady Anne's funeral; for he associated her with a time when he had been included in the life of a "real" family, mutually supportive, and inclined to favour the efforts made by relatives. He had not been an easy guest to entertain, although he shared his brother's interest in outdoor pursuits. He lacked the facile charm and tact which made it a pleasure to grant Charles's every wish. He lacked the modesty and grace with which Charles gave and accepted small gifts, and his acceptance of adversity. He fitted into their family circle with ease, but had no sense of humour, and took offence if his presence was disregarded, withdrawing into a defensive shell. Anne had the ability to distract him from his gloom, and persuade him that stubborn insistence on his mistaken belief was unnecessary and unfriendly. This was not always his experience in his own family and his brother often disregarded his sensitivities. He was amenable with the Carterets whom he had come to trust. For example, he accompanied George on an inspection visit to the Broad Street house, whose first-floor timbers had been recently installed. He admired the ground plan and the proportion of the principal rooms, then sat on a stack of timber, gazing at the carriages passing in the street. In a relaxed frame of mind, he began to recount a series of events which had clearly obsessed him for years.

'George, do you recall the business in 1657, when you were imprisoned in the Bastille? This, by the way, has nothing to do with your recent loss; in fact it has no relevance to anything happening now. You see, I have often wondered what they told you, was the reason for your imprisonment, and why they released you. You have never spoken of it. Did anyone ever explain?'

'I think, at the time, I assumed it was connected with my work for King Louis, in improving his harbour defences. It might have seemed less than patriotic to Cromwell, I suppose, to be assisting an enemy. Or, perhaps it was an on-going political, or financial, muddle, like the one I'm struggling to end with Parliament. I was never enlightened about either my arrest or my release. I was ordered, peremptorily, to travel to Marseilles and inspect their harbour work, the next on my list. I received another message in Marseilles, ordering me to report at once to your mother, the Queen, in Paris.'

'So, no other explanation was forthcoming? I suppose you just said, 'Thank you,' and returned to work. I would have been furious, if anyone had treated me that way.'

'Life has taught me to overcome setbacks, by getting back to work. It's the way I have to live. I am an optimist, I suppose, and have a childish belief that all will finally be well.'

'I may be able to suggest the cause, George, after all this time. Strangely enough, it may be that our fates in 1657 were closely intertwined. I may, unknowingly, have been the cause of all that happened to you.'

'Information came to me unexpectedly, when my brother insisted that I should negotiate the sale of Dunkirk. You know how annoyed I was to be forced to stand about in Paris when I wanted to be actively involved on the battlefield. Edward Hyde suggested to Charles that I could become a 'Gentleman Volunteer' with the French army, and my brother accepted his advice, to my delight. That meant that I retained my British Nationality, and was protected from danger. I served in the cavalry and got a reputation as an intelligencer and was, I was told, a good cavalry leader. I had some skill at assessing enemy positions, opening siege lines, and conducting convoys through hostile territory. In fact, I had a wonderful time, and Turenne made me a Lieutenant General after my work at the siege of Ligny and Mausson, in 1554. I was almost 21 at the time and longed for more responsibility.'

'Unfortunately, Cromwell unexpectedly signed a peace treaty with the French, and they decided to fight the Walloons in the low countries. I could not fight against the English who were their strongest supporters. I thought my chance of happiness had gone. Fortunately, General Conde had heard of my compromised status, and asked me to join him with the Spanish Army fighting to hold the Spanish Netherlands. I see you are looking confused George: you will understand my invidious situation, having no idea about my activities, I simply took any opportunity which arose, as you do, I think.'

'I thought the Spanish General Staff muddled and sluggish, and they may have known my feelings, I was not promoted and when we moved to the Spanish Netherlands to defend them against the French and English, Turenne and Manchester beat us at the battle of the Dunes. The war ended and Dunkirk was awarded to Cromwell. By that time he was actually dead and only Hyde, and Monck remembered we had been granted ownership of Dunkirk.

'At the end of the campaign, the Spanish offered me promotion and invited me to Madrid for my reward.' James continued. 'I travelled back with them, listening to them attributing blame to others. I decided I wanted no more to do with them and had heard that Cromwell's son Richard was taking over, instead of Henry, who would have been a good leader. I travelled with a few gentlemen and found that we were being pressured to go to Madrid. We left for the French border and safety. The notes I read were between English ministers in London and Paris, concerning a plot devised by Thurloe to capture me, then sell me to the English or French, as a hostage. He asked the French to hold you as a hostage of roughly equal value to myself if the need arose. This would have prevented you from carrying an agreement from Charles to Parliament in London. His plan worked. It was John Thynne who carried the document. Can you believe it, George?'

'Thank you for telling me, James. I shall enjoy telling Thurloe he was responsible for sending me to the Bastille, and setting up the basis for the restoration Fortunately we were both quite unaware of the fate our masters manufactured for us. Such is politics!'

'I am a little embarrassed by the fuss Coventry is causing about the navy financial deficit. I advised him not to act, but he had already spoken about it. Of course you are innocent: we all know that, but neither my brother nor I can intervene now it is the hands of Parliament. Whatever they demand, I am sure your accountants will demonstrate your honesty. His Majesty would want me to say that all that he owes you, will be repaid after the inquiry, or there will be unexplained amounts on your account.' The Prince had made Lady Anne's funeral an occasion to sail from Scotland to London, and he returned some days later.

# ~ THREE ~

## CHAPTER FIFTEEN

The years 1663-1665 were of great significance for the future growth of British wealth at home and British power abroad. The significant events might have seemed unimportant when first promulgated, and the unceasingly significant results of these small decisions fully realised much later. Faced with having his wishes questioned in parliament, Charles learned to allay opponents' concerns by passing the issue to sub-committees for investigation. There was a growing body of opinion that Britain was essentially weak in matters of government. This belief was held in France and Holland and echoed by the British press. However, there was a growing War Party in Britain which advocated the re-assertion of Naval power in the Channel, and attempts to blockade European ports and permit only British trading vessels to conduct trade. Strong attempts to capture some of the weaker African coastal trading stations were successful and Benin and Ashanti were opened up. These had been Portuguese posts, and Bombay also came under British interest.

As Naval Controller, James, Duke of York, made constant attempts to create a naval war chest and enlarge the fleet, arming them for attack and not merely for defence. Charles allowed this policy since it was unlikely to endanger his hold on power. As Commander of the Army, he lavished money on regimental strengthening, fine uniforms, ceremonial and training. Those who sought actual experience of battle, were permitted to form regiments to fight in the ongoing European wars. The best trained of existing regiments, were the Coldstream Guards, formed by Monck for the protection of the Commonwealth. They and their officers were rededicated as 'Guardsmen' and their efficiency became an example for the training and discipline of the subsequent guards' regiments from each of the national territories. Basically, all regiments were primarily for the King's own defence. He was determined that war would never again be fought in Britain. Future wars would always, from that time, be fought by proxy in Europe, or in a theatre of war in far distant places.

Returning, energised, from his mission to reorganise Scotland, James turned his mind to a concerted attack on the Dutch. English ship-building was having a resurgence, and The Navy Acts had provided Prize Money as well as a considerable amount in fines and confiscation of vessels, but, despite this a naval deficit of £1,000,000 remained. Clarendon was in despair but the Bishop of Munster, firmly protestant and a soldier at heart, offered to send an army to attack the Calvinist ruler of the neighbouring Dutch provinces, in return for £50,000 payable for three monthly instalments. His attack would be synchronised with an English attack on the Dutch in the North Sea.

Parliament had imposed a 'Window Tax' and a 'Chimney Tax' to raise money, but local inspectors disliked them. Many house-owners bricked up their windows and fireplaces rather than pay. London bankers now refused to loan more money to the King. George, however borrowed £28,000 on his own security as another loan, and devised a means for paying the Bishop £150,000 for his alleged expenses. This money was paid in three instalments into Navy funds where it could be concealed. Accounts were not due until the next year. The money was despatched in the form of expensive goods which, offered for sale by the Bishop, would raise the sum required. George used the good offices of friendly merchants in Spanish Flanders, whom he had met through Princess Eugenie, whom he had known for some years. Several towns in the low countries were supplied with soldiers from British regiments who promised to synchronise their attacks on various Dutch inland defence posts.

The Admiralty officers, from Pepys downward, knew of the essential weakness of the navy. When Clarendon again appealed to the Lords and Commons, they objected that they had expected to see victory as the result of their previous grant. The King expressed confidence in his brother's new project, to which he would give full support. Louis, eager to see the Dutch attacked, also made an allowance to Charles, to be used at his discretion. Prince James intended to lure the Dutch fleet from their home ports and force a decisive confrontation. He reached a secret agreement with the Bishop of Münster, who hoped to extend his power in Holland by invading the inland provinces, while the main Dutch forces were engaged in battle on the North Sea coast. The outcome was a further disappointment. One of the ships transporting precious goods, sank off Ostend. A second ship's cargo failed to find a buyer, and the expensive items had to be sold off at bargain prices. The third ship, loaded with Cornish tin, made very little profit. Cornish tin exports to Europe had been banned by the English Trade Acts made four years earlier. As a result, the Germans began to mine their own tin, and it no longer needed to be imported from Britain.

Despite these set-backs, the two fleets fought a sea battle off Lowestoft on 3 June 1665. James's flagship confronted the flagship of the Dutch Commander, Admiral van Opdam, in a direct full-on attack, and bombarded his ship until it was destroyed. It is probable that, with the Commanders fully engaged in this confrontation, neither fleet received any further orders, and would probably have adopted the usual response, to attempt to gain leeway so as to bombard an opposing ship with whatever arms seemed appropriate. They would next advance on a chosen opponent, bombard it, and pass on, possibly turning to make a second attack.

Left to their own devices, they would have acted in their best interests, on their own initiative. Several British ships proved to be structurally flawed and powder and weaponry was soon exhausted. Finally, the outcome uncertain, and under cover of darkness, the remaining British ships limped home. The battle was indecisive and an anti-climax. The British suffered very heavy casualties, particularly among officers and nobility, many of whom were among the best and most experienced of British seamen. One of the survivors was Captain John Lawson whose ship, the London, exploded in the Thames several years later. It was eight years since the last British campaign, and most seamen were untrained and quickly disheartened. Pepys, Carteret and the Admiralty, had used up all the investment poured into the fleet, and the coffers were empty once again. Prince James was sent north by the King, to protect him against any charges of poor leadership. In Scotland he successfully put down suspected plots against the monarchy. Further campaigns would have been impossible without ships. Fortunately their postponement had the after effects of The Great Plague as a justifiable excuse.

If it was in fact the 'Great Plague' which claimed the lives of the Carteret girls and Lady Anne, they would have been among the first Londoners to die. Whatever the cause of death, it would have been a great shock to their parents, who had exercised such care and concern for all their children. There were many other infections and fevers in circulation however and, crossing from France to England, they probably lost immunity to several infections. Plagues were endemic in Britain, Europe and the near east, and their severity reached a new pitch of intensity at approximately twenty-year intervals, from 1605 onward. Bubonic lesions of swollen glands, and bruising of the body, often preceded feverish convulsions, followed by a painful but rapid death.

The death of Lady Anne Carteret occurred shortly after the deaths of her grandchildren and its cause is uncertain and may have been simply the result of age and infirmity. The loss of Bessie's mother and George's mother-in-law, who had been his strongest advocate and supporter since his childhood, would have been a severe blow to them both. The little girls had been interred in Deptford; for Anne, the Carteret plot in St Peter's was proposed, but at this news the Dowse family offered an alternative, which seemed eminently suitable. Anne was the daughter of Sir Francis Dowse, and her connection with Hampshire, London and Oxford was stronger than that with Jersey. Sir Francis Dowse, Anne's great-nephew, who was Sheriff of Southampton, made a strong case for a ceremony nearer to the family lands, where many generations of the family had been interred.

Not since her childhood had Anne resided in her homeland. Marriage had taken her to Jersey, and its new customs and language, from which the Civil War had exiled her to France. In late middle-age, she had returned to England, where she had maintained correspondence and made visits to Dowse relatives whenever possible. She had been anticipating renewed relationships with the younger Dowses, when death intervened. Among the mourners were Dr. Philippe, Lory Hyde, Samuel Pepys, and many from the time of the sieges in jersey and exile in St Malo. Elizabeth and George missed her energetic support in tensely, and there children to whom she had been the ideal grandmother.

The London Dowses had settled in areas of the city where retail manufacturers had their workshops and which held no past family significance, and so Francis conferred with the Hampshire relatives. Thomas Dowse, of Kings Sombourne and Lesser Wallop, was pleased to be consulted, but had reached the final days of life. A Southampton burial was a possibility, but other places perhaps had a stronger claim for suitability. Giles Dowse, Rector of Broughton, had been restored to his living in 1660, and was the son of Thomas. He was in the process of carrying out his father's benefactions for the community, including Almshouses, a community Reading Room, and the construction of a dovecote, for which Royal Approval had been granted.

Precedence was granted to him despite some local reservations. He was a controversial figure and George remembered him as a tormented ex-soldier, seeking religious clarity he had served as a soldier in Flanders after graduating with Holy Orders, and he had learned some years later, that he had become Anglican.

Under the Commonwealth he had been sequestrated and he had been actively involved in the dubious actions of The Sealed Knot, which had not endeared him to his puritanical parishioners. Once restored to his living he had applied the new Anglican strictures with a degree of kindliness. His death may have prevented doctrinal disfavour. His burial service took place in Lesser Wallop, attended by numbers of family and a contingent of Carterets and Paulets. Also present was William Petty, soon to become the Earl of Shelburne, formerly in charge of the economic regeneration of Ireland and to whom George had been introduced by Sir Francis.

Before the Carterets left for London, the Reverend Giles Dowse insisted that they must spend a few days at Broughton: his wife had suggested the idea and would be hurt if the invitation was refused. The village was set in the heart of cattle raising country now providing food for the thriving sea ports of the coast. Sir Thomas's benefactions to the parish made in 1600, were much admired and the village school visited. After dinner late one afternoon, the ladies having taken a chaise to visit Mottisfont Abbey. Giles asked whether George knew about the early career of Sir Francis Dowse, his father-in-law.

'I knew that he had been a courtier and a lawyer, knighted by James I, and High Sheriff of Hampshire. He supported my naval ambitions and introduced me to Charles I. When Bess and I married, he always sailed over for family christenings, but we had little opportunity to talk.'

'I understand that, George. I was always in too great hurry to listen to stories of past events, but I think you should know about the services he performed for the King. I am sure they are in the State Papers, but let me tell you the story Sir Francis told me. At that time of course, Bess would have been a small child, and I expect has no knowledge of this herself. You may like to tell her one day.'

'Francis was among a group of young and highly intelligent young wits and lawyers, whose company King James enjoyed. He was inspired with enthusiasm for the new rationalism of Bacon and Descartes, and wanted to create a new vision for Europe, putting into operation the new ideas of government Kings who would encourage the new thought and replace the old medieval fears and enmities and encourage rule by agreement, rather than by force, as Christianity proposed. He gathered a small team of 'illuminati', and gave them a mission to go as Ambassadors to the crowned heads of Europe, to bring them together under his leadership, to rule by the new and enlightened ideals he had evolved during his long delay before gaining the British crown. He was convinced that only the British could succeed in the creation of enlightened government throughout Europe. This long embassy was a costly business and had great significance for the King.

'The team was small but well briefed and full of enthusiasm. It included Sir George Goring, Sir Francis Dowse, Sir Charles Lucas and Dr John Donne, among others you may not know. They spent two years in negotiation with the rulers and statesmen of Europe, reporting back regularly to King James, who was fully engrossed in creating the amalgamation of Great Britain, and with a new Bible and prayer book challenging the religious confusions of the past, which had resulted in the creation of social antagonism.

'Perhaps James and his courtier/diplomats were over ambitious and arrogant, although James received fulsome praise from other rulers, and convinced himself that success was imminent. Of course, as we know, the project failed, and the Austrian ruler, with the support of the Pope, attacked the Elector of Bohemia, throwing his ministers from the windows of Prague Castle in an attempt to stamp out Protestantism with one firm blow. In the war which followed, Bohemian independence was extinguished at the Battle of the White Mountain, and Frederick and James's daughter, Elizabeth, were forced to flee for their lives. Despite his best efforts, James failed in his project, and Britain's power to influence other nations was loSt Britain became effectively a religious pariah and future generations forced to live with the consequences.'

'Then, I suppose,' George responded, 'this caused King James's strange despondency, and abdication from a King's duties. It may also explain the savage anger and bitterness displayed by Goring, Lucas, and sometimes Cromwell himself. They were men whose high ideals were violently destroyed, and who suffered greatly in consequence. This is astonishing! I have always supposed that we can frame the future and construct it at our will: but perhaps the opposite is true and future events are controlled by the actions of the past, and these events control us.'

'Lucas would have known what responsible work his father had done for the King in Europe. His father was a senior figure in Colchester and would have been astonished when the Mayor was reluctant to welcome Marie de Medici who had welcomed him to France. The people of Colchester derided her and, although they allowed him to entertain her at Abbey House, they gathered a party of citizens intending to set fire to his house. He and his family had to run for their lives. This must have rankled within him for years, and the defeat of the new King at Worcester, would have been a last straw, I suppose. The siege of Colchester was intended as a just retribution for the insult done to his family and friends. It was an action of great cruelty and difficult to justify which makes his reputation for an act of heroism, difficult to understand.'

'There was real malice in their actions in the seige of Colchester despite having sworn on their word of honour, not to oppose the Parliament.'

'As ex-soldiers, Giles, I expect we have, in situations of great danger, compromised our integrity. A reason perhaps to attempt to negotiate peace, however unlikely it may seem.'

Years before, in the 1580s, 800,000 Londoners had died from a strain of influenza, identified by modern analysis. In 1664 a new plague, given the title Bubonic, made its way quite rapidly along the trade routes, to the coast of France and inevitably to Britain. Typhoid and food poisoning were equally common, and children and the infirm were always in the greatest danger while the population struggled to gain herd immunity or died, having lost the immunity they had gained in youth. Coming from the safety of rural Brittany to overcrowded and insanitary London, the girls may have contracted one of a number of infections to which they lacked immunity. Other family members and domestics were apparently unaffected, and the survivors remained healthy in the Southwark home during the early years of the Plague.

The infection raged throughout London, beginning in the overcrowded and insanitary housing areas to the east and north of the City walls, from which it spread towards the River as the river traders and suppliers of country food from inland, met and intermingled on a regular basis. Prince James's secretary continued his inspection of the Navy accounts and reported that George was "a person whose capacity for work seemed endless and his honesty beyond doubt". Thousands of Londoners died during the weeks to the end of December 1665, but it was during those years that trade and commerce accrued more wealth than would normally have been expected.

Strangely, it was the unexpected result of the Navy Acts, intended to restrict foreign vessels trading in English ports. It accidentally resulted in the importation of foreign imports which only British ships could carry. Transported with the goods into London and other towns, were the viruses. Charles sent a specific, but misguided, demand to George for the expulsion of French Galliots from the Port of London, and supplied Lettres de Marque he had signed in advance. In response George ordered Captain Waltham to bring all the men who could be pressed into service, to London and Portsmouth, where ships were undermanned. Philippe le Geyte, in Jersey, asked George to obtain an order from the Privy Council, expressly stating "pirates" were forbidden to use St Helier for trade. It was accompanied by a sealed note requesting the right to condemn any pirates to death by hanging. There is no evidence that George presented the demand to the Privy Council. George did not pass on this request, as it was a sealed document and unsigned, so the order was invalid. Whether or not any Pirates were subsequently executed is not recorded. In previous years, when he was island Governor, some had been executed without permission, but this was at the time when two parliaments vied for authority.

It was some time after these tragic deaths before George regained something approaching his usual energy. Philip had run the family business affairs in the meantime, with the aid of their team of clerks who had been trained under his father's supervision. George knew it was 'business as usual' as far as his official duty was concerned, but Coventry impulsively raised the vexed issue of George's bonus of 3d for every pound of naval business completed. Coventry had been instructed by Prince James to identify examples of financial wastage in the Navy office, and he come upon George's unorthodox salary agreement. He suggested that if George wished to be regarded as a gentleman, he should reject this unfair privilege. A "gentleman" should be grateful to fixed a salary, like every other Royal employee. The navy had great need of the over-generous award George was accepting, to the King's disadvantage. George decided to ignore the condescending tone of Conway's explanation, realising that Prince James must have raised the question: he could be meticulous about small details, often failing to see beyond the obvious.

'The King made the agreement to ensure that some of his debt to me was repaid, by this means,' George responded with patient moderation. 'He undertook to honour this arrangement. I leave it to you, Coventry, to inform him he was mistaken.'

'George, His Majesty is not a city businessman, and you should not take advantage of his generosity.'

'With the greatest respect, you are wrong, Coventry. His Majesty, as you well know, is salaried Chairman of the 'Royal Africa Company' a registered City Company, and receives profits from several others, such as the Levant and Tangier companies. I am Treasurer of several of these companies myself, and also of the Navy. Your own employer, the Duke of York, is a City shareholder and entitled to be regarded as a City businessman. Ask him for guidance in this issue: this is my best advice.'

As the epidemic spread from the crowded slums and the dockside areas of the City, George asked Pepys and others what steps could be taken to prevent the spread and contain the increasing daily death rate. The College of Surgeons answered that since 1515, a number of measures had been proposed, e.g., to isolate those infected in hospitals; to ensure access to food and water for those caring for the sick; and to ensure the cleaning of the filth lying in the streets and contaminating the water supply. The Company of Physicians had published clear directives which, if they had been made official requirements, would have curbed the outbreak of fresh infections. All these recommendations were approved by the Mayor and the City Fathers, and approved by the Westminster Parliament. Unfortunately, one hundred and forty years later, they had not been put into place, because of the building and administration involved, which would require additional taxation to cover the cost. Neither the City nor the government was prepared to impose such a tax. Once again sensible measures gave way to possible commercial advantage.

The measures which were put in place had the advantage of seeming decisive, while requiring minimal expense. They included the extermination of all cats and dogs. There was a public outcry preventing its full enforcement in face of which exceptions were made for hunting dogs, guard dogs, and lap dogs. Every previous epidemic had begun with a similar purge, effectively this exterminated the animals most likely to kill rats. People continued to believe that it was their fleas which spread the infection.

Sensible people packed their goods and retired to the country. These included the Lords and principal Ministers, the Surgeons, and Ministers of religion, including Bishops, and the King and his Court. Charles with wife and mistresses, went first to Hampton, then Windsor, and finally to Oxford, from which the students were expelled to their homes. Charles returned to Whitehall, with a smaller court, just in time to witness the Great Fire. In his absence, he published a notice advising the public that he would not be available for touching for the King's Evil, at this difficult time, to prevent the Plague spreading more widely among the unfortunate poor.

Pepys, George and a considerable number of the middle class business people, remained in London. Various reasons supported their decision. Some chose religious beliefs in support of their decision, e.g., God was punishing Britain for its lack of religious faith, or, that those who died had lived wicked and depraved lives, and were selected for punishment. Those who lived in squalor and depravity were rightly being prevented from endangering the lives of the devout and hardworking. Many fatalists believed that since there was no cure or reliable treatment, they would live as though impervious to infection, going about their business, but avoiding close contact when possible, and certainly avoiding crowds. Pepys sent his wife to live in Woolwich, and George's wife and children remained in Deptford. He continued to live in Seething Lane with a cook and cleaner.

Almost a quarter of Londoners died during the epidemic, but in the Westminster court newspaper,' The Intelligencer', Roger L'Estrange as its editor, recorded. "In this raging pestilence it hath pleased God to spare those public ministers, magistrates and officers upon whose lives the peace and order of the government so much depend, insomuch that I do not find this visitation to have taken away any person of prime authority and command." Heartless though this statement seems, it is a blunt assertion that those who were well fed and lived in clean and uncrowded homes, and could avoid crowds, were least likely to be infected.

George and Sam Pepys might perhaps have consulted the weekly Mortality Bills for each parish, which recorded those who died "Normal" deaths, separately from those who died of "Plague". The figures are at best estimates, because the Plague symptoms so changeable, and those making a careful diagnosis ran a considerable hazard. In Pepys' parish, St Olave's, Hart Street, the figures for August 1665, were 7 and 4: on 19 Dec., they rose to 237 and 190. This statistic is found in all the 'fringe' parishes surrounding London: parishes crowded with poor and insanitary housing for starving newcomers. George, might have been concerned with the fate of the Steelyard inhabitants of St Antoline's, Budge Row Parish, where a Dowse had earlier been a Priest. Their death rates were high. In August, there were 15 and 22: the December totals rose to a shocking 58 and 231! However, he would probably have followed the example of Pepys, who avoided Communion, and compulsory attendance and saw that the office was well aired. On his next visit to church, after an absence of some weeks, Pepys was surprised that the graveyard on each side of the approach path, was almost a shoulder height lower than the graveyard, overfilled to accommodate the number of bodies buried there.

## CHAPTER SIXTEEN

Philip Carteret and Will Jarvis met for a business meeting at the Carteret office in Broad Street. Will, initially George's valet, had shown himself as financially astute over past years and had taken a responsible role in the family business since George had noticed his instinct for detecting dishonesty in potential suppliers. He was paid a salary sufficient to rent his own home and perhaps acquire a family. It was that time of year when agents or clerks, acting for Lords of Manors, whose dues awaited collection, were dispatched to manorial holdings. On Jersey and across southern England, George was acquiring a considerable number of wealthy manors, many gifted to him by the King in repayment for previous loans. Manors were in the King's gift and no profits had to be declared in official returns. Their task was to collect annual rent payments and settle disputes peaceably between contentious tenants. If a tenancy fell vacant they allocated parcels of land where appropriate, and ensured that rectors had received their lands. Also, they were charged with the collection of the Farm tax, required by the government to cover Government expenditure, which were constantly increasing. County Sheriffs were empowered to forward these to Westminster and the Treasury, and Manorial Lords were an essential source of these payments. The national circuits to exercise legal judgement and try offenders were financed for the Ferme Tax.

'We will look at last year's accounts, Will, to see if there are outstanding matters. Then we must decide what to set aside for those who have lost a breadwinner in the Plague.'

'I think we could afford to be generous, since business is making good profits. The tenants have had a difficult two years with floods ruining their harvests.'

'When shall we be going, Philip? We will need to allocate several weeks because of delays caused by the Infection.'

'I think the end of the month will be soon enough: I will write to warn them to have their books made up. I'll not be travelling with you this time, because my father has several worrying matters in hand. I don't know whether the news has reached you, Will, but in a few weeks I shall be married, and there are preparations to be made.'

'I've hardly seen either of you for weeks, and I hadn't heard. Congratulations, Philip! I will be careful to bring all the payments back, you will need every groat, with a wife to keep!'

The deaths of two healthy daughters, followed by the death of Lady Anne had been a severe blow to the family. Elizabeth lost interest in life, constantly in tears, insomniac, uninterested in food and worst of all, losing the desire to meet her friends and quite unable to accept their sympathy. It was several weeks before she became aware of George's equally troubled state of mind. He had absented himself from meetings with business colleagues, meetings of the Privy Council, and parliamentary committees, which was quite unlike his normal behaviour. With the King and Court moving about the country, seeking to avoid any contact with infection, his absence was hardly noticed, fortunately. Many others among their friends were suffering from similar bereavement and Philip was alarmed by his father's lethargy and abstraction. People became once again conscious of their own mortality. It seemed strange that, with sickness spreading inexorably into the heart of the city, and the publication of the Death Lists, telling of the demise of former associates, trading profits should begin to show a strong revival.

Philip was in complete charge of business and indeed of most family matters. Fortunately no problems arose and their closest associates and friends offered help and sympathy. Admiral Penn, though no longer active in the Navy, was a tower of strength with finance and Pepys took every opportunity to strengthen his control of all aspects of naval activity. When the Pett brothers, the timber merchants, were suspected of malpractice over purchases, Pepys was able to save their reputation. The Navy emerged from the Plague on a much more solid basis than would otherwise have been the case.

It was Bess who recovered first from her deep depression. Edward, her younger brother, now an officer in the King's Guard, showed his concern, and urged them to consider Cranbourne Lodge once more, where alterations had begun earlier in the year. Now that George was to care for the Royal Forests, they decided to take up his suggestion, and, surrounded by pastures, trees and deer, and all the charms of nature, Bess regained her normal confidence. The house became their preferred home for several years to come and was convenient for travel to the City, and to nearby Windsor, almost unaffected by the epidemic. It became King Charles's residence of choice, with a much-reduced household staff. With Bess's encouragement, George began to regain his ambitions for his Children's future. He also made plans for re-foresting the depleted parkland having made a study of Evelyn's new book 'Sylva,' the first book published by the Royal Society. It was followed by Hook's remarkable "Micrographica" in 1665.

Philip's endeavours with trading and land management, were effective and his parents placed their hopes of future security, on his shoulders. With one daughter successfully married, they turned next to their sons. James, younger by a year than Philip, had, after a rackety start in the Navy, finally acquired some of the qualities necessary for an officer. He had three or four short-term Lieutenancies until, at last, his father felt sufficiently confident to enquire for a sound ship for his first command. James was offered the captaincy of a slave ship trading with the Indies. George concealed his considerable dismay and despite his personal distaste for the trade, offered congratulations, and expressed his pleasure that he had been selected for such responsibility. He hoped that his son would not be corrupted by the reputation for mindless brutality among officers and men, which seemed endemic in the trade. James was a well-meaning fellow at heart, though somewhat gullible. George reflected that since he was Treasurer for the Royal Africa Company, the most wealthy of all the slave trading companies, due to Royal Patronage, he might recommend better practice. He would make every attempt possible to ensure that high standards of conduct prevailed. Since Naval ships often guarded slave ships at sea, they might attempt to make improvements in return for protection. James's first important command might not create immediate reputation, or make him a strong contender as a businessman with wealthy daughters, but he might be able to smooth his son's marriage prospects in future.

George's own attitude to slavery is one of those matters on which he never expressed an opinion, in writing. I assume it was a subject where he did what seemed to be in the best interests of the King, his employees and, ultimately, of his own family. The Restoration and its re-establishment cost more than the national Ferme Tax could provide. The King felt compelled to fall back on the example of his Father. Neither of them possessed financial or legal training for their rôle. Nor did Charles show any real eagerness to learn from others, being indifferent to advice and with no desire to pursue detailed discussion. Since 1630, when his father had ruled without parliamentary consent, most European kings had gone their own way, generally taking all financial matters into their own hands, and creating Command economies controlled by their chosen ministers. They liked to amass valuable possessions, and spend money as though it was their right. British rulers had attempted to do the same, but were, unaccountable, hampered by powerful nobles, popular revolts, or by seething social unrest, caused by religious and social variables. Their interference in the affairs of overseas nations, whose territory they claimed, generally brought no benefit to any nation.

Britain in the 1660s had few products for export which other countries required, since the wool, like the tin and copper, once so much in demand, was now sourced within Europe. Britain had waged commercial war with Europe by banning the export of these products. This encouraged foreign enterprise, while impoverishing British workers. The Kings were forced to enter existing markets by military force, by acts of piracy on the high seas, and by forbidding foreign ships entering British ports, or sailing the Channel without paying taxes to Britain for the privilege.

It was some time before the King's ministers realised there were essentially three money earners which, if exploited, might supersede trading barriers, or European objections. These were: armaments, horses and slaves. In those areas Britain could trade freely, civil conflicts at home having given rise to technological advances in those three areas. The high standard of their advanced products was of considerable value in many countries.

The Civil Wars in Britain had produced the most advanced cannon, small arms, and saddlery in Europe. Secondly the wars produced a generation of highly trained soldiers, and officers skilled in man-management, willing to make their skills available to any country needing an army. Horses and their breeding were an offshoot of the wars, and one which was of particular interest to the King. Horse racing, on permanent tracks, replaced the Medieval obsession with tournaments, while the people gave enthusiastic support to an industry which provided them with excitement and the pleasure of betting, popular with the masses who had wages to spend. For many this would have been a new experience.

More important, in the long term was Slavery, the greatest money-spinner of the lot and with remarkable potential as a wealth creator. The Slave Trade was probably Britain's chief contribution to world trade and the result of British ingenuity and commercial drive. Slavery existed throughout the world for centuries before the Restoration. The Anglo-Saxon invaders of Britain sold Celtic slaves to Irish and European owners following the example of the Romans. Throughout the world, captured soldiers from defeated armies were traditionally forced into slavery to perform tedious work for the victors, as an alternative to death and starvation. Everywhere slavery was accepted as part of the normal social fabric. In Saxon England, socially inferior to the Freemen, and bound to provide service to their ruler when required, there were three orders of slavery. These could gain freedom by buying it with money they had earned from tilling common land. Below them were the 'Bordars' and the 'Cotters' who were entirely dependent on the employment offered by their employer, and possessed few, if any, skills. They were tied to the land of their owner, and prevented from wandering away.

Sir Francis Drake had brought black slaves on the Golden Hind, rousing the interest and approval of Queen Elizabeth. His successor, Sir John Hawkins, brought regular cargoes of slaves to London, where they became objects of interest and appeared sometimes, smartly dressed, in portraits of the wealthy. Many had come voluntarily to Britain as seamen and gained rewarding employment. The most inferior groups in society, the bordars and cotters, had been killed by starvation or by the Black Death and consequential epidemics. From that time, there were few menials offering free labour, since labourers were scarce and skilled menials demanded paid work from potential employers These adventurous Africans who settled were not slaves but paid employees. There was no provision in British law supporting, regulating, or even banning slaves, because those whose life was one of deprivation and inadequacy, and had neither work nor skills, died in their hundreds. There were, in consequence, no slaves.

It was the expedition of Carteret and Rainborrow to Tangier in 1629 to secure the release of Englishmen captured as slaves by Moorish pirates, that revived awareness of indentured workers and set a moral dilemma. Carteret explored the Gambia in a search for gold, a search which Prince Rupert commandeered. In addition, he brought African captives, gained in tribal conflicts, to England in exchange for glass beads and pistols. His activities gave rise to conflict with Holland, which initially held a monopoly of slaves, but Dutch interest was more recently concentrated on the wealth of the East Indies, rather than of Africa. Their vacant African factories were commandeered by Britain, and our trade in slaves expanded. These captives were exported to the New World, by exiled Protestants, to perform labours which the English found demeaning. By 1665 the so-called Three-way Trade was well established.

The Royal Africa Company was recognised with a Charter, on the Stock Exchange, within a few years of the new reign, Its Principal was Prince James. George Carteret was the first Treasurer of the company and remained a company member for the remainder of his life. Other traders included all the great and good of the century, including the King, Castlemaine, Locke, Pepys and John Milton. None of them, I believe, owned slaves personally, and may never have seen one. Bristol and Liverpool were the leading ports of transfer, with London a smaller participant. Those who took part in the trade gained great wealth, especially with the growing demand for sugar, first in England. The question remains whether this was moral dereliction on the part of the British public, and a conscious decision to treat some humans as an inferior species. Not for a half century would it become as great a scandal as the alleged Catholic Plots, which scandalised avid readers of the sensation-seeking popular press.

It is probable that the average English person was unaware of the suffering caused to thousands to provide him with sweet food. Carteret had chosen to give all his support to a King who had expensive tastes, mainly admired by his subjects, and regarded as extravagant by Parliamentarians. Whether or not Carteret approved, disapproved, or was indifferent to the growth of the Slave trade, is irrelevant, since his opposition would have made no difference. He was by no means a celebrity politician, as Shaftesbury was, nor was he an "Influencer" in modern jargon. Pamphleteers and news sheets provided only limited publicity and little intereSt

A case could have been made concerning the increasing numbers of men and women employed by the King and the Royal family, from grooms and farriers, to chamber maids ,builders and gardeners to service the needs of the Royal households, their farms and woodlands, and the greatest need was for ships, jewellers, and weavers of silks and satins. These were costly to invest in but rewarding in the long term. This is unfortunately lacking since all of these skills increased the national wealth, and demanded careful training. Many of the resulting products were exportable. This is one reason for the increase in trade in the years of the Plague and Fire of London. The arrival of foreign skilled craftsmen escaping persecution, also increased national wealth, although their presence was generally opposed by the unemployed who had few skills to offer. To some extent the new technical colleges springing up, provided accountants, surveyors and legal clerks which began to fill those gaps. Unfortunately the Slave Trade was Most rewarding trade in terms of profit and was acceptable because its basic invisibility made it non-controversial.

In the meantime, Philip was becoming an ideal model of a husband and father to the next Carteret generation. At the early age of twenty-three, he was financially secure, heir to a baronetcy, a member of the Royal Society, a mathematician and scientist, and a business man. He was not lacking in social skills, and had associated from childhood with the King and Prince James. He went to the races, was an excellent seaman, rode a hunter with Prince James, and enjoyed theatre, and took the waters at Bath and Tunbridge. He was also ready to make an advantageous marriage which would please his parents and, perhaps, ensure the future of the family. Wisely, his parents stepped aside tactfully, but asked him to make his choice of a wife, as soon as it was convenient!

Of course, urgency may have become imperative, since the plague had made personal plans for the future less certain of fulfilment than normal, since many and various causes might result in the sudden death of any individual. Fortunately, Philip did not need protracted thought. He had noticed Jemima Montague, finding her lively and attractive, whose large number of siblings were devoted to her. Their families had always associated, and Montagues and Carterets, were among those families most supportive of the Stuarts in exile. Both fathers were naval commanders. Edward Montague, Lord Sandwich, was the cousin of Sam Pepys, and it was a sign of great trust and confidence, that when George broached the suggestion to Montague, it was accepted at once. Naturally there would have been financial arrangements to make, necessary in an age of sudden deaths, to secure that children of the marriage, or the widow, did not become impoverished. The procedures would have been well known, but might take months or even years to complete.

Montague was involved in the Royal wedding, and spent months at a time in Spain, as Ambassador. Having naval commitments to complete, he asked Samuel Pepys to act as intermediary between the young couple, their families and the lawyers. Both families included lawyers who would secure favourable contracts. George and Bess were delighted by Philip's choice, and Sam had known Jemima from early childhood and had been a friendly and trusted "Uncle" in support to Lady Montague and her nine children. Jemima was a great favourite of Pepys. She was a bright child and had taught him to play cribbage. He took her to see the monkeys at St Bartholomew's Fair and also to see the lions in the King's expanding collection of animals housed in the Tower of London. No doubt he introduced her to musicians and the theatre as she reached her teens.

Edward Montague had extravagant tastes and was always short of money, and his wife was delighted that her daughter was marrying into an honest family. George was a very wealthy man. Pepys took on the arrangement with enthusiasm and recorded every detail of his actions in his diary, A June entry reads: "Sir George received the business [a dowry ie. a financial allowance to Jem] with great content, and promised what he could to render him (Philip) fit for my Lord's daughter." No-one would have been able to convey the extraordinary events leading to the wedding with such insight as Pepys. The diary entry for the following day reads: "To Whitehall again, where, after I had received Sir George's and his lady's full consent, Lord Sandwich did direct me to return to Sir George and give him thanks for his acceptance of this offer, and the next day he would be willing to discourse with him about the business. My Lord, I perceive, intends to give £5,000 with her, and expects about £800 per annum jointure."

On 2 July, he noted: "Sir George did send me word that the business between my Lord and him is fully agreed on, and is mightily liked by the King and the Duke of York." The relationship between the Carterets and the Duke strengthened considerably and they frequently exchanged visits. Anne, the Duchess was quite demonstrative, though, if there were other guests, the Yorks insisted on space being made for them to stand apart from uninvited contact with other guests.

The prospect of marriage between Philip and Jemima was so successfully arranged that it could take place only about a month later. The Banns of course had to be proclaimed on three preceding Sundays, as was required. Having barely a month concentrated minds remarkably. The King, when he was informed was enthusiastic and, as a sign of great favour, offered the Savoy Chapel for the wedding and the Palace for the reception. The calling of the Banns, took place in St Margaret's, Westminster.

Bess went at once to tell the good news to Frances Clarendon, her closest friend, before the news was made public. Frances and her Husband, Edward were shortly to move into their new Piccadilly mansion, Clarendon House. Elizabeth, full of her news, and noticing her friend's red eyes, added that the king and Prince James had offered their congratulations. Frances responded with floods of tears. Bess was used to her friend's overwhelming surges of emotion and did her best to sooth her and make general enquiries as to the cause.

Once the cause was clear, she was relieved that she had not mentioned the total lack of formality the Royal brothers had shown. Almost it seemed, they reacted as though to a family member. Bess had responded by congratulating the Prince on the recent birth of his new son, James, Duke of Cambridge. Earlier that day, the Clarendons had driven to St James's to offer congratulations on the birth of the Prince, offer their love to their daughter Anne, to offer their relief at the baby's safe delivery. The Hydes were astonished when a footman stopped them and requesting their names and business. Satisfied, he went away to inquire whether the Duke and Duchess were available, and returned to say that it was possible.

They were shocked but decided that an insult was not intended, that the doorkeeper must be a new employee and, after a lengthy delay, they were ushered into a throne room, and invited to approach the Duke and Duchess and to kneel, before kissing their hands. The Duke thanked them for coming, but regretted they would be unable to entertain them, and had them ushered out. Clarendon, never lacking in self-confidence, excused this insult as the impulsive action of a Prince adjusting to his new importance, in the line of succession. Frances, however, noticed the square-jawed determination on her daughter's face, and feared for them both, and especially her husband.

George heard Bess's account with some concern. All he had learned over the years, from friends and from his own observations, taught him that rulers had to re-evaluate their relationships on almost a daily basis. However close a friendship seemed, when it began to demand strong support, there was no guarantee that the ruler would feel obliged to respond in kind.

He had noticed that when Clarendon spoke in Council meetings, the King sometimes showed impatience, perhaps interrupting his flow, offering his thanks for his contribution, then inviting another speaker to intervene. Was this an indication of displeasure: if so, would Edward realise it? As a lawyer he had developed a very thick skin!

Perhaps there were other signs of change. For example, Lady Castlemaine, had recently given birth to another son, Henry Fitzroy, Duke of Exeter, and Clarendon had not only failed to offer congratulations but avoided speaking to her and interrupted her when she was being at her most charming. He spoke of her always as 'His Majesty's mistress'. In addition, George was aware that Clarendon often addressed the king like a domineering father might, reminding him, tactlessly, that he should be more careful of his dignity and public image. Hyde had been entrusted by Charles I with his son's guardianship, but his ward was now a monarch and over thirty years of age. He was no longer the King's Guardian, but his subject.

On one recent occasion, when the Carterets were entertaining the Hydes to dinner, George had suggested that sometimes Edward overstepped the mark. He did not take offence, but the nature of his response was not quite what George had hoped for.

'I'm sure His majesty is aware that I have the deepest regard for him, but have a duty to encourage him to responsible behaviour. I see, you think I speak out of turn: sometimes one has to remind him that his conduct is closely studied by potential enemies, who look for errors.'

In the next weeks, George began to notice other ominous signs.

In the meantime, naval accounts had been selected for discussion by the Commons. This followed the disappearance of the contents of the Navy Chest, for which the Petts were held culpable. They were England's finest shipwrights and were utterly reliable and honest. They had come upon the Navy Pension Chest at a time when there was no money available to complete an urgent order. The cash it contained had not been awarded as pensions for invalid sailors for some time: indeed there was a large deficit in payments. The Petts, who had acted with the best of intentions, had been exonerated. Unfortunately, the MPs were inclined to take an unsympathetic attitude to financial incompetence. They wondered why the Lord Chancellor had allowed it to happen. It appeared that Clarendon might be the next man to be accused, although he was probably unaware of the existence of the Navy

Chest. Unfortunately, it would certainly involve the part played by George when Navy Treasurer. He was no longer holder of that responsibility and Coventry had drawn attention to the complexity of the salary agreement between himself and the king. This could be made to seem irregular or even illegal by those who had no knowledge of what was customarily used as a correct payment procedure. There was no standard salary model to present as a traditional payment method. There was no generally applied scale of payments since career continuity was rare, and could be brought to an end without notice.

## CHAPTER SEVENTEEN

June to August were the months of 1665 when the plague was at its most severe and was spreading throughout the country. By coincidence these were the weeks chosen for the wedding of Philip and Jemima. The main seaports were soon affected and hundreds of deaths occurred in Bristol, Portsmouth, Ipswich and Norwich. The working classes were badly affected and received little general sympathy, though there were honourable exceptions and some attempts to alleviate harm. Gradually the rapid spread of infection overwhelmed them. On the whole the poor and unemployed were blamed for leading squalid and insanitary lives of general immorality, by their feckless behaviour, adding to the spread of the sickness, and too idle to undertake sensible precautions. Colchester's population, for example, was halved, and it was many years before the Borough regained its previous level of prosperity. Towns well inland also became infected. It was assumed that avoiding the sick people would prevent infection. It was not realised that it could be spread by contagion. Generally the clothing of the dead was saved for sale to pay burial charges. Some communities patrolled their parish borders, banning incoming or out-going travel. It was the clothing whose sale permitted the plague to infect the people of Eyam, Derbyshire, resulting in terrible suffering.

The weeks leading to the wedding were marked by unexpected reminders of the past, and relatives rarely thought of. Family changes in Jersey led to the wish to sell houses rarely used, and the disposal of furniture and possessions. Cupboards and boxes were regarded as useful, as were rolls of good cloth, linen, silk and satin which were generally re-used.

Bess, with forethought, brought to London some unwanted items for possible use by their married daughter, though Philip's marriage had not been planned at that time. Bess and various children had continued to visit Peyrol and the Ruby continued to make Channel trips.

Weddings were on Bess's mind one evening when she and George were discussing whether the planned wedding should be postponed. On the whole they decided that if you waited until the sickness was over, you might wait for years. 'Better perhaps not to buy things previously used, or go to crowded markets.'

'You remember, George, the long curtains from St Helier now hanging in the drawing room in Piccadilly. I have other items they might use in their house, when they buy one. I brought back some useful commodes, two of them with cool cupboards, they can place in their dining room. Your sister, Rachel was very helpful. After we had sorted out the things to send to London on Ruby, and they were ready to leave, she told me she wanted to take you some items from Mont des Vignes, which she thought you might wish to see. Clement inherited them with the whole contents. He has decided to sell it before they move to London to set up as solicitors.'

'Oh! Did she? She was always a hoarder. I expect it is a lot of old rubbish?'

'I said I would take it on the boat, if it was small, thinking it would be easy to dispose of later. It's not much, and I've thrown most away, but I saved a wooden box, and a toy boat, in case they bring back memories.'

'You mean a sort of yacht?'

'I'll show you. Here they are!'

'Good Heavens! The pond yacht! I'd forgotten all about it! I remember Reggie helping me to make it for him. It used to stand on top of the box on the window-sill in his room, pointing out to sea, He used to sail it on the pond. How very strange! Reggie! I remember it so well!'

'Do you remember the box, George?'

'I remember it used to stand on something, 'So that the Captain could steer the ship', or some such nonsense, he used to say. Why do you ask? I know Reggie used an old box to keep treasures found on his travels.'

'He always brought us gifts to amuse us, George, when we were small. We all liked Reggie and of course we will never see him again. I think you should open it, George. You may find it reassuring.'

'This is definitely Reggie's collection: here is a ptarmigan's wing feather, and a piece of fool's gold, a small cameo, and a piece of scrimshaw, and what are these? They are short notes, and they all seem to be addressed to me. They are folded in the Prayer Book my mother gave me, before I went to sea.'

'The first is dated 1633: I'll read them to you. "My dear brother, I am overjoyed to have been made lieutenant. Your good fortune was with me that day. Our mother said, "Put the letter in the box, and I will see that George reads it'. "Affect. Your Brother Reg."

'There are several more, in date order. I'm sure I was never told about them, Betsy. He or mother, must have added the others over the years. I am sorry we never seemed to be home together, or I might have read them... They all give the name of the ship he was on, so its like a list of his career and all the ships he had sailed on.... This one is to thank me, when he gave my name as a referee, and was promoted.... And this congratulates me on becoming an Admiral. Later ones mention his pleasure at meeting our children and his affection for you, Bess. In 1645, he mentions suffering an injury in a sea-fight and that his leg had mended nicely. The final letter records his appointment to the Dolphin, of the Irish Sea Squadron, as 1St Officer under Prince Rupert. '

George remembered taking six Naval ships to Jersey to prevent Parliament taking them. Prince Rupert had confiscated three others and taken them to Ireland. Two of them were sunk with all hands by Blake's Parliamentary squadron, in the Irish Sea This explained his twenty year silence.

He was suddenly overwhelmed by grief and guilt. He had never doubted that his brother was happy in his work and was content to believe that his progress was being followed with interest by the family. Perhaps writing the letters was a great support to him.

'I am sorry I never met him again, but you say he enjoyed his visits to St Helier, and he would have met Philip, I suppose. I remember he mentioned him once or twice: Sometimes I met an officer who would ask if I had a brother in the navy, because it was an unusual name. They all spoke well of him. I shall keep the box, and the boat. If I ever have a grandson, he might enjoy the yacht.'

'Don't forget, George, he always signed himself, "Your Affectionate Brother." You must always remember that.'

Pepys, in a diary entry, records that, pausing for lunch in a Gravesend public house, he enjoyed a meal and conversation with a Lieutenant Carteret, who was about to board his ship. The date, 1655, is consistent with Reginald's appointment to Prince Rupert's Irish expedition, which ended with the loss of two ships. Did Pepys ever pass on this coincidence to George? We may never know. It is possible: Pepys was a good communicator.

Bess was increasingly concerned to notice changes in her husband's manner, some she accepted happily, such as his new pre-occupation with the future welfare of the family, but others were of more concern. He was less impetuous and more inclined to depend on Philip and the clerks in the Broad Street office. He had suggested to Philip that William Jarvis should take the lead in manorial matters and take on two extra clerks to do the tedious searches through papers to establish the facts, and conduct interviews. Often there were unrecorded sub-tenancies, or garrulous country folk who wanted to know about the Dutch Wars, to divert enquiries into apparent discrepancies. He recommended Ezra 'Chones' as a deserving clerk. Jones, as Philip had been told, was grandson of Jones, the surgeon, during George's first cod-fishing trip to Newfoundland. Dr. Jones, now an elderly man, was a member of the Company of Physicians, and had worked tirelessly among the sick during the infection. While in Jersey, George had been saddened by the deaths of some of his childhood friends and astonished to meet their grandchildren, who recounted reminiscences of exploits which he had to take on trust, having no memory of them.

The wedding plans for Philip led to discussion on the subject of money. Bess was aware that their way of life was expensive, although George's earnings, and annual pension from the Navy Office, were generous *[footnote. Balleine, in 1947, estimated that Carteret was "worth £3,000,000". Independent Examination of the Navy Office Accounts for these years using "modern" accountancy practice, revealed that figure to be accurate.]

Elizabeth was aware that parliamentary committees often criticised the Navy accounts and that George became angry, feeling his honesty was in doubt. Pepys and Coventry independently checked everything and found them example of openness and accurate book-keeping, but it appears that neither of them was regarded as entirely reliable, because they were 'colleagues', and Coventry was Prince James's private secretary. The deficit was caused by the lack of government investment and this shortfall was never remedied. George, in 1664, began to think of disposing of the Navy Treasurer's Office, but would need to find a purchaser, prepared to receive standard salary levels. Fortunately, there were several willing to take on the task, confident that they could cure the deficit and stay in budget. Frances Hyde admitted she had similar anxieties concerning Edward. Many of his policies required the raising of taxes, and some MPs believed still that it was Cromwell who had led the party of taxation and they had relied on the

King to reduce or cancel the tax burden. Unfortunately, Hyde was unable to delegate responsibility, however trivial, and was accused of deliberate delay, although he worked long into the night, unable to find young men who understood confidentiality or basic arithmetic. Working at the office all night, he was often found asleep in the morning.

The Carteret household wedding plans took their accustomed course. A magnificent wedding was planned in detail by Bess and Lady Jemima, for both Philip and Jemima, lacked their parents' enthusiasm for ostentation, and were shocked to discover that almost everyone their parents knew, was to be invited. Carriages were booked, and preparations made in the City for ceremonial arches. The militia was called upon, as well as Naval officers, to provide guards of honour. Bess reflected sadly how much the little girls had enjoyed being bridesmaids at their sisters' weddings: the younger Montague girls would have to take on their place this time. This wedding was to confer political status on the Carterets, and Montague provided a large dowry for his daughter, while Philip made a will, leaving 40% of his estate, if Philip was widowed, to provide for their children. The Baronetcy would be hers in trust, if Philip died first, for their eldest son. The Bishop of London permitted the wedding to be celebrated in the Catholic Savoy Chapel by permission of the Queen and the young couple felt overwhelmed and wondered whether they would survive the ordeal.

At Court life continued to run on the physically active lines demanded by the restless energy of the King. The routines were varied on impulse and were principally concerned with outdoor activities. The Hunt and the racecourse were the main pursuits of daylight hours, alternating with falconry and rowing and sailing on the Thames. Charles and James were both superb horsemen and they and other courtiers set up flat-racing and steeple chases in the traditional hunting grounds in southern England. Challenge Cups to reward and increase competition and the variety of winners. And annual race meetings pencilled in for future years. James was a formidable huntsman and went out in almost any weather, often at considerable personal danger. On one winter day, when the stable-men were strongly against riding, warning that it would be too dangerous, James exercised his authority and led them out. Later that day he had a bad fall and continued hunting with a broken collarbone. Two days later, with heavy strapping, he was out again. James's bravery could not be questioned, in the hunt or on the battlefield, his strength of purpose was quite different from his brother's prevarication, or his flexibility.

When winter, or bad weather, forced the Court to entertain themselves indoors, there were lavish feasts, and new treats. Lady Fanshawe, recently a widow with children to raise, had turned to writing recipe books. Baron Crewe, of the Court of Chancery, had taken the tenancy of some of his Essex properties, Fanshawe had inherited from his father, after the Restoration settlement, the hereditary post of Royal Remembrancer, which was passed to his son in Ware. She supplied a dish named 'Icy Cream' and presented some for the King to try. Charles was delighted with it and it became popular at court and with those who kept an ice house for preserving food. Some were already quite familiar with it, but it was new to the King!

He was also fond of dancing, and of dancers, particularly dances where the woman was seized and twirled about, while running and jumping. His personal attendant, William Chiffinch, had many questionable tasks to perform among which was to encourage young women whose performance the King had found enchanting, to accompany him by way of the back stairs where His Majesty would like to express his admiration for their performance. Then there was gambling with card games or roulette tables, and someone might make a boastful claim to have seduced many noblewomen then present, stating it to be true, and bets would be placed on whether the ladies present would support his claim. Large sums of money were hazarded in these, and other ways, and fortunes lost and gained. Impromptu lotteries were also popular. They had been used in Holland, by the States general, as a means of raising money to build ships, schools and Universities.

It was a means for making gains for the community without levying taxes. No such noble aim prompted the British version which was aimed only to create profit for the promoter. Tickets for English lotteries, which caught on with the moneyed classes, were kept as low as five pounds each, although that sum was equal to the annual wage of a domestic housekeeper. Wealthy women might invest much larger sums on a weekly basis. All funds were distributed among those who bought winning tickets. Those who acquired wealth became the celebrities of their day. Country estates or 'killings' on the stock exchange financed the men, and they in turn, financed their wives and mistresses.

The Merry Monarch, amiable and friendly to all, enjoyed the freedom thus acquired and many lived for the day only, under the eye of their benevolent monarch, knowing that sudden death by plague could occur to anyone with no warning. Dryden replaced Milton as the nation's popular poet, and Wycherley's satires replaced Shakespeare in popularity. The up and coming favourite writer of the moment was the teenaged, John Wilmott, soon to become 2nd. Earl of Rochester, whose scurrilous rhymes and lascivious accounts of persons and activities among courtiers, alluded to the King and those lampooned proclaimed to the world the King enjoyed sexual pleasures above all. He was not only a forceful ruler, intolerant of opposition, but a man of the people: a merry monarch who could even laugh at himself and took nothing to heart!

While the Second Dutch War was in progress, and Plague entering English ports, the King and Courtiers, aided by actors, actresses, musicians and dancers, were performing "The Marriage Masque" written by Cleveland, with sets designed by Wren. It was commissioned for the King by Lady Castlemaine who would star beside his latest mistress,' La belle Stuart' as "husband and wife". While taking refuge in Oxford, the King had become infatuated by Frances Stuart, one of the Queen's attendants, educated in France, and seven years younger than Barbara Castlemaine, who had recently given birth. Charles was spending rather less time with her than usual. The Masque told a tale of lovers and the tribulations of their affairs before their final happy marriage was consummated. It was pantomime, designed to contrast the attractions of the two women now Barbara had regained her figure, and restore her power over Charles. Barbara played the beautiful bride, and Frances Stuart was the handsome hero, displaying her beautiful Legs. Their 'Marriage' took place in an elaborate bedroom scene, with much titillation and display of flesh, designed very much for the taste of the King, who was enchanted.

Charles enjoyed this Masque, but became impatient with Barbara, her jealousy and violent temper, and constant demands for money. He maintained his relationship with her, but continued to pursue others, particularly Frances. She remained reticent and therefore fascinating and unexpectedly announced her marriage to the Duke of Richmond and Lennox, despite his attentions. Charles was displeased and briefly banned her from court. Pepys records, however, that in May 1668, the king took a skiff and rowed to Somerset House, where he climbed the wall to be with Frances "which is

*Restoration and Retribution*

a horrid shame". Pepys was by no means a prude but he was one of many who were familiar with the King and his sexual incontinence. However, her beauty was so great that Pepys, whose devotion to Castlemaine was such that her portrait had a place of honour in his dining room, called her "the beautifulest creature he had ever seen". Even Clarendon remarked on her beauty. Frances was not impervious to the King's attentions including his love poems, which renewed her affection. Seeking an emblem to be placed on the reverse of the newly minted gold Crown coin, he had Frances drawn, seated on a rock, with the ocean and Navy in the background, holding a spear and shield displaying the British flag. She would, from that time be immortalised, unexpectedly, as Britannia wherever the image is used.

The second Dutch war was extremely popular with the general public, and there was a plan for a joint attack with France, by land and sea. The Bishop of Münster had appealed to Parliament for financial assistance in defence against a possible Dutch attack. A large British fleet would attack the Dutch coast at the same time. £20,000 was sent to the Bishop and a date agreed when both attacks would be launched. Weather, and the fact that the Dutch were forewarned, saw the English fleet confronted by a strong Dutch force, while the Stadtholder attacked the Bishop across the Rhine. A full-scale battle was fought off Lowestoft and the British suffered a humiliating defeat. The finest ships were destroyed and excellent seamen, including Sir George Menges and the Earl of Oxford, and many others, including hundreds of seamen, were killed. Prince James lost his flagship, but fought on to general admiration and gained increased popularity.

CHAPTER EIGHTEEN

The Carteret marriage preparations continued their prenuptial formalities and all seemed to be settled when Fate decided to show its hand. The plan for a wedding at the Savoy Palace had to be abandoned and George considered Deptford Church followed by a reception at The Belvedere. This was the latest of several speculative pleasure resorts, designed for the discriminating entertainment of the wealthy. Constructed on a hilltop south of Eltham, its high tower provided a superb panorama of the Thames and London, There were extensive gardens and pavilions for dining and dancing. It was quite near Deptford House, and thus very conveniently placed. However, at the end of June the Epidemic reached the overcrowded, squalid streets of the south Thames riverside. In a few days hundreds were infected nearby in Southwark, and the defensive gate to London Bridge. The disease spread to those who lived and worked there, and spread the infection to the south bank.

Deptford House was no longer safe and London guests could not be expected to risk crossing London Bridge. A country house, secure a great park and with a nearby Church, would have to be found. Lady Montague provided a solution. Her sister, Anne, had married Sir Henry Wright whose home was Dagenham Park, a rural estate in Essex, close to the Thames and surrounded with woodland and dairy farms. Largely well drained, former marshland, it was drained by the River Wantz. This was one of several streams and creeks running into the Thames. Pepys probably negotiated the agreement with his cousin, Edward Montague. Lord Crewe, Anne Wright's grandfather, who had earlier shared the moderate political views of Harrington and the Carterets. The Wrights willingly offered their home for the wedding of their niece, Jemima, at Dagenham Church. This building had recently been restored by the Fanshawe family, who owned the living. As former friends in St Helier, they would be delighted to provide the church and would attend the wedding also.

George notified the new plan to the guests. The Banns would be read in Dagenham at the Church of St, Peter and St Paul, within walking distance of the House. The Wrights would entertain the Montague and Carteret parents, and their engaged children, so as to establish the necessary residence qualification. An Anglican Marriage Rule stated that weddings must take place during daylight hours, and no later than mid-day. This would not present a problem at Dagenham, for one of Crewe's relatives could conduct the marriage ceremony.

In the remaining days before the wedding, a number of trips across the Thames from Dartford to the Wantz Creek, as plans were made by family members, beginning on the 19 July, and using the barges general use to ferry passengers across the Thames. Pepys was in his element, rushing between the Navy Office, Deptford House, Westminster and Dagenham, and recording every detail in his diary. Guests could stay at the Hall. The country areas east of London, mercifully, had few infections.

George was determined that the marriage must be performed in style, and decided that he would commandeer the Admiralty Barge for the family to cross and recross the river. It was very large and could carry the Admiralty Coach, drawn by four horses, and passengers. This would convey them to Dagenham House from the ferry, then carry the bride and bridegroom to the church. Any visitors would be impressed, even though there would be no procession through the streets of London. By co-incidence the church had been thoroughly repaired by Lord Fanshawe, before his unexpected death. He had been a guest of the Carterets in Jersey, when he was secretary to Prince Charles. The Fanshawe family had held the post of Royal Remembrancer since the reign of Elizabeth I It was his duty to ensure that every law and precedent pertaining to the Ruler should be borne in mind at all times, so that no privilege should be forgotten. Lady Fanshawe hoped to attend the wedding, and would drive there from Parsloes Manor, her home nearby.

Fate had an unwelcome surprise in store, however. On 17 July while checking the details, George noticed that Dagenham was not in the Diocese of London, but of the Bishop of Ely. Will Jarvis had to be despatched with urgency to St Albans, where the appropriate Bishop had a palace, and was fortunately at home. Will returned, exhausted, with the correct, signed, licence late on the afternoon of the wedding eve. The coach horses had been sent ahead earlier, and were being groomed in Essex. The great Admiralty Coach was loaded and awaiting the arrival of the family party. George and Bess, with Pepys and a few of their personal attendants, went to board the barge and watched, as the barge, with its heavy burden, was launched onto the waters. There it stuck firmly in the mud, and was immovable. It was almost low tide, and it could not be re-floated for another twelve hours at high tide.

George decided that if they returned to their house for the night, Bess would have no wish to complete the journey in the light of an early dawn. Therefore, he called up a wherry, and when it had been cleaned, the whole party was rowed to the Isle of Dogs, where there was a riverside Hostelry. It was usually the haunt of wherrymen and stranded Rovers, looking for work on a sailing ship. George, who happened to be wearing his Trinity House uniform and Master's badge, chosen as his wedding uniform, exercised the full weight of his authority and ordered decent rooms cleared for them. Bess, fortunately, entered into the spirit of the occasion, and feeling refreshed, though wishing for a change of linen, they set out by wherry next morning for the Wantz Creek to rejoin the coach. When they came to rest in the creek, sightseers came from all directions as the news of these strange visitors spread. Some thought it might be the Merry Monarch himself, coming to meet his people, but the sight of the golden coach, headed by a gilded statue of Neptune, with his great trident and surrounded with Nereids, was sufficient to satisfy them.

Finally, the horses were brought to the coach and persuaded into harness, and the passengers boarded. His watch having unwound overnight, George sent a footman on horseback to Dagenham Park carrying the Licence, without which the marriage could not take place. Pepys records his astonishment and admiration for Sir George's exuberant conversation and laughter. The whole family it seemed, were enjoying the experience, as much as Sir George. He, Pepys, was clearly extremely anxious. The roadway was very poor, and the journey slow. Sir George was absolutely in his element that day.

Entering the Park, they were directed to the Church and, as they approached, the wedding party met them coming out from the Church, where the wedding had taken place, just before mid-day by the local clock. Happiness broke out and congratulations were exchanged all round, and George and Bess regaled everyone with the tale of the wherry and the Isle of Dogs. In his diary, Pepys wrote:"Sir George, the most passionate man in the world and one with the greatest haste to be gone, did bear it very pleasant all the while, at least not troubled so as to fret and storm."

At the house, the wedding breakfast was put to bake, and half past five chosen to come to table. In the meantime, the ladies went to wash and dress for the occasion, and it was decided that Jemima and Philip would wear their wedding costumes, which had not arrived for the wedding. Men were instructed to absent themselves to view the Estate, not get in the way, and not to get drunk. They were to appear ready for dinner in their wedding costume, no later than five twenty.

The wedding breakfast was a success and the guests stood for the entrance of the Bride and Groom, followed by Louise Marguerite as bridesmaid. "So to dinner," wrote Pepys," and very merry, yet in such a sober way as never almost any wedding was in so great families." It would be natural, with the Plague not yet at its climax, for the guests to wonder how soon they and those they loved, would die a cruel death. But in the meantime, joy was unconfined! Brides and Bridegrooms were not exempted when the Gentleman with the Scythe came calling!

"That night, after prayers," Pepys recorded, "I got into the bridegroom's chamber, while he undressed, till he was called to the Bride's chamber, and into bed they went. I kissed the bride in bed, and so the curtains drawn with the greatest gravity, and so good night."

The newly married couple had several homes at their disposal and moved from Deptford House to Hurstbourne Park and Broad Street, now Piccadilly, to avoid contact with the plague, which seemed to have done its worst in London, before it moved far afield to inland towns, carried by travellers and the clothes they wore. The Carterets remained largely unaffected and Philip, with Will Jenkins's assistance, began their inspection visits to the Carteret Manors. Until recently this visit could have been swiftly made, but the Carterets had recently received more manors as further evidence of the King's generosity.

During His Majesty's sequestration in small towns in the home counties, for safety from infection, it seemed the King had discovered a drain on his income. Throughout England and Wales there were 25,000 Manorial holdings, administered by Lords of the Manor all appointed by the King, at his discretion, and each contributing annually to His Majesty's Treasury. They were also the most intimate aspect of the power of government in each locality. Since no assessment had been made since 1654, considerable sums might be needed for ten years of neglect. Much would depend on whoever had possessed the manorial land for the past ten years. Many of them had no living claimant, however, and George was selected by the King for yet another possible source of income. He might perhaps have hoped that Charles would repay his debt in the form of cash. But this was a scarce commodity, and a generous Manorial gift would cost the King nothing, and provide a means by which George could repay himself by his own efforts. Naturally, he would have to devise the means and method to pay for its collection.

He had been given six Manors in Jersey in 1660, which were already on Philip's list. New additions were: Leigham in Devon; Pengelly in Cornwall; Stapleford Abbots and Regis in Essex; Tregear and Burneyre in Cornwall; Plympton St Mary, Membury, Bickham, Elesham, and Saltram in Devon; were assigned and also, Loaxley and Westwood in Lincolnshire. The Jersey payments were easily collected, those in Devon, by the appointment of a local agent, and the Essex manors were within travelling distance. It seemed that Charles was once more repaying his debts by indirect means, but each was rewarding and enabled him to make improvements to waterways, re-roof churches, and sometimes make an educational grant.

The Plague sent the King to safety in the country and MPs. to their distant constituencies, causing a discontinuity in the committees pursuing existing government deficiencies. Parliament was losing sympathy with the King: the King certainly seemed disillusioned with them, and there was an avoidance of large meetings and decision making at all levels: Charles was less eager to seek the advice of his Privy Council, or the parliament. He was certainly more impatient with their sluggish discussions and obsession with the extension of the Test Acts, because they seemed determined to penalise those whose loyalty was well known, irrespective of their contempt for Anglican worship. Thousands of well-meaning men and women faced loss of employment as a result, and many chose to seek refuge in the new colonies, fearing prosecution.

Parliament, when recalled, clamoured for a new Dutch War but the fleet had not been rebuilt after the Lowestoft fiasco, and only small ships were willing to venture out to harass a few solitary Dutch vessels for plunder. Then some large war ships needed expensive re-fitting and there was no cash to provide it. A peace Treaty with the French, aimed at finding allies to attack the Dutch, provoked Protestant MPs, because it seemed to concede advantage to the hated Catholic King of France. This anger resulted in further Acts of discrimination directed specifically against 'Traitors to the Realm' ie. Catholics.

Charles had accepted the passing of a Triennial Act and began to rely on a new set of ministers, strong-willed enough, he hoped, to overcome opposition. The Cabal of six ministers chosen were a balance of Protestant and Catholic who made an attempt to add weight to Charles's weak situation and defend him against suggestions that he was attempting to seize Absolute Power, or favour one Christian sect. He had begun to resent the reproofs offered him by Clarendon, about poor moral standards and gambling. Clarendon demanded Charles should dismiss Castlemaine and her idle friends from Court, for the national good, and learn to control his lust. Clarendon conspicuously refused to acknowledge the existence of Castlemaine and snubbed her associates.

Charles was increasingly offended. Parliament was growing more and more sectarian, and extremist news sheets and pamphlets attacked non-conformity as an act of treason. Some blamed the plague on the moral turpitude of the King, and it, was seen as an expression of God's anger. This Plague was certainly the worst of the four major epidemics to afflict London during that century. The Members of the College of Physicians had sought refuge themselves when it became rampant, having no wish to fall victim themselves. They were censured for doing so, but they had published clear and sensible Instructions to prevent the spread of plagues, and republished their advice again forcefully. Their advice was ignored once again, and they were accused of wishing to curb individual freedom and attempting to bankrupt the country. Demanding that specialised hospitals should be provided to isolate those with symptoms, and providing carers to nurse and feed those who wished to isolate, was absurd and outrageous, and who would pay for that?

Neither the King nor Prince James was allowed to increase Naval expenditure and the financial situation made no improvement, and so George decided to sell the Treasurership as soon as possible, first gaining the King's approval. James Carteret, after an inauspicious start, was appointed Captain of the Royal Prince, a second- class warship. He was to lead a fresh attempt to recapture St Kitts from the Dutch. His small squadron was inadequate for the task and failed to achieve its aim, as the result of communication failures caused by the failure of flags for signalling ship to ship instructions not being interpreted accurately. One ship was lost, though the others avoided damage. His next posting, ironically, was to the 'Jersey' a smaller frigate, plying coastal waters and the North Sea. French ships were small and agile, and were well-equipped. Dutch ships were broad and slow moving, but had a useful shallow draft suitable for shallow seas. Either fleet could defeat a solitary ship with impunity. A number of British ships were forced to surrender and it is a shameful fact, that British sailors were known to surrender willingly to Dutch ships, if given the choice, since they were better employers, and always paid their crews.

The King's return to London from Nonsuch Palace, his most recent place of refuge, marked a distinctly low point in his relationship with parliament. They continued to demand war with the Dutch and the strengthening of the Test Acts against Catholic traitors. Charles asked in response, what amount they were prepared to grant to repay Naval Debts, to have new warships built. Parliament had increased his annual allowance to £1,800,000, but this did not repay his debt, which continued to increase. The Queen's Dowry had not been paid for two years, money which would have paid the standing army in Tangier, where it was about to be attacked by a Moslem army. Thomas Povey, an honest and wealthy City merchant, held the office of Master of Plantations, so the solution, to George's relief, was given to him to find. The former Sultan might have assisted, but his replacement had no wish to pay, what was intended to repay a debt owed to the Portuguese. The Duc de Vendôme, George's former protégé, had recently died, leaving his naval command to his teenage son. On this occasion, George was not able to cover the deficit.

By the time the Queen returned to London, from Oatlands, the whole City had heard of Charles's affair with Frances Stewart, and his lecherous activities in various safe houses while his people suffered. They also heard that Barbara Castlemaine had given birth to another son, George Fitzroy, in Merton College, Oxford, who was to be known as Duke of Newcastle. The country was in a state of shock following the deaths from the plague of almost half of London's working population, including craftsmen and skilled workers. Unemployed soldiers and sailors roamed the streets disconsolately, and basically the enthusiasm fuelled by the Restoration years had evaporated. Nell Gwynn was the King's newest lover, a kind and good-natured young woman, in Pepys' opinion. She had previously been introduced to him by Mrs Knipp, his constant lover, and Nell had sat on his knee, to his great pleasure, after a rehearsal. His own investments, largely in ships, which had been at sea during recent months, returned to port and added to the sudden increase in trading profits. New building schemes were planned or begun, and George's Piccadilly house was nearing completion. In the interim, he had been elected as Master of Trinity House, with a new ceremonial uniform, and a special sword, of which he was very proud.

# ~ FOUR ~

## CHAPTER NINETEEN

The summer of 1666 was almost unbearably hot but at last a refreshing south-easterly breeze offered welcome relief to the crowded tenements and corpse-filled graveyards of the City. At 3 am on 2nd Sept. Pepys was woken from his sleep by worried servants who said they could smell smoke. He dressed hurriedly and left the house to discover the cause. As the result of his prompt action the best account of the Great Fire is from his diary. From Pudding Lane it spread unstoppably westward, and then northward, before if settled down to the destruction of the trading warehouses of the port areas of the City. It raged westward again for a further three days, crossing the Holborn and the Walbrook, but with reduced strength at reaching the Tyburn. George and his family were largely unaffected by the fire, which stopped at the end of his street, where most buildings were of brick. The inferno of timber buildings on London Bridge made Thames crossings difficult. The dockside commercial area of the City was nothing but a charred ruin, requiring many thousands of pounds to replace. Small-scale house fires were quite common, and only a few set money aside as a safeguard, and Insurance cover was rarely sufficient. The City Corporation proved to be extremely resilient, however, and it soon recovered, gaining even greater wealth.

Fresh companies sprang up, replacing those made bankrupt, some of which flourished. The Gambia Company was one such but only marginally successful. The Senegalese tribes were small in stature and not suitable for hard plantation labour. In general they were not 'recruited' but encouraged to supply the English ships with fruit, vegetables and fish. Prince Rupert hoped that the headwaters of the fast-flowing river, might be a source of gold, or other minerals, and also provide a route to the unexplored interior. Results of exploration led to this plan being abandoned. At the river mouth, however, a town named Bathurst, for the Governor, was established, and a Governor's Residence and barracks built, asserting this as British Territory. Fifty miles up-river, on a rocky island, a military Headquarters was built, with barracks and slave quarters and a Factory for the grading and shipment of slaves. The local people were largely untroubled by these activities, and The Gambia remains among the oldest and most loyal British colonies.

The decades 1630-1660 saw the growing success of Carteret's investments in the East India Company. From small beginnings at the end of Elizabeth's established reign, it had taken on the power of Portuguese trade, City merchants financing determined efforts to reduce their trading concessions, until the Mughal Emperor finally gave them trading rights in specified ports. Once they were established, the three Dutch Wars and French co-operation, dealt a fatal blow to Dutch traders. This success was recognised by Cromwell in 1657, when a permanent joint-stock corporation was formed, allowing the company shares to be openly traded at the Stock Exchange. Two years later, Cromwell issued a full Charter and established a supply base on the island of St Helena for the use of British ships trading on the route between England and the Far East.

The St John's settlement continued to thrive, and the Labrador hinterland, explored by George and the Hudson's Bay Company led to vast expanses of the American continent, infinite mineral resources, and prairie lands where bison grazed. The forests and lakes, where bears and beavers were easily hunted, and fur, became a new source of wealth to Britain. Prince Rupert, deprived of a European throne, became an imaginative exploiter of the region which he referred to as 'Ruprechtland'. George had already established connections in the region and was an importer of its furs. Prince Rupert engaged intrepid explorers to explore the territory and return with reports and maps. The French had much the same intention and had fisheries and trading posts of their own at Montreal, Sault S. Marie, and elsewhere. In the next century the French submitted, after protracted opposition, to British hegemony and Canada, the second largest country in the world, became the most valuable British Colony.

George did not make the Atlantic crossing again as an adult, though James paid a visit during his tenure. George had continued trading with the trappers he had met as a teenager, but was astonished when he was hailed in London by yet another friend from the past. George must have remained relatively unchanged for, while inspecting the goods recently arrived at the fur wharf, he was recognised by Robert Gaiches, one of a small group of childhood friends with whom he had explored the secret woodlands and sea coasts of Jersey. Gaiches, as he had always been known, was large in build and jolly by nature. He was now running manufactures in London for luxurious fur winter wear, and bearskin hats and beaver-skin boots for soldiers. He had settled in St John, and worked for John Gyon, who George remembered as the General Manager of John Smith's business concerns. They agreed to meet at a future date, recall names and places from the past, and exchange reminiscences.

The home counties manufacturers of essential workaday products were as important to him as they were to other traders operating on a much larger scale. They were the iron workers, enjoying increasing demand for agricultural tools of all kinds, from ploughs to scythes and spades, essential at home and in the colonies. Other products from Dowse family workshops were saddles and harness, and carts for farm work and transporting heavy goods. Oxen required different harness and trappings. Weapons of all kinds were essential for use at home and for export where the rule of British law was often challenged. There was also the carriage-building trade for men of standing like Carteret and Pepys. The search for speed and a smooth ride added to technological progress. The extent of goods traded and methods of retail in an expanding market was as challenging as of goods for export. This exemplifies the rapid changeover from Monarchic control to Republican and public control.

Who were these friends who placed such trust in Carteret? William Povey, mentioned earlier, was a leading trader in this command economy. Cromwell had recognised his skills and put him in charge of the Office of Plantations, his task being to develop new outlets for British products, and setting up planned colonies, on a legal basis, to prevent unregulated dens of piracy developing. He, and a colleague, Sir Andrew Riccard, joined the King's Council for Plantations, and helped to formulate the Navy Acts. Povey is regarded as" England's first Colonial Civil Servant." He led a trading family, in essence, and worked hard to gain higher positions in British society. As a result of William's efforts on behalf of Massachusetts, Tom Povey, his cousin, was made Governor of Massachusetts. His son became Lord Chief Justice of Ireland. William was also governor of The Tangier Company, founded some time earlier. Part of Queen Katherine's Dowry, its trade was shrinking and there were threats from Moslem raiders. Charles realised that its income scarcely paid for its defending Regiments. At his request, Povey placed its economy on a stronger base.

Sir Nicholas Crispe, who died at the age of ninety in 1666, was already established as a City father when King James began his reign. He had considerable trade in West Africa in the 1630s, and led The Guinea Company from 1625-1628. He imported luxury goods, cloves, cinnamon, silks, ivory, calico, slaves, and sea shells for gentlemen to decorate their grottoes. These were becoming very popular. Between 1632 and 1644, he made £500,000 from buying gold for the King's use. He lived in Hammersmith, where he had a nearby factory making glass and china beads for the Africa market. These were made from strands of gaudy red, green white and opaque glass, cut in short lengths and perforated for ease of threading. They were produced in a variety of sizes, some round and some tubular, and were popular items of exchange for spices, copper ware or slaves. This intervention led at last to the total destruction of the Ashanti and Benin kingdoms, and the plunder of the Benin Bronzes and other examples of remarkable beauty. HI craftsmen specialised in the new engraved glasses for wealthy connoisseurs of wine. During the Civil War he had been a generous supporter of Charles I and, at his own expense, paid for fifteen merchant ships, fully equipped for use at sea.

When Charles I was defeated, Crispe's property, his house, collections, and factory were confiscated, but he supported the restoration and escorted Charles II into London. Glass for windows and churches was among their products and his pottery works produced "blue and white" Delft pottery. His property was returned to him and Charles appointed him to the Council of Trade in 1660 and The Council of Plantations in 1661. Pepys praised him for his inventiveness and new technologies and mentioned his plan for constructing a dry dock to George, who later implemented the plan in Portsmouth Harbour.

Sir Andrew Riccard was a famous ship owner and shared many of George's interests. In 1654, during the Commonwealth, he was M.P. for the City of London. He was well-connected and his daughter married Lord Kensington. At the restoration he received a knighthood, and was a good administrator of The Levant Company, living long enough to become a Director of the new East India Company.

Thomas Warner is memorable for his part in populating the New World settlements. St Kitts, in 1627, and Barbados, in 1631, both relied heavily on his efforts to discover poor but willing people, eager to leave England, seeking new opportunities. Between 1625 and 1649 he provided, as evidenced by his certified accounts, 30,000 settlers for the Caribbean Islands, and another 30,000 for the North American settlements. He also sent heretics, protestant and catholic, who offended against the Church of England, and convicts who had survived their imprisonment, and vagrants. Thousands were not strong enough to survive the climate and infections, or the endless toil of making a living. African slaves were healthier and survived for two years on average before a replacement had to be purchased.

So, in effect, George was among a group of honourable and wealthy citizens who were the backbone of the future wealth and reputation of the City of London. Though they were Royalist by tradition and inclination, and some, like George, had a personal attachment to the king, all could now see Charles's shortcomings, and had the skill to avoid his extravagance and attempts to gain the absolute power which his cousin, Louis XIV had been awarded by his ministers. They supported Royalty as an institution, and Charles as the present office holder, up to a point. Before the century ended, the City would dismiss one King, replacing him with a pair of rulers prepared to allow Parliament to gain control.

George created what was, in effect, the instrument of partial democratisation, through force of circumstance, rather than intention. By 1670, Charles had lost the power to demand obedience from the Houses of Parliament. The Commons in particular, had devised a programme of their own based on commercial gain, and the King was compelled to become a city trader if he wished to display the symbols of monarchy in public as well as private collections. The ceremonial traditions dating back to "Time Immemorial" were not likely to be financed by Parliament.

The insufficiency of his income was mirrored by the inability of the Government to repay its own debts. In 1667, Treasurer Clifford estimated the Government Debt at £2,500,000, of which Naval expenditure alone was £1,000,000. Not even George was able to stand surety for such sums, and the City financiers felt compelled to restore the expenditure lost in the plague and fire. However, he retained the trust of the King and in conversation with Pepys, George declared, on more than one occasion, "the king did nothing without consulting him" and Pepys recorded it carefully in his diary and asserted that it was true. These years saw George's most prosperous growth during which he became a millionaire. That he achieved this success while retaining a universal reputation for honesty, may not make him an exception, but it may imply that he was a rarity.

Medical facilities for the individual or for the populace at large, were basic and received small financial backing. European towns like Bologna and Leiden were much in advance in surgery and hygiene. Traditional 'Cures' were preferred and the College of Physicians was a voice crying in a wilderness of superstition. When threatened by the Plague, George, like most other citizens who could go to a place of refuge, left the citizens in the hands of the few enlightened doctors who remained, like Dr Jones from the Atlantic voyage. All sensible proposals to isolate and support the sick, and build hospitals, and close public meetings, had been rejected as too expensive. The only new contribution to the alleviation of the Plague, was a reissue by Culpepper, an unqualified fraudster, of his "Herbiary", published some years earlier, to encourage self-medication with herbal tinctures and ointments, with herbs culled from the fields and hedgerows. He re-published it, adding alcohol, which was popular, and other poisonous or damaging items. He also recommended regular blood-letting, and the application of noxious substances to the open sores. People who were unable to find specific items, like "eye of newt" were encouraged to find a likely substitute. He recommended the extermination of all domestic pets, which led to an increase in the number of rats.

Public and economic life ticked over hesitantly, George was probably consoled for their absence by the knowledge that his surviving children were dispersed to places likely to be secure. In early 1666, however, he received a message that his younger brother Philippe, Bailiff of Jersey, was unwell and losing strength. George found the Ruby was available and he and Bess set off for Jersey at once. It was a cold, crisp crossing but they arrived in time to be at his brother's bedside. Fortunately, it was not the plague but an illness which made digesting food problematic, making him increasingly weak. He had lost a great deal of weight and his sun-tanned complexion had a sallow yellowness. He was refusing to take more purgatives and vomit-inducing medicines, and would not be bled. Their doctor prescribed opium, which relieved his pain, but made him confused, and he preferred the pain to the treatment. He and George discussed their youthful agreement, and knew that their decision had been the right one. George promised to provide for his nephews and nieces. He realised how much he owed to his brother's willingness to take on political burdens. His brother died a week later and George began to realise that changes would have to be introduced: he would not be able to avoid responsibility.

They stayed for the funeral and George needed several weeks to recover his usual assurance and humour. Elizabeth become increasingly concerned about his solemnity and depression. The death of Cesar, Duc de Vendome, was another shock, though he was pleased that Cesar's son had thoughtfully sent him the news. On impulse, they sailed Ruby to Avranches and then to Ducey and La Potrel. Bess's relatives informed Duc Louis, Cesar's son, of their arrival, and George was greeted by Louis, and his younger brother, Francois. Landed in Jersey to commiserate. Louis was making progress with the French navy, but said they saw little action because the fierce English prevented them leaving their harbours! George remembered two small active boys, who thought his French accent was the funniest thing they had heard, though their mother reproved them. They had enjoyed his stories about pirates and spying, and retold them to their friends in gory detail. Their father had told them about his destruction of the Spanish fleet and that he owed all his success as Admiral to George's teaching. His first meeting with George was only the second time he had been on a ship, apparently, when he had been placed in command of the French Navy. He had been terrified, but after his first trip, had wanted to do nothing else, and had gained a good reputation for his command of the navy. He was deeply grateful to George and had instructed his sons to express his gratitude. They were welcomed to England and the court. Louis, the elder son, became cup-bearer to Queen Catherine.

Spring came to London with sudden warmth and the promise of a fine harvest later in the year. The preceding summers had been wet and overcast and in some areas starvation resulted. A succession of increasingly cold winters had left the ground cold and saturated and rivers and ponds frozen. London was a sad place. The optimistic energy palpable since the restoration had dispersed and isolation from Europe had returned, following a promising start.

Some explanation of the growing concern around the succession, which taxed Parliament and the press in the years to come, is probably required at this point. It is necessary to return to the birth of Edward VI in 1517. He had no child and in fact the Tudors produced few other Royal children or offspring. One result of this, and the accompanying Reformation, was that Britain made no alliance with any European country, until 1610. In that year Elizabeth, daughter of James I, married the Elector of the Palatinate, and gave birth to Prince Rupert. All earlier possible marriages had been

*Restoration and Retribution*

prevented by the execution of possible rivals for the British crown, or by death in battle, or execution for treason. Edward VI, Mary, and Elizabeth were all childless. James I and VI and Queen Anne produced nine children. Hopes for a strong alliance with a strongly Protestant Europe ended however, when Lutheranism was crushed as a heresy, and the much stricter Calvinism took its place. The teachings of Calvin were anathema to the Stuarts, and the Church of England and its doctrines lacked real credence in Europe, or indeed with many in Britain. Laud tried, and failed, to strengthen its doctrines, and enforce uniformity of doctrine and practice. The result was unfortunate since it offended those who honoured the Tudor settlement, and was anathema to the increasing numbers of Presbyterians in Scotland and in England. This was the matter which led to the War of Three Nations, formerly known as the Civil War.

Charles II had hoped for a son, but Catherine, after six years, had given birth to a stillborn boy. The King refused to divorce his wife, and relied on his brother, James, to provide an heir. James had nine illegitimate, children and a son and two daughters by his wife, Clarendon's daughter. There were multiple illegitimate children of the King, but none were legitimate. James Scot, Duke of Monmouth, married Anne, Duchess of Buccleuch in 1664, adopting her title. He was 18 years of age and had been born in Holland and was a contemporary of Prince Willem. He was considered" the most handsome man in Europe" and was charming but vapid, and untrustworthy. After his marriage, which produced four children, he added another five to his existing brood of four Illegitimate children. Unfortunately, he was easily persuaded, some years later, to challenge the legitimate succession by unscrupulous politicians. Certain elements regarded the future succession as uncertain since those next in line, were either foreign or Catholic.

London after the Plague was shabby and many buildings abandoned. Some shops and houses still bore ominous red crosses. There was a prevailing odour of death from the overloaded burial grounds and plague pits. In addition, the general squalor of the streets was increased by negligence, for workers and labourers were in short supply, especially those whose work had brought them into close contact with infection. The maimed and indigent still thrived, though fewer in number. Theatres and Gardens remained closed, and there was little to attract an audience, or entertain: even the bear-baiting pits were closed.

Shocked by the haggard faces of those he passed in his carriage, George arrived at the Piccadilly house and found Christopher Ewens in charge, assisted by two junior clerks. Philip, Will and young Owen, were continuing their Manorial visits, and post had arrived yesterday from Devonshire. They had found Devon clerks helpful, and established ways to fill deficiencies created since the last visitation. Ewens was Philip's choice of a temporary office manager, and everything was running smoothly. George enquired sympathetically about the health of their families, and found that they were too deeply shocked to be totally coherent, two of their colleagues having died in appalling circumstances. He did what he could to help and arranged that a bonus would be added to their wages, to assist their dependants.

Goods and invoices had continued to arrive and were being acted upon in the hope that contracts would be completed. George drove on to the Admiralty, where he found Pepys busily interviewing delivery drivers and making payments for goods signed off as delivered. Pepys was working at his usual pace, but with a reduced staff, and extremely anxious about the continuation of the Dutch War: there was no truce, despite the plague. George learned that it had been severe locally, and death rates were certainly rising. Sam was unable to be precise, but the Clerk of St Olave's Parish had told him of nine deaths this week," though I have returned but six". Pepys thought this false accounting was regrettable, and wondered if the same practice was followed in other parishes. If so, the death rate must be greater than the people believed it to be. He had recently visited Drury Lane and had seen several houses with a red cross upon their door and "Lord have mercy upon us" written there. In his diary he wrote: "sad sight to me,… the first of that kind I ever saw….that I was forced to buy some roll-tobacco to smell and chaw-which took away my apprehension." His greatest concern was rumours that Parliament planned to make an attack on the Dutch while the British were dying from plague.

At mid-day, in April 1667, George walked to Whitehall, and went in search of the Privy Council meeting. They generally met twice weekly. The King was in Oxford, but the Duke might be at St James's. Clifford was in the chair, one of the King's recent appointments, engaged as the King's spokesman to Parliament. He, a Devonian Royalist, had been surprised by the animosity in the Chamber toward him, who still believed the navy could overcome the Dutch, despite a lack of ships. He sought Carteret's advice, who responded with caution and expressed the belief that the navy would be ready with the coming of summer and favourable winds.

Carteret was thankful that he now held only a humble part in naval affairs: he knew how weak the navy was, and in no fit state to fight again. He had successfully sold his Treasurership of the Navy, and taken on the post of Treasurer for Ireland. That country had suffered greatly under the Commonwealth, but Petty's land distributions and the wise administration of the Earl of Ormonde, had resulted in a small economic miracle, and he had no anxiety about what the Accounts might contain. In fact he was fortunate to be absent from London for much of the next two years, and grew fond of Ireland. Naturally he enjoyed the chance to sail there and back when possible, but often managed to escape to Haynes, where he now had two grandsons, the latest named Philip. George had taken to the pond yacht, and sailed it on a constructed pond raised two feet above ground level to avoid any chance of drowning.

Some had asked Clifford about requisitioning merchant vessels, converted to fighting ships, and whether there were enough fire ships to create havoc with the enemy. The Duke strode in at this point, demanding a brief resumé, and asserted that the navy, as always, would be ready to serve the nation when the need arose. That closed down discussion, to George's relief, he hoped strongly that a need would not arise to prove the Duke wrong!

The Clerks of the Local Councils had been called in to report on the Mortality Rates for the London and adjacent parishes. Clerks were required to provide weekly returns of deaths under two heads, 'Predictable Deaths' and 'Deaths by Other Causes'. Many Clerks hid Plague deaths under the second heading or a euphemistic phrase, to prevent the probable closure of businesses which would probably result from the truth being revealed. For this would ruin hardworking shopkeepers and publicans. The number of deaths recorded in late April were surprisingly low considering the evidence visible in the streets.

Surprising causes of death were given, including 'Frighted,' 'Grief,' and 'Lethargy'. For some the 'cause' was given as "suddenle": "Teeth" accounted for the deaths of 111 persons in one week: (all were babies). "Infants," were considered the cause of 22 deaths in the same week. "Feaver" or "Spotted Fever' were probably nearer the truth. The dangers of making a close examination of the cause of death, with a disease so contagious, would naturally discourage close examination. In addition, the symptoms were many and varied, in response, perhaps, to new variations in the virus. At the height of the infection many overcrowded parishes reported over 4,000 deaths in a week. The true total can never be known, but a close estimate from the information available, led to a total of 70,000 deaths. This is a fairly recent estimate, but another suggests 40,000, an underestimate, the total must be closer to 100,000 deaths. Somewhere between a quarter and an eighth of the working population of 800,000 died.

Naturally, the economic results for London and the rest of Britain were marked. Many industrial concerns lost both owners and workers. Cloth workers were badly affected and there was a shortage of watermen and domestic servants. An influx of untrained country folk arrived to fill the vacancies however, and recovery began. George's wealthy friends suffered reductions in their profits, but their enterprise was sufficiently extensive to provide support. Louis XIV sent words of sympathy and an offering of cash for the King's use: the Dutch hoped to benefit from the financial disaster and their navy became more active in the Channel. There was fear of a Dutch invasion and anger at William the Silent, whose wife was a daughter of Charles I, and whose son, William, was heir to King Charles II. Some felt that he should provide finance to Britain.

Finally, the time came when Parliament decided that this humiliation was not to be tolerated, and to Clarendon's dismay, on 1 June 1666, seventy English ships confronted seventy Dutch ships and a battle lasting four days took place. Many ships were lost on both sides, and thousands of men. Three English ships collided and were lost. The newest generation of trained officers were reduced in number and Pepys mourned the loss of Sir Christopher Menes, who had always provided support and sound advice. The Earl of Oxford was killed: probably the most noble of the victims. Prince James had fought with reckless courage, and lost his flagship on three occasions. The King was terrified that the heir to the throne might have died. James was sent to Scotland for safety and to establish sound government, and George Carteret decided, once more, that he was fortunate to have little connection with Naval affairs. He spoke to Pepys several times, who had clearly decided that keeping the books straight was the first essential demanded of a permanent secretary.

This decision was confirmed on August 4, St James's Day, when a reinforced English fleet confronted the undefeated Dutch fleet yet again, in a one-day battle. The result was more of a success for Britain, but the Treasury was now completely empty, and a Treaty of Peace, engineered by King Louis, was agreed, which pleased nobody in Parliament.

Prince James asked Carteret for an opportunity to speak to him in private, accompanied by Coventry, and suggested that Philip could join them. George invited him to dine at the Piccadilly house. Coventry and Philip were the only guests, and the subject of the meeting was entirely confidential. It was not the first time James had used George, whom he trusted, as a sounding board. Once again, the naval expenditure was the central issue. James was disappointed the King had discharged him from office, and command given to a group of civilians. He spelled out their names, before speaking of them as a "Cabal". There would be yet another Parliamentary enquiry into 'losses' in the naval grants, and the poor repair of ships and their equipment. It all seemed so futile. Why did they suspect deliberate dishonesty where none existed?

Coventry said he had made a thorough inventory of accounts, and was forced to accept that no-one was stealing money and wished to apologise for suspecting George's honesty. MPs. rejected Coventry's judgement as yet another cover-up. They had no understanding of the ongoing costs of an army or navy, each of which required a constant flow of cash, which would always be an expensive necessity. Neither army nor navy could be on a sound basis with random or impulsive gifts of cash. James knew the King understood this, but no-one could force the MPs. to accept these facts. The King had heard that George was seeking a sound manager to buy the post of navy treasurer. He thought this was a wise step, but must not be taken suddenly or the banks would lose confidence in the pound, and bankruptcy would follow. George said that trust was difficult to achieve. The commons probably felt that they should be trusted to know in advance what estimates the finance was based on. In principle this might be a solution but he doubted whether they would be prepared to accept the estimate of what was needed. They would almost certainly not trust each other sufficiently to reach a decision. The Cabal, he said would need to be not only transparent, but have a detailed grasp of every facet of naval affairs, or the distrust would continue.

There were other serious matters concerning money and the King's new ministers. Arlington, a sound financier, had sent agents to discover why so many seamen had not been paid for months and why compensation for serious injuries, suffered in active service, was not paid. This information was available to them and Chief Pursers in Chatham and Southampton, had offered answers, but Arlington seemed dismissive. Payment was a relatively small issue, compared with the lack of shipwrights and the lack of fibre to make the ropes and halyards which drove the ships. After some reluctance, junior clerks were told to take his agents to inspect the Navy Chest. When the chests were unearthed and unlocked, they proved to be empty. Someone it seemed, and it was probably a wicked Cromwellian, had spent the money on weapons to defeat His Majesty. The shipwright brothers Pett, admitted they had used the money to repair the ships for the recent Dutch War, which seemed more important than payments to sailors. They had been dismissed for misappropriation of funds, common practice in most engineering projects. They had to be reinstated weeks later for the simple reason that they were the best shipbuilders in Chatham, and were irreplaceable.

James thought he should point out that, since no one person seemed to be to blame, the responsibility must fall on the Treasury. As Chancellor of the Exchequer, Clarendon must have been negligent he suggested. This was probably the next stage of the rift which later led to Clarendon's dismissal. MPs agreed that this must be his culpability for the loss of life on land and sea, and for insisting on waging war, knowing the Navy was unprepared.

'I see from your face George, that you consider this to be unfair, but there is no doubt that Clarendon is overwhelmed by the weight of his duties and important actions are being needlessly delayed.' James offered this to George by way of defending the Navy officers. 'He seems more concerned with building his Palace than with national affairs. Arlington asked him whether he wished for clerks to assist with legal issues, and was rudely rebuffed, I hear. I think he is under great strain and should accept an honourable retirement. Only recently Lady Castlemaine met him in the lobby, and saw him wince when, with typical kindness, she asked after his gout. The man ignored her and turned aside, Lord Rochester demanded whether his hearing prevented his hearing her kind enquiry. My Lord replied: "I am not in the habit of responding to the importuning remarks of Whores." I feel that my Lord exceeds the latitude given to a man of his age.'

'The King laughed when he heard it, but Barbara thought my brother was laughing at her. She refused him favours for two days, it seems, and only relented after the gift of a ruby necklace. I will also mention his high moral tone when he chooses to admonish my brother for moral turpitude: this is not to be borne! I heard my brother tell him he intended to pack a small bag and ride to Tonbridge alone for a quiet weekend. Clarendon replied, "I shall instruct your Majesty's Guard Regiment to accompany you."

My brother was annoyed, and said, "They are part of the small bag!' My brother is so tolerant.'

After the Duke's departure, Philip, who heard the whole story, murmured, 'I fear my uncle's days are numbered. I have heard it said that Clarendon forced the King to marry a Portuguese Catholic, although he knew she was infertile. Surely that cannot possibly be true, Father?'

'Of course, it is not, my boy. The queen has suffered two miscarriages, I am reliably informed. My Uncle Amyas often told me, Philip, that if you decide to serve a King, you should create a measure of personal security for yourself and your family firSt A ruler will always exercise the right to sacrifice any person, however close to him, to protect himself. You must remember the fate of Strafford and Laud. My family's safety has always been my first concern, Philip.'

# CHAPTER TWENTY

On Sunday 2 September, George was woken early by the sound of a window rattling and discovered that there was a good stiff south-westerly blowing. After several days of oppressively hot temperatures, it was a welcome change. He dressed hurriedly, and went down to find the dogs prepared to enjoy a world full of rabbits and sleepy ducks to chase. Sunlight was glittering on the Thames and ships moored overnight, and smaller fishing boats made a fine display with the wharves of the Limehouse quays visible in the distance.

The dogs returned to him, panting and, calling them to order, George led them along the lane and up the steep slope to the hill top, the highest point of his land. The Tower was visible and smoke beginning to rise from kitchen chimneys. At six on this Sunday morning, little activity would be visible until citizens roused themselves for Matins at their local churches. This was the one day of the week when the City streets would not be hidden by a blanket of smoke from the many London factories. Then he noticed a great column of thick, black smoke rising high into the air from a point beyond the Tower, it was being spread by the wind over the City rooftops. 'A house or perhaps some poor fellow's factory, going up in flames. Hope they get the water pumps out,' he thought. Calling the dogs to him, he walked back to the house along the ridge and was startled by the sound of an explosion. 'It must be large warehouse, to be audible several miles from London' he thought, before going to breakfast.

While entrusting the dogs to the stable lad, there came a second explosion, loud enough to set the dogs barking. 'Is it the wicked Dutch attacking us, Sir? That's two, Sir. Shall I run to the Docks and ask?' George advised him of his duty to attend to the dogs and, when that was done, to harness the horses for the small carriage ready for Church.

Emerging much later from church, Bess lingered, to thank the rector for what George thought was an extremely tedious lecture. Their fellow communicants were exchanging fragments of news: some said the explosion was from the gunpowder works, testing a shell: some said a ship had been destroyed: others believed the Tower of London was being attacked by a

French mob. George, feeling instinctively that all was not well, sent his valet to have the Admiralty barge prepared to be rowed to Tower Pier.

The closer they came to the Tower, the thicker the smoke, billowing like a winter fog, but constantly swirling and expanding as fresh outbreaks added to the uneven clouds. London Bridge was only partially visible and, as they began to moor the barge, smoke rose from the South side of the river: glowing fragments of paper, straw and cloth were mingled in the smoke and had ignited some material in Southwark. It appeared that the river was no barrier. It was clear that this was not merely an annoying house fire, but one which was increasing exponentially. Some means must be found then quench it before serious damage was caused.

He walked from the quay to Seething Lane and the navy office and met Sam Pepys who was also concerned. He was about to find a waterman to row him to Whitehall and inform the King of the emergency, since no-one seemed able to think of practical measures. He had been woken during the night by their maid who had smelled smoke. He and Elizabeth investigated, could see no obvious source, and had returned to bed. At six he had dressed and gone to investigate and realised that buildings were burning fiercely. He and a neighbour saw from the tower of All Hallows Church that Fish Street Hill, and streets and warehouses beyond, were ablaze and the strong wind driving smoke and flames rapidly westward. George watched Pepys on his way, noticing several boatloads of anxious families attempting to cross to the South Bank for refuge.

Surprised they were not escaping uphill toward St Paul's, he became anxious about his Piccadilly home and offices. He slowed his rapid pace, since people were going about their normal Sunday activities, and found his house was untouched. The housekeeper, although surprised to see him, offered him coffee and he sat thinking what help he could offer in this new situation. Somewhat refreshed, he set out for St Paul's and the Offices of the Lord Mayor, who would be taking charge of the situation. Each Parish, he knew, had Beadles, known by their hats and staves of office, and empowered to demand help from any citizen in an emergency. Militia? Would they be involved? He had never taken much interest in the administration of the City Corporation, but presumably someone would have taken charge.

Near London Stone he came upon a crowd of anxious gentlemen, haranguing a red-faced bewildered man in shirt sleeves and wearing a crooked wig. He was hardly recognisable as the Lord Mayor Bludworth who had delivered a fulsome speech at a recent Guildhall banquet. This was a man in the grip of total panic. George enquired after his well-being. 'His beadles had been despatched,' he said, 'to find buckets and flat brooms for beating out fires. Some had gone to fill the fire-cart barrels and attach the pumps. They had started filling it at the conduit, but had been pushed aside by house owners eager to fill buckets.'

'I expect they will lend a hand when they see the situation for themselves,' George remarked in an effort to calm him.

'The beadles have not returned with assistants, as I instructed. They have been seen defending their own houses.'

The flames were moving in the direction of the Lord Mayor's House. George left him fearing that the situation was already out of control, and might grow worse.

His own business affairs were mostly in stocks and shares, and assurance, and his ships were either at sea or in dock for repairs. There were bound to be goods in storage, some on the riverside, but newer factories were to the north and east of the city. The fire was sure to burn itself out. He called a carriage and set out for Whitehall. It was late afternoon and he was not surprised to find that the King and Prince James were in the King's library discussing the information Pepys had provided. Arlington and Lauderdale were present, having heard of the fire from passing strangers. The King had sent messengers to Privy Councillors, and Clarendon and Ashley were expected shortly. Some time later, a semi-formal meeting began. MIlitia and army officers were now also reporting that the fire was running unchecked, and George reported on the dilemma of the Lord Mayor.

George asked whether they could send soldiers to take charge of the streets and prevent panic and looting. Charles thought it might work but believed it might be forbidden. The City controlled its own business and the Law forbade the King interfering or entering the City, unless invited. James felt that they must make some attempt to help: this was an emergency. To do nothing would seem that their monarch did not care for their suffering.

Messengers arrived reporting that people were running in panic from the flames and small groups were calling for the death of Catholics and French spies: all were arsonists planning to capture London for King Louis. It was decided that, before night fell, the King and Prince James would take the Royal Barge down the Thames, through the City, to see for themselves what Londoners were facing. Rowed slowly past the Tower, they could hear at first hand of the dangers and pleas for help. These could not be denied and the King responded, after speaking to Bludworth. The Lord Mayor and Aldermen, granted permission for the King's guards to enter the City to beat out the fire.

George returned to Deptford House by barge. He informed Bess he was bringing forward their plan to move to Cranbourne Lodge and they would be leaving next day by carriage for Windsor Great Park. He had made a number of improvements to the facilities and believed that they were complete. He would remain in London until the situation improved because he knew the Dutch War might resume again at any time, and Windsor would offer the family greater safety.

Confident that his family were secure, George set about various unexpected challenges created by the speed at which the fire was advancing. The strong wind had continued overnight to drive the flames westward and the fire was leaping across streets and open spaces, creating new outbreaks. Since the previous evening the fire had spread along the riverside quays and warehouses, and had reached the London Bridge making it inaccessible. Further inland, India House, and Baynards Castle had been destroyed completely and also the Royal Exchange. Fortunately help was on hand to rescue some of the more important contents. George and others took a hand in rescuing the Exchequer Papers, which were dispatched by coach to Nonsuch Palace with the permanent staff. The Dowager Queen, Henrietta Maria, demanded to be rescued from her home in Somerset House, and was rowed to Hampton Court. The true arsonists, she said, were the heretical Londoners!

At Whitehall he discovered Prince James dispatching the last of the guards regiments to salient positions equipped with ropes, hooks and hatchets and instructed to create fire-breaks by pulling down houses and other inflammable articles. Householders were ordered to assist in the destruction of their homes if they had not already escaped. John Evelyn came from the King's presence where Charles was preparing a speech to deliver to parliament assuring them that no effort would be spared to repair the damage. " We have been predicting this event for years, George. Perhaps we will be able to design wider streets and stone buildings and remove the squalid warrens of filth and infection. I have been asked to draw up a plan for a rebuilt City."

Evelyn had taken his wife and son to see the fire the previous evening.

George walked to his house and noticed that the fire appeared to have stopped short of St Paul's, though some streets which he had walked yesterday were now burned. Finding a clean pie-shop open, he bought several and joined his clerks for a snack. Reaching Seething Lane some time later, he found Prince James who had come to see for himself whether the Navy Office and Admiralty were safe, which had seemed at risk. Pepys and Tom Hayter, one of the clerks, had loaded his best furniture and dispatched it to a friend in Islington. The Prince was reassured and returned to order fresh demolitions, and George found Pepys and Admiral Penn burying a box of papers in the Admiralty garden. As an afterthought, Pepys also interred a complete wheel of Parmesan cheese which was a recent, and much valued, gift.

On Tuesday the fire was clearly out of control. Prince James worked tirelessly among his troops, hacking and beating out new outbreaks with unrelenting energy and great courage. He had to be rescued at one point from being surrounded by fire, while working for over twelve hours with scarcely a break. His personal reputation as a leader was enormously strengthened. Despite all efforts, including some of the boys of Westminster School, who filled and carried buckets of water for hours on end, the Guildhall, and finally St Paul's Cathedral were both destroyed. Pepys saw the destruction of the house where he had been born and the streets he knew, all destroyed. The King commended his brother's efforts and observed the progress of the fire from his boat. That evening, at dinner at Whitehall, the Banqueting Hall filled with moths and butterflies and the Courtiers and their ladies, armed with nets, took part in a butterfly hunt with great enjoyment before settling down to cards and dancing.

On Ash Wednesday the fire continued to burn, but less fiercely, for it had now reached the marshland closer to Westminster where there was less to ignite. The wind was probably more gusty, for flying ash and fragments of charred paper, in addition to acrid smoke, blew as far as Windsor and Eton, thirty-five miles from the City. George discovered that during the night the fire had reached Piccadilly and damaged his carriage sheds. Oily smoke stains patterned the walls of the side aspect, which would need to be cleaned. The book shops of St Paul's Yard had lost £150,000 of stock, and their wooden buildings.

Potential opportunists finding fresh opportunities, and up to no good, were much in evidence, though the Beadles were watchful. Many were interested in awarding blame, on the basis that such a blaze must have been the result of a deliberate act. Mr. Farriner's bakery in Pudding Lane was accepted generally to have been the source of the blaze, and he and his family had been the first people to have made their escape from their burning house. He was sure that his ovens were cold when he inspected them in the middle of the night, and he was a much-respected man and supplier of Biscuit to the Royal Navy. Alternatives were the traditional enemies; foreign immigrants, Dutchmen or Catholics. Clarendon, the Chancellor, was mentioned as a malefactor, by unpaid soldiers and seamen, and was a suspected Catholic, though he was very strongly Anglican. For the third night, windows in his fine mansion were stoned. The warm weather continued however, and the homeless citizens camped in makeshift tents in Smithfield and the gardens of the Temple, (whose church was one of the last fine buildings to burn). Most of the homeless sat about listlessly, accepting offers of food and telling their story to anyone willing to listen.

George was one of the reconstruction committee, called together by the King. Architects and surveyors were asked to present plans and Hooke had been out and about with his visual ability to measure open or charred spaces, accurately. However, before any plans were drawn, many Londoners had moved back to the site of their home and were clearing it, so claiming the space as theirs. Many set up a camp on their site. Planners were to be presented with jealously guarded property deeds. Fires continued to spring up as smouldering cellars burst into flame and walkers sometimes fell into newly opened holes in the ground. The smell of rot and decay permeated the air for miles around and seemed a permanent feature. By 9 September the worst was considered to be past. At the Annual Meeting of Trinity House, George was once more chosen as Master. It did not deter him from his attempt to identify a successor as Navy Treasurer, for which he had not yet found a purchaser, although he had several suitable applicants. The King would make the final choice of appointee.

Business returned gradually to a new normality. The Royal Exchange building was no more and Gresham's College was adopted as a temporary base, forcing the Royal Society to fight for its space. The Exchequer remained at Nonsuch, but operated its current business in borrowed space. Very soon Philip and his two assistants returned from their lengthy Manorial visits, well satisfied with their success. The manorial system, though perhaps a primitive survival, was an inexpensive way of making fair decisions in the event of property and financial disputes. Problems which had rankled for years were resolved to general satisfaction, and rates for tenancies reassessed. George decided that, if he could hand over his naval duties, he would enjoy taking part when he had more leisure. Philip mentioned that he had stayed with the family at Cranbourne Lodge on his journey back to London, and that they were well, although his mother was anxious about George's health and the pressures of his duties. He was eager that he should hand on the Treasury, which was making him so unhappy, and buy a home in the country, where they could enjoy the fruits of his unrelenting labours. He mentioned, modestly, that he would take it as a great favour if Cranbourne Lodge was available for Jemima's laying in. George hugged his son warmly and offered his congratulations, adding that the Lodge would certainly be at Jemima's disposal.

'I hope, Philip, that when Broad Street is repaired, we can make it a temporary home because Deptford House, pleasant though it is, will go to my successor; and I cannot count on remaining Warden of the Forests. If that post is given to another man, we shall have no home. I know we could afford to buy a country house, because we no longer have any justification to return to Jersey. I suppose Hampshire might be a possibility, and convenient for London visits.'

'Mother hopes to take you away from your work place, father, you need to be able to get away from work, and Hampshire is too near London.'

'We can discuss it when she comes here. I believe I have found a purchaser for the Treasury, but the hand-over must wait until the new financial year.'

'May I make a suggestion, father? We went up to Lincolnshire to collect the dues and it is completely dependant on Hull, and a long way from a road leading to London. It is not a happy county, and many are moving there to avoid the Test Act, many local people are Presbyterians and planning to emigrate from Hull to America.'

'We came back by way of Northampton and Bedford. I have a strong feeling that it is the sort of country-side mother likes, and it reminds me of Hampshire. The Great North Road is convenient for travel, but is a day's trip to London, and quite accessible, though not close enough to make a brief visit. I noticed that land is much cheaper there than closer to London. You could build a fine house with parkland surrounding it, and you could construct lakes, and plant trees, and build orangeries, if you feel inclined, and make it a real family home.'

The autumn brought increased political tension and greater hardship for the majority of the population. The harvest was disappointing and the weather wet and cold. In some areas there was commercial activity, and the ports of Bristol and Liverpool expanded their trade with the American colonies, where the import of slaves increased productivity. Parliament remained obdurate on the subject of royal extravagance and Charles, in genuine need, sank even deeper into debt. As a concession to accusations of extravagant clothing, he imposed a set of Sumptuary Laws on those who lived at the Court. A new, simpler style of clothing for men and women was devised. Ribbons and displays of lace were discouraged and the use of brightly coloured, expensive material prohibited. Former more flamboyant 'Cavalier' clothes were discarded in favour of simplicity of line, and black, or grey and white, were the recommended shades.

Louis XVI was horrified that his cousin was too poor to reward his courtiers, and responded with derision, enforcing the same style of dress on members of his serving staff. Charles continued enthusiastically to purchase paintings, plant gardens and bring Italian musicians to the Chapel Royal to expand his band of '24 fiddlers', two of whom, Thomas Beltzer and David Mell, played on first-rate violins from Cremona. The Royal Observatory at Greenwich was also sponsored by the King, who appointed John Flamsteed as Astronomer Royal. A golden ball was lowered there every day at noon precisely using a mast placed on top of the tower, to indicate true mid-day to all the vessels on the Thames, and traders with deadlines to meet.

Parliament, increasingly determined to resume the Dutch War, set up yet another Special Commission to attribute blame for the failings of the Royal Navy. Pepys undertook to provide incontrovertible evidence that lack of adequate funding for ship-building, running repairs and payment to chandlers and crews was the reason. Pepys' proudest moment came at the conclusion of two days of grilling, when he succeeded in persuading the hostile Commons that the debt resulted from lack of adequate finance. The Debt was enormous, but the King declared the account closed. Government no longer had the trust of the City bankers, who refused to finance it by attempting to sell worthless shares. George was vindicated publicly, and sold the Treasurership to Lord Aingier, who bought it at a bargain price. To make up a shortcoming by the sale, the King appointed him Receiver-General of Ireland, with a guaranteed profit of £5,000 per annum, and also as Treasurer of Cork, worth £500 per annum. Unfortunately, the stalwart defence of

Admiralty poverty, presented by Pepys, did not result in increased estimates for the navy. He did, however, so impress the MPs. that he was asked to fill the parliamentary seat for Harwich.

The Duke of Ormonde, Governor of Ireland, welcomed his management skills and advice, and as a result there was a reduction in the internal conflict on the island. George crossed to Dublin, when it became inevitable, but retained his post of Vice-Chamberlain and Privy Councillor. He spent no longer in Ireland than necessary, since William Petty had created a balanced budget by rationalising land sales to owners who were likely to put in an effort. He now had leisure to spend at home, in Cranbourne Lodge, or Carteret House, London. Philip played an important part in discovering a suitable location to make a country estate, suited to the ambitions of his parents. He and his father spent time and thought considering a number of sites, eventually settling on land in Bedfordshire. At the same time, George was engaged in the committee replanning London, which would give useful insights when the plans for an estate were under consideration.

While plans for London were at the committee stage, the cause of the Great Fire of London became the hot topic, since it was highly unlikely that a bakery oven could have created such destruction. Rumours were rife throughout the City, and the media promulgated even more unlikely theories with no actual evidence. Clarendon, to his annoyance, was tasked with forming a government investigation to find the cause and bring to justice those who were responsible. One suggestion was that the fire had been started by an arsonist who was walking free in the City. This and other theories had neither supporting evidence, nor witnesses. Clarendon, and others who were witnesses, were convinced that the bakery was the source. The public and press, however were howling for a culprit, and financial incentives were offered for his capture.

Had it been a foreign Government? Surely there would be boasting about the damage? The "evidence" all pointed to Farriner's Bakery, though he was certain his ovens were cold. He and his family had escaped by way of the roof, because the first floor and stairs were burning. The family were certain of their innocence. George pointed out to the panel, that house fires often began as chimney fires, when brickwork become red hot, igniting adjoining floor beams. Such a fire might smoulder for hours unseen. Of course it was also as impossible to prove.

# ~ FIVE ~

### CHAPTER TWENTY-ONE

Then arose the strange case of Robert Hubert. He was one of many solitary and homeless men camping with others in the fields and open spaces within London. He seemed incoherent or confused but informed a member of the watch that he had started the fire. He repeated the claim to others and eventually was brought before a local magistrate. Under questioning, he repeated his story. He claimed to have come to London seeking work as a clockmaker and had been offered food and work by masked men. In exchange for food he agreed to place incendiary devices to start a fire. The information finally to the attention of Lord Clarendon, who had been dealing with a number of improbable claims, and investigating numbers of plots and suspects. Despite deploying his team of secret agents, he had been unable to arrest a culprit, or evidence of a conspiracy. No plot was disclosed and no foreign agents found. Clarendon and the King both found Hubert's claim implausible but felt it must be investigated.

Examined by skilled lawyers under oath, Hubert repeated his story of an offer from masked agents of food if he followed their instructions. He could not identify them because they instructed him in a dark room and took him, blindfold, to the place where he was to use the devices. His blindfold was removed so that he could see the building to be attacked. On the night of the fire he was led there again, the blindfold removed, and instructed to throw the devices and run away. The man who led him there, vanished. Afterwards he had run back to his campsite, to be told London was on fire and told the watch what he had done. Yes, the agents had given him some food now he was looking for work in Eastcheap.

He was escorted from the local court to Eastcheap by court officials, where he seemed confused and uncertain, until he recognised the shell of a former building, from which he led them through a series of burned streets and finally stopped, by a length of wall, and claimed to have thrown the incendiaries through a window. It was Farriner's bakery in Pudding Lane. The lawyers, Clarendon and the King were reluctant to proceed, but their visit to the scene of the crime had been made in day time and attracted a considerable crowd of witnesses. With great hesitancy, Hubert was brought to trial at the Old Bailey before a packed courtroom. George did not attend, considering that the court must dismiss the case for lack of evidence and witnesses. However, when the jury returned, they unanimously found Hubert guilty, and he was condemned to death. On 27 October, he was conveyed to Tyburn, though streets lined with howling Londoners, and hanged. Before his corpse could be collected by the College of Surgeons for dissecting, it was seized by the mob, torn to pieces, and allegedly eaten. The London mob, when roused, is a fearsome thing!

The Privy Council meetings were increasingly uncomfortable experiences for all concerned. There were often about twenty legal and commercial experts as well as vociferous MPs. and a scattering of Lords. The King, or sometimes Prince James, was Chairman and prepared the agenda. Clarendon was the main speaker on most subjects and spoke for the King, and also for himself as Chancellor. Notes were constantly passed between the King and Clarendon, the King frequently modifying his most recent statement in conformity with Clarendon's advice. Charles always made his amendments with great courtesy, but with obvious lack of interest. Parliament frequently questioned Privy Council decisions, but Clarendon remained inflexible in the House of Lords. Clarendon and George often shared their anxiety concerning the King's apparent disinterest, but Clarendon insisted that the decisions of the P.C. should always be accepted by Parliament, because the Councillors were experts whose decisions must be accepted. George realised that this attitude was unnecessarily confrontational, and resulted in confusion and inactivity.

Charles had begun to find the six members of his Cabal more amenable than the Privy Council. He felt that his persuasive attempts to achieve personal financial independence were failing for lack of strong supporters in Parliament to turn a tide of criticism. George Villiers, Duke of Buckingham and Henry Bennet, Duke of Arlington were men of his own age who had fought for him since the Civil War. Thomas Osbourne, Earl of Derby, was a Yorkshire landowner and a persuasive speaker, and Thomas, Lord Clifford had naval interests. The Earl of Lauderdale was Scottish and supported by Covenanters, and the last was Antony Ashley Cooper, formerly a strong Parliamentarian, but wealthy, politically active a man Charles wanted to bent to his will.

To the MPs. they were regarded as an extra-parliamentary faction attempting to overrule elected government and introduce rule by force. George deplored this pointless quarrelling. It was contrary to all the good that he had believed would come with the restoration, and he saw that the King was losing the will to take a stand on any reasonable plan which might endanger his personal hold on power. He was thankful that while he took so little interest in business or politics, he would never have the energy to grab absolute power. The thought came to mind that Charles had achieved his object and had seized the elements of political power by subtle means and without causing the antagonism his father had provoked by announcing his intentions in advance. If MPs opposed him threateningly, he could dismiss an advisor or two for going beyond his political brief. The Cabal had no interest in Trade as such, and collectively advocated War with Holland. Bennet and Arlington were supporters of Catholic toleration: Lauderdale and Buckingham were strongly Royalist, while Ashley and Danby were parliamentarians and strongly opposed to dissenters who refused to accept Anglicanism. All branches of opinion were represented, but none took precedence. Apart from the King and Carteret, none were interested in increasing trade and Charles and James were able to seize that initiative. When the time came.

Public opinion favoured war and the persecution of heretics. The Court was also divided. Lady Castlemaine was a Villiers by birth and a Royalist. Coventry supported Prince James. The common enemy was Clarendon. He was believed to be responsible for the failure of the English navy, for forcing the King to marry a woman who was infertile, and for supporting Catholics, who were planning to secure a future catholic successor. All these charges were untrue. By December 1666, MPs. were threatening Clarendon with Impeachment. Informed of this proposal, Clarendon addressed Parliament at some length asserting his innocence and honesty, and total Loyalty. Even his strongest opponent could not challenge this. Clarendon was utterly dismissive of the "plot" and the King assured him of his support. Opposition grew however, and it was evident to all that England was bankrupt, and cut off from trade by the well provisioned and armed French and Dutch navies. Trade by way of the Baltic was blockaded by Danish traders. In October Parliament impeached Clarendon for actions which had ruined the economy, had forced Britain into a war with inadequate preparation, and with possible treason.

These problems affected the population only indirectly and life continued with increasing inflation and epidemics and starvation in the depths of an icy winter. There was nothing unexpected in these effects. The Carterets passed an enjoyable Christmas at Cranbourne Lodge, and Philip and Jem, and also James, home between ships, joined them and the Penns. The Admiral took George for a long walk with the dogs to unburden his anxiety concerning his son, William. Apparently, he was continuing to behave irresponsibly and his father contrasted him with James Carteret. George attempted to reassure his friend, although James had a tendency to provoke fights and drink too much, he seemed to have 'grown up,' finally. He admitted to some reservations on that subject, which he kept to himself. He assured Penn that his son would improve soon, just as James had! William's faults included a tendency to introduce dissenting views in everyday conversation: some of the Admiral's friends had commented that this would not gain him friends in high places. He was also given to advocating religious toleration and universal education. Penn senior tended to blame himself for sending his son to Belfast, where he had adopted ideas from Scottish Covenanters. James Carteret showed no religious convictions other than his unfortunate worship of Lady Castlemaine. Perhaps his faith would soon be betrayed?

The Carterets' youngest surviving child, Louisa Marguerite, was about to celebrate her fourteenth birthday, and attached herself to Lady Jem, her sister-in-law, now that her elder sisters were living miles away. Philip announced at dinner on Christmas Day, that Jem, his wonderful wife, pregnant, to the joy of the family. Accepting their congratulations, he asked when Louisa was to be married, to his sister's embarrassment. Their parents had in fact begun to think of an eligible husband. They felt a lack of urgency, however.

At the new year, George and Philip made a leisurely trip to Bedford, and inspected several areas of land, occupied by houses which might be reconstructed, and adjacent land for purchase. Acquaintances who might have heard of land for sale were consulted and it was Lord de Grey who mentioned that there was a hundred acres of well-drained land south of the River Ouse, and with Bedford, a prosperous country town, conveniently close.

The present tenant was Samuel Butler who had published Hudibras in 1663, which had become a best seller and often reprinted. It was a book for its time; George decided that it derided principles which had only recently been admired. He could not understand why so many found it so entertaining, or why it was so popular.

Pepys, who was a tolerant man, had read it and thrown it away with contempt. When he heard his friends and colleagues laughing at its humour, he bought a second copy, and decided it was in tune with the raffish conduct and ideas of fashionable Courtiers. George probably shared Pepys' reaction. Pepys diary contains an undercurrent of support for the standards of conduct asserted by the Commonwealth: he was certainly very clear about the deficiencies of the King. If Pepys had not hurried in person to alert the King at Whitehall, that the fire in London was spreading out of control, he was far from certain that any preventative measures would have been offered.

In 'Hudibras' Butler wrote satirically about many subjects and attacked every one he met and every idea which came to his notice, and especially the Commonwealth leaders and their social doctrines. The 'honest' character Hudibras, is a mocking representation of a man of strong personal convictions in an age of disbelief. He wrote a second and third book lampooning religious beliefs and all they stood for, hoping for repeated success, but he misunderstood the spirit of the age, for Protestantism was becoming the symbol of Britishness and everyone was compelled to take Communion. He had hoped to make a fortune and buy a grand estate: he was living now in penury in a small farmhouse on land he could not lease. The Carterets could buy the land, of which the de Greys were part owners. George clearly understood the complex ownership structure and had its legality confirmed by Judge Crewe, Lady Jem's Grandfather, who arranged a legally binding handover.

# CHAPTER TWENTY-TWO

In early April, Bess accompanied George and Philip to Silsoe, where they hired horses and, accompanied by Lord de Grey, rode out to see the various qualities of the farmland and woodland. De Grey suggested a site for the house, on rising ground facing south east, with an open aspect across a valley, and prospect of North End Church. They decided that this would be their family home, providing the stability they so much desired. On the return journey, Betsy revealed a matter which had been on her mind for some time. It was a long journey to London and she cautiously told George her concerns about the state of the country, and the measures they should adopt if social unrest grew worse.

'What a wonderful day it has been, George.' She began lightly. 'I am so pleased to have found such a perfect site for our house. I had been trying to persuade your father, dear Philip, to reduce his work commitment. We have not had a home of our own since we were married, and left Jersey. I don't suppose he remembers, Philip, but this is our 25th. Wedding Anniversary, and I tell myself that the new house is an Anniversary present for us, George. And also, Philip, without your help, your father would still be saying, "When I have time, I'll give it some thought. Thank you both!

'I have been talking to Frances Hyde and the Queen's Ladies in Waiting, and we all agree nothing has been right since the Plague, and the Fire. I'm not referring to the loss of life, terrible as it was, or the loss of trade, though we are all suffering austerity measures. It is something else worrying us: something in the air- a new sadness, almost a mood of despair. No-one seems to know what to do, or whether any effort is worth making. Only the young seem not to notice and appear to be casting about with no real sense of purpose. I suppose the excitement of having a King again, which gave us all so much energy, does not impress them, since he is seldom seen, and seems to have lost interest in everything except his mistresses and the latest stage shows.

'How old is Lord Anglesea, who is taking on the Treasury? He looks in his mid-thirties and Ashley Cooper tells me he was too young to remember much about the wars which almost ruined us. Men of your age, George, need to hand over their good work, now it is effectively completed, to the next generation, who may have new ideas to bring back happiness. They can't be expected to live on our past achievements.

'Frances is terrified for her husband. George, you mustn't laugh: I am serious. He seems to antagonise everyone he meets with his high-handed manner, and constant criticism of any ideas save his own. He even contradicts the King. I have spoken very bluntly to Charles myself, in former times, as you know, George- but never in a room full of strangers.

'Clarendon must retire, George! I know he believes he is the only person who can save the country, but the country does not seem to agree! He has avoided Impeachment, I know, but we, Frances and I, are afraid that when the next crisis comes, taking us all by surprise, someone will suggest that he is responsible, and he will be dismissed or impeached. I can even envisage an Act of Attainder, George: and the King will not be willing to give him support, I think. I am quite serious.'

'I can see that you have doubts concerning mother's fears, Father,' Philip added, ' but I know the King attends Royal Society meetings very seldom, though his Observatory is an important achievement, and also Flamsteed's appointment as Astronomer Royal. But you must have noticed that on his morning walks in Horse Guards parade ground, he walks so rapidly, rarely stopping to talk to other walkers as he used to. You told me that he won't discuss anything seriously in Council and even in the House of Lords, he closes down serious discussions, and ignores matters which he should consider with care, or assign to a committee, or the Council. Racing, hunting and entertainment are all he cares about.'

'I think you are both worrying unnecessarily,' George responded,'for there is a great deal on His Majesty's mind at present. I think common sense will prevail and now that Shaftesbury had been made Lord Salisbury, he will realise he has the King's favour, and will stop his unreasonable demands. Clifford will be able to talk the Commons round, I think.'

'I well remember my father's shock when the King's grandfather handed all authority to Buckingham, and spent all his time hunting,' Bess interjected. 'Charles is doing what his father did, I suspect. He will try to find a man willing to take on his work, and let him take the blame. Who will he choose, I wonder? I'm hope it won't be you George, Thank God!'

'You are going to tell me to retire, Bessie. I know exactly what you two are planning. We have discussed this before, and I have been thinking about it carefully. This is why we have bought the Haynes estate. We can afford it, but I need a steady income if we are to make a success of it. Our business concerns are not sufficiently rewarding yet to live off the profits and I am looking for a short-term, but well-paid post, because I will need the King's support to retire from the Treasury. He must not have the impression I am letting him down- and don't forget, he still owes me money. If I can reconcile these issues, I will retire discreetly.'

'George, my dream of being the wife of a gentleman, retired and with a country estate, and with his own business is becoming a reality. I am quite happy with that plan and I will be able to persuade the Queen that it is what a man of your age should be doing. She will find a way to tell the King to support your plan, There will be no reason for him to be concerned about losing your support. The next thing we must do is to persuade our friends of our generation to adopt the same course of action, and we will begin with Edward Hyde.'

'I think you may have taken on an impossible task, Bess. He is extremely stubborn, and regards himself as indispensable: and I fear he may be right. He is the man who is holding the Country together at present, and he will be a great loss.'

'Not if he dies of a heart attack caused by anger and overwork, George.' George and Philip found that they were both in agreement on that point.

'Frances and I have thought of a plan which might persuade Edward to do the sensible thing, as you are , George. It's really quite simple, and I think you will enjoy it, and you will be in charge. I may wish to reply to your speech when you announce your retirement publicly.'

'I don't think a public statement is necessary, Bess.'

'Let me tell you the plan, before you refuse.'

'I suggest that we celebrate our joint twenty-fifth anniversary on 1st July, and invite all those whom we have worked with, and have meant so much to us during the past twenty years. We should celebrate our successes, and consider how to adjust to handing on our responsibilities to younger, physically stronger people. Perhaps to our children, like you, Philip, and Edward's son, Lory, can grow the seeds we have planted. We must, I propose, include all our children in the gathering who show such promise. I often feel that our preoccupation with the war and the Commonwealth, has distracted us from the nurture of our children. So many of us had to separate from them for our mutual safety, at a time when they needed us,

*Restoration and Retribution*

and they may feel excluded. We might name it a "Celebration of Family' event".

'Betsy, are you proposing to invite Prince James? I know how fond you are of him. Of course, he would be welcome, and his impressive wife. By the way, how is her latest pregnancy?'

'I take it you are in favour of a celebration, George? The Princess was low in spirit when I saw her last week.'

'Of course, my dear. I wish I had thought of a Celebration. Twenty-five years! A Self-Congratulation Event is a very good idea, and will probably appeal, especially to some of the men who never take their families to social events. If you invite the wives, I know you will certainly get their husbands. They will know no embarrassing disclosures will be aired.'

'I think it is high time we heroic survivors enjoyed an informal meeting and a fine meal before we are forced to separate by age and unforeseeable events. It will be something to recall in our dotage, George. Few of us will leave behind any lasting memories after our death: Edward and Cromwell will, I suppose, and perhaps our children might remember such an event and mention it to their children. It might even become a regular anniversary, perhaps.'

'This is beginning to sound a little depressing, my dear. You seem to be obsessed by Time.'

'Not Time itself, George; only by the changes it brings. Perhaps it's the result of all these clocks Philip brings into the house. The ticking of a timepiece is soothing: a chime seems like a dire warning.'


George was fortunate in having business interests: these and his large accumulation of manors, added to his family concerns, were sufficient to engage his interest and energies. The London house was re-plastered, its domestic offices, stables and carriage house completed, and their carriage installed, with lodgings for a Coachman, ostlers and an energetic butler, Smethurst, to attend to daily management in conjunction with their housekeeper. Rooms were set aside for office space, and Philip's workshop, and Elizabeth saw to the furnishing of the public rooms to be used for the Grand Reunion dinner and other entertainment.

Lady Jem's pregnancy was announced on 4 April and a combined celebration held for that announcement, and the completed purchase of Haynes Park, Bedfordshire. They had reached the conclusion that the existing farmhouse was not worth repairing. A careful demolition ensured that valuable timber, metal and stone was saved for re-use. George had always liked construction and was pleased when the King asked him to join an inspection of the shipyards of Deptford. He also wanted to view progress on the Queen's House being constructed at Greenwich for Queen Catherine to hold Court. Its rural surrounding would provide the fresh air she enjoyed, and for riding, picnics and archery contests. It was all as informal as the King preferred. One or two interested courtiers went with them, and a servant. But before they went on board, no Admiral's whistle sounded, The King took off his fashionable full-bottomed wig when on board, and hung it on a convenient bulkhead, revealing his bald head, and refusing assistance.

He made a lengthy inspection, and finally hunger intervened. George discovered the pub he had often used, open for business. A servant was dispatched there, with a note requesting a dinner for six. After eating, an inspection was made of the repair yards. John Evelyn met them at that point and invited them to see his recent plant collections. George had consulted him on plantings at Haynes Park. Such was the success of the day, that Charles suggested future trips to other dockyards to encourage the workers and assure them they would always have employment.

George hoped the King was sincere, although nothing new was being planned at present and even repairs depended on the good will of shipwrights. The warm summer which followed brought fresh breezes from the south and east. On the night of the 11 June, and quite unexpectedly, a lightly armed fleet of Dutch warships entered the Thames estuary and advanced as far as Gravesend. This town was the embarkation port for overseas travellers. That night a concerted Dutch attack on London's defences showed them to be totally ineffective and largely unmanned. The damage to buildings was slight, and no-one was killed. On 12 June, when the news broke in London, it marked the blackest day in British Naval history, before the Dutch conquest of Britain in 1688.

Admiral de Ruyter commanded this fleet, which attacked Upnor Castle and Tilbury Fort, the two fortified Military bases, built to protect London and the Medway shipyards. Neither was manned, and neither made a response to the challenge. The only substantial building within sight of the ships was the medieval tower of East Tilbury church, adjacent to the site of Queen Elizabeth's defiant speech against the Spanish Armada.

The whole of London heard the sounds of battle, and the news, when it broke, created panic and anger In the City. Pepys and the Admiralty were astonished and dismayed, and Pepys was so alarmed that he sent his wife and family by coach to Huntingdon, for safety. He believed a full-scale invasion of England would follow, against which there were no defences.

Invasion was not the intention, however. It was a response to the constant attacks by small, private, English boats on peaceful Dutch trading vessels. This was in contravention of the Non-aggression Treaty the English had signed. It was always difficult for the Parliament to prevent Englishmen breaking laws which most people thought were unjustified. De Ruyter prepared to return to Holland, once the action was completed, but Jan De Witt, the Grand Pensionary of the United Provinces, who was on board, overruled de Ruyter and ordered an attack on Chatham Dockyard.

Fireships were sent in to destroy ships undergoing repair, and two Dutch tugs were despatched to cut the lines of the Royal Navy flagship, the 'Royal Charles', the largest and finest of the English fleet. The pride of the Navy was towed across the North Sea into the heart of Amsterdam, and exhibited there to mockery by the citizens. The whole Dutch nation regarded it as proof of Dutch superiority.

George was in Bedford at the time, engaging builders for the house, but was mortified by the news. He was relieved, one assumes, that it did not happen "on his Watch" but told himself that he and the Admiralty had done their best to improve the nation's defences, all their attempts being thwarted by Parliamentary inaction and suspicion of the King's motives. He returned to London, not imagining he could prevent the disgrace, but hoping to instil a greater sense of realism in their future financial proposals.

He found that the London public demanded the punishment of those who had allowed such a national humiliation to occur. This created a difficulty. Everyone knew that Parliament demanded war with the Dutch and had spent money on a number of underprepared attacks. The King could not be blamed since everyone knew he was bankrupt and had been rendered powerless. The honesty of the Admiralty had been established recently by three searching inspections, so they were exonerated. George remembered his wife's warning concerning Clarendon, who had been the scapegoat for the errors of others. Would this disaster also be laid at his door?

Clarendon stubbornly defied public opinion, which was convinced he had encouraged the attack. The capture of the Flagship was not something for which he was prepared to accept the blame. George met Edward after he had spoken in his own defence in the House of Lords. He had made clear his constant opposition to war with Holland because they were a religious, Protestant nation, who should be our allies, not our enemies, He rejected any suggestion that resignation was his wisest course of action. Prince James, and the members of the Cabal spoke in his favour, but without success. The English did not want Protestants, who were regarded as republicans, like Cromwell: nor did they trust the King's ministers, whom they believed were basically Catholics, who would burn at the stake decent members of the Church of England, if they gained power.

Charles was seriously concerned and contacted Louis, asking for asylum for his family if it became necessary, and for financial assistance to pay his employees. Against Louis' advice, he refused to dismiss the Commons, or assume absolute rule. Louis advised him to abandon his throne and live in France, although he would need to become Catholic if he wished for a public role. Once he had prorogued Parliament, Charles may have hoped that national anger about these issues might subside. This prevented Clarendon from using the Lords as an arena to voice his indignation. Nominally he remained Chancellor and, fortunately, the views of his opponents were also silenced. In addition, the King's financial state worsened, since his annual allowance could only be paid by parliament, which could no longer meet his debts.

# CHAPTER TWENTY-THREE

Amid all this turmoil Lady Carteret's grand Celebration came to fruition. Planned essentially as a reunion of "old friends," with the hope of encouraging their children to retain their parents' belief in Monarchy, which was sorely needed in the present circumstances. Bess bore in mind that Lady Jem and Philip were expecting the birth of their first child in late June. They were living in the London house, and also Anne, now Mrs Stanning, who was just pregnant. They were all living conveniently close to the surgeries of the best Physicians in London. Louisa would also be present, and others visiting were Lady Montague and her youngest children, who still required her care. Fortunately, the house was large and most of the guests had London homes. Those children needing care could be placed in upstairs rooms with their nurses, and mothers would be free to leave the table when necessary. The whole plan seemed likely to be well timed.

July 1st dawned fair, but rather too hot for comfort, unsuitable weather for Jemima, Philip's wife, and Anne Stanning. Jem had experienced great discomfort, and Philip had wakened early, leaving her to rest while he released the dogs and made sure they had food and water. He met his father as he returned to the house, in conversation with Smethurst, the butler.

'Morning, Philip. Just checking that the waiters understand their duties. How is my daughter-in-law today? Was the change of bedroom an improvement - with less passing traffic?'

'She isn't awake yet, but she seemed to be more relaxed.'

'Not a good time of year to be carrying that great weight. Perhaps the baby will decide to join the celebration.'

'Don't joke, father: it is due any day. Jem is determined to enjoy the celebration: and is hoping to be a good example for Anne, by making a straightforward delivery. Stanning is at his wit's end and hoping she won't lose this baby, their second attempt.'

'We have the best physicians here in London, and your mother has informed them that nothing will go wrong with them. I saw Stanning just now, looking tense: I advised him not to visit his wife looking anything less than cheerful. I hear she is eager to be at the dining table and the little girls are attentive to both ladies, hardly leaving their rooms. Oh! Here is Stanning. Give Jem my greetings, Philip.'

'Nicholas, try not to worry! I'm sure all will be well. Her sickness will come to an end, probably quite soon.'

'I hope it does this time. She lost the first baby because of the sickness, I believe. I have another problem now. My father has been suffering badly from the stone for almost a year, and the doctors say it must be removed. I need to be in Devon at his side, to help with his public duties. Pepys tells me he should make a good recovery, but my father is not a young man. I can't leave Anne in London alone, so I hope she will be able to travel.'

'If there is any doubt, Nicholas, I recommend that you leave her with us. As her parents, we are as anxious as you. Think about it: coach travel in this weather would be better avoided. Excuse me, Nicholas, I see a carriage drawing up: our first guests are early.'

'George! Delighted to see you, and M'Lady Anne! Allow me to kiss your hand. I suppose muddy Essex has dry roads after this hot weather. I saw the Coldstreams parading for the King two days ago. He is very impressed by them, George. A clever demonstration of your swift change of loyalty; but the King enjoys quick responses!'

'Here is Bess, she will attend to you, Anne. George, let me lead you to refreshment, we old fellows are born survivors! Montague and Harrington will be here soon.'

'Edward! Jemima! I am so pleased you are here, and Catherine and her sister. Girls, you will find Louisa and the others upstairs in the nursery: we have planned some entertainments for you. Off you go!'

'We have prepared an early meal for close friends to begin at 1pm. and at about 4pm. other old friends and associates will arrive, and enjoy conversation and entertainment on the parterre, and in the orangery. The Moncks are here, but not the Clarendons, though they live very near, so I am not concerned. Then there is Tom Dowse, and Anthony may come after closing time at the factory. Philip is somewhere about and James will be here for the dinner, he is between ships at present, but has been serving at St Kitts.'

'Father! I've seen Edward Hyde's coach lumbering this way: I can't imagine why he is not using a small carriage!'

'He places great stress on position and status. I hope he sends it away; we don't want to block the street.'

'You probably know that Edward is being opposed from all sides at present, from the Court, Parliament and the pamphleteers. They are trying to blame him for de Ruyter's attack on the fleet; but you and I, Montague, know that he admires the Dutch.'

'I hear that you have persuaded Anglesea to buy the Naval Treasury post from you, George. I hope for another posting in England, and it may be my laSt I think Hyde would be wise to follow your example. Sir Edward Carteret believes that Monck may be planning to retire to the country, now that he has handed over his regiment, the Coldstream Guards.'

'That is very interesting: Bessy will be delighted!'

'Why would Bess be concerned, George?'

'This dinner is the result of Bess's desire to hold a celebration for all those who joined together to make the Restoration possible. She has seen the strain I have been under, to ensure that our success is not thrown away and wasted. Six years at the Admiralty is enough for any man; and I have other business concerns, with the colonies, to occupy me. Bess seems obsessed with time passing, and that we are ageing: so we should hand over to the next generation. I don't know why she is worrying about Time. She hasn't heard Newton and his theories, so I suppose it might be Philip, or even the King: they are both involved with clocks, time and navigation.'

'What is the connection between clocks and a reunion of old friends?'

'I'm not sure, but she has been in discussion with Frances Hyde, and believes that it is only a matter of time before Hyde is sacked or executed. She has tried to persuade him to resign, but, as you know, he is obstinate. She is the hostess of this dinner and she will be addressing us at the end of the meal and before the celebration for the successful purchase of our new house.'

'I had no idea, George So is this to be a farewell party? Surely not!'

'I've probably said too much.... And here is Harrington, looking subdued, and the two Dowses. They are both in manufacturing: the wife's family, you know! I must urge the ladies to join us in five minutes or so. Excuse me.'

'George! Can you not hear war breaking out all around you? Did some of the dogs just run past you? The girls were allowed to show their friends the puppies, but they have let them run all over the house. I will not have dogs in my dining room! I've sent James and the waiters to round them up and shut them away in the coach house. I am sending the little girls to you for a strict reprimand, and you must tell them they won't be allowed into the dining-room unless they are thoroughly chastened. Do not let them twist you round their fingers!

'Now here are the girls. Come along Louisa and Catherine. Sir George has something to say to you. When you have finished, George, the gong will sound and everyone must go to the dining-table in five minutes and no longer'

'Now don't look so frightened: you can tell me all about it, and then you will feel much better. No wonder your mother is so upset: it is a very important day! Now tell me how the dogs came to be in the house-you know they are not permitted….'

A long and confused narrative poured from them simultaneously, each adding personal supplements of their own innocence, and the sound advice ignored by the other, which they had offered.

'Well, that is a very sad story, and I am disappointed that such wise intentions were not heeded. You must remember that those dogs are very young, and make mistakes, and sometimes we all made mistakes, don't we? So, we must always try to learn from them, and not make the same ones again. I'm sure I don't need to say any more, so give me a big hug, then find your mother and tell her how angry I was, …and say you are sorry!'

The dinner was unusual enough to be a great success. Those present found that they enjoyed their dinner companions, at table, and Lady Jem and Lady Anne made valiant efforts to take part in the conversation, though they ate little. Lady Jem discovered a surprising need for cherries, and Anne confined herself to water. The little girls were charming company and sat very patiently during the speech. Sir George exercised verbal restraint and confined himself to expressing gratitude that they were able to attend and to ask Lady Elizabeth to reveal her unexplained purpose in bringing them together,

Her address was not long but it in its sincerity and generosity of spirit, very characteristic of the speaker. 'Yes,' she began, 'the dinner is intended as a reunion'. As such she felt that the present happiness was all that she hoped for. Family and friends, young people and old people were all together and sharing their memories of past success and tribulations. Perhaps they had not realised how much they shared: she would try to put the events into a new context.

'Whatever our present age, our lives have been shaped by the extraordinary events of the past twenty-five years. We are, all of us, survivors. Some are lucky to be alive and healthy. We all have felt grief for those who have not survived, whether killed in battle, drowned at sea, or whose lives had been cut short, as the result of illness. Those times are vivid in our memories; and now we contemplate the present time and the years of Plague and grief, the great Fire and the recent terror of the raid on the Medway. Even our youngest will never forget them.

'In all these events those who were left at home were left in fear and anxiety, wondering whether they would ever meet their loved ones again. Like Frances and Jemima, and many other women, I have remained at home, and in exile, wondering whether our husbands and sons would ever return; hearing dreadful rumours; or receiving no news at all, and telling puzzled children that all would be well.

'I was walking in the dusk at Cranbourne Lodge on 5 September, last year, and that dreadful wind was blowing, you will remember it had been for the past four days. It carried swirls of smoke and dreadful smells of burning wood, and tar and spices; and suddenly it seemed that the air was filled with coal-black snow, sticking where it fell, and I realised that it was fragments of charred and burning paper. I could imagine all the books in London bookshops and libraries burning, as they once burned heretical books when we were young. I ran to the house, terrified, trying to avoid the clinging fragments.

'When I looked in a glass later, I found one last piece firmly stuck to my hair. You have never seen this tiny piece of paper, George, but when you have examined it, please pass it round the table so that everyone may read it. This is what has prompted me to bring us all together. It contains only four words, but they seem to be all any of us really need to know about life. A sort of special knowledge to make us all question whether the trivia which fills our lives really matters. It is surely only "Now' that matters. We must think of the present for none of us can control the future, though we may be innocently damaging it.

'I am not one who gives credence easily to fortune tellers or horoscopes, but I feel quite sure that, with so much changing around us, we should consider changing some of our convictions which many find inappropriate and reject others, more suitable to our changed circumstances before we, like them, become obsolete. I am sure you will know George is hoping to find a replacement for the navy, to lead the navy with fresh vision. Lord Albemarle has shown the way by resigning his office, and James Harrington, who is here with us has decided to let his books survive or not, on their merits.'

'I think it is curious that Time itself should fascinate so many.' Clarendon was the first to responded. 'Philip has been telling me about the tendency of clocks to synchronise. I think Huygens has been experimenting with clocks also. Newton of course, is suggesting that time and motion are aspects of one thing called space, though for the life of me it seems pointless speculation.'

'If mechanical things may synchronise, is it surprising that two men should have the same thought at the same time, of that the whole of London could believe we must attack the Dutch.' Montague remarked.

'If that is so then we must reject the belief in Free Will as a divine gift given that we may all seek out the truth for ourselves,' Harrington responded.

'So, what then is Time?' asked Tom Dowse. 'Are you suggesting it is a substance? What do you think, Philip? Are the Illuminati of the Royal Society discussing it?'

'I know that Hooke is concerned, and I believe that Spinoza has given some thought to the matter.' Philip said. 'He once felt that God was perhaps an omniscient clock-maker who set the world going at the creation with a sudden explosion and sometimes resets it to keep time running on. I am more puzzled by Newton's idea that time is only a mathematical or geometrical concept and only existing to allow us to believe we are progressing to some destination beyond our imagination. Those are the basic principles of life. I feel like Hooke that if Newton is right, then God would have made nothing except sideboards, and commodes.

But may I follow my mother's ideas with some of my own. Let me explain.'

'Sir George, my father, loves the company of children, and I remember the wonderful time we spent when James, George and I were children, He taught us to swim and sail and built us tree houses and invented fine games. I know we all missed him when he was away from home; and he was often gone for so long that we thought he might have drowned at sea, like the fathers of boys we knew. I cannot understand where in Newton's plan, human nature and love enter his world of equations. Perhaps even so great a mind as Newton's has limitations, and he seems unable to encourage friendship, or publish his ideas for our benefit. Now that I am a father, I intend to follow my father's example in raising our children. I have a new use for my uncle's pond yacht.

'I know you connect me with time-pieces, but you must know that telescopes, quadrants and compasses are an equal intereSt I know my father and James will agree, when I say that great storms and fog are terrifying to all who go to sea, but what follows them may be more alarming by far. For then the question must be asked, 'Where are we?' Around us is the sea, which is rarely still, and the currents will be carrying us and the wind driving us onward, and we will fear unseen reefs, or sandbanks, until finally we arrive at a destination. Any coastline is welcome, but if it is unrecognised, it may not be friendly. Only a landing will reveal the truth.

'Telescopes and quadrants will not answer those questions for, whether it is day or night, you will not know the time because no timepiece works at sea and quadrants require sunlight. No chart can give you your position. A timepiece, unaffected by the plunge and swing of the sea, and utterly reliable, which would not rust or warp, would help to solve these problems. Even as a child I knew the problems my father would be facing. When my mother told to us not to worry, 'Your father is the best sailor in the world!' we knew that she was being brave to re-assure us.

'As you can see, our mother is showing her agreement'. I think every expert maker of timepieces hopes that he may be the man to devise a reliable chronometer. You probably know that the round world divides vertically into 360 segments so by measuring the distance a ship travels in an hour, one may estimate ones east and west position. If we draw 360 segments horizontally, we could, with aid of the accurate time, discover our position at sea. This would be of great value and save the lives of countless seamen and valuable cargoes.' The silence which followed was broken by George who stood, tapping the table for silence.

'Thank you, Philip, for that clear explanation of your research: I had not realised that you and your brother were caused such concern by my absences. Bess, my Dear, I know you have always allowed me to take considerable risks, because we both enjoy the opportunities life brings and have no desire to stagnate. I see that our sons have learned their bravery from you, and that Philip is determined to solve problems which he knows will improve the lives of many. Please let us drink a toast to Companionship, and Trust, and let us accept that Time must rule us all.'

'George! Have you escaped from your guests? I have been sitting still for so long listening to your son's lecture, that my leg is giving me hell!'

'I'll join you if I may, Edward. You will need your legs in good order for dancing this evening. I imagine you must be exhausted with all the extra tasks forced upon you recently. I hear you actually slept in your office two nights paSt'

'I was expecting to hear from an agent who was to report at five in the morning. I find that I work better under pressure-fortunately I have a sound constitution. Your Lady wife seems to have suffered badly from the effects of the Fire. Of course, Londoners live such peaceful lives since the Restoration, that they cannot take that sort of shock'.

'That business with Hubert must have must have been somewhat bewildering for the law to deal with, I would have thought?'

'Not really. I deal with so many cases of derangement, or those seeking attention by making false claims. I did my best to persuade the man to admit to the fabrication, but there was no sense in him. He was clearly seeking execution, and I suppose I provided for his need. I see you've taken to growing oranges, Carteret- and purchased a little place in the country too. Your wife will be better for a retired life. I hope we won't lose you on the Privy Council.'

'I'm not planning to retire from public life, but only from the Navy. I'm eager to rebuild London. Monck, I hear, is retiring from the Army. Have you any plans to pass on some of your responsibilities?'

'You mustn't listen to rumours, George. Most of these young ministers of the King seem to be idiots. I shall have to clear up the mess they make. No-one else can do it. I heard a rumour that the King thought that Buckingham would make a sound Lord Treasurer. That can't be true: he is almost bankrupt himself. You remember that trouble we had with his father. We were about to pass an Act of Attainder when he was shot by Felton, thank goodness. Do you remember, Carteret?'

George left Clarendon to continue pacing the orangery and returned to the house to find the next invited guests were beginning to arrive. He forced himself to ignore the qualms of guilt when reminded of Felton. Most of the ladies were invisible: as was apparent from their voices and laughter, they were upstairs with the maids, attending to their dresses or resting. The men were drinking the best London ale, and discussing the conduct of the war. In Clarendon's absence, he was the subject of strong criticism, mingled with great concern. Would the King recall parliament? If he did, would Clarendon be charged and Impeached? He was in charge of national finance, and therefore the loss of the Royal Charles was his responsibility. George wondered whether Frances Clarendon had appreciated Betsy's words. Clarendon had clearly not responded to the implicit suggestion of retirement, since he had not referred to it in his response to Bess: many felt he should have understood Bess's concern for his well-being. George felt that matters had therefore advanced too far for Clarendon to take a tactful retirement. He felt certain that Edward's fate was sealed, barring a miracle.

Drawn into the house by sounds of laughter and hearty greetings, George discovered the arrival of a steady stream of afternoon visitors. Most were friends and acquaintances, including Sam Pepys and his wife accompanied by Will Hewer. He took the opportunity to introduce them to Lord Brouncker and his constant lady companion. Their informal relationship was no longer questioned.

Bella smiled a greeting and remarked, 'We have been discussing the nature of Time itself, Mr Pepys. It was very profound and I'm afraid I was left wondering whether 'Old Father Time' was aware of this and whether, in due course 'Time will tell……

'Philip would probably refer you to Spinoza.' George responded.

'Brouncker, is he a member of the Royal Society?'

'He's a Jew and lives in Amsterdam under sufferance I'm told. Apparently, his opinions are too outrageous even for the Dutch. Hooke is the man to talk to: he may already be 'working' on it.

For an excellent mathematician, he is a genius for instant answers: I feel that if there is no obvious answer. Better not to waste time cudgelling your brain, Eh?'

When it seemed that the last of the guests had arrived, the great salon was cleared of most furniture so the preparations for dancing and music could be made. By means of whose long-standing relationship with the Chapel Royal, and Charles's Twenty-four fiddlers, a considerable number had volunteered to put aside their sacred anthems and overtures, and indulge in a selection of the latest popular music from the theatres and taverns.

An interval followed the first three sets, so that partners could be changed and refreshments taken. The first violin struck up a melody soulful and heart-warming, and the ladies hushed their husbands, and Sam Pepys was called upon to perform his latest popular song, 'Beauty Retire.' Accompanying himself on the lute, the violins joining in with the repeated final line. In response to requests, he gave an encore, then he and George led their partners onto the floor for a second set of dances.

Lady Hinchingbrook, Jem's aunt, expressed to Bess her pleasure that the Carterets were to rebuild Haynes Park. 'We will be relatively close neighbours, my dear. I shall introduce you to the Spencers when you have settled in. I believe you have met the De Greys. By the way, when is Jem's baby expected; she is enormous!'

'It could be any day: we have Surgeon Frazier standing by, in case of problems.'

'I think I saw your daughter, Anne, leaving the party just now. I hope she feels better soon.'

'Frances! No! Don't try to stand, I have some smelling salts here. Try to take deep breaths. I'll send a waiter for water.' 'Thank you, Bess. I feel a little dizzy, I am afraid, and I would like to lie down. I don't want to force Edward to take me home, he is so relaxed this evening, and he will want to stay and talk.

'I must thank you again, Bess! You tried so hard in your speech, to persuade Edward to offer his resignation, but your charming story about the fragment of writing, I'm afraid fell on deaf ears.'

'I had hoped that George and Monck retiring might persuade him, I didn't expect him to be affected by my story. In fact, Frances, it is not a story, but the absolute truth. Here is the water, I think you should take your carriage back to Clarendon House. You need to reSt I'll tell the coachman to return for Edward later: I can see he is talking to his usual group of admirers and will be talking for hours.'

On returning to Clarendon House early the following morning, Edward discovered his wife semi-conscious in her bed, and it was revealed by the doctor that she had suffered a life-threatening stroke. With care she made only a partial recovery and for some weeks lost her ability to speak and the use of her right arm. Clarendon's fate was sealed and he lost his post as Chancellor and was impeached, and sent into immediate exile. A short delay was permitted for the sake of his wife. His sons, however, did not share his disgrace and his impeachment was postponed out of sympathy for his wife. Her subsequent death finally permitted his impeachment and exile.

Other significant changes occurred coincidentally at about the same time. Prince James and Anne had a son on 4 September, named Edmund, Duke of Cambridge, and so the line of heirs apparent seemed secure at last. Anne, James reported, was very weak, and he was concerned about her and ever grateful for her generous love and devotion to him, which he feared he had betrayed in the past, but never again.

# ~ SIX ~

### CHAPTER TWENTY-FOUR

In London business continued as usual. On 3 July 1667, the Committee charged with the rebuilding of London, met in Whitehall to consider the redesigned plans submitted by Hooke, Wren and Evelyn. George was the first to arrive, Carteret House was being renovated following the Celebration and in preparation for the two imminent births. George excused himself, pleading urgent business at Court and felt a weight lifted from his shoulders as the door closed behind him.

The King was the only one in the room and three large plans were spread before him. They were beautifully drawn and although there was nothing recognisable in them, that was inevitable since familiar buildings were destroyed. The sinuous line of the Thames was clear and the Walbrook, Tyburn and Fleet rivers, and the Tower and London Bridge were identifiable at last. The planners had clearly attempted to provide something modern and well-planned, and suitable for the capital city of a wealthy, forward-looking nation eager to display the most advanced of modern design.

The first plan, seemed all straight lines, squares and rectangles, and was Hooke's contribution, but buildings, not shown, could be fitted into the geometric shapes. Measurements of the many plots were supplied! Wren's plan tended toward circles and crescents, scattered with squares and gardens. One large square was labelled 'St Paul's'. Although the site was only indicated, Evelyn's plan was complete with inserted buildings of a regular height, behind a sinuous Boulevard along the river bank where palaces named for the nobility were all equally noble and uniform. A parallel street contained churches interspersed with Guild Halls. The riverside boulevard was concluded beyond Westminster by a line of intricately planned pleasure gardens with groves of trees. Trees also featured throughout his inner-city plan.

'I see you are taken with Evelyn's plan, George? My family also approve your choice, of gardens and palaces: so like Paris. But the cost, George! Who could finance either of them? Not I, and I don't think Parliament will be likely to levy more taxes.

Charles placed Evelyn's plan before him. 'Where on this plan George, is the location of the wharves and warehouses?' The King gave him the disarming grin, generally used to avert expected criticism. George placed a finger squarely on the centre of the projected boulevard. 'I believe you are beginning to find the need for larger wharves and warehouses. Will the South bank be used for commerce and shipbuilding?'

'Impossible, Sir. They must be on the North bank beyond the Tower; That's where the manufacturers work.'

'I can see I shall never have a fine city like Bologna or Milan. Do you know Wren? When I was in Oxford in 1665, I was taken with the Sheldonian Theatre and its roof seems to defy gravity. It is the shape of the Roman Theatre of Marcellus but is a new original concept. Our new buildings must seem to speak for us and our ambitions, George.

During this and subsequent meetings, it was decided that land owners must be permitted to construct new buildings of brick and stone, and leave fire breaks between structures. Strand and Cheapside would be widened and straightened and landowners compensated for the land they lost. The Bishop of London was to provide details of all churches destroyed, and a team of Architects engaged to create new designs for them. A series of walks would be undertaken by the Committee to decide which buildings were worth restoring and which should be rebuilt, using fire proof stone where possible.

A few days later, George escaped from the house once more to avoid the squalling of George, his newly born grandson, whose appetite seemed insatiable, and rambled with Wren and some others among the wreckage created by squatters in the garden area of the old London Convent, whose orchards had sloped down to the Thames. They had come from St Paul's and George had not been aware of the dignified range of buildings on the North and South sides. Cromwell's death had delayed the completion of a church planned for the eastern end. The front, with two plain pairs of doors, was in plain faced stone, with a recessed area suggestive of large windows. The plain gabled roof projected some distance forward covering a paved and sheltered area, and was supported by four massive stone pillars of no particular order.

'What is it, Christopher? Not a church, surely?'

'This building scheme was financed in part by taxation under Cromwell's Government. Every large-scale development must of course have a place of worship for the needs of the local people. As you know, once the medieval churches were emptied and whitewashed, they were equally suitable for worship, market halls, auction houses and school rooms. They were full of wasted space, and repairs were difficult for a lack of old-fashioned stonemasons. This one was designed like a tithe barn. Large, so that hundreds could stand and see and hear the great divines invited to preach the gospel.'

'I wonder what you will design to recreate St Paul's?'

'One thing is certain, George. It will be difficult, because it will have to be replaced. Only a few things survived the fire, including John Donne's memorial and only a small amount of stone remains usable. Most of the stone was cracked by the heat, which was so great that the stone melted into strange shapes. Do you realise it was the largest of all the cathedrals in Great Britain? It cannot be rebuilt as it was originally, but its replacement must be large enough for the Christians of London to pray and show the power of the Church of England as the heart of Britain.'

'I dread the thought of a 'Tithe Barn' of that size and height. It would be horrid and terrible.'

'I agree, George. I hope for inspiration!'

'I'm going to ask those labourers why they are digging a hole at the side of the building. Surely no-one has come back to claim his buried treasure, or his Parmesan, like Pepys.'

'Forgive my curiosity, Master, but would you tell me why you are digging?'

'I thought I would have to satisfy your curiosity, George, before long. Don't recognise me, do you? Newfoundland, George? Cod fishing? You taught me to read Do you still draw like I taught you? Le Sueur, Pierre! Remember now?'

'Heavens! Petit Pierre. I can't believe it. You've changed somewhat. I think you would be able to pull a fishing boat ashore single handed! May I introduce my friend, Christopher Wren? He has been analysing this building for me. What are you digging?'

'I saw you at the iron works last Wednesday. You were trying to have bronze cast. I'm Kit by the way, Pierre: pleased to meet you.'

'Excuse me; I can see they have struck gold. If you wait you might have a surprise.'

'So, you and he used to fish in Newfoundland, and now you're the King's right hand man.'

*Restoration and Retribution*

'Pierre le Sueur et Cie is the premier makers of bronze statuary to the King of France.'

'The King is not so eager for my help as he was, I'm building a home far from London.'

'Several children, I suppose, George? I have six. Ah! That was the sound of a shovel striking metal. This may be interesting'.

'I became a grandfather, yesterday for the first time.'

'Congratulations! Look they are digging round something and it seems to be wrapped in sacking. And here, like a crow seizing its carrion, is M'Lord! I must speak to my employer.'

Turning aside, George was face to face with the florid face and huge wig of the Duke of Buckingham. 'I gather you are on the reconstruction committee, Carteret. None of your 'generous loans' at enormous rates of interest. On this occasion I shall be counting every pound: now the nation's finance is in my hands. Clarendon was dismissed from office yesterday and His Majesty honoured me with his neglected task. Now, let me see if these yobs have caused any damage.'

Wren rejoined him as a sizeable object, swathed in tatters of rotten sacking, was hauled to the surface and carefully unwrapped. An equestrian statue of King Charles I was revealed to public gaze. Villiers made an inspection and nodded approval as le Seuer removed some accretions of London clay.

'A fine piece of work, eh, Wren? My father commissioned it many years ago as a gift for His late Majesty, and it was not completed and delivered until 1642. In the circumstances, to save it from damage at the hands of the mob, I had it concealed in this holy place respected by Puritans, who had no idea what they were protecting.'

'I had thought we should commission statuary to replace those lost in the fire. This would be a fine first contribution, Your Honour.' Wren observed.

'Yes, indeed! I shall have it placed on a marble plinth at the entrance to Whitehall where it can be seen by former friends, as a reproof to their enemies. I take it, by your face, Carteret, you do not know of Clarendon's dismissal? He ranted at His Majesty for fifteen minutes at the Privy Council meeting two days' ago. The King showed forbearance, mentioning that he and his friends were well aware of his faults, but most accepted that he tried to correct them. After the Meeting he took the man aside, received his chain of office, and instructed him to leave the country as soon as possible.

I understand he has been somewhat slow in obeying.' So saying the Duke took his departure.

Having seen the statue loaded onto a cart, George decided that his young namesake, George, might be enjoying an afternoon snooze and there might be an opportunity for rest. It was not to be, however. He found Lady Jem and her mother, relaxing in comfort, while young George, limbs flung wide and breathing heavily, slept. Hushed to silence, a maid bearing coffee entering at that moment, George was ushered into the vestibule by the older woman. There he was informed that Bess had been sent for urgently, to attend the bedside of Frances Clarendon, who had suffered another heart attack on receiving the news of her husband's exile.

Philip had gone in support of his mother and possibly to express sympathy with the earl, and offer his own and his father's assistance. Philip was aware that Henry and Lawrence Hyde had been informed and had been assured by the king that their father's exile would not be to their detriment, although the King would appreciate it if they could expedite their father's departure. The king explained that he was about to recall parliament, and the members would call for an Act of Attainder against their father. He would be bound to grant it.

Charles ensured that Clarendon's exile was broadcast and the news came as a great relief to the less supportive members of parliament who believed that Clarendon was in favour of toleration for Catholics. Clarendon's devotion to his wife was well known and his sons did what they could to relieve his distress. He had begun, as long ago as 1643, to keep a report of the proceedings of Parliament and of the King and court, for use when untrue accounts of events circulated. He had added, from time to time an account of his own actions and motives, and described exactly the characters of many of the personalities shaping the events of the Civil War. Following the Restoration he had added an account of its progress and subsequent events. Charles II had been aware of this and had probably contributed memories of his own actions.

Clarendon pleaded for continued access to Privy Council and other state papers so that he could transform the material into a complete account of The Civil War to inform posterity of the importance of the events. Nothing similar had ever been attempted in England. Charles had read considerable sections of Clarendon's book, and found it extremely uncomfortable reading. He not only rejected the request for access to State Papers, but also forbade its publication. Initially, he proposed to confiscate all that was in Clarendon's possession. He permitted the writer to continue on condition that if anything came to his notice which he thought to be untrue, Clarendon would be arrested and tried for treason. None of his writing was to be published in Britain or abroad on pain of death.

Lady Clarendon failed to respond to the best medical treatment available and died on 8 August 1667. Her widower found a new home in France but remained in England at the Great Tew estate to perform his wife's obsequies and burial in the family vault there. He continued to assert his innocence and the injustice of his dismissal, spoken to him by the King in private. He hoped for a trial by his peers. He continued to practise law and prosecuted several who denied him legal justice. Despite the friendship the Carterets had demonstrated for him, he did not fail to prosecute George Carteret for the felling of a line of mature oaks marking one boundary of his estate. The Hydes had always been advocates for tree protection.

This action against George was in reference to the felling which had taken place the previous autumn. A Parliamentary instruction had, because of a dearth of mature oaks for ship building, instructed landowners to fell oaks not fully mature. George, as Royal Forester, was ultimately responsible for the cull which was performed by government agents, appointed by the Sheriff of Oxfordshire. If George had been aware of the felling, he would not have challenged a government order, and Edward would surely not wish to be seen as a privileged landowner. His action had not been illegal, and the case was dismissed. No apology by George could repair the damage caused.

Young George was a large and healthy boy whose peremptory demands were always loudly announced. Fortunately, Jem had an easy delivery and was not one to demand a lengthy lying-in. She was needed to assist with Anne, whose sickness was no longer constant, and lend a sympathetic ear to Bess, who was deeply saddened by the misfortunes of the Clarendons.

George was delighted by his grandson and Philip was bursting with pride although, when congratulated, he was modestly dismissive. Jem was showered with attention and gifts. Her younger sisters were frequent visitors, and Edward Montague sent a congratulatory message from his ship. His anxiety was reserved for the members of the Royal family and its supporters. Perhaps because he had less frequent involvement, the departure of Clarendon from the Privy Council did not seem to have created a more co-operative situation in council, and the Cabal, who were strongly opposed to him, were now open to criticism from all sides. They seemed to become more open in their views and disparaging about the actions of others. The central unspoken dilemma concerned money, religion and the succession.

Following a meeting of the Rebuilding Committee, George was taken aside by Prince James, who offered his congratulations to Philip and Lady Jem on the birth of a son. That said, he stated that Princess James and he would be grateful if Lady Carteret, and he, would join them at St James's for an informal meal the next day. George accepted the invitation and it was clear that James had nothing to add except to say a plain carriage would collect them after mid-day. Decisions taken included the rebuilding of the Guildhall, the centre of City government, the Stock Exchange and the Exchequer: these were to be priorities, and the plans for St Paul's would be opened for tender.

Bess was not surprised at the invitation, and expressed her suspicion that Anne, (Princess James) was probably concerned about their children. 'He and Anne usually come to visit us in a plain carriage, and if we are not to take our own coach tomorrow, there must be confidential matters to discuss. Anne will naturally be upset by her mother's death. She and James felt unable to attend her Catholic funeral, poor things!'

When the one-horse carriage arrived at the palace they were conducted first to a cloak room and then through glazed doors into a covered terrace open to the sun and fresh air, looking over the parterre. The Prince greeted them warmly expressing his pleasure at seeing them after the terrors of the past year. He led them to an alcove where Anne was seated, on a couch supported by cushions and, though she smiled with pleasure in greeting them, George and Bess were shocked by her sallow complexion and stoutness. Chairs were brought and they sat talking of Anne's parents and the difficulty they had found in offering help. James wanted to help his father-in-law, and had to make their offers through Lawrence and Henry, since any direct help they offered would be seen as political interference: they might consider it to be behaviour expected between father and sons, but more reprehensibly, they would be supporting a disgraced statesman punished by impeachment, and an enemy of parliament. In addition, they would know that the King was increasingly irked by Clarendon's open criticism of his actions. This might be seen as an attack on the King's judgement.

The Carterets indicated their entire understanding with their difficulty and Anne said that her mother had expected the Privy Council to instruct her father to resign. She had come to appreciate Bess's words about the need to recognise when retirement was the best course of action, which she believe Edward had understood but had chosen to ignore. He had strongly reproached George and Monck, for choosing to retire at a crucial time, when their advice was essential. She remarked that her mother's last coherent request was to offer thanks to Bess for her kind intention.

Once any misunderstandings had been clarified, James's mood lightened, and he called footmen to set a table and chairs, before an elaborate picnic was brought, and wine poured. He reminded George that in St Helier, he had enjoyed being in the open air, when possible.

'I often see you riding in the Park: do you enjoy hunting, Sir, as you used to?'

'I hunt at least twice a week during the season, and now we have a racecourse at Windsor, we can run on the flat, or steeplechase throughout the year. The King and I were swimming in the Thames this morning, and turned it into a race. I beat him home. Of course, I'm younger than he is, which made the difference!'

'I gather you had a very fine retirement party, Sir George, I hope the Navy will continue to have your sound advice. I've been sidelined after the Medway raid, and I learn it is to be run by a committee. I believe you will be included or it will be a disaster. I fear there will be further expenditure reductions.' James paused and seemed to gather his thoughts, as though preparatory for something important. George noticed that Anne's attention was on her husband as though they had agreed on what was to follow. Both Carterets resigned themselves to an overlong account of some personal grievance: an aspect of James's mercurial nature, and his tendency to act precipitately and be torn with regret later.

'I don't know if you were in London, or involved in the Fire last year,' he began, 'and you probably don't know that His Majesty, allowed me to take the Guards Regiments to help delay the spread of the fire. I was amazed that the Lord Mayor and Corporation gave permission for me to march an army into the City. It was a great compliment - you will remember my father was forbidden to enter the City without permission after he tried to arrest those five MPs. I know the Aldermen believe I am a danger to the citizens, so they must have felt very worried.

'We went in on Tuesday and toiled like slaves until Friday - and we were successful! I was delighted, and the Mayor and Corporation came out in their robes to thank us. I will never forget it! It is wonderful to be cheered. I hoped that they might have seen that I was not their enemy.'

'No, Anne, please don't cry again. The fact is, George, it all ended badly: in my experience, my actions are plagued by misfortune. You and Bess are the only people we can speak to in confidence, knowing your discretion. I may not discuss this matter with my brother, who continues to find me untrustworthy. I seem to fail him constantly, he dismisses me from the navy, then sends me away to govern Scotland, or sends me to Paris, anything to undermine my confidence. I think he would have preferred it if my young brother, Henry had lived, and I had died. You have younger brothers George, but I know how much you trust them.' The prince ground to a halt, and George hoped that he would overcome his reluctance to speak, and come to the point. His brother must have found his hesitancy annoying.

'I know you have both faced dreadful losses recently, the deaths of Lady Anne and two more of your daughters. I can barely imagine your grief and here you are, going about your lives as though you have somehow been able to set sorrow aside. You must believe that I wished to present my sympathy to you in person, but had to think of my brother's safety, and stay by his side in Windsor.'

'We appreciate your sympathy, Sir. We heard of the sad death of Prince James, who survived the usual perils of infancy. He was like your shadow, always chattering and showing you his discoveries I sorely miss my daughters, and the loss of my mother-in-law, Anne, was a dreadful tragedy. Not only had she educated the girls, but without her assistance I would never have gone to sea. She persuaded my father to appoint my brother to take on my administrative tasks in Jersey, allowing me to join the Navy.

'Enough about me, James: are you able to explain the cause of his death? Was the Plague responsible?'

'No, George, I was responsible! I was dealing with the fire: hoping to prove my worth to my brother. It was a difficult time, Anne was soon to give birth, and I wanted to be at her side. James wanted to know where I was going, for he had seen me arriving, black with smoke, to change my clothes and sooth my burns. Anne showed him the clouds of smoke, and said I was helping to put out the fire. Then he saw the Westminster School boys, carrying buckets of water. He wanted to be allowed to help me, and asked his tutor to take him, and was refused. On the fifth day, when I was fighting to save the Middle Temple, a laundry girl saw him struggling with a bucket of water in the stable-yard pond, and in danger of drowning. He was pulled out, protesting loudly, and cleaned up. He was so pleased to tell me about his adventure.

'I was angry that his nurse had left him alone. She had seen him playing happily with toy soldiers, not wandering about!' Anne murmured. 'The next day he was full of life and I was with him when he became feverish and was sick. Dr. Frazier thought he might have swallowed pond water. He was very sick, which was a good sign, for then he slept and later woke feeling better,'

When he saw me, he smiled and said, 'Father! I went to bring water. He grew feverish, and died that night. I tried to avoid distressing Anne, but she insisted on seeing him, and collapsed from the shock. The new baby we were expecting died soon after birth, to our distress. We managed to baptise him, Edgar, just before he died.'

Anne intervened at this point, 'Dr Frazier has tried to relieve the constant pain I have. He tells me it will not be possible to carry another child.'

The men walked in the parterre while Bess remained with Anne, attempting to help her deal with the anguish she felt. She was inconsolable at the fate of her parents and the loss of two sons in one year. An earlier son, Charles, had died aged one.

'George. Has the King mentioned to you that two of his nephews have died? He has said nothing to me, even when we have been riding or swimming. I believe I have failed him again!

'I have several living illegitimate sons, and he has at least seven to my knowledge, but none of our sons can become King. Queen Catherine and he have been married for sixteen years and, as yet, she has had two miscarriages. He is devoted to her and is often with her, and even goes to the archery butts with her and fishes with her on the River Lea. He won't think of divorce, and remarriage, and neither of us seems able to produce an heir. I am my brother's heir, and Mary, our daughter, is next in line of succession.

'I understand that that wretch Ashley Cooper, is encouraging the Duke of Monmouth to assert his right to the throne, because he is an outspoken

Protestant. I am a communicant of the Church of England and so are my girls. Anne, of course has always been a Catholic, and so is the Queen. Ashley knows that the Anglican succession is safe with us.

'The King and I have tried, like Clarendon, to encourage religious toleration, but parliament wants to impose Conformity. It is driving some of the best people in Britain to settle abroad. I don't know how it will end, and the King seems to be afraid of provoking unrest by making any public statement.'

'You know you have our sympathy, Sir,' George responded. My advice is to remain patient: Difficult situations sometimes resolve themselves, if not stirred up. Worry less, like your brother, if you can. Racing at Newmarket begins next week and I hear Old Rowley is the horse to watch. Anne may regain her strength soon, and one day, when we have completed Haynes Park, you will honour us with your company. It's relatively close to Newmarket.'

## CHAPTER TWENTY-FIVE

The remainder of the year 1667 was marked by the growing tension between Royal supporters and parliamentarians. The term 'Tory' was an increasingly pejorative label for anyone who supported the meagre standards agreed for government in the Breda Declaration. The clearer standards set by the Cromwell administration, had been utterly refuted in the hysteria of the restoration. 'Whig' was a term used to annoy politicians who wanted firmer lines of demarcation, with, particularly, limitations on Royal powers over army and navy, They even demanded that all government ministers should be Anglicans. These issues bedevilled British life for the next twenty years, resulting in mass emigration, biased political and legal decisions, and, inevitably, led to the burning of books, and the executions of the innocent.

George's Irish appointment was a welcome change and brought him into close contact with Lord Ormonde. Placed in charge of Ireland following the contentious rule of Henry Cromwell, Ormonde managed, by fair and just means, to reconcile the Presbyterian/Catholic antagonism, encouraging commerce and industry. Ireland began to be economically sound. George's task was basically a supporting role. It was not unlike the policies he had adopted in Jersey in the 1640s.

Westminster Whigs, having dismissed Clarendon, soon discovered another target, in the form of Ormonde. He possessed many of the qualities which they deplored. He was a Royal appointee, and an old friend of the King; the linen trade he was encouraging and improvements in agriculture, were undermining English trading rights, and trading with France and America. He was a committed Anglican, but had the strong support of the Catholic Archbishop of Dublin and therefore was a dangerous Catholic supporter. Therefore he might do what Strafford was alleged to have promised, ie. to bring an Irish army to murder loyal Protestants in England.

Charles attempted to refute these accusations, but this was considered a demonstration that the King himself was a closet Catholic, like his brother. James, who was an Anglican communicant, began to think more about his personal religion. It was against this background that George took up his appointment. Like Ormonde, he was also a Royal appointee and parliament had not been consulted. George decided that once the King replaced Ormonde with a Whig applicant, he would seek a purchaser for the Treasurership. Irish economic success meant that he sold his post at a good profit. The new Governor imposed the required harsh restrictions on Catholics and the island became impoverished, although the poor were willing recruits for English regiments.

Young George Carteret continued to flourish in the quiet of the Bedfordshire countryside, and was soon able to walk, and then to talk. Jem, and the Carterets and Hinchinbrookes, became good neighbours, and met local families, including the Cromwells, who had reverted to being careful landowners. Sad news, however arrived from Devon, where Anne Stanning had died giving birth to her child. The daughter survived and passed into the care of her grandparents. Stanning, Philip was displeased to learn, was already seeking a new wife. George and Philip had joint trading concerns to run, and increasing trade and administrative business, involved in the expanding line of colonies on the eastern seaboard. Fortunately, the Piccadilly house was easily adapted for office space. Stock Exchange trading was on the increase, and moved into a new Exchange building in the following year.

The new Haynes Park presented a strong landscape feature with its newly created vistas of trees and lakes, which had benefited from Evelyn's advice. Most of the following years, saw George and Philip travelling to their manorial holdings to see that everything was in good order. It usually required a team of four, including clerks, who always patronised a local hostelry, to smooth local relationships in the countryside.

Until November, Clarendon remained in England, determinedly working on his History and protecting his inheritance for his children, and his reputation. He seemed to believe that his demotion was a trivial oversight on the King's part, that he would be restored to favour at an appropriate time. Parliament finally insisted that he must be forced into exile, and Clarendon once again ignored their order. An Act of Attainder was rushed through both houses, as a direct result, and with the King's total agreement was signed into law. If Clarendon returned to England, it stated clearly, he would be executed for Treason. There was no alternative and Clarendon set up a new home, in November 1667 in Rouen.

His departure created yet another hiatus in the management of the

Royal Africa Company and the English possessions on the American coaSt The African venture had made a number of false starts, caused by lack of investors, but became more popular as it began to produce the promised wealth. The whole west coast of Africa, and the East coast of America, was claimed by Charles as British possessions. This was hotly contested by the Dutch, who had historic proprietorship of both coasts, and also the naval strength to justify their claims. Carteret was now the leading proprietor of America, but could not drum up regular investments to keep the colonies solvent, and fed, when adverse weather or smallpox prevailed.

The Dutch Wars, of the next decade, were the result of these problems and the Command Economy under De Witt, in Holland, was entirely aimed at overseas domination. The resulting war was strongly contended, Britain only gaining control of New York and New Jersey with French assistance in threatening the Dutch inland states in Europe. Britain had entirely failed to make any headway in the East Indies; and was being denied access to African resources by the superior power of the Dutch navy, and their well-defended coastal ports.

Clarendon's exile left Carteret standing alone and unprotected. Charles needed constantly increasing supplies of cash, denied him by parliament. The increasing trade in slaves between Africa and America was the obvious answer, but it was not until 1673 that it became possible. Hitherto the De Witt brothers had made Holland the wealthiest nation in Europe by their close and democratic rule of every aspect of Dutch life. The four landlocked Dutch provinces however did not share the wealth of the coastal 'United Provinces' which controlled international trade. The crux came when the French Army marched into the four inland states and they were captured by France. The remainder of Holland was then open to invasion, and the people blamed the De Witts and threatened them with treason. William of Orange was a mere Duke, but he offered to lead them to victory if he was created Stadtholder. He attacked the French and allowed the De Witts to be brutally executed. His mother was a sister of Charles II and he was a Protestant and finally married Prince James's daughter, Mary. Each of them were half Stuart by birth and therefore both were heirs to the Throne of Britain.

At Christmas, 1667, Lady Elizabeth mentioned Amyas Carteret, who had ceased to be as frequent a visitor as he had been. George, with some regret, mentioned Amyas to Jarvis, who replied with the fact that he had seen Amyas very recently. George penned a rapid note, and despatched a clerk to deliver it to his address. The response arrived the same day. In his reply Amyas regretted that his health was making him less active, but that he would appreciate it if he could visit Carteret house that afternoon. He added that he had unexpectedly been contacted by an old friend on a matter of some urgency. George replied that he would be available at any time that afternoon.

When they met George was pleased to see that Amyas had not lost his energetic manner, showing reliance on a walking cane. He no longer wore a sword. Greetings and family enquiries over, Amyas got down to business. He had recently been asked to meet by an old friend, John Thurlow who was known to George, and wanted to disclose some disturbing matters, which he felt should be conveyed to the Authorities with some speed. Amyas pointed out that he no longer concerned himself in matters of state but suggested that he, George, would be the best man to inform. Such was Amyas's concern, that George agreed to meet him the following morning at his Lincoln's inn home.

Once Cromwell's Spymaster, he now had no official powers since the restoration, but such was his ability that Clarendon had paid him a salary to continue to work for the good of the country. He had the support of Monck and had to relinquish his post as MP for Ely before he was removed. His information, gained by trusted spies, helped Clarendon to nip in the bud numerous plots to sabotage the Restoration or assassinate the King. When George paid his visit next day, Thurlow revealed that he had a high regard for George, and trusted him implicitly. He hoped that he would listen to his concerns as matters of great importance. George was astonished when Thurlow suddenly addressed him as "Milton", the name given him by a secret British agent, in the years when he was working in France.

Thurlow disclosed that he no longer felt free to continue his espionage efforts, since the dismissal of Clarendon (whom he had trusted) and his probable replacement, whom he was reluctant to trust. He felt that the 'CABAL,' now in charge, had conflicting interests concerning the powers of government and the Toleration recommended in the Breda Treaty. It was certain that the King was bankrupt and while paying off his greatest debtors, would probably renounce his remaining obligations, if he could find a way

*Restoration and Retribution*

to finance himself with minimal government assistance.

George was amazed at the shrewd understanding of national affairs Thurlow displayed and asked him to explain his deep concern. Thurlow predicted social unrest in the future between the dissident Protestants as the King suggested allowing Catholics and small dissident sects to play a full part in public affairs, including the Army and the Navy. Ministers were divided on these questions and Shaftesbury and Osborne were sizing up each other and preparing for conflict. The King would be forced to make invidious choices.

George remarked that perhaps Thurlow was unnecessarily alarmist: after all, with all his confidential information, he had played no part in saving the Commonwealth Government when Cromwell died.

Thurlow justified himself by asserting that no-one believed that Cromwell was about to die. Even his wife considered that he was merely undergoing one of his personal crises, when he doubted his own worth and lost his personal faith. They had several candidates to replace him, if he retired, including Ireton and Henry Cromwell. The former had devised a new constitution, and Henry Cromwell was his father's chosen replacement. George was surprised by this news, and asked what went wrong. Thurlow explained that, at his unexpected death, Henry Cromwell was in Ireland, taking control in place of Ireton, Oliver's son-in-Law who had died from typhoid. Since it was mid-winter, storms prevented Henry's delayed return, and he, Thurlow, had persuaded Richard Cromwell to head the government until Henry's return. Unfortunately, other army officers had insisted on making Richard's appointment permanent. The rest is history, as they say.

George complimented Thurlow for his efforts, and for accepting the new situation created by his failure with such foresight. Thurlow felt encouraged to be open concerning his present fears. He agreed with George that much political unrest existed beneath the surface of increased trading strength and the new attractions of legalised gambling, horse racing and public celebrations following Plague and Fire. Two matters concerned him at present. The first was the growing strength of secret plots and conspiracies disclosed every day by his agents: they were doubling in number every month, and Constables and Magistrates were hard pressed to keep up the rate of prosecution and punishment. Fortunately, many folded up due to incompetence or informers. Fortunately, they were so disparate in their aims that none had yet found a leader to make them formidable. But that time would come, he was sure.

'I believe that I may have become an object of interest to one of these groups: someone holding a grievance against me, may be planning my harm. Possibly I have information to his disadvantage, or may be seen as a growing threat. I may be myself in potential danger. I had news recently from one of my best agents of a plot to kill the King. He came to me by appointment and with every precaution and after dark. His visit was brief and he went on his way. My neighbours include retired judges and magistrates and we work together for our mutual protection. We had spoken while under close surveillance by neighbours I can trust. His visit roused no fears.

'As one of my few legal duties. I stand in for local coroners under pressure of work. I was asked to perform a post mortem recently on a body dredged from the Thames. The corpse was quite decayed, but I recognised it as the body of my visitor. He had been cruelly mistreated before being killed by a blow to the skull with a blunt instrument, perhaps a mallet He had no identification on him. I could not identify him, and never learned his name, though I knew him to be honest and trustworthy.

'Some days later, my neighbour remarked that he had noticed a stranger lurking in the field on several occasions and, opening his door recently, had surprised a man standing in his porch, who hurried away ignoring his challenge. I have taken the precaution of setting my friends to watch my house while you are here, and I can tell you that no-one has observed your presence.

'I am confident that you will be able to contact those agents at court who are at your service, so that they must be more than usually watchful'

Taking notice of the warning, George mentioned the incident to the King, who knew of Thurlow's reputation, and notified the agents he employed as Lord Chamberlain of immediate danger. He took Jarvis into his confidence who promised to ask his friends among the city underworld to report on public speakers who were gathering large audiences, and to alert those with intimate knowledge of the Lincoln's Inn Fields.

In the meantime, George and Philip were experiencing an influx of successful trading ventures. For some time, partly at the suggestion of Lord Brounker and Samuel Hartlib, they had collected Stock Exchange reports for the past few years, and made a painstaking effort to produce statistics to show the trends in exported goods which seemed most rewarding to

*Restoration and Retribution*

investors. In 1658, while George was trading from St Malo, he bought a book written by Blaise Pascal, a French mathematician, who had amused himself by throwing dice, and had found that any particular number could be expected to land uppermost after a consistent number of throws.

He had memorised the accuracy of his prediction quite easily for only the numbers 1-6 were involved, and found he could, while throwing dice repetitively, count the falls of each number and win the bet, if he was competing with another thrower, His claim was that there were natural laws of "Probability" and that they could be applied to trading ventures, if the prevalence of certain materials could be formulated.

George realised that he based his own trading ventures on his memory of previous successes, and tried out Pascal's theory during dice challenges among his friends, after experimenting with his son. He found that his chance of winning increased by a considerable percentage. He knew that when playing card games, he often won by being able to recall the card played by his opponents and retaining the card which would win the trick. His commercial gains of the past year were evidently the result of their labours with statistics. Fellow Royal Society members were fascinated by the dice throwing game, but his fellow traders dismissed its application to trading practice, preferring to rely on their 'Instinct' which also brought them success at the races.

Shortly after setting his agents to work at Thurlow's behest, he heard talk at Gresham's of the remarkable successes of a professional gambler, who was frequenting the more high-class London gambling clubs. Gambling and purchase of Lottery tickets were the latest craze among the wealthy and their womenfolk. Barbara Castlemaine was an irrepressible gambler, betting hundreds of pounds on the throw of a die. She generally lost and the King smilingly paid her debts, although Carteret discovered that Charles was visiting her less frequently during her current pregnancy, and had told her he refuted her assertion that he was the baby's father. She should look to John Churchill for child support. Barbara was told that she must take responsibility for her own losses. As perhaps a final Royal gift, she was given Nonsuch Palace in compensation.

Repeated success at the gambling tables generally resulted from a conspiracy of deception, but a few continued to make consistent gains despite increasingly close observation

Carteret's curiosity was roused and he and Philip went as observers to his preferred club, and studied the flow of cards and dice with great care. Mingling with other observers, they realised that cheating was not taking place. George and his son compared observations and concluded that others shared remarkable memory for the game in hand, and George's own retentive memory.

Philip and he had just decided to bring their observations to members of the RS among whose members was Sir William Petty, knighted for reorganising the finances and land ownership of Ireland, and an old acquaintance. Among other friends were French bankers, and Italians, where the science of money valued as gold and silver had developed into a science. These were collectively referred to as Lombards in London. In Edinburgh William Law, a wealthy goldsmith, was about to inaugurate the first Assay Office, encouraged by Prince James, who was determined to place firm standards for the coinage. London, in 1678, was not ready for this move, in part because the stability of money was subject to wild fluctuation to accommodate the whim of the King. Thomas Neale was master of the Mint and Groom Porter to the King: a link which would have to be broken in the interest of closing a dangerous conflict of interests. Proof of probity was constantly being demanded. Neale was an unscrupulous property speculator, and among his Royal duties was the provision of playing cards, dice, and gambling equipment for the royal palaces. He was a compulsive gambler himself, and was said to have run through two fortunes at cards. Gresham, who had set up the first bank to lend money on credit, had died before he had achieved his aim. He had planned to place the money market under firm regulation and create a Bank of England. This would have set a firm standard for gold, the basis of all trade, Gold was minted in many countries and since many coins had been "clipped" to forge other coins, there was no certainty of their value. In the interim, those seeking to borrow genuine gold, would apply to the London Goldsmiths, who would demand security on any loan. They were no more prepared to provide loans to the King, whose debt was unfathomable, and George, despite a large income, could no longer sponsor loans for the King at his own risk.

# ~ SEVEN ~

## CHAPTER TWENTY-SIX

During their discussion of the King's renunciation of his debts, a waiter brought a message 'Mr Jarvis wished to speak to Sir George urgently.' In the reception area Jarvis informed him that a Mr. Thurlow had been attacked and viciously beaten by a stranger that afternoon, putting his life in danger. Jarvis had received from him a request for another meeting with George that day. Full of concern, George summoned a carriage and went to Lincolns Inn.

Thurlow was at home being treated for his grave injuries. His attacker had used a crow-bar to break open his door then turning it on Thurlow. He had been thrown to the floor and beaten, but the cramped space had protected him, and the instant arrival of Amyas and a Constable had brought an end to the attack. They were approaching the house from two directions when a nondescript passer-by some yards ahead, launched an unexpected attack on Thurlow's door, bursting it open. Thurlow had been taken completely by surprise and not seen his attacker. Fortunately, the culprit had been detained while escaping. Amyas had thrust his cane between his legs as he ran, and the constable, slow-moving but heavy, had fallen on top of him before attaching handcuffs. Thurlow was slowly recovering and expressed gratitude to his rescuers.

Carteret later engaged a man to remain with Thurlow, round the clock, for care and protection. Amyas and he walked back to his lodging together. The attack had occurred earlier, and in broad daylight, and Amyas and the constable had arrived by chance. The attacker had been dragged before the nearest Magistrate who had no hesitation in remanding him to await trial. He wondered whether the attacker might have previously killed Thurlow's agent. He might ask the prosecuting magistrate to enquire. It did not appear to be a random attack, but had the attacker thought he would not be observed?

'Amyas, I think I must speak in confidence to the Magistrate. Thurlow was eager to tell me that there was a real threat to the King's life. The trusted agent who warned him, died by drowning following his visit. He may have attempted to silence Thurlow, who might hold information.'

'The attacker seemed less than professional, surely? To break and enter in daylight and injure Thurlow's legs!'

Amyas interjected, 'Perhaps, George, it was intended to frighten him. A threat of worse to come, and to warn witnesses that we might receive the same treatment. Do you think that is possible?'

'If that is so, it implies a genuine plot, organised by a clever manipulator. I believe I must speak to the Magistrate, and perhaps I will send Philip to tomorrow's hearing. What did you say his name is?'

'Edmund Godfrey: he is quite well known and very thorough. He actually represents St Martin's ward, but happened to be spending the day with his brothers who are his partners in a building-supply firm, and the Constable had spoken to him earlier.'

'I've met Godfrey. I didn't take to him, but he has a sound reputation for thoughtful and fair questioning. He will probably get to the truth. I will speak to him before the hearing.'

When George told Godfrey that he feared the attack could herald a plot against the King, and the attacker might now fear discovery, he found Godfrey ready to support the suggestion. His first impression of the attacker had been the man was too stupid to have planned the attack: but he would investigate his identity, and question friends and neighbours who knew him. If he was part of a plot, he would extract the facts. He would imprison him in the meantime for common assault, and make further enquiries.

The hearing next day was inconclusive. William Brown was as simple as Godfrey had thought. He was an unemployed drayman formerly employed, and then sacked for giving the goods he conveyed to anyone claiming to be the named recipient. He had no home and ran errands for money. He had been offered a pound if he found a crowbar, broke into a house and beat up the owner, who was a murderer. He was supposed to collect his reward at the Waterman's Arms. But he had been arrested before he could make his claim and was broke. He couldn't remember his employer's description. "He was ordinary looking," was not helpful.

Philip added that Godfrey had undertaken to send constables to question Brown's acquaintances, and there was a surprisingly long list, for such a nondescript person. The enquiries produced nothing to his discredit, though he was well known for being gullible and inept. He was sentenced to a month's imprisonment, and Godfrey had the church commissioners provide him with food while serving his sentence. Both he and his victim thrived: Thurlow began to receive further messages about plots and conspiracies, and Jarvis and his contacts confirmed and added to this information. Jarvis offered, with some diffidence, that several mentions had been made of 'Israel' and 'Tongue,' gaining some notoriety from impromptu hell-fire sermons, particularly when plied with gin. To those seeking cheap entertainment, he would rage about the wicked behaviour of MPs, business men, and members of the Royal family, whose immoral activities he described in lurid detail, adding on additional perversions at the suggestion of his audience. He was surprisingly inventive, and some of his audience were disposed to be convinced by his tales, for they were certainly popular currency in the slums and alleys. Some of those questioned on Brown's behalf, also believed that the Lawyers at the Inns of Court led lives of deep depravity. Brown might be performing a public good, it was high time somebody exposed them!

Unfortunately, less than a month later, when Thurlow's carer went to his help, having heard him cry out, he found him semi-conscious. Several hours later he died as the result of a stroke, confirmed by a neighbouring surgeon. There was discussion subsequently about whether Brown should be tried for murder. It was finally decided that it would not be appropriate. At the end of his sentence, Brown was released to an anonymous fate.

The Carterets and other scientists among the RS members, had heard of the improved Scottish financial situation and met William Law, a new appointee, who impressed them with his knowledge of capital investment. They learned that in the previous century, Cardano of Padua University had experimented with dice and discovered 'probability' as a valid proposition. Galileo had come to the same conclusion, and it was one of the 'evil practices' for which he was tried. This was a century before Pascal reached the same conclusion. William Law was quite frank about his strange talent with predictable patterning of numbers. At least one of his sons had similar talents, and had joined the local Philosophical society, assisting Scottish businessmen to trust him with their order books, to study 'trends' in the market. Scottish businesses began to flourish, aided by the firm government imposed by Prince James, their popular regent.

Carteret and some others gained new insights from discussions with

Law, and together they attempted to introduce new practices to the London Stock Market. They had limited success for business was increasing steadily and most traders preferred to keep to their profitable and well-tried systems. They attempted to convince Treasurer Buckingham that it could help to fill the yawning gap in British national finance. Part of the discrepancy was due to Buckingham's incompetence, not unknown to Carteret, who favoured the new theories.

His friends were sympathetic, but if the Minister of Finance did not support the scheme, it could not have essential legal status. As a result, British trade continued to be directed by impulses of the moment, or memories of similar questions raised in the past. The improving rate of British trade inhibited any change. In European Universities, lecturers addressed students concerning new insights into algebra, the calculus, and the geometrical theories of Pascal and Fermat. Philip Carteret knew both of these men from his studies concerning time and motion under Huygens. He had broached one aspect of 'Time' in his response to his mother's innocent question on the subject several years earlier.

Louis XIV was all powerful in France and a remarkably perceptive ruler. He possessed the political strength to impose on his country an entirely new order affecting every aspect of life, and with remarkable success. His aim was to unite the several large nations of France into a united, powerful Kingdom. He imposed a unified legal system, and Courts of Justice. He created a French Academy to define and order a national French language, in part defined by Boileau, to be taught and printed throughout the country, and a scientific society through military academies in which the students would learn mathematics, surveying, engineering, and he financed the plan generously by encouraging the development of new industries to produce the finest china, glass, silks and satins, vineyards and refined spirits. All was intended to make France the acknowledged centre of European culture. These enormous ambitions demanded unlimited sums of money which were provided by the fact that France was the largest European country, with a population of seventeen million, and the largest amount of agricultural land in Europe. Fortunately, it also enjoyed a temperate climate. As his plan grew, it demanded a growing supply of money. Even France began to outgrow its financial means.

Louis and Charles wished to gain the admiration of other nations by other means than the tradition of invasion, conquest and despoliation. Attempts to raise envy were made, to show the attractions of economic and fiscal probity and the benefits experienced by the ordinary citizen. Louis was able to create a standard form of Christianity, and by means of the Academie Francaise, to create a national printed language and deny publication to any other. By controlling the French Treasury, Louis was able to invest in the creation of new industries and set new standards in products, directing scientists and academics to develop new theories, and put them into practice.

Charles was not in charge of a "Control" economy as his cousin was. He exercised considerable personal power, but could only exercise it to the extent permitted by industrialists and a parliament, eager to prevent Charles from spending, or increasing the amount gained by the Treasury in the form of taxes. The result was that the languages of the British nations remained and were taught in schools and published for public consumption. In France a national curriculum was emerging, and engineering and the sciences were taught to army and naval cadets. This was one area expanded, and academic studies, languages, the arts and philosophy were others. The King and the Church encouraged the growth of universal education and public sponsorship was available. There was a university in every large town, or a school of higher education.

These developments must be understood if one is to understand the unique situation in which the Carterets found themselves. They were well settled in London by 1670, and their children were well adjusted to British ways. As with parents everywhere they experienced the same concerns as parents of all times and nations. They would have been anxious about uprooting such tender plants and expecting them to adjust to very different educational programmes. Philip, aged 18, proved himself an able manager, trained in accounting and wise in investment, so it was the younger ones, particularly the girls, whose future was uncertain.

Philip had been educated as a child at the grammar school in St Peter's parish. As in France, the school was taught by a Regent, an Oxford graduate who had matriculated from one of the Jersey schools, and had chosen to return to guide the next generation through to university or to more traditional farming, fishing, and trading opportunities. Philip had been a willing pupil and in London aged 18, he was better qualified than all but a few British youths of his age. Taken from St Helier to St Malo, he passed naturally to the Education centre of Rennes Cathedral, where men of the Calibre of Descartes, Pascal and Fermat found employment. He was invited to join the intellectual cream of England when he joined the Royal Society, bringing with him his fascination with clocks, motion and lenses, having worked beside Huygens. He was a valued participant in their exploratory science.

James had followed his brother through the same process but, like his father, had a practical turn of mind. His father, George, had fought a determined battle against being sent to University, and had joined the fishing fleet, and grown up to be a strong-minded team member. James was born impatient and restless, eventually following his father into the Navy.

The girls were left behind in St Malo, where they were receiving a sound classical education, and developing their intellectual capacities, under the tutelage of well-educated Nuns of a famous teaching order. English boys and girls had no opportunity to study of this quality, available in France. Therefore the girls were to remain with the Nuns, until their parents could make a settled family home where their intellectual capacity would not be wasted.

In Britain the situation was different. Basic education before the Reformation and the Dissolution of the monasteries, had been generally available, but not compulsory. The dissolution closed 2500 Monasteries and over 200 Convents, many of which were education centres. Thus thousands of boys and girls were fortunate if they managed to acquire even basic skills. Edward VI permitted the opening of a limited number of Grammar schools, which taught Church of England beliefs, and tolerated no questioning. Boys learned to despise Catholicism and Presbyterianism as heresies. Bibles and prayer books printed in Latin or Greek were to be burned and only new books printed in English, and approved by the Stationery Office were to be sold.

The Commonwealth Government realised that Britain was falling behind in technological and academic skills, and that the two existing universities, educated boys whose parents could pay for them to attend, irrespective of their ability or personal wishes. Thinkers like Petty, Hartlib, Locke, Evelyn, and Challoner, had begun, as far distant in time as the reign of Charles I, to support the creation of fee-paying schools in the London area, where boys and girls could be educated.

When Elizabeth Carteret brought her two elder daughters to London, she had found Mrs Basua Makin, whose educational programmes were being copied by other school owners and were run by intelligent women for girls. The academies for boys, which taught skills needed in the new industries, gained a measure of support from ambitious employers, who were searching for mathematicians and accountants, but also surveyors, and potential engineers. Obviously, the ability to write and read would be an essential for those skills, and sensible boys, impatient with boring books and tedious writing, picked up these skills as a necessary hurdle on the way to success. In 1674, Pepys invested in a new Royal Mathematical School, encouraged by the King. Evelyn was paying favourable visits to several girls schools which had sprung up, unnoticed, in Wandsworth , Hackney and other areas where the newly rich had chosen to live.

The difference between the French and British systems was that one was universal and had a structured curriculum, and the British model was randomly scattered, and should have had a national organisation: even one like that devised for horse racing and breeding, depended on the devotion and idealism of individual owners. Thus, they varied in quality and an organisation would have been an advantage, since without it, education ended on the death of the owner, or his insolvency. Education was subject to the whims of fashion, and might fail or succeed when a social celebrity sent their children to a particular school to be educated, or withdrew them, having quarrelled with the owner. Such education was based on what poorly educated parents thought was desirable, rather than on academic challenges devised to encourage the young to think and discuss.

If there is ever a search made for a new Heroine of the movement to support female equality and emancipation, Mrs Basua Makin, should head the list. Her book, "An Essay to Review the Ancient Education of Gentlewomen,' published in 1675, and dedicated to Mary, Princess of York, deserves study. She presented alternative curricula, to provide for girls of varied levels of ambition. Half the time in school should be spent studying Dancing Music, Singing, Writing and Keeping Accounts, with the other half dedicated to Latin, French, Greek, Hebrew, Italian, and Spanish, but those who insisted might 'forebear the languages' and learn only Experimental

Philosophy. Her Schools were popular and were influential among Quaker communities in Britain and America, where Mrs Anne Bradstreet learned from her example.

It is unfortunate that the Educational reforms proposed in 1625 by Charles I were rejected. The great educator Comenius had earlier become famous throughout Europe for his educational programme beginning "at the mother's knee". In London, Charles I invited him to devise an educational programme to educate every child in Britain and establish an educated and intelligent society. The proposal was to have built a Grammar School for boys and girls in every town with over two thousand inhabitants, and a University in any town of more than 5000. The old Savoy Palace was donated as the headquarters of the educational programme, where graded text books would be published in English, and teachers trained to staff the schools.

The Parliamentary rejection of the King's 'extravagance' included this programme which, it was feared, would create a population of obedient workers, slaves to the Royal Tyrant's Will. It was rejected, but Cromwell reserved it for future consideration. Although it has never found favour in Britain where national schemes, are always viewed with suspicion, because equality of education might undermine the class system. It took root in Scandinavia, and the Educational programmes devised by Commenius, were adopted throughout the United States: MIT being one offshoot.

Another drain on treasury resources, was Louis' undertaking to make France the most Catholic Nation in Europe. Protestantism had outlived its welcome, it seemed. Massacres in Europe, restricted it to a few minor princedoms. It had suffered utter defeat everywhere except in Britain, Scandinavia and a few German Duchies. The Dutch republic had become a Kingdom in which Catholicism and Judaism were barely tolerated. Previous French rulers had waged genocidal crusades against all nonconformists. It now fell to Louis to remove the remaining Huguenots by any means available. The last bastion of Protestantism lay in the French banking system. Protestants had been encouraged for many years because strict Catholics were reluctant to charge interest or make money "breed". This rule was quietly relaxed and Huguenots either dismissed or persuaded to transfer their considerable wealth to Britain.

London and Edinburgh received enormous benefits from the influx of

French bankers who introduced stronger standards. The banking system in France was weakened and the King was inclined to try paper money and regulation of credit to speed up trading and bring larger, taxable profits. His bankers were reluctant to adopt the idea, although many approved it as a possible move in future. This delay prompted Louis to recommend the idea to a meeting of the Parliament but the delegates were strongly against the move. It was not accepted until the early years of the next century and Law's son, John, was the agent of change.

.

## CHAPTER TWENTY-SEVEN

In Holland the new Dutch government were most concerned with replacing the former, egalitarian regime of the De Witt ministers, with a more authoritarian government led by the Prince of Orange /Nassau. The previous freedom exercised by Dutch traders was curtailed, and reduced naval protection led to the loss of a number of African forts. William created a new monarchical constitution to ensure that his new, strengthened Royal Family, would have heirs and continuity. The Africa Company in London was restructured with a new Charter, headed by Prince James, and with George as senior executive and no longer treasurer. The earlier Gambia project was reduced in scale, and West African ports in Ghana opened up for exploitation. There were several strong Kingdoms there, including Benin and Ashanti, of long standing and ruled by kings, operating under a strong administrative structure, supporting a cultural, legal and commercial system, and social systems, which ensured that justice was fairly administered. Trade expanded with other kingdoms, as far as East Africa and the Arab lands of the North, and was properly organised. Under British control, the possibilities were infinite, and at first, trade in silks and cotton flourished along with spices and wood and metal-ware, equal to that produced in Spain and Italy.

These Kingdoms were extensive with many large, prosperous and properly administered cities and towns. The first travellers from England noted their fine buildings and planned cities, well-kept roads, and their excellent agricultural skills. The craftsmanship of their goldsmiths and metal workers in bronze, exceeded anything previously seen in England, and samples were brought to London. Traders began by offering cheap cloth and beads in exchange, but it was not acceptable. The only goods comparable in value to their products, were guns and shells. These had the effect of leading to the destruction of their societies.

These kingdoms were self-sufficient, and the goods on offer to them, heavy blankets, saddles and harnesses not suitable for camels, ploughs for oxen to draw, were not appropriate. Soon, and by force, the traders began to take what they could, beginning with the gold. The Dutch had relieved the tribes of their criminals who were sold on as slaves. The British began to test Africans for their potential as labourers, and as the demand grew, so did the provision of an increasing number of slaves. New and larger ships were commissioned, with lower decks fitted out to hold either closely packed commercial goods, or slaves. The Three Way Trade grew to supply the ever increasing demand for slaves to augment the productivity of the American colonies.

The increasing significance of Slavery led to the economic success of Britain and the financing of the Monarchy, which gave rise to grave moral concern to the Carterets and to many others, concerned with the political tension it created. George's instincts faced a personal dilemma, the result of many years involvement in the suppression of slavery. In the early years of the century, no coastal port of Europe or the Atlantic coast of America, could prevent their ships and seamen being captured by raiders from the Mediterranean ports, where they were sold into slavery. They saw the destruction of coast and inland communities in Britain by frequent raids by slave ships.

As Captain and Commander under Charles I, he had patrolled these coasts tirelessly in a constant attempt to alleviate the twin problems of smuggling and enslavement. With Rainborrow he had engaged on behalf of the King in diplomatic efforts to secure the release of British slaves and restore their freedom. When the King was executed and the Commonwealth established, George, with his own naval force continued the policy, and freed Jersey from slave raids.

He encouraged the British practice, long established, of freeing slaves held on foreign ships, bringing them to England, where they could enjoy the freedom of every British subject. Men and women of colour had been a small, but growing, percentage of the British population for centuries, and had led productive lives at every level of society. George himself had commanded ships with crews drawn from men of all nations, whatever their colour or religion. He presumably knew if they were good seamen and, if prepared to work as part of a team, they were welcome, and could be appointed officers by merit.

However, civil unrest in Britain culminating in the Restoration, brought about changes, some advantageous, but some of questionable morality. Among the latter was one which George, as Naval Treasurer, was obliged to read, among many others. This stated the Rules of Precedence governing naval operations. He came to the astonishing realisation that the year 1641 instigated a significant change in the national attitude to slavery. The result helped to make slavery acceptable. He was able to trace this terrible outcome to the arrival of an English trading ship, the 'Star,' commanded by a captain with an exemplary reputation, which arrived in Barbados with a cargo of black Africans. The ship was suddenly lacking a chief officer, and he had brought it safely to harbour after an Atlantic crossing.

1641 was also the year when Monarchy was replaced by Republicanism. It was also the year when George lost his command of the British navy, which he was well qualified to perform, to be replaced by a government committee ignorant of established practice. The Captain, in this invidious situation, sought the advice of the harbour authorities, who decided that the slaves should be sold on the open market to defray the cost of their transport. Thus, by chance, a British trading ship by-passed the normal practice, to seize the ship and free its cargo of Africans. That was the year, it seemed, when traders and ships' captains, formerly eager to establish sound relationships with African rulers; became less scrupulous than formerly, when Middleton and Drake were careful to respect the lives and freedom of African crew members. Many African men had freely signed on for the exciting prospect of a life at sea, from a natural sense of adventure, and a number came as welcome visitors to England where they were entertained by ordinary families. Freedom to travel has always been normal behaviour in the young who naturally wish to see the world. Drake's commercial success was due largely to a young African who came on board in Morocco, and who remained on board with Drake, as a valued member of crew. Because he was bi-lingual he made possible complex commercial agreements, aided by his ability to negotiate. This practice became customary in future years as a sensible trading measure.

The 'Star' episode created a new precedent and Africans began to be forced on board at the point of a gun, against their will and in contravention of the laws of their land. During the next twenty years, a steady increase in the number of such vessels began, and records show that between 1663 and 1667, 6,000 slaves were delivered to the plantations by the Company of Royal Adventurers Trading to Africa, which was founded in 1663. It delivered more than 30,000 enslaved Africans, exported through London, and Liverpool. Later, Bristol became the trade Headquarters and offices. Slaves often passed through these ports, although direct transport, via the Azores, was preferred, to make a more humane crossing, in two five week stages. This was to ensure the cargo arrived in good condition. At no time was Slavery sanctioned in Britain, but the trade in the British colonies flourished as a result of an aberration, since slaves were not held in Britain. The substantial profits of the trade however were gained by British traders and investors. Slaves therefore were rarely seen, except by those who worked in the docks: therefore most of the population could claim to be ignorant of the trade.

The profit gained by the King and the partners in the company was considerable, although it was never sufficient for the King's needs. MPs. Continued to criticise the extravagance of the Court, however the income from slavery and generous grants from Louis XIV, gave him freedom from Parliamentary control by restricting his income. As the rewards increased, it enabled Britain under Queen Anne, to take on the armies of Europe with a good measure of success. From its origin as a private company created to benefit the Royal treasury, it became an increasingly important public company, The Royal Africa Company, under its next Charter, traded legally on the London Stock Exchange, which itself gained international power and influence as a result. The proceeds enabled benefits to be felt in America. On the whole the colonies were expected to become self-sufficient by means of their own efforts: slavery assisted this process. Initially, George earned £700 per annum, a sound return supplementing his other trading ventures, and manorial income. Shareholders at that time might buy shares, priced at £200 each, and with no upper limit. New share issues, at ever higher profit rates, were frequently issued. In contrast to this level of wealth, a British Housekeeper, running a fashionable country residence, and a town house in London, might be paid £20 annually. The contrast is striking.

Once more, George's conscience would have troubled him. All his instinctive love of freedom, as a man of Jersey, and instinctively independent by upbringing, must surely have troubled him. He realised that he was denying to other humans the freedom he had always sought to defend. Amyas, of course, had often warned him of the danger of placing your integrity at the mercy of a monarch, or indeed of any employer, but to deny the right of freedom to such an increasingly absolute and cynical ruler as Charles II, Supreme Head of the Church of England, might be viewed as treason, as it had been for Clarendon. He might perhaps have consoled himself with the thought that he was acting in the interest of his family. Equally, he may have gained reassurance with the knowledge that philosophers such as John Locke, and leading Christian Bishops were his fellow investors. Once again, on this occasion, his loyalty to the king overrode his more humanity, but moral disquiet would surely have increased as he grew older.

Anne Stanning had died in 1668, but Sir Nicholas increased his future success by being sponsored by the Carteret clan. He was appointed to the household of Queen Catherine, and became a cupbearer. As an MP, he played an active role in defence of the Royal Prerogative, and sat on seventy Committees concerned with trade and social affairs in the South-West, as Assessor and MP for Penrhyn. His son, Andrew, by his third wife, was entitled to a considerable fortune and extensive property. Despite his early promise, he died in a Soho tavern brawl.

The husband George supported as suitable for Louisa Carteret, was Sir Robert Atkins, whose father had fought for the king in the war with Parliament. Robert was in his late forties and a successful lawyer. His knowledge of the laws concerning government was second to none. He gave valuable advice on the administration of the colonies and the slave trade and, later on, the aggressively antagonistic threats to the King, waged by Anthony Ashley Cooper. Robert and Louisa were married in St Margaret's, Westminster, and the congregation included Prince James and John Evelyn, the Carteret local church in Woolwich having burned in the Fire. Rev. Giles Dowse was among several participating ministers. Atkins later produced "The Power, Jurisdiction and Privileges of Parliament": a legal handbook held in esteem for many years.

Louis, a son of the Duc de Vendôme, the former colleague of George while in France, was suddenly dismissed from the Queen's household for "compromising" letters sent to the confessor of his grandmother, Mme De Maintenon. This accusation was made by Ashley Cooper, as an indication that French catholic courtiers were a danger to British decency. The Queen had entertained him with her household at Somerset House, but the accusation was dismissed by the popular press, who held the Queen in high regard. She and her ladies frequently made excursions into the countryside where they held picnics, in popular places of recreation, and she enjoyed talking to passers-by and sharing her delicacies. This attack was, in fact, an ominous sign of the growing hatred of the French, which soon became a major issue. Among valuable sources of income to the Court was the export of fine race horses, bred in English studs, in which the King and Duke had financial interests. They were the main export to France, and were very profitable, but a greater variety of French products were being brought into Britain. Both Royal Princes took part regularly in races for 'Plates' or 'Cups', the prizes sometimes financed by their winnings.

In the year of Louisa's marriage, a second son was born to Jem and Philip. He was given the name Philippe and baptised at North End. George discovered more about the life of Sir Giles Dowse, whom he had met long ago when he was employed as a lawyer's clerk. Having ended his military career, he was torn between Anglicanism and Catholicism. He had learned from Thomas Dowse, that John Donne, the writer and Dean of St Paul's. had been tormented by the same doubts. Also, that an earlier Sir Francis Dowse had travelled with Donne to Europe to attempt to gain support for a binding peace treaty. H had read some of his writings and spoken to none other than James Hay, owner of Pyrgo Park, who had led the peacekeeping mission. He had, as a result, taken Holy Orders with the Bishop of Winchester, and was appointed Rector of Broughton, remaining until he was sequestered, in 1645. He had regained his benefice at the restoration and was intending to remain there for life.

Perhaps he learned from Giles that writings and endowments are likely to ensure that a man is not completely forgotten soon after his death. Good works may create a degree of immortality. Giles had created an educational trust, and endowed almshouses in his parish. Many others had performed similar generous acts. Fired with good intentions, or possibly guilt for his role in the growth of slavery, George wrote to the Governor and Deputies of Jersey offering them a gift of land and money to enable boys leaving the Grammar Schools, aged thirteen, to be offered scholarships to Oxford Colleges to defray their expenses. Ormonde, who was Chancellor of Oxford University, supported the idea.

To alleviate seasonal unemployment in the island he also offered to fund a training establishment where the unemployed could benefit from retraining. These suggestions were acknowledged and committees formed to develop the idea, but in the long run, neither offer was taken up. A possible explanation might be that Carterets had played a dominant role in the island for many years, and it resented interference, and his plans might be viewed as a plot to seize permanent control. George did not repeat the offer so perhaps, as an instinctive islander, he understood their unspoken refusal. Work at Haynes Park continued in the meantime.

As one of the two main proprietors of the new colonies in America, the other being Lord Berkeley, George was regarded as something of a reliable advisor in all issues, governmental or commercial. In truth, mismanagement prevailed, in part for lack of financial backing or serious attempts to secure continuity. Admiral Penn's Son, William, who had caused his father such anxiety, had now inherited a fortune and concluded that the equality of persons and belief in peaceful co-existence of the Society of Friends, was the way forward. Pennsylvania was successful because money and hard work were expended. Its influence spread. Other colonies were torn apart by doctrinal conflict or overweening power struggles. There was no colonial office to guide and develop, but George was nominally in charge from New York to Southern Virginia.

The King's ministers saw a chance that the Royal debt might be eased by an integrated management structure for the Colonies. It was already too late, since many of the colonies had been founded on divergent principles and believed that other communities lacked in integrity. George, however was appointed to 'The Board of Trade and Plantations' in 1670. Worthy men like John Evelyn were co-opted and weekly meetings were imposed. Animated discussion ensued about contributions, payments listed for the services the Board might impose on them, what increase in numbers of imported slaves would be necessary, and the costing of each slave. George did what he could, despite opposition. He was the only member of the board who had set foot in the New World. Few of the members had ventured outside England. The system they finally agreed on was in most details the Feudal System imposed on England by William the Conqueror. Tyrannous rule, compulsory belief and a permanent underclass of unpaid serfs included. These were exactly what the colonists had emigrated to avoid.

Some good emerged from extra parliamentary committees: one was Evelyn's desire to create a secure hostelry for old soldiers who had no home or family. Pepys, Carteret and Wren were prime movers of a plan which finally succeeded, in the form of the Royal Hospital. George was rewarded for his efforts by being granted the Administration of Carolina: in addition, he became Count Palatine of the Bahamas. On the other hand, he had one complete success: he sold the Treasurer's post in Dublin to Lord Aungier, who was able to assist Ormonde, whose reputation was now being undermined by the Whigs and Ashley Cooper. This led to the arrest of Bishop Talbot of Dublin, and of Dr. Oliver Plunkett, Papal Emissary in Ireland, and ruined the Irish economy.

The autumn of 1669 was marked by Pepys' decision to travel to France for a holiday. He had begun to have serious concerns about his failing eyesight, and had not taken a holiday from his work commitments for nine years. His navy Office duties finally discharged, he consulted John Evelyn and planned a detailed itinerary of European towns, buildings and significant individuals which were felt to be essential to ensure the benefits of such a plan. Elizabeth Pepys, and her brother Balty, had fled from France for security from persecution, and settled in London, where their father found profitable employment. Samuel had married Elizabeth when she was an engaging girl of 15 years, and he was a bachelor aged twenty-eight, already deeply committed to hard work and financial success. The trip was a great success and he reported in his diary the pleasure given by the change of scene. It might well have marked the beginning of a new chapter in the account Pepys gives of their often-strained relationship Their return was greeted with the delivery of a family coach and Pepys records his delight when he and Elizabeth took it to St James' Park on a warm autumn day. Elizabeth, already feeling unwell, developed a bad headache, which in the following days became a fever, leading to her death. She was only 29 years of age.

Pepys was extremely distressed, and had already decided that his deteriorating sight was in part due to the long hours engaged with his lengthy diary entries. He added a brief paragraph mentioning his decision but did not record his reaction to the bereavement. This saw an end to his diary. His friends and colleagues noted that he had withdrawn himself from his usual activities and was rarely seen for three weeks. Many wrote letters expressing their sorrow and sympathy, some of which survive and also some of his own sad responses to their expressions of grief. The portrait of his wife he had commissioned, remained in his possession for life and, in addition he had a memorial placed beside the Admiralty pew in St, Olave's Church where they had often sat. On his death he was interred with Elizabeth.

George and Bess knew the couple well, as colleagues and close friends and much of our knowledge of George's career and personality are shown in the frequent references to the Carterets in his diary. His affection for their family is clearly displayed in the vivid and affectionate account of the arrangements he made for the marriage of Philip Carteret and Jemima Montague. His frankness about his own life and those of his associates, and his sturdy defence of his employer against the charges of corruption levelled at George by his political enemies, are made credible by being conveyed in code and bound in identical boards as the rest of his library, remaining untranslated and unpublished until years later.

His account of the first ten years after the Restoration has been adopted as entirely trustworthy, and the secrecy of its writing assumed to demonstrate the honesty of his assessments. Elizabeth's life-like portrait bust in the church, gained Sam's approval and conveys her personality showing her engaged perhaps in lively conversation. Although Pepys found her extremely attractive, they had little in common. Elizabeth retained through her life a preoccupation with fashionable clothes, hair styles, and embroidery. Pepys made great efforts to encourage her musical talent, but was distressed to find that most of the lessons he financed passed in animated conversation. At social occasions they performed his latest songs, she sang to his lute accompaniment.

As to his Diary, the proliferation of new source information available in a digital age, demonstrates that Pepys had his prejudices which undermine complete accuracy, and fail to tally in every respect with many different sources. They show him to be willing to grant favours, and be bribed, in exchange for gifts, and to be unscrupulous in financial dealings. He certainly made a great deal of money while Navy Secretary and concealed the means by which he made such gains. He was certainly deceptive in the process of selling the Tangier naval base, to the disadvantage of Mr. Povey, who deserved to be better rewarded.

The new year of 1670 arrived with strong winds, sleet and then heavy snowfall. The Thames above London Bridge froze solid. This freezing was not a regular event, though it had become more frequent in recent years, Leaving Gresham College after a meeting of the Royal Society, George greeted William Petty, whom he had seen little of, engaged in arranging his cloak to provide maximum protection. The re-allotment of farming land was Petty's special responsibility and, as a gesture to convince the native Irish that he was personally committed to the agreement, he had purchased unclaimed land holdings as a personal guarantee. So, as an Englishman showed confidence, Ormonde, who was an Irish-speaking native of the island, began to purchase land in England to demonstrate that he had no ambition to be King of Ireland. Both gained the support of parliament.

'Foul weather, George, and worse to come, I hear. It hardly ever seems to be light. I believe you have retired to the country: How is dear Bess? You are grand-parents, I think.'

'We have two very active grandsons, in fact. I had hoped to enjoy some leisure when I gave up the Admiralty, but I've been given a heap of other responsibilities. Fortunately, as Plantations, Privy Council and Rebuilding London require short meetings to approve plans, with luck we can deal with a good number of matters in one day.'

'I was a little upset by the experiment of putting a cat in a bell-jar and removing the air. They took it out unconscious. I wonder if it will survive?'

'It was a blackbird last meeting, which fell off its perch. When it was released it flew out of the window, Clever fellow that Hooke, finds us something to see every time, but I wish he would put his mind to new ideas: improvements to old gadgets may be useful, but we need new inventions.'

'When I was at your party in '67, Philip showed us his microscopes and magnets. I was impressed by his determination to improve means for better navigation. Has he had any success?'

'He thinks the answer lies in making a completely reliable clock: that will require investment, and no-one is prepared to lend without certain success. Perhaps someone will offer a large prize or award to the first man to make one.

# CHAPTER TWENTY-EIGHT

In Parliament, stalemate persisted. Charles's requests for additional subsidies, or preferably, a regular increase in income, flexible to inflation, was again refused, only small subsidies being awarded. To keep parliament in check, and avoid persistent questioning of a King's right to make appointments without discussion, of government ministers, was of central concern to parliament. There were fears that Charles was, perhaps, tempted to revert to absolute rule, which his father failed to implement, and they were wary of providing an opportunity. However, Charles was too indolent and eager to remain popular, to persist. On the other hand, European considerations suggested another means to augment his income.

Throughout his reign, Charles discussed matters of State with his cousin, King Louis, and these exchanges took place with increasing frequency. He was in constant correspondence with his sister, Marie-Anne, Duchess of Orleans, Louis' sister-in-law, and his correspondence with her was beneficial. They were not the only intermediaries: there was a small body of extreme Catholics, contemptuous of the complacency of their co-religionists who were prepared to discuss a possible uprising. Improbable as it was, the proposed Indulgence movement might suggest that Charles might be sympathetic to their desire. They discussed the Treaty between England, France and Holland ending the Dutch War in 1667. Charles claimed that he had always wanted a close Treaty with France, except 'R" (possibly Clarendon), had dissuaded him. If Louis was now willing to agree a treaty, binding them to joint action against the Dutch, he would offer his navy to take part in such an action. Parliament, he suggested, wanted to avenge the Medway disgrace, and would provide money. He, Charles, would need to be solvent, of course, in case of a reverse. Following further discreet discussion, this personal agreement was signed in total secrecy. Charles accepted an annual pension from Louis to guarantee his continuing loyalty, and allow him to ride out parliamentary opprobrium The Treaty of Dover, (1670) was signed, and George was probably one of those few who knew of the agreement, although it would surely have been a further cause of concern.

This generosity on the part of Louis XIV was deep and he and Charles were not only cousins but acquaintances from childhood. Charles had spent his most formative years at the French court, and had absorbed lessons in Kingship from the King, Louis' father. His father's example remained clearly in mind throughout his life. He shared the family love of ships and the sea and his capacity for thorough research and record keeping in matters which he esteemed, ships, horses and the arts. He loved his children, and he had their affection. He spent time with them and invested in their future.

One example is Henry Fitzroy, Duke of Grafton, born in 1663. He loved ships and his father gave him the opportunity to make it his career. In 1678, Henry joined the Happy Return and sailed with the Mediterranean fleet, returning the next year. The same year he sailed on the 'Leopard' serving on the Turkish coast and in Malaga. He seemed to enjoy it, but Charles become anxious with the Franco/Spanish war beginning, and cut short his career. He was a popular choice when selected as Master of Trinity House in 1682/3, and subsequently was made deputy Lord High Admiral. Prince James's son by Sarah, elder sister of John Churchill, the Duke of Bolton, was also a cadet until joining his family in exile. Charles and James were familiar with ships' crews, and recorded references of cadets likely to make officers and officers suitable as captains. At navy Board, when making new appointments, they were ready with their notebooks' to support or reject potential candidates. Many Captains started their careers as deckhands, and rose to be Captains as a result. The quality of British officers benefited from royal insistence on appointing those with ability whatever their social background.

'By God! Is that you, my old shipmate? You're looking a little rounder in the waistcoat since I saw you last. Good to see you though, Brother. What are you doing down in this part of London? Not your usual scene, I should think'

'I could ask you that Jim, but I wouldn't wish to embarrass you. Where have you been hiding?'

'In plain sight, old lad. Partly about the Court, hence the smart outfit. What do you think?'

'I think you have been wasting money. Did you do well on your last trip?'

'Well, thank you, George! The Mitre is just round the corner: they've made some improvements. If you are interested, and have time, I'm happy to talk.'

'Agreed, but if you don't mind, I would like to go round the block on the way. I promised to look in to see how our new wharfage is coming along. There's an upturn in trade coming, and we have to be ready for it.'

'We don't have a problem in Chatham. Naval ships are being laid down even now.' The inspection took some time, Philip introducing his brother to some of their employees before they found a table at the Mitre.

'I heard about poor Anne's death when I was in Plymouth, but the funeral happened the day I arrived. She was a lovely sister: I was being set on by a couple of lads once, and not getting the best of it, and Anne sailed in and landed some good punches which saw them off.'

'You're between ships, I suppose, Jim. So, why visit the Court?'

'Can't do any harm to get to know some of the new Council who are MPs. Tom Dowse has introduced me to some helpful men and I've introduced myself to the Duchess of Portsmouth: she likes to be helpful to smart young fellows, I have found, so I go around with her and young Rochester. He's amazing, handsome as the devil, plays the fool, swears like a trooper, comes out with a stream of smutty rhymes; drinks and gambles, although he's six years my junior. The King is so pleased with him that he has been given a pension for life.'

'I heard that some MPs think the King is a spendthrift who favours the French and Catholics. He owes thousands to businesses and wastes them on gambling, horses and mistresses.'

'That's the Whigs talking, Philip. They are just jealous and want places at the trough with the rest of the hogs. The Royalists are right! We should all live for the day, as the king does. Long live the merry Monarch! Our father seems to have it right. He's found you a wealthy aristocrat for a wife, and our sisters are all married to men with land and money. The Carterets are certainly rising in the world. Philippe in St Ouen finds it quite amusing, to see father grovelling in London for any scraps the King throws him. I just follow his example, Phil.'

'Don't forget, James, when we were very young we were exiled from Jersey, without a penny, and father had to find ways to feed us and educate us and support the King, with any skill he had and great bravery.'

'Yes, but don't forget that French business: he was working for the enemy, the French. He was a pirate and a traitor!'

'I can't tell you now, but he was lucky to survive. He always has several

*Restoration and Retribution*

irons in the fire and is everyone's friend: his front door is always open to useful opportunities, but he always has a back door unlocked to be able to make a rapid escape.

'You remember the offer he made for bright boys to go to Oxford, and build a training centre for the unemployed?'

'Yes, I thought it was generous.'

'Did you? You forget, when the fishing is over they spend every possible hour growing the food they live on: they are not unemployed. Jersey has good schools: you and your brother were well educated. You refused to go! The States will never accept his offer. Every islander votes for the delegates and the Jurats and they will never vote for those proposals. They would be handing over power to England if they did.'

'You forget, our father and Amyas spent years persuading King James not to tamper with Jersey's constitution, and they won. He would never betray them, James.'

'Phil, like you, I remember the wonderful games he invented, and he taught us to sail, and swim, and took us on board ship with him when he sailed to St Malo, but I also remember the card tricks, and the three cup trick, one with a cob-nut concealed. I've seen him at the King's table gambling for real money. He is always reluctant to play, he will be 'expecting an urgent message,' after about half an hour, a messenger arrives, and he leaves the table with apologies - and with his winnings. He beats everyone. That is because he is so good with figures. No wonder the King is bankrupt.'

There ensued a pause during which a waiter brought fresh coffee, steak and vegetables. Both agreed that more talking was necessary. James re-opened their discussion.'

'I apologise if I have informed you of matters you are unaware of, Philip. I suppose it is because I rarely see our father at home that I have seen him in different surroundings. You work closely with him, and are central to all his activities, and cover for him when he cannot be in two places at once. George Carteret, our father, is an amazing man. The King and Prince rely heavily on him, and his advice and negotiating skills, and I admire him as much as you. He always identifies the essential point of any problem and acts on it at once. For example: you will have heard tales about the St Kitts operation to relieve the islanders, which failed because our ships became separated in avoiding shoals. Malicious pamphleteers made much of it, speaking of incompetent favourites' being made Commanders. Me, Phil?

Can you see me as a Royal favourite?

'I don't, Jim. It was a communication confusion over rocks which had not been correctly charted. Fortunately, the weather was in your favour that day. I read the full report.'

'Thank you! I'm glad you read the report. I am grateful that you troubled to search it out. I realised at father's retirement party, why you were working on clocks and magnets. You and father both understand that a necessary change of course, decided by the Commander of a squadron, can only be clumsily conveyed to the other ships by a Loud-hailer, or hanging out a group of signal flags. The first only works if ships are close together and someone is on watch, the second depends on the limited number of flags available and the eyesight of the man watching. That is why you are making your experiments. I realised, after thinking about your speech that day, that you were probably thinking of my safety also and saving my reputation. I am very grateful!'

'There was also father's brother, Reginald. No-one knows why his ship sank in the Irish Sea, but Prince Rupert said that he was lucky himself, to avoid some uncharted skerries not on his chart. Most sea battles seem to end in a state of chaos, with the first Commander back in port reporting victory, whatever the outcome.'

'James, will you be in London for some weeks? Perhaps we could go to see Haynes.'

'I'm expecting to receive a new commission shortly: the Admiralty have exonerated me and I shall be leaving for the African station. It's a Royal Navy mission intended to protect the slave ships from being captured by the French or Dutch. We can't allow them to ruin our most rewarding trade. The King would be furious. Lady Castlemaine has a constant craving for sugar: towering castles made of crunchy sugar are her favourite food at present.'

'And in the short term, James?'

'I'm meeting our father tomorrow morning: he may have an heiress lined up for me to marry, but I shan't take the bait. I prefer to make my own choice. This afternoon I am visiting Damaris Page's house of specialities, in the East end, with young John Wilmott. He's a frequent visitor, but it's my first. As a respectable family man, I won't dare to invite you to join us. Wish me success!'

# ~ EIGHT ~

## CHAPTER TWENTY-NINE

Philip Carteret stood reading to the end of a speech made by the unfortunate, but morally sound, Aurangzeb and, paused, deciding whether or not to buy a copy of Mrs Behn's play. He had seen it performed recently and wondered how many in the audience believed, like Rousseau, that in some part of the world, there were people living, entirely untouched by envy or anger. Holding it open, he asked the stall-holder whether he had any plays by George Etheridge.

'You don't find noble savages in West Africa nowadays, Philip. Their leaders are becoming professional slave hunters for our merchants.'

'The book-seller returned and offered "The Sullen Lovers", and Wycherley's, "A Country Wife."

'Rochester regards Shadwell with utter contempt for writing sentimental, insipid rubbish. I think I shall buy both of them, please; I'll lend them to you, Philip, when I have read them,' his father promised. I saw 'The Country Wife' last week: it is very popular at Court, because the "hero" is in search of country girls to ravish. He boasts of his sexual prowess, but the joke is this, he is in fact impotent. I suppose anything may be the subject of humour today. The young louts at court have picked up his constant oath to repeat as many times as they can.'

'You must mean "Stap me vitals!" I expect. I wondered where they heard that.

'Evelyn was with the King on Tuesday evening to talk about the Covent Garden buildings: Charles was being distracted by two of the ladies, and discussion was impossible. Mrs Carwell and Nelly Gwynn, wanted him to award a prize to the one with the most beautiful breasts. They invited all the ladies to take part. When Barbara Cleveland's breasts were awarded the prize, Nell recited the first verse of a poem that Rochester: had written, 'Quoth the Duchess of Cleveland to Councillor Knight,'

"I'd fain have a prick, knew I how to come by't.

I desire you'll be secret and give your advice:

Though cunt be not coy, reputation is nice."

'It's very clever I suppose; I can't quite recall the rest, but I expect someone has a copy.'

'The King enjoyed it, I expect. Your mother tells me about the sexual innuendo bandied about. It may have begun then when Prince Rupert lost his verbal memory, and began using oaths to fill the gaps, like drunkards do. It's become the latest fashion. I'm afraid the King has lost interest in matters of state. He won't recall parliament now they have given him money.'

'He hates to ban people from Court, or sack Ministers of State. He never wrote to Hyde to dismiss him from office. He simply asked him for his Seal of Office, put it in a drawer, and told him to go away. It was Parliament who passed the Act of Attainder for the king to sign,' Philip stated, with inside knowledge, probably.

'Castlemaine is seldom with him now: she still claims that her last baby girl is his. He and everyone else, heard her boast that John Churchill was the father, and he does not deny it. Barbara will be expected to leave the court: Charles has paid off most of her gambling debts, I am told.'

'The middling sort in London seem to enjoy the same plays as the King, and Rochester's rhymes are known everywhere. Some hack printer will pirate a collection of his stuff, I expect. I was with the King and some others on his barge, and when he walks in the streets, he said, workmen call out cheery remarks: "Good on you, Old Rowley!" They like the idea that the great racehorse is being sent to stud. You see he enjoys the things they enjoy, and doesn't mind what they say.'

'He told us the vital skill of a politician is to tell difficult people to "Fuck Off." His father should have tried it, but was too well-mannered.

'Rochester took him up on that, and made an instant Rhyme:
> "Here's Monmouth the Witty,
> And Lauderdale the pretty.
> And Frazier, the physician;
> But above all the rest,
> Here's the Duke for a jest,
> And the King for a grand Politician".

Sadly, while everyone was laughing, Prince James sat there, anxious, and trying to understand the joke'.

'That sounds like James, Philip. He is getting increasingly stuffy as he gets older. Of course, he is no longer the slim, sensitive teenager who left Jersey in tears. He's overweight, despite all his exercise, and set in his ways, but we still exchange views regularly. Your mother, by the way, has become

Lady in Waiting to Queen Catherine: it was Frazier who gave advice about Anne's sickness. His daughter is also attendant on Her Majesty. She is a great favourite of the King and your mother copied out one of Rochester's poem for me to read:

> "I swive as well as others do;
> I'm young, not yet deform'd;
> My tender heart, sincere and true,
> Deserves not to be scorned.
> 'Why, Phillis, then, why will you swive
> With forty lovers more?'
> "Can I," said she, "with nature strive
> Alas I am, alas I am, a whore".

However amusing it is, I hope I have not shocked you? I came here intending to buy a seascape or two, showing well-rigged ships and a coastline. I need at least one more for my new study.'

'At least the King can appreciate a joke, even when he is its object: the pity is that he refuses to be involved in governing the country. Nothing interests him except women, plays and gambling. However, I still find him considerate and good company. He is the man we chose as a King, so we must live with our choice. None of us is perfect, but I had expected more effort.'


'Bess, you are the world's best house-keeper. Beef and oysters are the perfect combination. Oysters as good as those, must have been caught on the East coast.

'It is wonderful to be able to relax with you over good food, and fine wine. May I suggest, my dear, that we empty our glasses and go upstairs, there are one or two matters I would like to put to you in private'?

'George, you are talking like a lecherous old man in a Wycherley comedy. The King seems to behave like one of his characters. It seems to be affecting the behaviour of Princess Mary who seems to be empty headed. Neither she nor Anne had a governess to guide them with firmness. It is so unfortunate that their mother died, and Edward is totally preoccupied as Chancellor. Prince James takes very little interest in them.

'I haven't told you I had an unexpected visit from our James, yesterday.'

'I had hoped to speak to him myself about his next posting. How much money did you give him? Did he say he would visit us before we move to

Haynes?'

'He wouldn't accept money, George. He had hoped you would be at home, but he is to join a Royal Navy frigate in Southampton, and is leaving London today. I gave him two pairs of gloves. I am relieved it is not a slave ship. I am sure it is not good for decent young men to associate with poor, unhappy slaves They must regret their loss of freedom as we would, and may have apprehensions concerning their owners.

'I can remember the Arab raiders visiting Jersey trying to capture slaves, and the militia seeing them off. It is a demeaning way for any decent man to make money.'

'His ship will guard the African coast from Arab and Spanish raiders, so that the slaves can reach America safely, without fear of attack at sea.'

'But it's still about slaves, George. Can you not find him a post where he won't have to see them?'

'I always hope that he will come to work for me, eventually, but I have nothing to offer at present.'

'George, do you think James drinks too much?'

'I think it's quite probable! I hope he has a taste for good wine, and leaves rum alone, because it is really harmful. Philip tells me he smokes sotweed, which can develop into a habit. I suspect he is already addicted to alcohol.'

As she emptied her glass, Bess wondered if there was any way they could persuade him to stop drinking. George doubted whether anyone could persuade him. A man must have strong will-power and learn to restrain himself, but our son seems to have few restraints.'

Bess sighed regretfully, apparently in agreement. Changing the subject, she asked, 'Have you had any news of Amyas? I thought I might see him about the Court, but not so. He was such a good friend to us, and he did not come to our celebration. He was helpful when I first came to London. I hope he didn't die during the Plague!'

'Come along Betsy; time for bed! I was talking to William Petty recently, and he said Tom Dowse had visited Amyas recently. I think it may have been Amyas I saw in Bond Street: he was going into a shop, and carrying a walking cane.'

'If you can find him, George, ask him to come to dinner here, or perhaps he would like to visit Haynes? We must look after our old friends, George!'.

'I expect you are thinking about the Clarendons and Elizabeth Pepys.

What a shock it was to learn of her death! We must have more consideration for our young friends also: no-one is safe it seems. Philip and Jem are so caring of those two little boys. I wish I had spent more time with our two, Bess, when they were small, but I had to work hard for us as a family.'

'Our children have never complained that you neglected them, George. They remember wonderful times you spent playing with them and remind me of many things of which I have no memory.'

'The London celebration party you arranged, was so opportune, Bess. It is almost as though you knew that good fortune cannot last forever. I would never have bought this place if you had not set me thinking of other aspects of life than making money. I love this place and its tranquility and we seem to be surrounded with families who share our views about those things that are most important.'

'I'm surprised that you spend so much time at court, I thought you had sold off all your governmental posts.'

'I have, my dear. It's trading and business matters which I spend time on. I attend the Privy Council Committees once or twice a week perhaps, but only when I am sure there are matters of importance to discuss. There are changes in progress at this moment which I know nothing about. The Cabal seems to be losing its grip on public affairs: two of them are dead, or dying, and Shaftesbury and Danby seem to be fighting for power. There is worry about who will inherit the throne when Charles dies. James's appointment as Commander for the new campaign against Holland had been well received in general, although Shaftesbury found it necessary to regret, he had decided to turn Catholic.'

'What is Charles's opinion?'

'He is confident that James will stick to his promise to support the Anglican Church, and when he marries again, his son will be raised as an Anglican. I think he is beginning to feel that Parliament is setting out to oppose him, and his response is to listen to their advice and refer it for future discussion. So although he never refuses them, neither does he follow their wishes. Nothing is happening as a result and he goes to the races and the theatre, rather than Parliament. He told me his only duty is to sit and listen to them: he feels that they have the advantage of outnumbering him 500 to 1 while '500 Kings' shout instructions at him. He refuses to take this seriously: this was his father's mistake. He claims to believe that he is safe from danger while they continue to quarrel among themselves.'

'Is anyone running the country? Is anyone actually in charge?'

'Parliament passes legislation whenever it needs to avert a crisis but makes no plans for the future well-being of the nation. The Courts and magistrates perform their functions and the farmers and traders exercise their skills, and pay their taxes, and the country somehow continues to manage itself. You have heard of Tom Osborne, he has just been ennobled as Lord Danby. I think the King is grooming him for Lord Chancellor, in the hope that MPs will see him as a fine organiser who will gain a dominant force in Parliament and enable the King to exercise his sovereign power.

'He is very clever, and confident that he can control the various factions, and is rather like Strafford. However, Strafford was scrupulously honest, and I believe that Danby is not. I'm happy to wait and see, but I have no wish to be involved. Sooner or later there will be a crisis, probably about France or Religion, or possibly both. In the meantime, I shall walk out to see whether the new lake is lined and ready to be filled by the next year's rainfall.'

## CHAPTER THIRTY

Tom was the first friend George saw next day who was able to answer his enquiry about Amyas, with the astonishing news that Amyas had asked him for news of himself and Elizabeth. Amyas was less politically involved than in 1668. Tom mentioned that he was apprehensive about where the government ministers were leading them. 'He sees indications which alarmed him, and he had some concerns he would like to share with you, George, if you could spare the time. He would welcome a private meeting at his house at Lincoln's Inn, and would be available most days after 10 00.a.m.'

'Thank you for your help, Tom. I shall visit him tomorrow morning. I have always valued his advice. How is your nephew, young Tom? Is he still working for Pepys?'

'He enjoys the work. There is a greater range of trading interests, because every minister and their accounts, are subject to parliamentary scrutiny. He has a good brain for figures! Danby recently offered him employment and, I am pleased to say, he decided against the offer.

'I wonder, George, did you ever meet my eldest sister, Esther?'

'I was not aware you had a sister, Tom. She didn't attend the family conclaves, did she?'

'No, she was married before that time. About five years ago, she was widowed with a certain amount of property, and married again. Her new husband is Henry Paulet. Strange isn't it, the way our families continue to bond over the centuries? I think you used to know him. I remember the Privy Council ordered you to assist him in conveying six horses to France?'

'Yes! That was soon after the siege of Basing House. We had other trading business later. Is she happily married?'

'I believe so. It was a big wedding: Winchester Cathedral was full. Most of our old friends were there, I expect. They have a son who must be about four and out of death's clutches for a few years. I will try to introduce you; they are very good company, and I think the boy is close in line for the earldom. I think the last Marquis left no direct descendant, and Henry's father was next in line, and he was also dead. That would please "the old woman", your grandmother, long dead. I recall her being opposed to your marriage. Amyas seems hale and hearty: he is looking forward to your meeting.'

George visited Amyas next day in the sheltered, sunny corner of the range of aged Greys Inn buildings occupied by some of the best legal brains of the time. It dated from a time when lawyers, like monks, lived a life of obligatory celibacy, Family ties would have been impossible in earlier times, when Masters of Law had to accompany bishops or nobles, providing instant expertise at whatever time of day. Some, as they grew old, were financed by the Inn, as teachers imparting their knowledge of Case Law to the next generation, though knowledge was increasingly provided in learned tomes, in Latin, even at that date.

Amyas' legal training, gained by years of active practice and a good memory, had brought him financial rewards and a retirement home. Thurloe, Cromwell's advisor and spymaster, lived a few doors away. He and the Crewe family had been supporters of Parliament, though after the execution of the King, had supported the restoration.

They reminisced about Sir Philippe's generous support for Amyas, one of whose sisters had given birth to him as the result of an overwhelming passion, though the identity of the father was never revealed. Sir Philippe and he, had, together, persuaded King James, whose fine legal mind was taxed by having to defeat the legalistic trickery of Cecil, and the complex tissue of lies woven to deny his undoubted claim to the English crown. Somehow James was persuaded that the independence of Jersey and Guernsey offered security to the British mainland at no cost to him: better to keep the British connection than hand them to France,

George had never heard this story before but said that he had learned a great deal about the skills of overcoming stubborn minds and strong opinions by the skilful use of language and argument, and Amyas' skills had been employed by Anne Dowse, Sir Philippe's wife, and her father, Sir Francis. George thanked Amyas for teaching him the skills of successful negotiation, which he had employed in French and in several languages, for, with the Middle folk or labourers, Latin was of little use. He had also introduced George to London, its streets and people; the rules of courtesy, and how to dress well, but inconspicuous

'I remember introducing you to Pym after King Charles put you in charge of the Navy'. Amyas reminisced. 'Pym tried to spoil your pleasure by hinting that it would be a brief appointment. You pointed out that if that view was correct, the King possessed legal authority to dismiss him, whereas Parliament did not. Pym did not'.

'I don't remember saying that, Amyas. I often think of Pym and Hampden; they achieved so much in a short time by way of regulating the powers of the king and the parliament. I was all in favour of the Restoration, as most of us were, but I had not realised that Clarendon had deliberately framed the terms so that Pym's new laws of government were cancelled. I suppose the Declaration of Breda achieved a peaceful restoration, and Charles II wanted a very short document, re introducing the Monarchy, the Church of England, its Bishops, and the Nobility to all their former power. As a result, all that Hampden had hoped to achieve, and Pym and the Commons had written into law, was cancelled at a stroke.'

'George, I cannot forget that day when the King summoned Pym to Whitehall to negotiate a peaceful settlement of the national dispute. The King realised and accepted, the justice of the new laws, and the moderate restriction of some of his power. He and Harrington had agreed that he would concede Pym's proposals, and accept the new role of Parliament. I believe I know why it did not take place, as intended.'

'I had no idea, at that time, that matters were close to a sound conclusion. I was at sea with the fleet, so I heard nothing about it, though Harrington has always told us all that the King understood the reasoning and justice of Pym's arguments.' There followed a pause, while Amyas added sea-coal to the fire, after which he began to disclose an extraordinary story.

'I have come to the conclusion that John Thurloe was correct when he suggested that you might be a trustworthy recipient of some hazardous information. What I shall tell you was information pieced together by Clarendon, who was in charge of a team of Government Investigators,-sometimes called spies,-though 'listeners' might be more suitable. Thurloe, after Cromwell's death, was unable to counter Clarendon's changes, and to save the new constitution from attack.'

'I will mention a confidential meeting between the King and Pym in 1642. You will not know of this event: Harrington would have been too discreet. Both men had reached a point where an agreement was inevitable. Pym would not have risked his reputation and his life, if he had any suspicion of treachery on the King's part. Harrington told Clarendon that the deed was as good as done. Please remember that both men had been negotiating for several years; Pym was, at the time, dying from a terminal illness, and hoped this could be his final success. The King was finally convinced that the legal acts which parliament had passed, did not endanger the powers of monarchy, but clarify them, and create unity. Both men longed for peace.'

'So, what went wrong? This information came to me from Lucy Carlisle, Henrietta-Maria's lady-in-waiting. The Queen had been furious at the escape of the Five Members and Pride's armed raid on the Commons, and demanded that the king should make a summary arrest of all the MPs. and have them executed. In tears, she had asked Charles if he had no consideration for her life and those of their children: he must act as a King and Ruler should, and enforce law and order. Charles loved his wife dearly, but usually over-ruled her instinctive intolerance of compromise, or 'weakness'. He was extremely tired, having gone from triumphant reception in the streets of the capital, to see the same crowds become a howling mob demanding his death, a few days later.

'Before going to the meeting with Pym, and fully prepared to sign the essential agreement, Charles had decided he should inform the Queen of his next intention. She was so angry that she had raged and thrown vases and slippers at him, and threatened to leave him, and escape to France for safety with their children. Charles began as always, to reason with her, and assuring her that all was for the best and they would all be safe and regain the love of their people. The agreement confirmed his power and was not a danger. Lucy believes that the Queen now sensed victory, and knowing she would win the argument, become calm and reasonable.'

'Charles,' she said, ' I expect you are right, but Pym is a nasty little man and has left his wife! Don't let him claim victory. Offer him an Earldom, and a country estate if he will withdraw his demands: he will do anything for money, middling people are all greedy for money'.

'Charles replied, 'He had been amazed to discover, that Pym was an honourable man.'

'I did not realise that.' The Queen was heard to respond. 'If he is so honest why don't you made him your Chief Minister to take the place of Strafford? He would then do all that you have agreed, or you could execute him for treason if he fails.'

'The King went straight from her presence to his meeting with Pym. A table had been prepared, with the paper-work set out, and pens, ready for signing. At the last minute, the king remarked, 'You know Pym. now that I know you better, I regret the difficulties that have come between us. I would be honoured if you would become Lord Chancellor, for I am sure, with your persuasive skills, and my authority, we could pacify the Nation.'

'Pym was furious, George. Lucy heard him say that it was a cheap and unworthy suggestion. Surely the King could not set aside the months of tedious negotiation for a cheap trick showing them both to lack sincerity, and truSt 'I refuse your insulting offer, Your Majesty, and I shall inform the Commons of your duplicity.'

'Pym left the meeting rigid with rage and disappointment, knowing there was no going back. That evening the Royal family left for York, and Civil War became inevitable. What happened next, you will know. In deference to the Queen, King Charles decided to take decisive action. His decision was to force Parliament to defer to his authority by taking command of the army and leading them to London where they would seize control and establish military law.'

'It was ill-judged, since no preparations had been made and news of the raising of his Royal Standard, declaring war on Parliament, reached London at once where Parliament seized power and took necessary measures with the authority of the Royal Seal'.

'Thurloe has no official powers, since the restoration, but he remains loyal to the authority of parliament and believes that there are threats to our national sovereignty in existence which must be crushed before they overwhelm all that we believe in.'

George had learned a great deal that he had been unaware of, since he had been largely concerned in preserving the interests of the King in defence of Jersey and opposing the remnant of the Navy, which had fallen to Government control. He had seen that Amyas was urging him to take urgent action, and arrived at Thurloe's house at the time recommended. Thurloe, invited him in, and spoke to a neighbour briefly, mentioning that he would be grateful if visitors could be informed that he was not at home.

'Thank you for accepting my invitation. I consulted with Amyas Carteret and I hope he has given you a clear indication of the part played by unofficial agencies in the forming of government action. I am not referring only to Queen Henrietta, whose influence on her husband was in nobody's interest, or to the anti-Clarendon party, which has finally destroyed his reputation.

I imagine you will be concerned by the secret activities of the cabal, and at present, by the machinations of Danby, but perhaps as an honourable trader, you are insulated from the secret influencers at work, hidden from public notice, and engaging secret agents as spies on those who may threaten them and their plots.

'So, I want to turn to our present situation. You know there are strong differences dividing the Country: parliament is adjourned, the King has trapped himself and turned to self-indulgence. There is a political stalemate, and no-one can make a decision. Only the Declaration of Breda defines government power, and there is now a vacuum, which is open for anyone to seize power. You may say lies cannot survive for long, but some agitators will seek out means for distorting facts to their advantage.

'Political extremists are trying to establish their radical policies and attracting considerable attention, our MPs cannot reach a coherent response. They have conflicting agendas, and no common ground.'

'We traders have to share threats to our livelihood. Thurloe and I find that the King is not willing to confide in the Privy Counsellors he chose for himself, so our discussions are generally inconclusive. I suppose you fear the middle sort may rise against this king as they did against his father?'

'Can you really imagine London apprentices leading a revolution? No, George, because there are no Pyms or Hampdens providing a lead. In fact, most people are cheerful, most are well fed, and we have a King who seems to share all their joys and sorrows, as a good king should. You may be unaware, George, how in recent years royal agents have unveiled a number of conspiracies aimed at overthrowing Government and assassinating the King.'

'I am shocked! Who are these secret conspirators? Not Catholics surely, they are constantly interrogated, and protestant dissenters are escaping the country in droves, not rebelling. All of them fear arrest and imprisonment and do not know who will suffer when the axe falls.'

'Have you forgotten the Fifth Monarchists and The Sealed Knot?'

'No, Amyas. They were all madmen and Enthusiasts and the Monarchy is restored and the King has a reliable heir. I assume they have all disbanded.'

'Not so, George. They remain dissidents, but the younger generation is growing in size and influence. In some ways, George, you are surprisingly cushioned by fellow traders, and their code of honour. You were once an investigator on behalf of the King. I used to lead a group of agents, placed in the families of important royalists undermining the King's plans. Lucy Hay was one of many and you were another, known to me as Milton.

'I cannot imagine who you mean, Amyas.'

'George, you surely wonder how news of the Princes' intentions and religion, become widely known. You attend Privy Council meetings. Do you trust Ashley? He and Danby employ dozens of spies and many traders whose businesses have been bankrupted are willing to tell all they have learned in confidence to anyone who will pay them. Some are so eager they are willing to invent slanders in exchange for payment. I fear that someone with a cunning mind will collate these lies and construct a plot intended to destroy Parliament, or a plot to overthrow the king, or assassinate him. Somewhere there may be a concealed Guy Fawkes!

'There are others I'll call The New Royalists, I expect you know who I mean.'

'I'm sure you don't mean Prince Rupert?'

'An interesting choice of personality, who comes readily to the mind of many, I am sure. but not Prince Rupert himself, but his reputation, his Cavalry charges, his colourful dress, and lurid vocabulary, his energy and way with the ladies. His flowing hair, lacy collars and cuffs, chivalry, the charm of the Devil; are you with me? Have you noticed them, in Court, and parliament, at the races and theatres?'

'Well, I have, but it's only about trivial fashion and dress, and making an impression of virility for the ladies, surely?'

'It is certainly 'all that' but, this is the new generation, who have been brought up on the heroism and daring of their fathers and grandfathers. They want to recreate the violence and excitement of the past and imagine the honour to die for the King. If these groups came together, they could be a dangerous force. It may seem unlikely to happen, but Hyde predicted it. Recently one of my former colleagues came to me, to confide a growing conspiracy. I told him I had no acquaintance with seditious activity, but he was aware that we, George, were old friends. I warned him that in the event of matters coming clearer, he was to inform me.

'There have been a number of conspiracies discovered since the restoration, but Clarendon's agents exposed them all, and the leaders were executed. A recent one was to ambush and kill the King and Prince James, while returning to London from Newmarket. They selected a lonely road near Rye House. Fortunately, our agents heard of it, and all were captured and executed.'

'I know the Government has always had agents installed in the household of any family of importance, including the Royal Family. Are you wise to trust the word of an Agent with no credentials, Thurloe?'

'Two events since his visit prompted me to contact you on this matter. Many plots and counterplots have been exposed since the Restoration. The King has been made aware of them and has dealt with the culprits firmly. He takes comfort in the fact that his brother is his heir and that killing him will award the throne to James, now a declared Catholic, and that will deter them. However, there are other possibilities in the shape of the Duke of Monmouth, and Prince William of Orange Nassau. Neither of them would dare to attack Charles, but when he dies, either might take up arms against James. I will try to keep you informed of any developments, but you would be wise to engage some of your trusted employees in keeping their ears to the ground, since their lives might be endangered, and so might yours, George. The King's family may be infiltrated, George, and the same may happen to yours. You must be circumspect.'

'You mentioned two occurrences which had alarmed you, Thurloe. You have already confirmed my own suspicions and doubts about our present national dangers, and I shall heed your warnings, but I gather there is a further matter of concern which you are reluctant to divulge. I hope you will trust my absolute discretion, since we are now of one mind, despite our previous political differences.'

'I know I can rely on your discretion, or I would not have approached Amyas and Tom Dowse about my wish to arrange this meeting.'

Before responding, Thurloe poured more wine.

'I mentioned my conversation with a former agent. You will not be surprised that following that meeting I heard no more from him. However, as one of my few remaining legal duties, I sometimes serve as a Justice of the Peace. By an amazing coincidence I was asked to attend the postmortem on a body dragged from the Thames. The corpse was quite decayed, but I recognised it as the body of my former agent. He had been badly treated before being killed by a strong blow with a blunt instrument to the back of the head. He had nothing on him by way of identification. I knew him as an honest man, and regretted his death, although I did not identify him and did not know his name.'

'Mere coincidence?'

'Perhaps. But my protective neighbour saw a cloaked man leaving my entrance porch, just before my agent departed, and saw him walking in the same direction. These walls are not substantial, George. If he was listening he might have heard something. My visitor had Thames mud on his boots when he arrived and possibly intended to cross the River again.

'My neighbour would have come to warn us, if he noticed anyone lurking, but of course a passer-by may have noticed your arrival or departure, George. I advise you to be on your guard, my reputation may endanger you.'

In leaving, George expressed the hope that no harm would come to either of them

# ~ NINE ~

## CHAPTER THIRTY-ONE

'Have you details of Oates biography, Amyas?'

'Certainly not, George. I would not commit anything like that to paper. I have always destroyed any "evidence" in the form of letters, or notes. That sort of thing is so easy to produce and disclose as 'evidence'. I have an excellent memory and so have you. Oates was born in London in 1649 and his father was a dissenting preacher. He became an Anglican rector in Hastings, and had three sons and daughters. Poor, and lacking intelligence, Titus was offered a place at Westminster School. Dr. Busby dismissed him soon after and he may have taken work in London. He gained a place at Gonville College probably by producing false references, but kept dubious company, and left shortly after. Further deception gained him a place at St John's, Cambridge. I do not know why he made these changes, but he was inducted as a rector, and returned to Hastings where his appalling behaviour lost him his living. He obtained an army chaplaincy by unknown means but two years later, became a Catholic convert, and continued to wear his clerical outfit and function as a priest.

He next took up posts as a seminarist or a lecturer at various colleges in France and Spain, including Rouen, and Salamanca. He awarded himself a Salamanca Doctorate and returned to England as a Jesuit missionary and public preacher. He was certainly an excellent rabble rouser. He was asked to leave most of his posts following accusations of uncouth conduct, drunkenness and lechery which have caused his expulsion from every post he has held.

'In due course he renounced his vows asserting that his fellow priests were guilty of sexual immorality, naming one with whom he had worked. This Priest was subsequently de-frocked on the evidence of forged letters and the gift of a Rosary. He has an excellent memory and retains descriptions of rooms in buildings where plots were hatched, the private studies of College principles, the names of individuals and their foibles and has always had an incredible ability to appear plausible.

'I hope you can find more information on this unscrupulous man who is becoming well known for revealing criminality among Roman Catholics at all levels of society. I would approach the Minister in charge of Seditious Acts myself, but they seem to switch ministers around at a whim. I have not met either of the last two. It may be, I suppose, George, that Oates has planted agents of his own in key posts, even perhaps in the Court. I do not know what to do next and you may have useful contacts among your employees. I fear that anyone found by Oates to have an interest in his actions, may not live to tell the tale, but may be implicated in his 'Great Plot'.'

'I will follow up your suggestions and find a man I can trust. Perhaps he will show his hand and find himself arrested?'

'I suspect, George, that he will divert the blame to the individual who accuses him. Oates will be able to supply evidence of his accuser's guilt. He can turn any occasion to his own advantage and is always believed.'

'If you have any other information, let us meet in Whyte's. Are you certain no-one has been listening at your door, Amyas?'

'The neighbour who informed me previously, has been keeping watch.'

'A sound precaution, Amyas. I have no desire to meet a sudden death: I have avoided it so many times in the past.'

Carteret, having shed most of his responsibilities, acquired new ones. He had sold the Irish Treasurership to the Lord Treasurer, Southampton, to set up a new governing body to assist the development of the American and Caribbean settlements. It was named the Committee of Plantations. Time passed with less stress and urgency, and his flourishing business concerns and manorial responsibilities were shared by Philip and his efficient office staff. In 1671, Philip and Jemima's third son was born and named Edward: a third healthy boy. Unfortunately, Jemima died shortly after, so Bess shared with Philip the care of three small, lively boys. The family were now securely settled at Haynes Park where the household was increased by the addition of nurses and a governess.

After their son James's successful tour of duty in the Royal Navy, George was asked to recommend a Governor for the expanding colony of South Carolina. Observing promising signs of increased responsibility in their son, George recommended him for the vacancy. Such was George's reputation at Court, that the King approved his appointment. George was a little concerned at his lack of diplomatic experience, and advised James, to work with Philippe La Hogue, a Jersey relative, governing the New Jersey colonies with success. He would give sound advice and help and hoped that the cousins would be mutually supportive. Perhaps he might make a return visit to America and renew past impressions and old acquaintances.

In March that year, a coach bearing the Arms of the Duke of York drew up, giving rise to considerable consternation. It was not the Duke, but a secretary, asking Lady Carteret to return to London and the bedside of the Duchess of York, who was in poor health and longed to see her. Elizabeth left at once for St, James's Palace, knowing that the Duke would be grief stricken.

Having considered the possibility of sedition mentioned by Amyas, George made discreet enquiries among those at the Court and in the City. He confided in Philip, and in his one-time valet, Will Jarvis, who had employed those who had learned new skills in accountancy, surveying and drainage. He was surprised to learn that Philip had acquired a grasp of coster jargon. Will and other employees had very little contact among the governing classes but deep roots among the small business owners of London. George, in the expanding commercial world, had expanded his city connections by remaining at his post during the Plague, in his Broad Street home, ensuring a semblance of normal life and sharing dangers among his employees. The nobility and senior Ministers had left London for safety and the King had departed for Windsor.

There were of course, public servants and doctors who continued to serve their patients with disregard for personal safety. They suffered greatly from the infection and public order depended on the Parish Vestries, volunteers caring for the material needs and moral conduct of parishioners. The western areas of the capital including the adjacent areas of St Martin in the Fields and Whitehall Palace itself, were less affected. The Hospital of Greenwich, managed by the Mercers' Company, had connections with the Wood mongers' Company. Edmund Godfrey was its current Master. He was also a leading member of the St Martin's Vestry, and a Magistrate well-known for refusing bribery who often investigated the specific needs of those asking for his aid. He had been educated at Westminster School. He and his two brothers, Michael and Benjamin, were hardworking, ambitious businessmen, and associates of Papillon, a gold merchant and former financial advisor to Louis XIV, who had reluctantly exiled him to retain his Huguenot beliefs.

On one occasion Godfrey had, uncompromisingly, found the Earl of Portsmouth guilty of the murder of his duelling opponent, in the course of a street brawl. The High Court fearlessly agreed with Godfrey's sentence, and the Earl was sentenced to death. He was reprieved by the House of Lords. Lord Albemarle, formerly General Monck, who had effected the return of King Charles to England, and had been side-lined afterwards, for having served under Cromwell, took charge of public order, which was in danger of getting out of hand, restoring order and preventing looting. He also aided Godfrey by coming down hard on traders guilty of hoarding goods to increase demand so as to charge higher prices.

Many accused of plotting against government, whose only 'crime' was the accusation that they might be Presbyters or Papists, owed their freedom to his determination to demand conclusive evidence. In 1666, he was awarded a knighthood for his devotion to the poor. It is possible that his uncompromising honesty was offensive among criminals who may have conspired to silence him. No one escaped his pursuit of justice it seemed. Dr. Fergusson, an occasional Royal Physician, had lived well beyond his means to such an extent that his debtors finally applied for his arrest as a permanent bankrupt. Godfrey found him guilty as charged, and sentenced him to detention in the Debtors' prison. The Doctor appealed to the Lord Chancellor who decided that, as a Royal Servant, he was exempt from this law, and he was awarded a Royal pardon. A more canny magistrate would have learned to be cautious, but Godfrey contested this decision as an injustice.

George, and many businessmen applauded Godfrey's honesty and offered the hand of friendship, but Godfrey seemed to have little time for social gatherings. He attended public meetings and was, like George, one of the group who went as a welcoming party to Dover, to greet Henrietta Maria, Duchess of Orleans, Charles's younger sister, and also his favourite relative. Godfrey deplored the extravagance shown, and the depravity displayed by her French attendants, who displayed immorality far beyond that shown in Charles's Court. This strong reaction seemed strange, for Godfrey was known for his easy acquaintance at all levels of society: his associates including members of the Court and Judiciary, prisoners, and the wealthy, Anglicans, Catholics and Dissenters. These characteristics made his sudden violent death appear inexplicable in view of his scrupulous reputation.

Later in the year, La Hogue wrote to George accusing James Carteret of undermining his administration in New Jersey, by suggesting that the appointed counsellors be given more authority than he permitted. George wrote to reminded his son that he must go to Carolina, where he was expected, and attempt to devise a constitution there, bearing in mind the object of these colonies was to make money for the British Treasury. He should be content to learn from his cousin, and not to reprove him.

In 1670, the King's financial situation was eased to some extent by the Treaty of Dover, although his expenditure and debts continued to increase. The Treaty was negotiated by his sister, Henrietta Anne, aided by Clifford and Arlington initially. But the death of the former and the ill-health of the other led to their treaty being placed in the hands of Danby. His success in bringing the Treaty of Dover to a successful conclusion, gained him power, new titles and income. However, there was also a Secret Treaty which his sister negotiated with King Louis on her brother's behalf. The first part, ensured that Charles would join with France in attacking Holland and support Louis claims in Spain. The Privy Council would have supported this, and the concept of French naval support, and Pepys, in a strong address to the Commons, gained an extra £700,000 worth of support. The Second and secret agreement was an agreement between 'gentlemen,' (which neither King could claim to be), that in exchange for nine hundred million livres, Charles would accept Roman Catholicism as his faith. "when the Kingdom will permit". The greater commitment accrued to Louis.

Despite the financial gift, his debts continued to mount. Castlemaine found her hold on power threatened by Eleanor Gwynn and Louise de Karouelle, daughter of Mazarin, known to the English as "Mrs Carwell". She was often to be found in the fashionable shopping arcades of London, and her outgoing manner, did not endear her to the general public. The pamphleteers had named her "Squinabella" and held her in low esteem as yet another French prostitute. She was given half of Barbara's suite of rooms, redecorated, and expressed many disappointments with outburst of temper, and the creation of huge debts. She was more compliant than Barbara, however, who demanded financial support for Bridget, her latest child. Charles denied that he was the father of this one, and suggested she should ask the help of John Churchill, said to be the real father. Nell Gwynne was his new favourite, but never attained the success of Mrs Carwell, Duchess of Portsmouth.

*Restoration and Retribution*

It would be helpful to have a clear view of Carteret's opinion of the King's actions during the 1670s. It is clear that embezzlement was not involved, for he retained Royal favour, judging by the generous gifts of manorial holdings, and his final exoneration from further charges of extortion during his navy treasurer-ship. He remained MP for Portsmouth and a Privy Counsellor, and in addition, a Gentleman of the Bedchamber. He seems to have been able to accept the King's moral shortcomings and much criticised reluctance to involve himself in matters of state or to come to any firm conclusions. He sometimes failed to attend timetabled meetings, sending James in his place. Those who attended preferred those when James took the chair. He was thorough and preferred firm decisions following brief discussion. The King often ignored the decisions he made.

It would be unjust however to accuse Charles of neglecting to defend the welfare of the nation, and to be interested only in trivia. It is true that after setting up the Royal Society he took little further interest, but this left the members to form its policies. Some financial support would have achieved more collective action, but his most significant contributions were the National Stud and the Royal Navy. His growing commitment to the spring and autumn horse-racing sessions, created a valuable new industry as the seasons lengthened, and race tracks became more permanently used. This provided employment for increasing numbers of workers, from jockeys to saddlers, and most European countries were aware of his search for bloodstock. James and he were regular participants at the races, though James was more interested in fox hunting and breeding hunting horses.

Their chief mutual interest however was sailing, and the creation of a Navy capable of combating any restriction on the right to trade freely and to ensure that Britain could respond effectively to any attempt to invade Britain. When Charles arrived in St Helier on 24 April 1646 he had taken the helm of his "Bold Black Eagle' for several two hour shifts, and Carteret had a ship built for him, with two masts and stations for twelve pairs of oarsmen. Instructed by Carteret, Bowden and Mainwaring, Charles was a natural yachtsman and two years later, in 1648, when ten Parliamentary warships defected to the King, Charles took charge and led them into the Thames estuary on 29 August. He narrowly escaped capture displaying reckless courage and waving a pistol in defiance, refusing to go below deck for safety.

Charles 1 had begun to create a Royal Navy and had several ships constructed by Peter Pett, including the 'Sovereign of the Seas' the largest ship of war existing in any country. Prince Charles aged 7 was present at its launch and his total devotion to ships began. Under Parliamentary rule, twenty new Third, Fourth, and Fifth Raters between 1649 and 1651, and another thirty ships were built between 1649 and 1660. In all Parliament added two hundred ships to the Navy. Exiled in Holland, Charles made use of a native Dutch 'Jacht,' moored conveniently below his apartment. In Jersey once more, where he was proclaimed King following the execution of his father, he took command of his ship and sailed it between Jersey and Normandy. Prince James remained on Jersey until the next spring and learned there the rudiments of sailing. Following the Battle of Worcester, Charles made his escape to France on a collier named 'Success'; later Charles bought it and had it renamed 'Royal Escape,' mooring it on the Thames at Whitehall as a precious trophy.

During his reign, Charles created the largest British Navy ever built. Despite financial restrictions made by parliament, in 1688 there were no less than sixty each of Third and Fourth Raters available which had been designed, constructed and manned by the Royal brothers. In addition Charles acquired the first of a number of yachts as a gift from the Dutch in 1660. Redesigned and made larger over the years, they became increasingly popular among the wealthy and speed trials and challenges became popular. Gone were the days when to join the navy was a sign of failure: the King and the Duke created a trend when their illegitimate sons, Charles and Henry, passed their tests and became active naval commanders. Together and separately, frequent visits were made to inspect building progress, to be present on sea trials, and to inspect the dockyards and dry docks. By 1688 there were 20 large yachts the largest and most impressive named 'Fubbs' Charles's pet name for Mrs Carwell, otherwise lampooned as 'Squintabella'.

Charles frequently sailed alone into the Thames estuary, for his own pleasure. Sometimes he mentioned his destination, but he was often found to have made visits to dockyards and been invited to share a meal on board. Pepys mentioned a visit they made to a new ship, when the King removed his full wig, hanging it on a nearby post and made his visit showing his increasing baldness. On one solo trip he was surprised by a severe storm near the Nore eventually running his ship safely onto the beach at Leigh-on-Sea. Guests, friends, mistresses, Ministers and businessmen, were taken on sea trials with the King at the helm. Evelyn was on one such trip and was very impressed by the King's skill. He persuaded the King to land him at Gravesend on the return journey, which was convenient for his home in Woolwich. Among the most regular passengers were the Carterets. George Carteret retained his fascination with ships and their construction, and his views and advice were constantly sought by both brothers and received the title, Lord Admiral.

The cost of this boom in shipbuilding seemed extravagant to the frugally minded, but the spending power it created made a strong impression on other rulers who established that British power should not be underestimated. In fact, shipbuilding was the largest industrial employer in Britain and the King's involvement provided an organisational drive and coherence which made it the basis of Britain's international reputation. It also made Naval careers available to men of all classes of society and gave them an influence and social standing extending to the Royal families of future generations.

Charles gave full support to the new Dutch War, making two lengthy trips to Portsmouth to show his support. For the first he was accompanied by the Queen and Shaftesbury, and for the second by the whole Privy Council, including George.

At this time, Princess Anne, Duchess of York, died following the death of her final son, and King Charles was determined that his brother and heir to the throne, should marry advantageously. If he was to succeed in attracting a wealthy heiress from a powerful European Royal family, he would require a central role in Government. To this end, Charles promoted him to a senior role in the Navy.

James came to commiserate with the Carterets that November, following the death of Jemima Carteret, Philip's wife. Philip had rapidly been a devoted husband and father, following his father's example, and he was for some weeks a broken man, unable to cope with business or other interests for unhappiness. The whole family went into deep mourning and Jemima was laid to rest in the newly constructed family vault in North End Parish Church. She had brought great joy to the family and, fortunately, Edmund, the baby was weaned and healthy before her sudden death occurred. She had not displayed signs of illness before her death. Her mother and siblings learned that it had happened in her sleep, astonishing and perplexing the whole household. From butler and housekeeper to boot boy, sorrow was palpable and friends and neighbours were also affected. Philip was grateful for his father's attempts, and a few days at sea, in the yacht 'Anne' helped to distract him from being laid low by the sorrow. Their eldest grandson, also christened George, was touchingly eager to find ways to console his father and younger brothers for their loss.

Now that Charles was solvent, having received 9,000,000 Ls. from his cousin, he decided to promote his side of their agreement. He had undertaken to support France in an attempt to destroy the power of Spain, by attacking together their European provinces and islands, and their source of gold in the Americas. If this was to work, it would be necessary for France to capture Spanish Flanders and the Rhineland provinces of the Dutch republic. Parliament was recalled and informed that the Dutch Wars would recommence that year and money was awarded to strengthen the Navy. His next step was to abrogate £1,000,000 worth of his long-standing debts to the City. This was surely inevitable and a long-held intention. Fortunately, George had received all he was owed, although much of it was in terms of manorial holdings, and Public Offices.

Turning next to the uncertainties surrounding the religious establishment in England, the King introduced a Declaration of Indulgence to the two houses of Parliament, in accordance with the promise made in the Statute of Breda, to introduce religious Toleration. In essence, in return for individual compliance and regular Church attendance, statements of private belief would not be required. Many people, after the Civil War, had become sceptics concerning religion. Many, like Pepys, found the revival of the banned Church of England, merely a Royal foible which could be tolerated for the sake of monarchy. He attended Matins regularly, listened to the sermon, and awarded marks for thought, then went on his way. Religious devotion, once conspicuous throughout Britain, was less commonly observable. The Anglican Church and its Coronation ceremony were the basis of Charles's authority. The King re-invented the Church, and the Church crowned him King, and head of the Church. To devout Christians, Dissenters or Catholics, this was unacceptable, and enforcing their compliance an absurd condition of social and legal acceptance. The Declaration was, fortunately, found unacceptable by both Houses, although they agreed that a settlement was much to be desired. Charles withdrew his request, setting up a court of enquiry to report back with an acceptable solution in 1674: he accepted a monthly allowance of £10,000, payable for three years, to cover essential expenses and encourage effort on the part of the committee members.

Satisfied that religious contention had been laid to rest, since neither House had demanded penal measures against dissenters, it was now time to clarify the royal succession. James should marry a second time, his legitimate son, the Duke of Kendal having failed to survive his first birthday. As a 38-year-old widower, there was optimism that eligible ladies might be available. The King seized the opportunity to bring his brother forward in an important public role as a leader of the aggressive policy toward the Dutch. A great naval victory was required when Holland was distracted by a French land invasion which would make Britain's power the equal of France, and Prince James the leading military hero of the age. Charles appointed his brother Commander of the Royal Navy and Lord Admiral of the Fleet for the war at sea against the Dutch republic. Charles next placed a "Stop" on the Exchequer, so that all finance was made available.

## CHAPTER THIRTY-TWO

Prince James was delighted to be permitted, at last, to play a role commensurate with his birth and powers of leadership, in a situation which would display his skill as a Commander. It was decided that the War against Holland would be reopened. British naval vessels were faster and more agile than the Dutch fleet, and a battle in the open seas was likely to be more successful than an attack on the Dutch mainland. Those who were conversant with Naval matters were apprehensive about the state of the ships of war and the merchant ships which would be taken into service at this time of national danger. Those who supplied lines, sails canon and gunpowder engaged new workers: also the provisions suppliers and the authorities set about recruiting new crew members with offers of good pay. The London populace were grateful for the employment opportunities offered and came solidly behind their popular King and his heroic brother.

James welcomed the new phase offered to him: the high Command, a future marriage, and the probable birth of a new male heir to his future throne. As a mark of fresh resolution, he took instruction from the Pope's Legate, and became a member of the Catholic Church. The news was not "buried" although the preparations for war were the topical issue and the Prince rode on a wave of popular anticipation.

He began to select the most reliable and experienced officers he knew. They were insufficient in number. George, a professional seaman and Admiral had, for many years warned of the inadequacies of the English fleet. James had to call upon the loyalty of former captains and commanders, many of whom were retired, or suffering the effects of naval hardships and injuries, or, like George Carteret, were fully engaged in the commercial enterprises financing the latest venture. He must have had insight into the problem and its causes. There was a whole missing generation of naval captains and officers. King Charles and his brother would, in normal circumstances have had sons in their late teens, eager to serve their country. The sons of the Cavalier Parliamentarians, had neither military nor naval training. George was exceptional in that both of his sons had a measure of military training. Both were fully trained naval officers, and James was already serving in the naval Caribbean Station. Philip had completed his naval training before joining his father's business with a young family to provide for.

Among those recalled was Edward Montague, 1st Earl of Sandwich and father-in-law of Philip Carteret. George and Montague were of similar age. Montague, on the other hand had been sent to remote Diplomatic posts, and, although he had been an excellent Commander, he had not seen active service for two decades. He may, perhaps, have felt a need to repeat the successes of his youth and volunteered to serve Prince James from motives of simple loyalty.

In an act of personal gratitude and, as a great compliment to his oldest friends, Prince James appointed Edward Montague, Commander of the Blue; the last of the three Squadrons which composed a battle fleet in the days of sail. James himself would lead the three Squadrons of the battle fleet, from the vanguard vessel of the Red Squadron; the second, White Squadron, would be a Squadron of French Warships, led by Admiral d'Estrees, a French Admiral, who had been trained as a captain when George had led the French fleet against the Spanish. As a gesture of friendship to the Carterets, Edward invited Philip to join him as Personal Assistant. Philip was a competent Captain and qualified for the task, although sailing battleships was outside his experience. He was known to be more concerned with measures to improve the safety of trading ships and their crews.

Montague's flagship was the Royal James, and its captain was Richard Haddock, regarded as the finest Captain of that age. Haddocks had served as Commander of Royal Yachts on many occasions. Montague knew his own tendency for impulsive decisions, and Philip would provide a useful voice of restraint. The Dutch were commanded by Admiral de Ruyter, and Grand Pensioner Cornelius de Witt, who had been responsible for the destruction of the British fleet in Chatham. I suppose one can make a guess at the reaction of Philip's parents at his new role. There would have been pleasure that Philip was to have the opportunity to demonstrate new skills and improved reputation; pleasure that Montague had chosen his son-in-law to share his honour; also Philip's grief, might find the challenge a healing distraction. They were relieved to find that the Blue Squadron would be the last to fight and might not be required. Of course, they could not attempt to prevent a thirty-year-old son from accepting the invitation, knowing his firmness of purpose.

The British and French combined fleet assembled off Spithead, where they met the French fleet on 7th.May, and many ceremonial salutes were fired to celebrate their strong alliance. The Commanders had met in conference already, and Prince James had published a standardised plan which combined simplicity and clarity. Each of the three squadrons would follow closely behind the Red flagship, keeping to the pace of their squadron leader. When the Duke reached their chosen battle station, battle orders would be issued, by messenger skiffs, flag signals and megaphones. It appears that the Duke did not announce this and, bearing in mind that the finest ships' captains had died in the earlier campaign, it is probable that inexperienced and retired commanders would have read the book.

De Ruyter, who had read the book, so was fully aware of these plans, decided not to wait to be attacked. He had set off the previous day, hoping to trap the English fleet setting out from the Medway and wreak destruction there for the second time. Approaching the estuary, he was informed that the fleet had already left to rendezvous with the French White squadron off Spithead. De Ruyter considered sailing into the Medway and demolishing Chatham docks, but the defensive castles were ready, on this occasion, and he revised the plan again.

The Duke, "very eager to get up with the Dutch fleet", beat up Channel and on 16 May, caught sight of de Ruyter's masts. This process of preparation had so far taken eight days. The weather was fine and James immediately raised the Union flag and, as this instruction was reported down the line of eighty ships, the three squadrons, in correct order, formed the 'line of battle'. All was in accordance with the Duke's "Instructions for the Better Ordering of the Fleet in Battle." This instruction Manual had been written and printed by the Duke during his previous time as Naval Commander. Whether it had been read and committed to heart by the Navy is an open question. Montague and other retirees, were probably unaware of its existence.

These instructions were first issued in preparation for the First Dutch War and designed to keep the ships one hundred yards apart. This was to enable the ships to cover the full length of the enemy formation and attack at close quarters, while holding the weather gage. It was a fresh naval innovation and subsequently adopted for all naval battles. The Dutch usually formed their ships into small groups, then launched several attacks on individual ships. Unfortunately for the British, de Ruyter had studied the

Duke's textbook and instructed his fleet to form the same line of battle. This would be a considerable shock to the British. De Ruyter was prepared, if the opportunity arose, to attack individual ships. In the event this flexibility led to tragic consequences for the Royal James.

Meanwhile, it took the best part of a day for the British fleet to space out in a line spread over three sea miles. The Dutch fleet would be expected to form a similar line, facing them. The fleets were evenly matched, but it was late in the day and, because the wind direction did not favour the Dutch, de Ruyter withdrew his ships to the safety of the shallow sandbanks off the Dutch coast, to await an improvement in the weather.

Observing this, the Duke anchored his ship west-north-west of Southwold Church tower, and his squadron anchored nearby. Montague and his squadron, overpowered by a rising wind, anchored slightly north of them, and d'Estrees to their south. It was now 23 May, and the Duke decided that since his ships were running short of water and food, he would instruct his Squadron Commanders to send boats ashore for supplies. On land in Southwold, he instructed the Mayor to close all approach roads, and ordered the townspeople to stay in their houses. All this was done according to plan. The Duke however gave no instructions to his commanders, nor did he mention his intention to stay overnight on land or have his ship beached and careened. His omission to convey his plan to his ships is astonishing. He was either over-confident or incompetent and his lack of action inexplicable.

The Duke created a land base at the Sole Bay Inn, and held a dinner meeting there with his officers but apparently gave no instructions. Meanwhile he received regular bulletins on the progress of the Dutch, and the changing weather conditions. It was four days before the wind direction became favourable again, and supplies were still being brought on board. James received a report that the Dutch were still in port and loading supplies. Careening was well underway, and a whole fleet waiting and running short of food and water.

Before sunrise on 28 May, a French scout reported that the top sails of the Dutch fleet could be seen above the horizon. Fortunately, the winds were light and the fleet would have three hours to get into position but considerable concern ensued. De Ruyter's action saw his line of battle was facing a ragged English fleet in some confusion. The high Channel tide was flooding southward and the wind east-south-east, therefore the Duke ordered Montague's squadron to confront the Dutch on a northerly course. James's Vanguard ship was gradually re-launched and since the Red Squadron was unready, Montague was instructed to lead, his ship directed by Captain Haddock. Thus, the planned order of battle had been reversed. D'Estrees, wishing to respond appropriately, asked for clarification and was instructed to follow the wind to the South. He assumed that the Duke would take the second Squadron's position, which it did, and the French fleet took on the post previously allocated to Montague's Squadron.

The two British fleets attempted to get into line, but Montague's Royal James was now far ahead of the rest of his Squadron. The Duke, whose ship had been renamed the 'London,' instructed his fleet to support the Blues, although the London was the last in that formation, and improbably, attempting to lead from the rear. De Ruyter seized the opportunity and ordered his ships to form small, random groups, including fire ships, and had no difficulty in picking out Montague's ship. Captain van Ness was ordered to go after 'Royal Charles', the Duke's ship, and van Ghent was instructed to intercept Montague's 'Royal James', flying the Royal Ensign from its Quarter-deck.

By 9.00 am. The Dutch had full benefit of wind on a perfect, warm summer day. The 'Groot Hollandia' attacked Montague's flagship, launching broadsides then, at close quarters, flinging out grappling hooks. As a result the ship lost her upper deck guns and her gun crews. A fire ship then attacked and Royal James was engulfed in fire. Other British ships blundering through the smoke, assumed the 'Hollandia' to be a victorious British ship and gave three cheers.

The Master, Captain Haddock, had given the order to cut the anchor cable, and Philip went to supervise the mast men. However, the fire ship had set the sails and masts on fire, and soon the 'Royal James' was on fire from stem to stern. The order to abandon ship was given, and the survivors launched two boats. Haddock filled his boat and rowed off. Philip and his father-in- law managed to get the Royal Ensign into a second boat and rowed off in search of an alternative flagship. It may be that they paused to rescue seamen who had jumped ship, but whatever occurred, in the smoke and confusion, their boat was lost, and never seen again. Those on board were assumed to have drowned, including Edward Montague and Philip Carteret.

The Battle continued. De Ruyter inflicted spectacular damage on the

British fleet. The Duke, according to the senior lieutenant on his ship, was "General, soldier, pilot, master, seaman… and most pleasant when the great shot are thundering about his ears". Sir John Cox, the Duke's captain, was shot while standing beside him; Narborough took on his post. The Duke's second flagship was destroyed, and he moved to a third, the Michael, and ordered the hulk of the James to be searched for survivors. He sailed on in pursuit of the Dutch, then transferred to the London, gathering up leaderless ships and joined in the pursuit of Dutch ships already being pursued by the French squadron. The chase continued until the following day. The Dutch then made for their home ports, and British ships, having deep draughts, abandoned the chase. In London, the reaction was muted. A British Victory was not proclaimed.

Parliament was highly critical of the outcome since it should have concluded with the defeat of the Dutch and the capture of Holland. However, despite these reservations, the county as a whole was delighted that Britain had achieved another great victory. James' reputation reached a remarkable high point, and the King decided that the time had come to strengthen his own reputation with an attempt to complete his long delayed promise of religious toleration. James may have justified his religious conversion.

In all, the Battle had occupied twenty-six days. The cost of the expedition increased the Naval debt considerably, but did not end the War. In 1673 another attack was made, led by the Duke of Monmouth and Prince Rupert. The Dutch were outnumbered but the superior fire-power of the allies was no match for the strong coastal defences among the sand-dunes, and no landing was possible. At the same time, the Bahamas, was given to George Carteret, possibly to console him for his loss.

Parliament finally refused funds to pursue the war, and there were accusations that the Duke had not made sufficient effort in his campaigns. A peace with the Dutch was negotiated which was extremely unpopular with the Dutch, whose trade was suffering. Their Commanders were made national heroes, and the de Witt brothers, who had created the wealth they had enjoyed were blamed for incompetence, and were dragged to Dam Square, and publicly dismembered by a howling mob. Their bodies were then eaten. The Stadtholder who had led their army made no attempt to save the De Witts, and was crowned King. King Charles and Prince James, sent their congratulations. As William's uncles they made plans for their

Stuart relative to visit England. He received a welcome and was regarded as a Protestant hero to Londoners, and Shaftesbury promoted his interests as well as those of the Protestant Duke of Monmouth, who was the more energetic, handsome and entertaining in manner, though more cunning. James, Duke of York, if he wished to succeed to the throne, now had two rivals.

In Britain the groundswell of opinion was strongly critical of the Government and its ministers and attempts were made to place the conduct of war in the hands of Parliament. Financial crisis led to the recall of Parliament, but the members insisted on dealing with the Declaration of Indulgence before any other business. Charles had belatedly introduced an act ensuring full toleration to all existing religious sects. If he felt this proposed act, incongruously coming from the Governor of the Church of England, would gain compliance, he was sadly mistaken, since there was little regard for either Anglicanism or the King at this time.

George and Elizabeth, after some days, learned of the deaths of Philip and Edward Montague, and the families combined their mourning and began to make plans for the care of the young of their families. Three small boys were now orphaned and even the eldest and bravest could be forgiven for falling into inconsolable grief. Great effort was devoted to restoring them to some sense of security following the loss of their parents who had been so central to their lives. The very unexpectedness of their losses weighed heavily, and they wondered whether their grandparents would abandon them to strangers. They had seen their mother conveyed to the family vault but there was no formal burial for their father. The bodies of the dead from the Sole Bay Battle were gradually washed upon Suffolk beaches, and there was hope that some would be identified, but even those with distinctive features or tattoos could rarely be named. They may have gained consolation from public recognition as national heroes who had given their lives for their King and country, but individual corpses were consigned to unmarked graves in remote churchyards.

At the end of the battle, ships, some damaged beyond repair, limped away seeking the nearest port, there was realisation of the number of ships, seamen and officers lost. Prince James who had fought for control of operations with great determination and had commandeered less than three ships, each destroyed as he led them into attack.

No consolation other than praise, was awarded to those who died on the Royal James, fearlessly taking the fight to the whole Dutch Fleet, while others did not dare to. It was reported, officially, that Philip had died bravely, attempting to save lives, which was probable. The boys might be consoled that their father was a hero, but the adults were rocked by yet another death in the family.

# CHAPTER THIRTY-THREE

George looked his age, every one of his sixty-three years, following this disaster and wore his grey hair long. Perhaps they hoped that Philip's body might be among the thousand washed ashore on the Suffolk coast during the autumn gales. Edward Montague's body was found in a fishing net, though only recognisable by his Garter sash. The Duke came to commiserate and offer help and friendship, though he, at the time, was suffering from serious reputational damage at the hands of his brother. The popular press attempted to assert the bravery and determined leadership of the Duke, but Charles sent him off to Flanders to assist the French campaign. The Dutch provinces had suffered severe damage and had only been saved by flooding their polders, creating severe economic damage. Meanwhile, the former concerns regarding the King's integrity and the deeply held hatred of Catholic treachery and conspiracies grew in strength.

At this stage the Cabal disintegrated and, by political sleight of hand, Thomas Danby overcame the Shaftesbury clique, when he began to claim that the King was a secret catholic and dependent on the French. Danby, according to Bishop Burnet, who was a confirmed gossip, "a plausible speaker who gave himself great liberties in discourse but did not seem to have any great regard for the truth." He attempted to revive the fine old Cavalier standards, supporting the King, Parliament and the Church of England.

Parliament was provoked into acting by the pamphleteers and demands of their constituents, and fear of the projected Act of Toleration. The Commission defining Toleration was forgotten and Danvers put forward the proposal for a Test Act. Previous acts had excluded Catholics from living in London, or any Chartered town with elected aldermen. The new Test Act demanded that Catholics must be removed from any public office unless they took Anglican communion regularly, in an Anglican Church, a commitment expected of all loyal Englishmen. In addition, they were required to state publicly that they rejected the Doctrine of Transubstantiation and the communion of saints, as false and heretical superstitions.

Since the object of the book is to illuminate the actions and beliefs of

*Restoration and Retribution*

three families and their close associates, it is necessary to show that they were as divided about the wisdom of this act as they had been during the disputes of the civil war. The majority of Carterets, Dowses, and Montagues had no difficulty with this declaration, but not all, and the Catholic Paulets, presumably, reached some diplomatic compromise. One cannot guess how many decent citizens suffered psychological injury having to reject all that they had always believed. King Charles was angry that he had been prevented, by this Act, from resolving the religious tensions which undermined his government. It might have been pointed out that the King himself had insisted on recreating the Anglican Church without reference to parliament, and that body was not respected throughout Britain. His acts restoring monarchy and a House of Lords had created complications which Cromwell's Government had circumvented.

The Duke of York absolutely refused to deny transubstantiation, and consequently was compelled to relinquish all his Government offices. Many ministers and military office holders were replaced by professed Anglicans. In Ireland, the new Governor, the Earl of Essex, chose to ignore the Test Act, since the wholesale dismissal of Bishops, and public administrators, would have created social chaos in a predominantly Catholic nation. English parliamentarians had always paid scant regard to the interest of the non-English nations of Britain. He was faced with some antagonism from those who wished to see a persecution of Catholics, acting instead against dissident dissenters who instigated acts of violence among protestants, which they accused Catholics of performing. When their lies were exposed, some became rebels and brigands instituting raids and murder in peaceful communities. They were named "Tories" from their attempts to undermine and discredit the peace. Shaftesbury and his disparate supporters adopted this term for their opponents, the Royalists. Such was Shaftesbury's antagonism that Charles dismissed him to protect him from a charge of treason. Charles finally disbanded the Cabal but awarded ex-members further ranks of nobility. Arlington and Clifford became Earls and Shaftesbury, was made Earl of Salisbury. Clifford, who was Catholic, duly resigned his office, and died shortly after.

The King was forced by the Test Act to make many changes. Now that his brother had lost his posts as Naval Commander and as Warden of the Cinque Ports, he appointed a committee of twelve Commissioners, including George as a leading authority on all naval matters. The President appointed was his former employee, Samuel Pepys, with whom he enjoyed a close relationship. In private, the King commiserated with George on the loss of Philip and Edward Montague and restated his intention to repay the money George had lent him and to elevate him to the Peerage in the near future. By way of a memorial to Philip, the captured Dutch province closest to New York, was given the name "New Jersey". George and his cousin, Dr. Philippe de Carteret, remained as Gentlemen of the Presence Chamber, and the King made Sir Edward Carteret, a Colonel, in his retirement from active service. He was also appointed Gentleman Usher of the Black Rod, who preceded the Monarch when invited to address the Lords in their Chamber. In the following year he was also appointed Keeper of the Little Park at Windsor. Cranbrook House was placed at his disposal, and he retained a London house adjacent to St James's Park.

It was Clifford, before his death, who had recommended Thomas Osborne, a Yorkshireman and excellent administrator, as Lord Treasurer. He was, fortuitously, a practising Anglican and therefore acceptable to the Commons. He had business interests in the City, and George was well acquainted with him. Danby, whom Burnett had accused of lying, was impeached, dismissed, and later tried and executed for plotting against the King. Salisbury lost all his political offices but began to promote the interests of James, Duke of Monmouth, who had declared his allegiance to the Anglican Church: a direct challenge to his Uncle, James, the heir to the throne.

The changes occurring at this time aroused considerable interest in the popular press of the day and the opinion-forming pamphlets, a large number of which were distributed daily. George noted, idly, that many appeared to promote the interest of the Dutch trading community and its desire for closer relationship with a fellow Protestant nation. This was hardly the view of the King who was firmly non-partisan, and could not be responsible. Gossip in the hall of the Stock Exchange had it that some of his fellow traders were accepting 'loans' to assist in the purchase of stock. These 'loans' were offered by Dutch merchants who were also publishing the pamphlets recommending a Dutch alliance. George greeted this news with dismay. He continued to believe that an oath or a promise should be binding

At Whyte's one morning, he ran into an old friend, Sir Edward Knight, who was gaining a reputation as a breeder and exporter of racing horses, with stables on the Hampshire Downs. He mentioned that he was looking for shipping space for the regular transport of horses to the continent. He was heading a loose consortium of breeders who needed suitably adapted ships and wanted a long-term arrangement. The Dutch had offered, but refused to trade with France. George expressed interest and observed that Portsmouth would be easily accessible: he was having a jetty extended to accommodate larger ships at that time.

They adjourned to St James's Park when Knight remarked that he had information that might be useful for him. 'There is good reason for us to be seen talking. The king intends to ride here today, so we can mingle with those who come to cheer him on.'

They arrived in time to see the King and his brother contesting energetically for a victory. From their position it was impossible to see who had won. The riders leapt from their horses, roaring with laughter and each boasting of his victory.

'Carteret! What are you doing here?' the King shouted, as they walked over." Which of us won?'

'From this place we could not judge, but you seemed to be neck and neck'.

'There you are, James. What did I say? I know you, don't I? Epsom races wasn't it. You are Knight, the horse breeder. How is Old Rowley serving your mares? I trust my namesake is giving satisfaction.'

'Very well, Your Majesty. Carteret and I are planning a shipment of four-year-olds for France. If I'm not mistaken, your brother's horse is one of mine; Bishop, isn't it?'

'Yes, one of five from the forty in my stable at Whitehall. Very fine horses! Good bye to you! I'm going to walk very quickly, brother, to confuse any assassins who might be planning my death. Though, with you as an alternative, it's probably unlikely.' Prince James, ignored the implied criticism, and rode back to the Palace.

'He can make a joke at his own expense, then.'

'He is always relaxed, Edward. He tells me he takes life one day at a time, and successfully avoids controversy. He gives his ministers their head, and watches the result with detached interest, and never judges. What did you want to tell me, Edward?'

'I have been told that several business associates of yours are in receipt of payments from the Dutch Stadtholder to promote his interest as an heir and a Protestant, who will always favour them in trading agreements. You may know this already, but perhaps you do not know that some of the King's Ministers are receiving pensions which could be doubled when King dies. William is to be proposed as his successor.'

'That is news to me, although Charles was restored with similar assistance, so it will not be a surprise. Is there more?'

'Nothing which can be verified, except that many of the Pamphlets in circulation, originate in Amsterdam: sometimes they hint at events known only to those in the closest Court circle. You will probably be aware that assassination plots are being constantly made, though fortunately, most are prevented by our agents and are quite inept.'

'Thank you, Edward. I always thought you might work for a certain retired lawyer; hence that savage attack made on you in 1637. Fortunately, I got you to a good surgeon who saved you from permanent injury.'

'So, it was you, George! When I regained my wits, I thought I remembered hearing your voice. Permit me to offer my belated thanks.'

Although the slave trade was closing down operations in the Gambia, it was decided to retain the port of Bathurst as a fuelling post for trade with Bombay, originally a Portuguese possession, now a British possession. which formed part of the Queen's Dowry. Spices and scintillating fabrics were in great demand, as can be seen in Lely's paintings. The reformed Africa Company was relaunched and opened to new shareholders so that in a few decades, almost any serious share buyer would have investments in the trade. There were increasingly good returns, though many investors would not have known that origins of their profit, or the sugar they consumed, came from foreign plantations where slavery was a common practice, although not sanctioned in Britain

In private gossip following a Privy Council meeting, George heard the disturbing news that James, his son, had been involved in stirring up a rebellion in the Jersey colony. He had advocated the overthrow of the British Governing Council, and encouraged farmers and shopkeepers to expel their representatives from Government House. Fortunately, a naval squadron had been in the area, and the rising was put down. Philippe le Geyt brought this news of his reprehensible behaviour to England, and presented it as a formal report to the Privy Council. There was an embarrassing meeting for

George, who was invited to absent himself, while the report was read. A reprimand was despatched to James to adhere to his contract and obey his instructions.

George was not held responsible, although he had hoped that James was gaining common sense and was disappointed. It seemed that James was sympathetic to the advice of Penn's son. The seeds of the movement toward American independence were planted early in the settlements, whose trade was required to pass through British trading companies. They were not permitted to trade directly with the Europe or with other colonies. They received a relative pittance for all their labours. This unfair situation might have gained support in Britain had it become known, but the general public and the press were too busy with imaginary religious plots to attend to other issues.

James himself was unrepentant and predicted that the Colonies would gain freedom in the long run, and attempted to draw attention to the unfair restrictions imposed by those appointed to office. A rebellion finally broke out and James attempted to end it with a coup. He failed. He appeared to have boundless energy and since arriving in America, he had acquired a wife and a daughter. His wife, was Francoise Delaval, daughter of the mayor of New York and an heiress to the Delaval family of Northumberland. Their coal mines were providing great wealth and their influence was strong in north of England circles and in New York. They had eloped and were married by a Minister in a neighbouring colony. They had been given a home by the bride's father, but James, rumour had it, had taken to drink and wife beating. His wife's father had been forced to rescue her. In 1674, he and his young daughter left America for Europe seeking to live at the London house. Parental supervision did not suit him it seemed, but he nourished happy memories of his childhood in Jersey.

Coincidentally Mr Poindestre, a St Helier industrialist, had asked George to send quantities of woollen knitting thread, to support a new venture, the manufacture of warm woollen socks for fishermen. George provided it and suggested that James could assist with this venture. It is a commercial act recorded in Privy Council records. Unemployed fishermen, idle in times of bad weather, were from that time seen walking the streets of Jersey, while knitting. Bess was delighted when she heard that James had named his daughter Elizabeth, and sent gifts to St Ouen such as might please a five-year-old, with an affectionate letter to James, with advice on the education of girls. George, ever practical, arranged for £200.00 to be paid to James annually. A sufficient amount for a country gentleman to rent a house and servants.

Some events of 1674/5 illustrate the varied life of a Senior Privy Councillor. Drama and music played an increasingly large part of the King's life in his declining years. His father James's Court had a reputation for extravagant entertainment and Masques. His sons Charles and James and their mother had all played parts in elaborate masques performed in the palaces, and Charles was eager to revive the tradition. John Crowne, a favourite musician at Windsor, was asked by Charles to write a colourful show full of magic and transformation in the story tradition of Ovid but without the usual sexual undercurrent. He intended to involve the Princesses Mary and Anne, and opportunities must be provided for them to dance, sing and act. It was produced, with music written by Nicholas Stiggins, an ambitious young composer. Its plot was ingenious but appeared to lack resolution, although the settings and dances were spectacular. The audience was not impressed by the princesses, who seemed unable to master their lines or adhere to: their speeches which were mainly redistributed among the cast. James, although fond of his daughters, considered that academic education was unsuitable for girls. They took little exercise and painted watercolours and played the Harpsichord: the greater part of their day was spent in embroidery and dancing. James presumably expected to pass his throne to a son. In the event when each girl at last inherited the throne, they were bewildered and out of their depth, with dire consequences.

The most spectacular occurrence of these years was the discovery of numerous bones buried deep below the Tower of London. They were assumed, with little justification, to be the two vanished sons of Edward IV who disappeared during the reign of King Richard III. It came at a time when the Hereditary principle of Kingship needed reviving, within the face of several possible 'heirs' being promoted by unscrupulous politicians. Charles and the Anglican Bishops proclaimed the undoubted validity of these bones, which were reburied with ceremony and pageantry in Westminster Abbey, the event observed by a respectful and enthusiastic crowd. For Charles, it was an assertion of the timeless principle of Royal Heredity which must be maintained. It was certainly a decisive occasion, on which he placed great importance, occurring as it did at a time of dangerous political upheaval when so many changes were made.

## CHAPTER THIRTY-FOUR

George and Elizabeth continued to play a supporting role in Prince James's life as he came to terms with his increasingly problematic political status. Following the death of the Duchess of York, and the Sole Bay battle, James had little time for his daughters. They were mere children and needed to be protected from the effects of their mother's illness. Efforts were made by their personal attendants to distract them, with dancing and music. They had no formal education or instruction, such as they might have received in an ordinary noble home. It was considered unsuitable for a lady to be taught any practical skill. Their future husbands would be able to mould them in wifely duties after their marriage. Both girls were confirmed members of the Anglican Church, and James was already wondering where to search for husbands in an increasingly narrow field of eligible Anglican suitors.

James spoke to his old friends, about his personal concerns, having no-one else in whom he could confide. They, of course, listened and expressed sympathy, as they had always done. However, they were increasingly unable to offer helpful solutions, rather than mere advice, owing to James's very specific problems. He was no longer malleable. Anne, his wife, had become a Catholic in her teenage years as a part of her French education. Teen-age devotion to her faith had modified when she fell for the charms of the young, vigorous James Stuart, but when pregnant, she accepted an Anglican wedding as politically necessary. She had attended Anglican communion with her husband, as he was bound to do, as brother of the Head of the Church of England. Following the births of her daughters and sons, she had found a stable group of supportive female friends, among whom was the Queen. The King and her husband, had extra-marital affairs and children by a number of mistresses; a familiar situation for many wives. The Queen remained staunch in her adherence to Catholic doctrine and practices, and to the King, and Anne returned to the faith of her youth, from which she gained solace. This faith was now her consolation as she awaited inevitable death.

James had initially refused to marry Anne, who was a mere passing fancy. In the confusion of events surrounding the King's restoration, the

King had insisted on his brother's marriage to the daughter of his chief minister, and James, as always, complied with his brother's wishes. This forced marriage had, over the years, become a happy relationship. Anne, with her optimism and humour, reconciling James to the thoughtless manipulation of his wishes and feelings by his brother. Some months before his wife's death, James had gone through the process of spiritual exercises before being accepted into the Catholic Church. The Test Act and loss of all his Offices, was the unexpected and unwelcome result of his brother's policy. Nevertheless, he was determined to keep to his new faith in the knowledge that he had signed a document asserting that he would always be a true Protector of the Anglican Church, if he became King. The Carterets agreed that there were rumblings of discontent at his Catholic conversion, among many of the Commons. However, out of loyalty to his late wife, he was determined to abide by his decision.

They shared their grief with James, who had lost wife and children in the same few months they had lost a daughter and son: all were concerned with national events which seemed to offer no resolution. To add to their grief came news of the death of Amyas Carteret, ending a long and precious relationship to which a solemn and well-attended funeral seemed to do less than justice for a man of such sound judgement and friendship. James promised that he would ensure that George's business concerns would receive support and that his connections with the Navy would continue, together with the Plantations Committee.

In the following months, George continued work on the reconstruction plan for London and, at Wren's request, on the planning committee for the new St Paul's Cathedral. There were enormous numbers of churches which required rebuilding, over seventy had been destroyed in the Great Fire, and each required an altar to be placed at the eastern point, a font and a pulpit, from which the rector or vicar could deliver a sermon. Suitable housing for the rector's family was the concern of the community. On the whole a rectangular building was favoured, with side aisles if the site permitted. A separate bell tower was preferred and baroque simplicity and large, plain, glazed windows required. No statuary or ornamentation was expected.

The amount of time spent discussing how such requisites could be expanded to the size of a Cathedral sufficiently large and dignified to impress the many expected viewers, and with the awe and architectural splendour of a National Religious Monument, was the cause of prolonged contention.

Traditionalists wanted something 'Early English' like Canterbury or Salisbury, but this was rejected as redolent of Catholicism and superstition. St Anne's, Covent Garden was a less controversial shape but would dominate the London skyline like a gigantic barn. With a bell tower added it would look absurd. Wren produced a variety of designs, and the model finally chosen was ostentatiously large and high but based on early Roman basilicas, with the addition of transepts to create the shape of the crucifix, two bell towers, to increase the height of the flight of entrance steps and a Roman portico. The crowning marvel would be the first architectural dome in Britain, designed to amaze the observer, and create aural resonance for doctrinal sermons. Thus St Paul's would echo with the words of doctrine and the Gospel, while its rival St Peter's in Rome, would resound with empty harmonies and the repetition of superstitions. Its construction roused consternation, but when completed it became an object worthy of the city and astonished the world with its size and symbolism.

Prince James continued to attempt to find a role at an increasingly frivolous court, where morals were mocked and honesty regarded as an embarrassing display of bad taste, His brother demanded that he should marry as soon as possible. Again, James came to George and Bess to complain of his misfortune, and the way fate, in the form of his brother, blighted all his attempts to achieve happiness. He bitterly complained of his brother's unkindness and his moral fragility, and happily ignored the fact that he had a good number of Illegitimate children himself. Parliament had demanded that his bride should be Protestant. James, still in mourning, chose the widowed Lady Beleyse, of whom he had grown very fond, and who had helped to console him in his loss. She was a lady in waiting to the Queen, and was attractive and mature with an adult son to inherit the title. The King refused to permit it. James, he stated, must find a bride from a noble family who could bring a personal fortune, the possibility of increased national trade, and the possibility of an heir.

They could see that James was unhappy with his lot, but many people would consider themselves fortunate to have his privileges. They noted that James was no longer the slim, serious minded and affectionate young man he had once been. Full in the waist, with a bull neck and a stubborn set of the jaw, he was now assertive and had fixed ideas which he would permit no-one to question. Once he had decided on a course of action, he refused to be challenged. In some ways he was becoming as uncompromising as his father. Bess agreed with George on this assessment and shared fears of what might be the outcome, if he inherited the throne.

Few European rulers were prepared to allow their daughter to marry a heretic, even a recent convert, who was prepared to rule a heretical nation. Finally King Louis persuaded the Duke of Modena, who was in considerable debt, that his sons would benefit from a French defence alliance, if he would offer one of his two unmarried daughters to Prince James, the British heir apparent. The chosen lady would probably become the next Queen of Britain. Parliament in London was not consulted, since foreign affairs were solely for the King to decide. Protestantism was an essential and several solutions were already available to the King to select a protestant succession. Among them was the new Dutch King. Meanwhile some Parliamentarians would be willing to legitimise the Duke of Monmouth and crown him, or alternatively, an act could be passed to crown his daughter, Mary, following the death of Charles, thus by-passing James entirely.

They noted also that the sordid break-down of the marriage of Lord Roos, his wife, and her long-term partner, had been adjudicated by the House of Lords, who had granted a divorce, without reference to the King or the Archbishop. This gave Parliament the right to divorce married couples. Was it possible that parliament could divorce the King and Queen? Probably not, but it led to a new suggestion, that the King should take the succession into his own hands, divorce his infertile Queen, and marry a woman capable of bearing a son. He would, of course, be following a pragmatic example set by his ancestor, King Henry VIII. Charles rejected the suggestion issuing a statement that he would never divorce his wife, to whom he swore lifelong devotion.

Louise Carwell replaced Barbara Villiers as lady in waiting to the Queen, in company with Eleanor Gwynn, leaving all these questions unanswered and they remained the King's favourite mistresses until his death. On 30 September, following a proxy marriage in Modena, Maria Beatrice of Modena, aged 15 years, arrived in England and on November 21 became Duchess of York, the Duke being 35 years older than she was. An Anglican ceremony was conducted at one of the Queen's Catholic Chapels, and a special permit issued by the Cardinal of the British Province. At approximately the same time, James, Duke of Monmouth, married the Duchess of Buccleugh, who brought with her a considerable dowry. He was at that time father of at least one illegitimate child, and the marriage was doomed to failure, by his serial infidelity, and his abandonment of his wife. His Royal pretensions led him to lead a rebellion against James when he became King. Executed for treason after the Battle of Sedgemore, his challenge to the heredity principal was rejected. Finally, on 9 May, a Peace Treaty with Holland was agreed and the situation which weakened British trade was finally resolved. These events would have been fully understood by the Carterets who were amazed at the extent to which concepts of honour and stability were being cast aside. Their son, James, seemed to have anticipated these destabilising codes of conduct with his own disregard for custom.

This treaty created peace between Britain and Holland, and allowed British regiments to take on other duties, many lending their support to Louis XIV. William's attitude to the agreement can be judged by his anti-Catholic propaganda and bribes to influential English MPs. William's suspicions were based on his personal insecurity. The Orange/Nassau family originated in a small French province which they had abandoned and had inherited a little land in rural Holland. His father, William the Silent, gained status by marrying Mary, daughter of Charles. Her marriage was unhappy, producing one son, whose health gave constant concern. At the Coronation of Charles II, he was a small child of 7, and Pepys described him as "a pretty boy". He became adult and an energetic soldier during the period when the United Provinces, nurtured by the de Witt brothers, created a European power to be respected.

With the overthrow of the de Witts, following the Dutch War, William came forward and imposed order, when chaos ensued. At the signing of the Peace Treaty, he was chosen as Stadtholder, a role equivalent to Lord Protector, the civilian title held by Cromwell. Holland lost much of its democratic government at that point, an aristocracy was created, and women denied authority. By consent it became an absolute monarchy. France lurked on its border as a constant threat, and William feared that his British uncles might conspire against him. He had the advantage of being third in line to the English throne, giving precedence only to any legitimate son of Charles or James. He felt that he deserved greater respect and active support from both. Charles pointed out that his virtual control of a united Holland was the result of the British defeating Republicans, so that William owed his power largely to Britain. As a subject ruler he should be grateful. William regarded himself free to pursue his own interests and began to influence members of anti-Catholic associations, including the Green Ribbon movement supported by Shaftesbury.

George became aware of William's plans through friends at court, such as Dr. Philip de Carteret, a colleague of George now that both were Gentlemen of the Presence Chamber, who accompanied the King in his rigorous early walks. His long, loping stride was becoming faster to avoid assassins and those who might criticise him. Crispe and Povey, long-time business associates, who were members of the Plantations Committee, had both been offered inducements to support William's claim. Many, uncertain about their future security, accepted bribes from various ambitious pretenders since secret deals potentially benefited giver and recipient. An established tradition of British law said a bribe accepted did not create an obligation for the recipient to honour the agreement. Such income was always undeclared to accountants.

The leading trader in the Slave Trade on the stock market, was John Ward, said to be the son of the John Smith who had bought Sir John Hawkins' shares on his death. Trade with the American colonies was growing exponentially, and several generations of Dowses held leading rôles in the public life of Massachusetts. In the next century, one Dowse who was a Senator of the state, offered advice concerning slavery to Jefferson. James Carteret's misjudgement of the mood of the time could be regarded as a sign of future moves toward independence, a rehearsal for later events.

Philip's sons where thriving under the care of Bess, who was a devoted grandmother, and among the Queen's ladies. George was concerned with the planning and financing of the Bedford estate and its farms, and was employing efficient managers and gardening staff. Bess was blessed with a remarkable house-keeper named Mrs Gosling, who ruled the domestic staff fairly, but firmly. Their individual concerns meant that they were often apart, but each accepted the situation in the hope that it would be to the benefit of the next Carteret generation. Their own line of the family was growing increasingly slender: Philip's three sons were the family's strongest hope.

George discovered that as the King spent increasing time on "leisure " activities, his persuasive skills dealing with Stage managers and musicians, was frequently called upon. He had acquired a feeling for the arts, and sang a round when necessary, and enjoyed spending afternoons at the theatre and after dinner he, Pepys and Hugh Montais, spent enjoyable time in the theatre and afterwards with Mrs Knepp, and other actors, in Vauxhall Gardens. George renewed his former relationship with Mrs King, now playing senior roles in Beaumont or Wycherley plays. Jane King, was still playing young roles, but she and Molly King spent leisure hours with them in after-show partying. As Vice Chamberlain George was easily persuaded to join the changing personnel of the Navy office.

At this point the King made him a Lord Admiral and the King's interest in the navy became his main occupation. He may well have welcomed the opportunity to avoid the petty squabbling of politicians and the effort of attaining a personal balance between opposing factions. While at sea he was saved stress and obtained an intimate knowledge of his ships and the men who built and sailed them. He demonstrated a thorough knowledge of these matters which contrasted with his well-recorded inattention in other meetings and his impatience with detail. In naval matter he was meticulous. He attended hundreds of meetings every year busying himself with provision and prices, the interviewing new officers. His many notebooks reveal that he regularly noted his observations of the abilities of young cadets, noting their strengths and weaknesses, so that years later, when a promotion was requested, he could refer to his own notes to suggest named candidates deserving promotion. Carteret, when Treasurer to the navy, had kept similar notebooks, and he and the King analysed their impressions and observations and generally found themselves in agreement.

Many of these Navy Office meetings took place on board ship, or in a shipyard, and captains and officers were expected to give their opinions and justify them. Prince James was often also present and kept his own notes, and was pedantically thorough: no doubt the brothers exchanged information. Sinecure appointments became quite rare: their own sons were expected to show improvement and increasing ability. The number of meetings increased as the Navy grew in size and, during the 70s, Charles attempted to spend weekends at Windsor, when he was not at sea. Sunday morning, after prayers and exercise, was the time for the Naval Officials to meet. Pepys, more at home in a City Office, disliked having to travel to Berkshire for meetings, even more than he disliked meetings held in an inn in Newmarket.

The minutes Pepys wrote up from his notes, rarely listed the names of those present, though the Chair was often named. Only the decisions reached are mentioned, and details of contention are only once stated in his printed records. On this occasion Pepys' brother John, not Samuel, took the minutes which show that strong opinions were stated; the King inclined to support those who were likely to suffer from a proposal to save money at the expense of unqualified workers. Prince James proposed that their sensibilities should be over-ruled as unimportant since they had little influence. The Prince's view won the argument at the meeting. Subsequently the King and Pepys, reversed the decision. The King generally got the result he wanted, even when anti-royalist politicians had a majority: the King was always better informed and armed with facts. Collectively these insights in to Charles's diary belie the suggestions amusements, laziness and lechery were his main occupations.

William Jarvis was now virtually running the Carteret commerce, and young Owen Jones, with Tom Hayter and Christopher Ewens, were sharing the management of the Manorial holdings. Thomas Hayter and Hugh Morlais, were engaged to assist Pepys' legal team, now given the title The Court of the Six Clerks, now given legal status as magistrates, which Government Ministers relied on for drawing up legal contracts and ensuring accurate book-keeping. All this was of enormous help to George Osborne, Charles's chief minister, who was ennobled as Earl of Danby for his skills in financial management. Pepys' sturdy defence of naval expenses earned him praise and the offer of a ministerial poSt He became an MP. but rejected Aldeburgh in favour of Harwich, which provided better access to trade with the Low Countries. The East Anglian market was expanding with considerable population growth and Harwich, and the new London docks in Stepney and Limehouse were growing rapidly as trading ports with Africa and the Indian sub-continent

*Restoration and Retribution*

# ~ TEN ~

## CHAPTER THIRTY-FIVE

Despite the efforts of the London Gazette and its editor in support of the King, antagonism to the Court grew to an alarming extent. The King was not personally attacked and continued to exercise daily in the Parks, on the river and in the tennis courts. Racing was as popular with the people as it was with the King. A body of opinion, however, suggested that he was being betrayed by deceitful courtiers and by his mistresses, and was too easy-going. He did not know that the army, law and church were increasingly in the power of catholic traitors. Corroborative "evidence" could be produced. Nobles travelling by coach were sometimes stopped by angry mobs and beaten or robbed as suspect Catholics. Nell Gwynne on one occasion had her carriage stopped by a mob who thought she was Mrs Carwell. Allegedly she wound down her window and announced: "I may be a whore, but I am a Protestant whore!" Parliament steadfastly refused to increase the King's allowance, accusing him of wasteful expenditure. Compared with English noblemen's salaries, Charles's income was meagre, but the estimates for the upkeep of his mistresses and children, was a constant bone of contention. If his eight children had been legitimate, Parliament would have been compelled to provide much larger sums for their upkeep and independent households. He himself took great care of them and encouraged them to take on real responsibilities from which income could be derived.

In 1675, Parliament, echoing the concern of the pamphleteers, demanded a new Act to compel the expulsion from Britain of all Jesuits and Catholic priests, and to forbid their employment in any government office. It also demanded changes to the constitution to exclude any Catholic from the Succession or from employment in any post in the army or navy.

A powerful rabble rouser, Israel Tong, demanded at public meetings, that the House of Lords should adopt the same restrictions. Charles made it clear that this proposal would be treason against the Queen of England. This was reluctantly acknowledged, since Catherine had earned public affection for her devotion to her philandering husband, and her friendly conversations with the people she met when shopping, or visiting one or other of the Spas or public markets. Charles announced firmly that his Catholic Italian barber, who shaved him every day, would not be replaced by a razor-wielding Protestant. Many of the jockeys and trainers at the races were Irish Catholics, it was admitted: the sport would be ruined if they were forced to resign.

Fortunately, it was pointed out that Tong and his supporters were demanding Constitutional change, which only the King could make. Anyone proposing alterations, was committing an act of Treason. Tong was compelled to moderate his invective, and turn his hatred on those less able to defend themselves, but the size of his audiences grew and demanded an act of conformity. It has been estimated that from 1580 onward, persecution had reduced the numbers of Catholics in Britain to a small minority. Following a hundred years of persecution 1% of the population perhaps remained Catholic, but rational argument lost once more, and the Act of Expulsion from all public offices was passed.

George kept open his contacts in the East End and docks, speaking to office clerks on the commercial implications of the law. Some were in favour, some against, and suspicions and slanders began to emerge, some names were mentioned, and particular hostelries were named, as places where dissidents met. The forces of law and order were often reluctant to refute the accusations of Titus Oates. Tong and Oates had become a prominent team and the names of crypto-Catholics were broadcast freely. Mrs Carwell was abused for trapping the King into a Catholic den of foreigners. Many citizens were named as suspects, and abused in the pamphlets. Royalist sympathisers responded with vituperative attacks on dissidents, or those believed to be anti-royalist plotters. The King, as Pepys discovered, seemed to have no comment to make, and had probably hoped that matters would eventually come to a head, when the Law could act to put down any criminal actions. If a crime could be supported with evidence: naming names was not in itself a crime: if in future, the Royal Family was accused of bias or treason, this would be the moment to act. Oates seemed to be gathering a following, and his generous benefactions to the poor, who claimed to have suffered at the hands of heartless Catholics, gained support, so the poor were encouraged to tell the stories of their unjust treatment. Lurid fabrications were passed round in the popular press. Names of those offended were not always mentioned, but their physical description was generally sufficient to identify particular persons.

George and Bess found the whole persecution incomprehensible and fortunately they appeared to have the strong support of their employees. It was one of those moments in their lives when they wondered how the Restoration could have led to such cruelty and injustice. To some extent these harsh religious laws allayed public anger, certainly there was a lull. It was perhaps due to the massive rebuilding programme of London churches, and a determined effort by Anglican Bishops to reinstate effective rectors and ensure the attendance of their parishioners. Other sects had no wish to be less demonstrative of their religious loyalty, particularly the dissenters. It made the conspirators more eager to identify vulnerable victims, and this time they would be of high social status.

Life at Court proceeded largely unaffected. King Louis had made an additional sum of 1,000,000 Lvrs. available to his cousin so that he did not need to go cap-in-hand to Parliament. To reassure the fears of the Protestants, and perhaps the anti-Catholic lobby, Charles arranged the marriage of Princess Mary, James's elder daughter, to William of Orange. This indicated Charles was strongly supportive of the new Protestant monarchy; as a gesture it cost Charles nothing.

Perhaps George feared the political confusion in the country, and perhaps he found the demands of public life uncongenial. Or did he recall Bess's wise words of advice given ten years earlier? For self protection he began to put his affairs in order; there had been several family changes since his last attempt. Haynes Mansion was completed, and established on a sound financial base. His business was thriving, but he needed to think of the future. He may have begun to feel the effects of age: though healthy, he was growing old. Much more likely was a growing anxiety about the influence of provocative elements among the general population, and the pressure they were exerting on MPs. Control by bribery, threats of violence, or blackmail was certainly practised by Shaftesbury. What if there was a return to protestant Republicanism? What would happen to those who held Honours, the Lords and the Baronets?

New conspiracy theories were being specifically levelled at members of the Court. George was aware of the King's derision when a slight aquaintance, Christopher Kirkby, whom he had met at a chemical lecture, made a point of warning the King of a plot to kill him. The warning was given while walking in St James's Park. Charles had often heard warnings of this kind, and dismissed this one until, several days later, he was informed by a guards' officer, that a man with weapons had been seen to follow him. The man arrested was Kirkby, son of a vicar, and when asked the source of his information, he reluctantly mentioned Israel Tonge, an elderly, dotty vicar. When Tonge was brought for questioning, he gave a garbled and unlikely tale of a plot involving Jesuits, King Louis XIV, and sacked Catholic officers, to kill the King, and proclaim James, his Protestant successor, as a replacement king.

This seemed to Charles to be so absurd he was sent packing, but later ordered to provide names of informers and written papers, which he claimed to have read. When he did so, there was astonishment, for he produced Rev. Titus Oates as his source. His licence to preach had never been withdrawn, which lent a certain credence, although there seemed no evidence that it had been annulled. These papers, he asserted, had been seen and authenticated, by a well-respected Magistrate, and had been given to him by a close friend, who claimed to have been present on the occasion when Sir George Wakeman had spoken of attempts to poison the King. The magistrate mentioned was Sir Edmund Godfrey. The "plot" was growing more complex daily.

Questioned in depth, Oates produced a fusillade of accusations against a number of eminent men among whom was the Catholic Archbishop Talbot of Dublin: Wakeman, a fine physician, who had attended George's daughters, and Anne Hyde accused of collaborating with Edward Coleman, secretary to Maria, Duchess of York. The son of an Anglican rector, Coleman who was a recent Catholic convert, seemed to relish the thought of persecution, and had some time before, served in the York household, and become an enthusiastic, but reckless and gossipy, letter writer. Some of his correspondence was with the French secretary of Mrs Carwell and one letter speculated sadly, on the unlikelihood of Catholic toleration. The Council found this to be incriminating, and Coleman was imprisoned to await investigation.

Bess and George were in London at this time, and were appalled that such a thoroughly decent man as Dr Wakeman could be accused of treason. George's anxiety was increased by the accusations being made against men and women of unquestionable loyalty. Oates was able to produce notes taken, he claimed, at secret meetings, and signed and compromising letters, and several witnesses of treachery who each gave independent but corroborative accounts.

Bess was a friend and frequent companion of the Queen, and George himself was known to have close contacts with the inner circle of courtiers with whom he had enjoyed long-term relationships for many years. Among the Queen's household, for example, was one old friend, Sir John Grenville, Master of the Stole, who had been present at Bess's Celebration Dinner, ten years earlier. During the Civil War, he had been the stubborn defender of Starr Castle in St Mary, Scillies, while he and Bess were defending St Helier, on behalf of the Prince of Wales. Even Admiral Pennington's son, Lord Edgecombe, who had also attended the dinner, in place of his father, under whom George had served in his youth, and who had defended Pendennis Castle in Falmouth against attack, was apparently being implicated. George began to fear for his office employees. If his senior officers were accused, how should he react? He knew nothing of their religious beliefs, and had no intention of asking them. If he defended them against attack, where would that place him? What did they know, or suspect, about his own beliefs? If he failed in their defence, would that condemn him? It was an intolerable dilemma. He supposed it was one faced by many hundreds of others. No-one could feel safe from attack; all shared apprehension and dismay.

If he and Bess were attacked or accused, what would be the fate of their grandchildren? They might be made Wards of Court if their grandparents' land and property was confiscated. It was Bess who came up with a protective measure which might provide the children with the security of a noble family of solid Anglican credentials with little public presence or standing. Granvilles and Carterets were of the same Norman stock and Bess had suggested that their son, George, and Sir John Thynne's daughter, Grace, could be legally betrothed. This could be a form of insurance for the next generation in the event of their parents' deaths. Children were unlikely to be accused of treason.

One of Sir Philippe's sons, from St Ouen, had spent two years, during the Royalist uprising in favour of Charles in Devon and Cornwall, under the command of Sir John Thynne, who lacked a son and heir. If the marriage came about, it could secure the future of both families. They knew families who had experienced the horrors of constitutional laws being arbitrarily overturned, since the coming of the Tudor Dynasty. In addition, Grenvilles, Carterets and Monck, shared distant family connections.

In the meantime, the ever-resourceful Will Jarvis imparted more information concerning Rev. Oates. Some among his younger relatives, not blessed with his social advantage, had been gossiping openly about occasions when they had heard the man ranting and they impersonated his affected manner of speech. He was vituperative in his criticism of the effete manner of "Courtiers" and used to imitate a mincing walk and affected speech, laced with fashionable oaths of a prurient nature. He was equally capable of speaking in the manner of a lawyer or of "a man of the cloth" with a serious manner and intensity. Relaxing among his intimate circle, he ordered his followers to perform acts of violence against those termed "enemies," bribing them with money and food. Those who proved "Unreliable' were ostracised by the inner circle and might be subject to a beating by unseen assailants. George recognised the affected mannerisms, used to create derision and anger, similar to those used in the comedies of Wycherley to convey the manners of society idols. The rabble Oates was attempting to rouse to action, found their inspiration in the character of Mr. Horner, in "The Country Wife" or Sir Foppling Flutter, in Vanborough' popular comedy. The whole "plot" was nothing more than an elaborate fantasy constructed by a malicious mind. Surely in time it would be exploded by its own ammunition.

The King himself sent for Titus Oates to attend a parliamentary committee to be questioned on his sources and to repeat and substantiate his accusations. He was a convincing speaker and had new evidence to present when doubt was cast on his accuracy. Charles took pride in his ability to judge character, an ability which saved his life on a number of occasions. There is evidence that Charles questioned Oates in private concerning plots he asserted were being hatched in Somerset House, the Queen's residence. The Queen's household consisted largely of Catholic believers, nuns and priests. Charles established by thorough questioning, that Oates' description of rooms where plotters had been heard, were inaccurate and so was his claim of familiarity with the building. Oates had to admit that he had not personally heard plotting, but had been told of these activities. He also asserted that he had been present when the Spanish Ambassador had discussed the possibility of an invasion. Asked to describe the Ambassador he described a tall, sallow faced individual with a fine moustache. Charles asked whether he was perhaps mistaken, for the Ambassador was a short gentleman with ginger hair. Oates was not ridiculed, nor threatened, but his credibility was damaged. The King was convinced that the man was a liar, but no-one was able to expose his lies. The King could bring forward no documents or witnesses to refute him. If the King had presented his knowledge before a Judge, it would be dismissed as hearsay.

Oates was able to enter into extended scenarios with great facility: asked to provide eye-witness, signed statements, he produced documentation, forged letters and witnesses were readily available, and not always easy to expose as liars. Charles was deeply concerned with the breach of security which had allowed him to enter Somerset House and endanger the Queen. Oates was detained on one occasion and placed under guard in Whitehall Palace. Would the plots continue to spread while he was under surveillance. Oates was spied on by government appointed agents, producing no results. William Chiffinch the King's personal agent was able to discredit the reputation of several of Oates' informers, but not the evidence they presented. Oates would have understood that an accusation against the Royal family would have been an act of treason and so, in one sense, Charles may have been challenging Oates to take the last fatal step. Some of the Royal family were, in fact Catholic, and there were priests always in evidence and masses held daily in Royal chapels. One surprise was the discovery that Oates and Tonge were lodging together in the same house. This house, agents discovered, belonged to Kirkby, the chemist who had warned the king of an assassination attack to be made in St James's Park. He had, of course, been questioned earlier but his knowledge of Oates and Tonge was a revelation, though no-one could demonstrate that a crime had been committed. Kirkby was an anti-monarchist and involved in the plot which failed, leaving him to be arrested. Oates never attempted to impugn the Royal family, aware of the penalty, he made no attack on these obvious targets. Oates, to the King's knowledge, was a Paper Tiger whom he was unable to eliminate.

The whole plot may be seen now as a tissue of lies involving a circle of conspirators in thrall to Oates, who paid them to lie, forge, and launch physical attacks on innocent opponents. London was seething with aggrieved criminals, forgers, thieves and ex-soldiers, damaged by years of brutal service. Thurloe's warning had been timely, but five years later the Anti-Catholic frenzy was continuing to grow in power. Prince James had finally married. The news of the marriage was greeted with consternation by Shaftesbury and the anti-Catholic party. In London the 5 November celebrations were postponed for a week, but the partisan crowds, dressed derisively as nuns and priests, processed to a bonfire where a large wax effigy representing the Pope was flung into the flames. The effigy contained dozens of caged stray cats, whose screams of agony were greeted with cheers and applause. Oates and his gang rode in triumph on a wave of hatred whipped up in support of the indefensible, as will often happens throughout the ages, even in Britain. By October 1678, it had begun to seem that the tide was turning, that the King's indifference to Oates and his revelation, was making it seem a nine days wonder. Perhaps in the fullness of time a new scandal would become popular and Oates and company be forgotten.

As a Privy Counsellor, George played his part of these events, knowing that the King continued to feel secure from present threats. London was a small city, in which 'The Ton,' ie. "The Establishment" were all known to each other. Londoners in general would be unlikely to feel personally threatened: they would feel that Oates was channeling hatred of Catholics on their behalf as their spokesperson. Oates had managed to create and identify "guilty men" among them. Queen Maria's ex secretary, Edward Coleman, a popular man about town and fluent French speaker, had several old friends in France with whom he exchanged amusing letters, sometimes lampooning English public figures: he was also the Queen's secretary. His letters fell into the hands of Oates, and when brought to trial, his letters were judged to be treasonous. He was sentenced to death and executed in December that year. Coleman had been for some time a popular host, who numbered Hyde, Samuel Pepys, and the Carterets among his wide circle of friends. Many who had been breathing sighs of relief that the threat had ended, found it was only just beginning. It was unfortunate that though Coleman's friends knew him to be innocent, though perhaps reckless, no-one dared to speak in his defence, believing that they would become the next victims.

It came to the notice of MPs that although Catholicism and its practices were banned, there were still five Catholics ruling the country from the House of Lords. Oates unexpectedly named them and demanded that they should be arrested. While gossip was rife, and Londoners were assaulted in the streets for 'looking Catholic' the plot was expanded. While the torrent of accusations intensified, on 17 October, a body was discovered in a ditch on Primrose Hill. Carried on a cart to a constable's house, the corpse was identified as Sir Edward Berry Godfrey, a magistrate of unimpeachable honesty. Carteret knew him well from the time of the Thurlow attack and knew of his exacting standards and scrupulous honesty. He had been reported missing by his family five days earlier, having failed to return home on 12 October. The weather had been fine that night and, after dining with friends, he had chosen to walk the short distance to his home.

At first it was assumed that he had gone to his office, or to St Martin's. This was proved not to have occurred so constables and friends had made enquiries, and published posters asking for information, though nothing was forthcoming. Primrose Hill was a popular destination for Londoners seeking fresh air. On the weekend of the 12 October, fine weather had attracted large crowds. Some locals made a search of the ditch with some care. An amateurish post-mortem revealed that he had been run through with his own sword, which had been left protruding from his back, and his cloak had been flung over his body. His possessions were found close by, including his wallet, complete with money. He had been beaten about the body, and his face was red and swollen, possibly choked by his neckerchief, which was never found. This suggested he had been strangled, viciously beaten, and then stabbed to death.

There were no witnesses, and no rumours or accusations spread by word of mouth or in print. His body was not concealed in the undergrowth but quite obvious. Its appearance, since theft was not the motive, was a matter of growing speculation. It might be that the killer was being protected by powerful friends. It was a sensation which spread rapidly throughout the capital. Those who knew the man, speculated that he might have punished a criminal who sought a vindictive revenge. This seemed unlikely, since he was famed for his scrupulous judgements. Clearly there would have to be a post-mortem. Only two weeks later were hospital surgeons called to examine the corpse and establish the cause of death.

The result was inconclusive for the body was too decayed for their current procedures. The most obvious cause of death was a well-placed blade. However, a surgeon noted a second wound had been inflicted, made ineffective by striking the sternum. Neither his clothing, nor the ditch was blood-stained, and no-one had seen blood where the body was found. Despite efforts to find the killer they were not successful. The absence of bloodstains made it possible that Godfrey had met his killer elsewhere, but had not attempted to resist his attacker, and had later been deposited in a place where his body would be discovered. George noticed that Godfrey and Thurlow were known to each other and both had died following an unexpected attack. He did not suspect a plot by Oates agents since neither gentle man was remotely Catholic. On the other hand, both had flourished under Cromwell. His feeling was that both attacks were made by supporters of the Sealed Knot or Fifth Day Adventists who had been guilty of killing and attacking many opponents of Charles I.

' Wait, George,' advised James Knight. ' many believe that this is only the beginning!' They had met once more at Whyte's.

'It seems that the plot is a complex one and expands by a mysterious process of multiplication.'

James continued to present a web of coincidences demonstrating how deeply the plot had progressed. George and others were puzzled by the lack of blood and wondered if the body had been concealed for five days and where it might have been. Perhaps the corpse had been taken there but killed somewhere else.

An octopus may be forced to release its victim from one tentacle, only to grip by another one. Sir Edmund's clerk revealed that his employer was the magistrate who had taken Oates' first deposition on oath, and later met and talked to Tonge and Oates together. There was a connection with Coleman also. Edward Coleman was young and wealthy, and a generous host. He had corresponded widely and among his friends were numbered the French Ambassador and the Confessor of Louis XIV. When Coleman was detained, in the St Martin's division, Godfrey was the Magistrate on duty and had advised Edward on his response if he was summoned to answer for an offence in court. Godfrey had given Coleman an informal, but strong, warning about his activities, and advised him to live quietly at home.

Further inferences regarding Coleman's treachery, were circulating already, and some correspondence came to public notice. He had written supporting the restoration of Catholicism, and claimed that thousands would rise in support of an invasion. Popular opinion in the streets asserted that Godfrey had been killed because he knew too much. The Green Ribbon Club, a protestant organisation with Shaftesbury's support, began to speak of a 'Popish Plot' which was about to be launched on an unsuspecting populace. Women armed themselves with pistols: a Catholic widow was

*Restoration and Retribution*

strongly advised by a J.P. to marry a Protestant as soon as possible, and Christopher Wren, the Royal Surveyor, was ordered to fix padlocks to all communicating doors in the home of the Spanish Ambassador, and organise a search of the cellars of the House of Commons for explosives.

The threat became so potent that Parliament was recalled and cautionary actions recommended. Agents were appointed to find the murderer. As suggested by James Knight, another tentacle seized its victim. At the opening of the House of Lords, the bastion of British Law, Oates commanded to address them, and chose this opportunity to level charges of treason against five Catholic peers who were present: Lord Arundell of Wardour, Lord Powys, Lord Petre, Lord Stafford and Lord Belasye, allegedly plotting together to kill the King. These were all elderly and hitherto honourable men who led obscure lives, practicing their proscribed religion in peace. They were arrested at the order of the Lord Chancellor, and imprisoned in the Tower.

This was not all, for on 7 November, Shaftesbury demanded the exclusion of the Duke of York from the Privy Council and introduced a Bill in both Houses, to debar Catholics from sitting in either House, or to serve in the Army or Navy. The result of the Test Acts had been to make these the only professions open to Catholics. Their expulsion would result in the decimation of the defence forces, since both were reliant on Irish recruits. He failed on this occasion to prevent Catholics from serving in the army, and Danby managed to oblige the attendance of Prince James at the Privy Council, since he was his brother's heir, if the King was incapacitated. The King refused to permit the Queen's household to expel Father Huddlestone, or her confessors. Huddlestone was a valued old friend, instrumental in saving Charles from capture after the rout at Worcester.

One can imagine the anxiety which these wild accusations caused for all those who may have been directly implicated and, in the case of the Carterets and many others how soon would they be named, and what would be their accusation. To be named a conspirator was sufficient to undermine a reputation. Trust in the victim's integrity would be broken. And if, as often happened after the accused was brought to court, evidence was conjured up, how could one make a defence against a case based on a forgery? It was not unlike the charges of witchcraft brought to court before the Civil War. Concrete evidence was required before a charge could be made, but an inability to recite a prayer, might well be caused by memory failure in old age. While they were deeply concerned for their own safety, they were deeply involved with those whose lives were lived at the heart of State affairs. They feared for the reputations of their close associates.

It seemed, however that they were to be spared at this time but it was their old friend Samuel Pepys who was the next victim of slander. Pepys was being forced to defend himself against charges of complicity in a plot to bring about Absolutist rule, by means of an uprising. At about this time, the news of the murder of Archbishop James Sharp of St Andrews became known. This roused considerable disquiet throughout the Kingdom and the suggestion was raised that Oates and his team might be extending their usual slanders to include physical assault in another country. Sharp had been set on by a gang of four ruffians in broad daylight. His murder had been systematic and brutal and carried out in the presence of his daughter. The culprits were never identified, nor was the killing followed by other assaults, so an Oates' connection seemed unlikely. Sharp was leader of the Scottish Anglicans, however, and as Bishop, he was critical of the standing of anti-Episcopalians and Covenanters, which may have caused extreme offence.

# CHAPTER THIRTY-SIX

Such was Bess's concern at the shock these events made her husband anxious and react with his familiar exclamation 'Dio mio!', only uttered under extreme provocation. She suggested they should leave London and go to Bath for a few days of leisure. The company of lively young people might work wonders for his low spirits even though the waters tasted frightful. They took rooms in Timothy's Hotel, convenient for the Assembly rooms and the Abbey for Sunday communion. However, whenever the dance or game of cards ended, conversation returned to the naming of those accused of plotting that day. George was drinking coffee and reflecting on the changes which time had wrought, when young Rochester, walked past, bowing in recognition. Although he had been resident there for several weeks he looked unwell, and was avoiding company. He attended Matins daily, it was said. Not his usual occupation at the Spa. It was believed that he was far from well.

'Sir George!' exclaimed a familiar voice. Looking up, he saw James Knight and invited him to take coffee. 'My wife is having a gown adjusted for tonight's ball.'

'Matters seem to be going from bad to worse, James! These accusations against Pepys are outrageous. You were right when you predicted worse events. Tell me, is this an accidental meeting, or have you news?'

'You must judge for yourself, George. It was certainly not Pepys's clerk Atkins, who killed Godfrey, as has been suggested. I can tell you the reason for Godfrey's murder. You may not know that Oates was dismissed from Gonville, Cambridge, when it was discovered that he had exposed a fellow cleric at Oxford for immoral sexual conduct. The student subsequently killed himself. The Master of Wadham met the master of Gonville quite by chance: and happened to enquire after his former student, now at Cambridge. He learned that Oates had been embroiled in a similar situation at Oxford. On this occasion his accusations were spurious. The Master of Wadham suspected that happened in Cambridge, and Oates was a malicious attention seeker, with persuasive ways. He had suggested a change of University to provide Oates to correct his conduct as a mistake of youth.

'Two days before Godfrey's death, he had been at dinner with the Master of Wadham and Oates's anti-Catholic accusations had been discussed as a matter of public concern. Wadham told Godfrey of his suspicions, and Godfrey had agreed that he would charge Oates with causing the death of a student and with immoral conduct. It was certainly a disciple of Oates who performed the murder, and he is under arrest. However, those concerned suspect that their own lives may now be in danger, whether or not they bring charges against Oates.'

To say that George's fears for the safety of Pepys, Grenville, the five bishops and the Irish Bishops, and others who might yet be accused, caused him extreme anxiety, would be an understatement. It was as though a net was closing around those who were his close friends. Was his anxiety similar to that experienced by Hyde when he was being slandered? Should he follow the advice Bess had given him? Surely as a mere businessman he might be in no danger.

He watched the progress of Pepys' hearing with increasing horror, and provided some of the supporting evidence which saw Pepys released on bail. But the main accuser was a formidable opponent, and claimed to hold supporting evidence, and so the date was set for his trial.

Oates had the support of a news sheet "The Intelligencer" which produced detailed plots and slanders aimed at those who feared to defend themselves or could not afford the costs. The evidence against Pepys was circumstantial but difficult to refute. One of the Jesuits arrested, named Fogarty, had, as Pepys admitted, been a musical tutor to his wife, Elizabeth. In addition, Morelli, a musician, had been paid by Pepys, and written a lament for Elizabeth, which he and Pepys had performed, at a memorial service. He was a Catholic and Pepys with great haste had him removed to a safe house deep in Essex. Shaftesbury had already, by this time, named Pepys in the House of Commons as a genuine danger to the general public. Samuel Atkins, one of Pepys' clerks was arrested next for being an accessory to the murder of the Magistrate, Godfrey. He was imprisoned in Newgate and questioned closely while held in chains. He refused to admit the charge, despite strong pressure, although Shaftesbury questioned him personally, and threatened him with hanging, "If he did not make some discovery". Questioned in Parliament on the subject, Pepys' own alibi was decisive:

he had been in Newmarket with the King on the fateful day and the King would confirm it, if Oates chose to implicate him. Nothing came of it, but reputations were being destroyed in the process.

Pepys was deeply offended by the charges and determined to refute them by exposing them as lies. His investigation, which was expensive and thorough, revealed that Atkins had been partying with friends on board the yacht, Catherine, from which his friends rowed him home "Much Fuddled," as they stated. At his trial Atkins was acquitted and released. His companions asserting the truth and the boatmen who had assisted lent his support. On the same day, three other men, facing similar charges, and who were accused of uttering treasonous statements in the public streets, and who were equally innocent, totally confused, and lacked friends to support them were condemned to death and hanged at Tyburn.

Pepys' opponents next suborned three confidence tricksters to accuse him of dishonesty and malice. Three plots were launched concurrently. First was by a former Master of a merchantman dismissed for drunkenness. Pepys had appointed him to deliver goods to several purchasers who did not receive them. The man had in fact sold the goods, stealing the payments and pretended to be a shipowner. Sam had sponsored him, believing him to be trustworthy, and naturally dismissed him. He was seeking revenge and claiming that he had been unjustly accused. At the trial Pepys, fortunately, had supporting evidence in writing and other witnesses whom he had also deceived.

The second accuser was his own former butler, John James, who had been dismissed after being discovered by Pepys in the bed of a serving woman in his own house, by Morelli, the musician. James swore on oath, that Pepys was a Catholic, and Morelli a Jesuit. Again, his accusation failed though it was reported in pamphlets.

The third was a so called 'Captain' John Scott. He produced copied charts to prove his authenticity, and claimed Pepys had paid him to convey secret official charts and strategic naval information to the French government. The depths to which people could sink to ruin opponents was a shock to Pepys, to his friends, and terrified other innocent men who realised how dark and squalid the political situation was becoming. Again Pepys was able to produce clear evidence to the contrary.

It was a sign of the depth of hatred directed particularly at Catholics and, by implication, at courtiers and ministers, and especially the Duke of York, whose heroic reputation was deeply offensive to those opposed to religious toleration and who hoped to be rewarded when Monmouth or William of Holland became king and enforced compulsory Anglican membership on every British subject. There was no doubt that the paymaster behind this movement, was a former chose friend of the King, the Duke of Buckingham, who was deeply in debt, and had been an inept Lord Treasurer. He was being "supported" by Shaftesbury. In the Common's Chamber, on 7 May, as a result, Samuel Pepys, a man of scrupulous honesty, was charged by Justice Harbord with 'Piracy, Popery and Treachery'. He immediately rose to refute the accusation but nevertheless, later that day, was committed to the Sergeant of Arms, and on the following day resigned as Secretary to the Admiralty and as Tangier Treasurer. On 9 May he was taken to the Tower. That morning, George emerged from a Privy Council meeting, at which the King was forced by public opinion, to exile the Duke of York to France, for his own safety. The King's manner on this occasion shocked George and others present by his apparent disinterest. He sat, largely inattentive to the parade of Oates' and Shaftesbury's accusation against James, and Oates suggestion, that he should divorce the Queen for the sake of the monarchy. His responses were disjointed and inconclusive, almost dismissive, and George wondered afresh whether the torments undertaken by those who had supported the restoration, had been wasted loyalty. Charles sprawled in his seat, playing with his dogs, or his codpiece, his mind clearly elsewhere. Finally, he prorogued parliament, and they were dismissed.

He exchanged greetings with several old friends, embarrassed to be unable to tell them that their names had been mentioned as complicit in the Popish Plot. He was appalled to discover that Pepys had resigned his posts and constituency, and was about to be imprisoned. Then there was Bess, known to be a confident of the Queen, would she be implicated? Thank heaven that Dr. Philippe had died last year, and also his old friend Sir John Grenville, an associate since the West Country rising, who had tried to hold Bristol for Charles I.

He went at once to the Navy office to offer his support and heard of the arrest of young Atkins, Pepys's clerk. Meeting Evelyn outside in the street, they planned his support and were pleased to hear that Pepys had

*Restoration and Retribution*

gathered evidence to defend Atkins successfully and established that Scott, his accuser, had a distinctly shady past. As Pepys pointed out, nothing could absolve anyone from baseless charges, not even protestations of innocence. The best defence was to attack and discredit the 'evidence' and its provider.

He had set out thoroughly to investigate the credentials of Captain Scott. Houblon, Evelyn and his lawyer got to work also and St Michel, his brother in law investigating in France. On 20, June, Pepys was released on bail of £10,000 of his own surety and £5,000 by each of three other advocates, to await trial.

George took some comfort, but was shocked that the reputation of a man like Pepys could be so unjustly ruined, George Wakeling, sometime surgeon to the Queen, was arrested next, and the Lords also, remained in prison. George had painful reminders of those occasions when his own honesty had been questioned. The threepence in the pound furore, the tedious Parliamentary investigations of naval finances and, of course, it was Pepys who had produced evidence of his honesty in the form of certified accounts which passed the closest examination.

Evidence! Evidence! What evidence could he produce to help Pepys? How could he defend himself if charged with Popery and Plotting? Such charges were abstractions that evidence could not refute, any more than those condemned to death in Guernsey for 'witchcraft'. "Look out for my sword!" might be a telling response to a physical threat or an insult, but would not serve to defend his integrity. But perhaps even integrity was insufficient? He remembered Amyas and old Sir Philippe who advised against relying on a King's friendship. Obligations to subjects might always be put aside if the life of the ruler or the country was felt to be threatened. It was clear to him now that Charles would rather sidestep a confrontation even one involving a friend or relative, such as his brother: but that knowledge left him feeling abandoned and exposed. His consolation was that the King continued to hold him in high regard. The King continued to patronise the races with popular reaction. He also gained a measure of peace when he took one of his yachts and a few friends to sail on the Thames. Meals were always stowed away or provided by a surprised innkeeper and they ate what was available.

Lady Elizabeth was enrolled as a Lady in waiting on the Queen, and later, on Princess Anne as an heir to the throne. The grandchildren were well cared for and remained in the country until George was seven, when he joined the family of the second Lord Sandwich to be instructed in those skills essential for a Baronet, a title he would inherit from his grandfather. Now well into his sixth decade, Carteret planned to provide the youthful George with a possibility of joining the old Nobility. While visiting Sir Francis Dowse, recently confirmed Sheriff of Southampton, George had met Sir John Thynne, a junior member of the Thynne family, builders of Longleat House in Wiltshire, owners of vast acreages of Wilshire and land throughout the South and West of England. He had only one child, a daughter, named Grace, aged 7. Sir John and George were both eager to provide security for their children if they were rendered helpless by the acts of politicians or ill-health.

A document was drawn up and given legal status by Parliament which betrothed the two children. When they both reached the age of eighteen, they could consent or accept the arrangement by mutual agreement. Their possessions and any inheritance would be shared as a jointure, and passed on to any descendants. The agreement was later confirmed in his Will. His daughters were married and seemed to be settled happily in Kent and Wiltshire respectively. Anne Lady Clarendon, died in 1671, to the distress of Bess, but she had become a staunch friend of Mary and Anne, Clarendon's daughters. Clarendon himself had died in exile in France, leaving his History of the Revolution unfinished. Charles had forbidden him to publish it and threatened him with death if he defied the prohibition. The French King would perform the sentence if Hyde remained in France. This decision had no penalty for his children and Henry became Lord Clarendon on his father's death, and Lawrence, the lawyer, became Lord Chief Justice under William III.

While the Carterets were experiencing the political turmoil of the financial crisis of these years, when the King renounced his debts and flung countless numbers into bankruptcy, while inherent religious disputes centred on the irreconcilable chasm between doctrine and faith, roused fatal events, they would surely have experienced deep concern about the future. The whole Oates conspiracy originated in the long-term over-reaction to the possibility that the Anglican Church might be undermined by foreign agents. Folk memories of the Armada and the gunpowder plot were encouraged by Anglicans who believed that the 'True Faith' would be increased by encouraging the idea that Anglicanism was in danger.

Christianity had during the past century disintegrated forming many sects, large and small, each eager to claim that their own beliefs and practices were more 'True' than the others. Toleration of religious differences, which Charles had promised to introduce, was bound to fail when the King reinstated Anglicanism, in total contradiction of his promise. The next step was for the Government to make Anglican doctrine and communion compulsory by law. Other sects were discouraged and catholicism, because of folk memories of past threats, became subject to strong disfavour. As contention grew, and legal sanctions caused real suffering, and so the ground was ploughed for Oates and his like to sow their seeds of conspiracy.

George may or may not have known the degree to which King Charles was implicated in the whole business. His close relationship with the King had made him party to the Dunkirk sale and the import of gold, lowering the value of the currency. How far was he aware of the secret agreement between Charles and Louis and the annual financial awards made to Charles for the remainder of his life, not to mention the random donations to protect the king's solvency? Surely, he must have realised that some 'Arrangement' had been reached. The unofficial French treaty cannot have remained totally unknown. Secret agents operate today, despite Official Secrecy laws and M.I.6 but no such laws existed in Carteret's time. Oates promulgated the belief that, even at court there were catholic plotters at work and proved it in the case of Coleman! How many agents were paid by Oates? Perhaps Oates was aware of the French agreement. He had open access to Parliament and the Court and had spoken in private with the King. Charles dismissed Oates as a fraud but took no action against him.

How much did George know? How much did he suspect? There is no suggestion of course that Charles was breaking the law himself: Law did not cover his actions or these issues. As the conspiracy rumbled on, destroying reputations and trust in its efficacy, perhaps George developed fresh rules for the "Game" which he had begun to construct in his earliest years of tuition under his Uncle Amyas. As one who understood numbers and patterns perhaps, he created a new game 'Royal Chess'. In this game although every effort was made by the black and white parties to defend their King at all costs, in his version the Kings were playing covert games concurrently in opposition to their protectors. Their Protectors might fail to bear in mind that they were only employees. If their Employers felt in danger or dissatisfied about their reputation, they could attack their agents and would use the freedom to ignore the accepted rules of the game and sacrifice any of their own players, whether knights, bishops, pawns or even the Queen, to ensure their survival. As Amyas had said, if you work for a powerful ruler you must ensure that you guard your own dependants and remember, you will remain disposable at all times. His relationship with his King was basically an informal friendship based on their mutual interest in ships and the sea. Even in this situation George could observe with some admiration the skilful way in which Charles gained the friendship and trust of others.

George spent the years 1670 to 1678 moving between Haynes and London. He continued on the Privy Council and the Plantations Committee, where his colleague was John Evelyn. There were a number of changes to the Navy office and its management during these years, and for a short time the King had to concede that the Committee alone should select officers because the Commons supplied their wages. They should select from a list of candidates. The only lists available, however, were those made by the King and Prince in their round of inspections and interviews. Effectively, nothing changed. Charles was an adroit committee man, and if forced into a position where he felt his authority to be under stress, he would appoint James as Chair, or appoint a committee to investigate. Pepys was a constant secretary and wrote the minutes, discounting dissention, and recording only the final outcome. The minutes were always taken as read, not made available except to the king. Recent research demonstrates the extent to which Pepys adjusted the record to suit the interests of the Navy Office and the king.

The full membership present at any particular meeting was rarely noted but of over 300 meetings in a two-year period, the King was present at about 250 of them. Prince James attended at least 200 which reveals for the first time that the brothers spent many hours engaged in the business of government. These were not the only Committees which engaged Charles's interest. This Information has only recently become available. This legend of the Charles "The Merry Monarch" was largely the creation of writers eager to create historic tales for the glorification of the British Imperialism, based on sturdy British morals. Pepys Diary has been taken as an eye-witness exposure of the actions in which he played a part. It should perhaps be viewed as an attempt by a shrewd autobiographer to justify his own actions and demonstrate his own organisational skill. The reconstruction of the

*Restoration and Retribution*

Navy was the work of the Kings for whom Pepys was one among many executives who carried out the Kings' instructions. Among them was Sir George Carteret, and many other fine seamen whose names are forgotten. Carteret certainly deserves to be more than a mere footnote.

It is clear that George was a constant presence at court until about 1678, when his health began to curtail his activity. He was almost seventy years of age and had outlived many of his contemporaries and most of his friends. The Royal brothers had known and respected him since their childhood and, in an age when kings were prepared to make themselves available for advice or confidences, George was visited by them and knew their children. Both Kings took a strong interest in the Carteret family, attending weddings and other celebrations, and George performed until his last illness the function of Vice-Chamberlain to the Court.

At one stage Pepys wrote in his Diary "Sir George told me that the King does nothing without seeking his advice." This was shortly after the restoration and he certainly always listened to the opinions of others politely, provided they were concise. I am confident that, in his declining years, George was companion to the king on many of his many fair-weather trips to sea. Perhaps the King on one day of fine sailing weather, nodding toward the horizon and remarking on the group of small clouds far ahead. George would respond that in a cloudless sky, there are always small clouds above Jersey and Guernsey. It seems likely that the king and he may have recounted memories of past events of the early years in Jersey, and his first sailing boat and life at the castle.

The King was on occasion, ready to speak openly about past events, recalling every detail. On one occasion, when he and Pepys were together, the King told the story of his escape from Worcester after the defeat of his army. Pepys recounted it in vivid detail, including concealment in an oak tree and in a priest's hole, shared with Father Huddlestone. Pepys lacked the close familiarity which George and his family had. A contemporary title given by others critical toward George's role at Court was "King's Fasciender, "a dubious term denoting a man of business. George certainly performed a remarkable variety of executive functions, but was less physically active as he grew older. Perhaps it was his presence and companionship which made him a constant companion. In modern parlance the term "Consultant" comes to mind. He seems to have been reserved as a sounding board running a varied and reliable Royal consultancy. The strength of this relationship survived well into the next century, and many of the Carteret family played significant parts in the final years of the Stuart monarchs, and beyond. Visible proofs are the several memorial tablets and elaborate tombs displayed in Westminster Abbey, and the portraits in museums and in Jersey, Longleat and Ham House.

The endless machinations of the Oates conspiracy seemed to have no end. People began to regard it as something they would perhaps have to learn to live with. The accused were from all classes of society, the accusations made were liberally provided with observers, or eves droppers, almost always in pairs or groups, and observed in places the victim was known to frequent. Imprisonment, public questioning before a Justice of the Peace was humiliating, destroyed reputations, and even provoked bankruptcy and suicide. A number of priests were exposed, tried for Treason by illegally living in England, and hanged, drawn and quartered. Parliament proposed that Prince James, no longer a national hero, should be barred from inheriting the throne: that Monmouth must be made legitimate: that Princess Mary, Queen of Holland, or her husband Willem should be made next in line to the throne. All these were ignored by Charles, though were quite popular in the streets. Shaftesbury lent tacit support to popular opinion and eventually went too far for Charles to ignore him. He had supported the suggestion that Charles should divorce his infertile wife and choose another who would provide a Protestant Prince. On this occasion, Charles issued a public statement that he would never under any circumstance divorce the Queen.

There seemed to be no resolution and streets of the city provided no answer, other than further attacks on "foreigners". The sight of friends or fellow businessmen disturbed him for he no longer knew whom to trust, he shrank from the sight of those who recognised him, whom he had to reassure about his health, saying he was well, he was merely puzzled. Coffee was of no help but increased his anxieties. As he walked on, unsure where he was, but hesitating to ask any of these total strangers who spoke to him. On he walked, passing bookstalls, beggars, markets-where he was jostled: through parks, graveyards, one with skulls over the entrance arch, which seemed vaguely familiar. Memories came of 1627 when, he was a member of a delegation sent by James I to the European monarchs to persuade them to settle their religious differences and unite in forming a unified force for universal peace. His fellow delegates included Wren, John Donne,

Restoration and Retribution

and Sir John Lucas. The world seemed about to enter an age of peace and justice: there was little to show for it now! He remembered his father-in-law, Sir Francis Dowse, had spent two years negotiating with foreign rulers, early in the reign of James I, and although the attempt failed, Francis had received a Barony for his effort. Their voices whispered around him, and his legs seemed to lose strength, or sense of direction. It was growing dark and he could feel rain on his face when a voice he seemed to know, said, "Good Evening, Sir George. I'm on my way to Broad Street. May I walk there with you? If I take your arm, we may avoid the worst puddles altogether."

Haynes Park became his refuge in the coming months. He was unable to remember travelling there, but Bess assured him that he was safe and he was enjoying his food again. One day he recalled someone assisting him to Broad Street: perhaps he had dreamed it. 'It was Sam, George,' Bess spoke gently. 'He is coming to visit us in a few days: he will be able to meet Elias, your nephew. I think you might like to show them our Parterre, which is beginning to fill out nicely.'

George made his will, ensuring as far as was possible the financial security of the family and asking Sir Edward to assist his widow and grandchildren. He led a quiet life, sitting in a wheeled chair on the terrace, enjoying sunny, autumn days. His grandsons were lively and good company and he found that he was able to remember stories about storms at sea and secret missions and protecting ox carts loaded with gold. He thought some of the stories might be true, though the detail was lost in time.

Smethurst, the Butler, and the footmen were very attentive, although he tried not to rely on them, his legs seemed to have minds of their own. Christmas was particularly enjoyable, however, and family and friends appeared in great numbers, including Lady Jemima and Lady Fanshawe, who brought her children and told amusing stories about Portugal and its Court. She was a close friend of the Queen, and her husband had translated the poems of the Portuguese writers into English. Pepys came to visit after Christmas, and they spoke about their memories of Elizabeth, and that was a special pleasure. He could remember being anxious about Sam, but he seemed very cheerful, so perhaps he had been wrong to worry. Pepys wisely did not mention his arrest and brief imprisonment for having employed a Catholic violist to teach Elizabeth. The repercussions of the Oates plot were to continue to plague the innocent during the next five years, culminating in the Glorious Revolution almost ten years later.

George regained a little strength in the New Year, and insisted that he must go to London to see the accounts and check on his ventures. There was no refusing him, and Bess decided that a slow coach journey and meetings with old friends might reassure him and put his anxieties aside. He and Bess set off in the brisk weather of the new year, 1680, they were assisted by Margaret her Lady's maid and Alexander Westlake who had been his personal servant since Jenkins had joined the office staff. They reached Broad Street on 7 January. The officers and staff were welcoming, and new year gifts distributed. A short visit from a recently arrived trader from New Jersey brought them news of affairs in the colonies. When the account books were inspected the new accountant recommended by Petty, was introduced and praised for his excellent book keeping. George was increasingly concerned about the possibility of insolvency, and needed frequent reassurance. He went so far as to badger 'Lory,' Laurence Hyde, now Charles's Lord Chancellor, for the return of money he had loaned to his father, Edward Hyde, to alleviate his exile.

One afternoon Prince James made an informal call and spent two hours with the family. He assured George, with great firmness, that His Majesty had included George in his New Year's Honours list and he would, when they were published, be officially created a Baron of the Realm with the title Lord Carteret of Haynes. His eldest Grandson, George, would inherit the title Lord Carteret, when the time came. It would be passed on to his future descendants.

Towards the end of 1679, George became a virtual invalid, cared for with great devotion by Bess, who had much to fear for a future without his financial support for their dependent grandchildren and Haynes Park itself, which had yet to reach its full agricultural potential. Fortunately, the little boys were not in danger of becoming Wards of Court, and had loyal family support, although James, their son, was effectively also a dependent, and likely to remain so.

His Nephew, Elie, at Haynes on a visit, recorded in a letter to his lawyer father, in Jersey, "Sir George is not what he has been. He is, alas, now but a cypher. One or two must be joined to him, that he may do something."

On 12 January, George complained of feeling tired and dizzy. He went to bed and George Wakeling came to provide medical advice. George asked for the curtains to be left open so that he could see the constellations of the stars. In the early morning hours of 7 January, he suffered a severe stroke and died the following day. After embalming, he was taken back to Haynes Park, of which he had been intensely proud, and buried in the Carteret Chapel of Haynes Church on 12 February 1680, the event being postponed for travel arrangement to be made by old friends and, probably, some of the Jersey family members.

The last Will and Testament of Sir George is as follows:
"Sir George Carterets's Last Will and Testament, proved (with a schedule of
debts & c,) 14 February 1679.
My wife Dame Eliazbeth Carteret the sole executrix. The poor of Hawnes in
Bedfordshire, Wingfield, Berks., and of several parishes in Isle of Jersey. The
church of St Paul in the town of Bedford. The poor of said town. Have contracted
several debts amounting in the whole of ten thousand pounds. Trustees appointed,
vizt. the Right Hon. Edward, Earl of Sandwich, the Right Hon. John, Earl of
Bath, the Hon. Sir Thomas Crew, Knt, son and heir apparent of the Right Hon.
the Lord Crew, my brother in law Sir Robert Atkins, knt. of the Bath and one of
the Justices of the Com. Pteas, and his brother Edward Atkins of Lincoln's Inn,
Middlesex, Esq. My lands in Ireland. My outrents in the Isle of Jersey consisting
in wheat an other grain. My Plantation of New Jersey. The Island of Alderney.
My grandson George Carteret at one and twenty years of age. My son Capt.
James Carteret. Philip Carterett my grandson, second son of my son Sir Philip
Carteret deceased, to have the manor or Lordship of Langton juxta Horncastle,
Lincoln. To my grandson Edward Carterett, youngest son of my said son Sir
Philip Carteret deceased, the manor and lands of Wyberton, Lincoln. To my wife
my moiety of the manor of Plympton Devon, the capital messuage of Saltram
&c. &c. for her life and next to my grandson George Carteret. To wife one third
part of manors, lands &c. in the Isle of Jersey for life, then to my said grandson
George Carteret. A similar disposition of my manor house of Hawnes, Beds and
other estates there. The Rectory of Plympton Sy Mary, Devon, charged with an
annuity of twenty five pounds per annum to my servant Alexander Westlake.
Bath 17.

In this three volume historical series I have attempted to recreate a
detailed picture of the remarkably varied activities of this remarkable
government official whose incredible energy and capacity for hard physical
and mental effort remained strong until the last few months of his seventy
years. Energy and foresight enabled him to survive a Civil War, confiscation

of his property, exile to France, the iniquities of the Acts of Obligation, the Great Plague, the Great Fire, and the terrors levelled by Titus Oates, the populist hero. He survived penury in exile by new employment and returned to England and safety with his large family, having saved the life of Prince Charles and proclaimed him King before the States General in St Helier within a few days of the beheading of Charles I.

He was the main financial provider for the Restoration and equipped the renamed 'Royal Charles' and 'Royal James' for their triumphant return to Dover. An astute business man and investor he rarely lost money and also invested profits from the restored Royal estates and new merchant ships and horse breeding enterprises. In the long run this made Charles II a sponsor of the Arts, Architecture eg. St Paul's, of the Royal Navy, parks and gardens and also provided for his many mistress and children. As a result, parliamentary government sprang into new life and Charles II was able to walk among the crowds of well-wishers which surrounded him whenever he went on walk-about.

George Carteret was not popular with the New Nobility, who envied his success, but his colleagues in financial circles were fulsome in their praise. Lord Chancellor Clarendon described him as: "the kindest of friends…a bad man to cross."

Samuel Pepys, his clerk, became a close family friend, and defended the accuracy of Carteret's accounts before an official Parliamentary Enquiry. He wrote: "he is the most passionate man in the world. I do take him for an honest man."

Sis James Coventry, accountant to Prince James, wrote: "he is a man who do take most pains and gives himself the most to do business of any about the Court, without any regard for pleasure or advertisement; and he retained work he amid the revels of Whitehall much of his Jersey Puritanism". Fortunately, he was motivated not only by "the Work Ethic" but by devotion to the needs of his family. He deserves to be better known, as an early representative of the self-effacing Civil servant class.

Printed in Great Britain
by Amazon